The Highland Fling

Other Titles by Meghan Quinn

All her books can be read in Kindle Unlimited

Getting Lucky Series

That Second Chance

That Forever Girl

That Secret Crush

That Swoony Feeling

Brentwood Baseball Boys

The Locker Room

The Dugout

The Lineup

The Trade

The Change Up

The Setup

Manhattan Millionaires

The Secret to Dating Your Best Friend's Sister

Diary of a Bad Boy

Boss Man Bridegroom

THE DATING BY NUMBERS SERIES

Three Blind Dates

Two Wedding Crashers

One Baby Daddy

Back in the Game (novella)

THE BLUE LINE DUET

The Upside of Falling

The Downside of Love

THE PERFECT DUET

The Left Side of Perfect

The Right Side of Forever

THE BINGHAMTON BOYS SERIES

Co-Wrecker

My Best Friend's Ex

Twisted Twosome

The Other Brother

Stand-Alone Titles

The Modern Gentleman

See Me After Class

The Romantic Pact

Dear Life

The Virgin Romance Novelist Chronicles

Newly Exposed

The Mother Road

Box Set Series

The Bourbon Series

Love and Sports Series

Hot-Lanta Series

The Highland Fling

MEGHAN QUINN

Montlake

Text copyright © 2021 by Meghan Quinn
All rights reserved.

Published by Montlake, Seattle
www.apub.com

Amazon, the Amazon logo, and Montlake are trademarks of Amazon.com, Inc., or its affiliates.

ISBN-13: 9781542025225
ISBN-10: 1542025222

Cover design by Caroline Teagle Johnson

Printed in the United States of America

To my mother-in-law, Sue, and her sister, Wendy, for always posting weird articles on social media. You inspired this book.

Prologue
BONNIE

"What the hell are you doing in here?"

A frightened yelp escapes my lips.

My arms flail.

My legs launch me a good two feet in the air—at least that's what it feels like.

The mug I've been holding slips from my fingers and shatters on the ground as a pair of ferocious green eyes meets mine.

Oh dear God . . . this is how it feels to be seconds from your death.

Kilty McGrumpyshire.

Wearing nothing but a pair of jeans undone at the waist and an intricate MacGregor clan tattoo woven over his right pec and down his arm, he looks positively murderous.

I've seen this look before.

He's Kilty McGrumpyshire, after all. He's known to frown more often than smile.

But this is a next-level murder look.

Like he actually just might pull the trigger and let his Scottish fury rain down upon me.

"You see—"

"Don't fucking lie to me, Bonnie."

That Scottish accent purrs in my ears, makes me weak in the knees, begs me to rip my shirt open and expose my heaving bosom.

Here are my breasts, you man beast. Take them as you want.

"Well . . . ?" he presses, folding his arms over his impeccably built barrel of a chest.

Does he really expect an answer?

When he's barely dressed.

Hair mussed.

Lips moist . . .

Good God, things have gotten out of control. I can't process a single thought without sexualizing the man standing in front of me.

It's all his fault.

How is a girl supposed to get anything done when there's a hot Scot prancing—well, not really prancing, more like strutting—yes, when there's a hot Scot *strutting* around with his shirt off, displaying his perfectly proportional nipple-to-pec ratio?

It's next to impossible.

I blame him. I blame him for everything.

Well . . . I guess if we're playing the blame game, I also would like to throw some blame toward my best friend, Dakota, who got me into this mess.

Let's move to Scotland.

For six months.

Get you out of this rut you're living in.

Find joy in the Highlands.

This six-month endeavor has done nothing but make me realize how extremely horny I am, because instead of enjoying this country's beautiful culture, all I can think about is lifting up every kilt that crosses my path and checking for underwear.

I'm a Pervy Pervertson.

And it's gotten me in trouble.

Deep trouble. I was only supposed to be here for six months. I was supposed to forget about the brutal breakup with my now ex-boyfriend, ignore the fact that I'd been fired for the third time in three years, and admit that I have zero future ahead of me.

Instead . . .

I've become grossly attached to a goat named Fergus.

Emotionally invested in a town known by tourists for its Castration Stone, used by the Serpent Queen.

And I've fallen for the man who is currently staring me down, waiting for my response.

If I want to get any answers, I'd better start from the very beginning.

From the moment Dakota handed me her laptop to look at a post.

A post that would change my life forever . . .

CHAPTER ONE
BONNIE

Cake consumed today: One slice . . . okay two . . . fine, FIVE, FIVE LARGE SLICES.

    Jobs fired from: One, making that a total of three jobs in three years. What a brilliantly terrible accomplishment.

    Eviction notice: One, and not because we didn't pay our bills but because we turned a one-bedroom into a two . . . illegally. Oops!

    Days since last male-induced orgasm: Sixty-five, and it wasn't even a good orgasm, just a twitch of gratification. A blip. Barely a pulse of pleasure.

    Relationship status: Dumped and painfully wallowing in self-pity. Thank you very much, Harry.

    This, my friends, is sad lady status. Enjoy.

"We're doomed," I whine, slinking down into the velvety soft cushions of our thrift store couch. "Why did I have to eat all the cake? Cake would make this all better right now."

"Because your life is a mess."

Dakota Dalton.

Fierce mother hen of our shared one-bedroom apartment, best friend since I was nine, and can be persuaded by any variety of cake, just like me. She's working that whole Meg Ryan circa *Kate and Leopold* vibe with her blunt shoulder-length blonde hair and take-no-prisoners style.

She's my rock.

The reason I'm not lying on the bathroom floor and purposefully giving myself toilet swirlies—thus is the current status of my mental health.

"How can you possibly be scrolling through Facebook right now, knowing we're bound to be homeless in a few weeks?"

"Alcohol," Dakota says, bringing a pink plastic cup up to her mouth and draining its contents.

"This is all my fault."

"How is this your fault?" Dakota asks, pausing at a funny meme of a sickly-looking SpongeBob serving food.

"I don't put good vibes out into the world. This is God smiting me." I hold my fist up to the air. "I'll be better, you hear me? I won't eat all the cake anymore. I'll give Dakota two-thirds of every sheet cake I make and take a measly one-third. That's love. 'Share with thy neighbor' . . . something like that." Pleading, I continue, "And . . . and I'll really apply myself. Use this brain you bestowed upon me to truly max out my potential. I won't go out with guys like Harry anymore. Guys who want one thing and one thing only: the sin of the bedroom." I rub my temples, hoping and praying that any kind of zippity zap from above strikes me with an idea on how to get us out of this mess. "And I plan on really sending out my résumé. I'm not sure I want to do the personal-assistant thing. It's not as glamorous as I thought it was going to be—one person can only pick up dry cleaning so many times before losing their mind. But I'll find something. This weekend I'll, uh . . . I'll take a career assessment test. Yes, perfect. I'll take a test. Multiple, actually. I'll take five . . . no, ten. Ten seems like a good number. You like the number ten . . . Ten Commandments and all." I smirk at the big guy. "I'll take ten career assessment tests, and then I'll apply to jobs that best fit my talents. I'll make something of this life."

"When did Anita have a kid?" Dakota asks, completely oblivious to my pleading.

"Do you think I should add anything?" I whisper from the side of my mouth.

"Huh? Oh, uh . . ." She taps her chin. "Maybe something about His hair."

"I don't know what God's hair looks like. Do you?"

"Uh . . . white and flowy?"

I look up toward the cracked ceiling. "And your hair is . . . magnificent. Do you use Herbal Essences?"

"I don't think He needs to shower," Dakota says, clicking on a picture of Anita's baby to get a better look. "And He sure as shit isn't using Herbal Essences."

"Why the hell not?" I ask, sitting up and staring down at my friend.

"Because He's God. Why use Herbal Essences when He created Paul Mitchell?"

Valid.

"What do you think He smells like?"

"Lightning bolts and cotton," Dakota answers dreamily.

"He's not Zeus."

"He could—" Dakota sits up. Her back stiffening, her mouth falling open, her eyes widening.

Detecting that something huge is about to happen, I clasp my hands together. "Did He . . . hear us?"

Dakota shakes her head. "No, but check this out." She turns her laptop toward me, and my eyes lock on a shared article from her crazy aunt Wendy—a perpetual oversharer of weird shit on social media. Ever wonder why you've found yourself caught up watching a video of an old-timey cowboy teaching you how to make huevos rancheros on a rusted metal garbage can top? It's because of people like Aunt Wendy.

Trying to get my drunk brain to focus, I read the post out loud. "Help wanted. Looking for two friends to manage small town coffee shop in Corsekelly, Scotland for six months. No experience necessary, all expenses paid, including free accommodations. Applicants need a cheery disposition and a thirst for the Scottish Highlands." I look at my best friend, eyebrows cocked. "You can't be serious."

"I have a thirst for the Highlands."

"Do you even know where the Highlands are?"

"In Scotland."

"Where in Scotland?"

"In . . . the Highlands."

Rolling my eyes, I push the computer back onto her lap. "You're drunk."

"Bonnie, don't you remember the results of your genetic testing? It said you were one-sixteenth Scottish. Don't you want to visit the lands of your dearly beloved ancestors?"

I point my finger fiercely at her. "Don't you dare throw my ancestry on the line like that. You know I love a genetically completed family tree."

"Come on, this is the perfect opportunity."

"Dakota." I shake her. "Are you hearing yourself? You are asking to apply for a job in *Scotland*."

She grows serious, and even though her eyes are glazed over from the tequila, she looks down at her hands. "I know it's been a year since Isabella broke up with me, but it's been difficult to move on."

Oh . . .

I lean in slightly to catch the distraught look on my friend's face. Maybe this really isn't about me but . . . about her.

Isabella was Dakota's first girlfriend.

Yes. FIRST. GIRLFRIEND.

Isabella was the girl who helped Dakota finally identify with herself.

And then Isabella went and broke Dakota's heart.

First love is hard enough.

But first love that brings on the realization that you're gay . . . now, that's a whole other level.

"I can understand that." I reach over and give her hand a squeeze. "I can't imagine what it would be like to be in love and lose it."

"It's been hard." She glances at her computer screen, moves the cursor over to "Apply," and clicks on the link.

"Uh, what are you doing?" I ask, starting to panic that she might actually be serious about this.

"Applying."

"Dakota—"

"Isn't this exciting? We're going to run a coffee shop in Scotland!" she says as she types her name into the application.

Wow, okay. I've heard of nervous breakdowns after serious break-ups, but I've never witnessed one in person.

I need to proceed with caution.

"Oh, sweetie." I pull her into a hug. "You're delusional. Maybe I should lay you down and bring you some cake. I can put an order on DoorDash and have some sugary sweetness to you in twenty-five to thirty minutes."

"I'm not delusion—"

"Shhh," I whisper in her ear while gently pushing her back against the couch. "You poor dear. I should have seen the signs. Losing my job has really turned me into a blind friend, but I see you now." I grab her chin and force her eyes to mine. "I see you, Dakota." I pat her shoulder. "Now, you just lie here while I order the cake, and we can try to figure out how to handle all of this. Don't worry—we'll keep this mental crisis to ourselves."

"I'm not having a mental crisis."

"Oh, honey." I wince. "That's what everyone says when they're going through a mental crisis."

Grabbing my cheeks, Dakota brings me inches from her face, tequila fresh on her breath. "I'm not having a mental crisis. We are going to Scotland for six months, where we will take care of a coffee shop in a small town called Corsekelly."

Carefully, I lower her hands from my face. "Honestly, I think you've lost your mind and you're frightening me a bit. I'm unsure of what to do . . . should I call your parents? This seems like a 'time to call the parents' moment."

Dakota sets her computer on the coffee table and turns toward me, frustration etched across her face. She can apparently sober up in an instant because she looks at me with clear, serious eyes. "The timing is perfect for both of us. You don't have a job—"

"Well aware of my unemployment status."

"We are being evicted."

"Which I take full responsibility for."

"And we both need a change," she says, her voice growing soft now. "I can't think of anything better than whisking off to Scotland for the summer."

"What about your job?"

"You know I can do my graphic design work while we're there."

True. She just rents a workspace so she doesn't get stuck in our dank apartment trying to feel the creative flow while she hand draws pretty pictures on her tablet for multiple social media influencers. She's paid well, she's self-taught, and she can take it anywhere.

If only I were an artist like her—then all our problems would be solved and we wouldn't be talking about moving across the world. Unfortunately, I've never truly found out what I'm good at. I was kind of hoping Los Angeles was going to help me with that, but all it's taught me is that celebrities are particular about their coffee orders.

I scratch the side of my head. "But . . . we don't know anything about Scotland."

"We didn't know much about Los Angeles, and we still moved here." Yeah, and look where that got me. My parents' disgruntled faces flash through my mind. I'll never forget the looks they gave me when

I told them I wasn't going to college but instead pursuing a dream in the "business industry," hopefully working my way to becoming a party planner or "something fun like that." Yeah, used those exact words.

"Uh, we drove up the 15 from Hemet. We didn't take a plane to another country," I say. "I already made a big move, and I have nothing to show for it."

She nods in understanding, but it doesn't change her long sigh as her shoulders slump. A defeated posture if I've ever seen one. "I need this, Bonnie. I need this adventure, something to get me out of here, away from the memories. I know running away isn't the answer to my problems, but I just need a chance to breathe, at least."

I study her. Vulnerability shines through the tough armor she wears daily. "Did something happen?"

Her teeth roll over her bottom lip. "It was the day you were fired. I ran into Isabella . . . with her new girlfriend."

"What?" I practically shout. "And you didn't tell me?"

"Because you'd been fired. You needed me, so I held it in, but it's been eating at me. They were so happy and—" Her bottom lip quivers, so I quickly pull her into a hug.

"Shhh, it's okay." I squeeze my eyes shut and hold back the onslaught of curse words I want to call Isabella. I rub Dakota's back, my eyes traveling to the open laptop. "You really want to go to Scotland?" I ask, still in denial that this is real.

Dakota pulls away and wipes at her eyes. "I really need this, Bonnie, and I think you do too. Let's get you out of this rut you're living in and find joy in the Highlands. This is our chance to reset, do something different, and just live freely for a few months."

"So you're dead serious? You want to move to Scotland for six months and run a coffee shop, even though we know nothing about coffee."

She nudges me playfully. "You know coffee—you've been retrieving it for the past three years. Plus, you learned how to work that one espresso machine when you worked for Lisa. You were making all sorts of drinks by the end."

"And getting a coffee order wrong was the excuse she used to fire me."

Yeah, got a coffee order wrong. It was embarrassing, to say the least. But Daloria Day—America's sweetheart—was looking for a reason to fire me. We didn't get along.

She waves her hand at me. "Semantics." She shakes my arm. "Come on. Accommodations are set, job security for six months, and the promise of adventure. Tell me you're in."

Damn those big blue eyes staring back at me.

I want to do this for her, but . . . there's an inch of fear trying to take up space in the back of my mind.

I moved to Los Angeles, and I still haven't found myself.

And now I could move to Scotland . . . to find myself. How could that possibly be any different? This is just one more risk that probably won't pay off. I wanted nothing more than to prove my parents wrong, and to prove the five universities I applied to my senior year in high school wrong too. I wanted to show them all that I'm worthy, that I have potential. But all I've done is prove to the world that I'm dispensable.

Will it be the same in Scotland?

I glance at Dakota as she quietly mouths, "Please."

Damn it.

Damn it all to hell.

We might not even be picked—there's no guarantee.

Smiling, I say, "I'm in."

And that's how I ended up in Scotland for six months. Fun story, huh?

Well, thanks for stopping by, hope—

What's that?

Leans in

What about the hot Scot?

And the Castration Stone?

And this Fergus fellow?

I mean, if you really want to know, then I guess I can tell the rest of the story. But prepare your hearts, because this is one hell of an adventure.

CHAPTER TWO
BONNIE

Cake consumed today: *None, and frankly, I don't think I can function properly.*

Job offers accepted: *One, and I have little to no experience for it.*

Days since last male-induced orgasm: *Seventy, and I wiped a cobweb from my lady area this morning.*

Current residence: *Scotland, apparently.*

This is what they call making a decision on a whim. Let's hope it doesn't bite me in the butt.

"No way am I driving that," I say, folding my arms over my chest. "This was your grand idea—you drive it."

Surrounded by stone buildings that look like they've been plucked straight from *Mary Poppins*, Dakota and I stand in front of our rental car, four large bags by our side and a rope in hand. Cars speed right by us, filling up Inverness's charming, if narrow, city streets. There isn't a tree in sight, just wall-to-wall cement and stone, but the spectacular architecture is making my mouth water—and I've never thought twice about architecture until this moment.

But even though we are surrounded by magnificence, it doesn't negate the predicament parked right in front of us.

A MINI Cooper.

Our form of transportation.

An itty-bitty green MINI Cooper.

Such a petite vehicle normally wouldn't be an issue—they're adorable—but when you have to cart six months' worth of luggage two hundred miles into the mountains, it doesn't scream "practical."

But don't worry. The rental company provided twine to secure our bags on top of the roof.

Oh, and in case you weren't aware, the Scots also drive on the other side of the road . . . and the other side of the car.

"Please, Bonnie, I can barely hold it together."

My beautiful best friend who thought of this brilliant idea—traveling across the world to sell coffee to strangers—forgot one minor detail: she suffers from horrible motion sickness. She spent our entire flight with her head in a bag while I rubbed her back and prayed to Jesus she wouldn't throw up on my leg.

"Can't we call an Uber or something?" I ask.

"No, this is the car Finella and Stuart arranged for us. Plus, I don't think Ubers drive out to Corsekelly. The town is really small."

"Dakota, that is a clown car." I point to it. "And you expect me to drive it through twisty, windy roads with two hundred pounds of luggage while navigating the opposite side of the road?"

"You're never one to back away from a challenge." She tries to smile, but it's pained. "They're expecting us in a few hours."

I sigh and move around the car. "The hospitable thing to do would have been to pick us up." I fold down the back seats and shove a suitcase in the rear. I lift up another suitcase and shove that one in as well. When I realize that's all that's going to fit, a light sweat breaks out over the back of my neck. Oh shit. I turn to Dakota. "Uh, so now we have to use the rope?"

She glances down at the thick woven cable in her hand. "I'm thinking . . . maybe?"

"Fine, I don't care. Let's just get them loaded up."

Together, we lift the first suitcase up top and then the second. How on earth are we going to—?

"Awright, lasses, dae yi'll need some hulp?" a deep voice says from behind me.

Ehhh . . . what?

I spin around to find a tall man with bright-red hair on top of his head and framing his face from ear to chin. He's wearing a charming smile and a tempting kilt. What I wouldn't give for a touch of Marilyn Monroe wind right about now.

"Umm . . . I'm sorry, I didn't quite understand you."

"Och, y'er American. Dinna fash yirsel, y'er in guid hauns."

Blinks

Mentally cleans out ears

Blinks again

"You told me they speak English here," I hiss at Dakota.

"They do." She looks as stiff as I do.

Snagging the rope from my hand, the rental car guy moves around the car like a ninja, strapping down the suitcases and securing them better than I ever could have. If I did it, Dakota would have to spend her first week in Scotland nude.

Dusting off his hands, he surveys his work and then turns to us. "That shuid dae it. Whaur ye aff tae?"

Oh God, I can't understand a damn thing he's saying. I want to say he's speaking English. I can recognize some words. They're in there, and he's acting like we should know what he's saying, but it's not translating.

Sweat creeps up my neck.

The corners of my lips flatten out, and I wince. "I'm sorry. Little jet-lagged. Uh, can you repeat that?"

He chuckles and plants his hands on his hips as he rocks back on his heels. At least he's a jolly man. "Where. Ya. Aff. Tae."

Aff tae.

Aff tae.

Off . . . tae.

OFF TO!

Good grief.

"Where are we off to?" I nearly shout, feeling like I just answered a *Jeopardy!* question correctly.

What is, "I don't understand a damn thing this man is saying," Alex.

"Aye." He nods.

Okay, totally know what "aye" means. Man, we're on a roll now.

"Corsekelly," I say.

"Och. Aff tae see th' Boaby Stane?"

There goes our streak.

"Boaby Stane?" I ask.

"Aye, Boaby." He taps his crotch and then pelvic thrusts at us. "Boaby."

"Boaby?"

"Aye."

Tap. Thrust.

Boaby . . . Boaby . . . uh, drawing a blank.

"Ya know. Boaby." Tap. Thrust. "Boaby." Tap. Thrust.

Dear Jesus, what is happening?

I clutch Dakota's arm. "He's hitting his crotch. Is he asking for payment?"

"Boaby," he says slowly and then scratches the back of his head. "Err, Americans say 'penis.'"

Boaby is a penis?

So he is looking for carnal cash. Good God, that's bold.

I need to get us out of this situation, and fast. "Yes, sir. We are aware you have a penis," I blurt. "I'm sure it's quite sturdy, given your

17

ability to strap suitcases to a roof, but if you're looking for payment, I'm sorry to say we're both lesbians. Lovers, actually. This is my lover." I grip Dakota even tighter. "We would be terrible at anything you're interested in. Fumbly hands and terrible mouth diameter."

He wipes a hand down his face. "Penis . . . Stone," he enunciates, trying very hard.

Well, there you have it, folks: he's trying to communicate that he's currently erect.

His penis is hard as stone. That doesn't make things uncomfortable at all.

"My God," I whisper to Dakota. "They are forward here." Turning back to him, I say, "Congratulations on your erection, sir. Quite a feat to accomplish in the middle of a city." I give him a solid fist shake. Solidarity. "Keep up the good work—"

"The Castration Stone." Dakota has spoken up . . . finally, despite being hunched over and completely out of it, thanks to the flight. "He's not boning out—he's talking about the Castration Stone."

"Aye." He winks at Dakota.

Okay, now I'm really lost.

"I'll explain in the car." She straightens up but still looks like she might puke. "We got a job at the coffee shop in Corsekelly," she explains to our knight in wooly tartan.

"That's ye twa lasses? Ah saw th' advert, ya know." He chuckles. "Need directions?"

"Directions." Now, *that* I understood.

"Maybe you could write them down?" I ask. Pretty sure there shouldn't be a problem with English on paper.

"Sure." He chuckles some more.

I reach into my backpack and hand him my notebook and a pen. As he writes, he says, "Canny oan th' roads. They're wee'er ere."

Wee-er. *Giggles*

18

He hands me the paper. "Juist follow th' A82 tae A887. Follow signs to Loch Duich." He winks. "Guid luck."

"Did you catch that?" I ask Dakota.

"Hoping you did."

"'Tis on th' paper." He guides us to the car and opens the doors for us. When he closes them, he hands us the ends of the rope. "Haud oan ticht." One more wink, and then he takes off.

With one hand clutching the rope that tied the suitcases and the other holding the directions, I look over at Dakota. "Uh, is this rope not secure?"

She glances at the rope in her hand as well. "Looks like it's not."

"Well, this should be fun."

◆ ◆ ◆

"Oh my God, the cars are going to hit me!" I scream as I drive down the road, one hand on the wheel, the other wrapped in a death grip around our trusty rope.

"Stay in your lane and they won't." What lane? The streets in Inverness are tiny. The painted lines are faded, some are zigzagged, and the stone buildings are practically on top of us, offering no visibility.

They may be pretty, but good God, they do nothing to help the driving experience.

"They're coming for me. They know I don't belong here."

"Just focus!" Dakota screams, clutching the dashboard with one hand, the rope with the other.

"I am focusing!" I scream back as a car zooms past us from the other side. "We're going to die!"

◆ ◆ ◆

"What in the fresh hell does that say?" I ask, hanging my head out the window as I try to read a street sign. Still stuck in the city.

Still being attacked by oncoming traffic.

Still trying to figure out why there are no trees!

"For someone who's worried about getting hit, you should be more concerned about keeping your head in the car," Dakota says, her voice full of fear.

"I can't see—this windshield is so small."

"Turn right. Google Maps is saying turn right."

"I think I need to turn left."

"I'm telling you to turn right."

"And I think you're wrong . . ."

"Stop staring at me. I told you I was sorry," I say, feeling the heat of Dakota's peeved gaze.

"Are you listening now?" Dakota asks, still pale from the ten minutes we spent on the side of the road so she could throw up. My left turn resulted in a rather scary downhill road that brought us face to face with an oncoming tour bus.

"Listening." I give her a charming smile.

"Stay on this road, and do not turn unless I tell you."

"Aye, aye, Captain," I answer with a smile that does nothing to help the green tinge in Dakota's cheeks.

Please don't let her throw up in the car.

"We're GOING TO DIE!" I scream for what seems like the tenth time as we merge into the inner circle of a roundabout.

"AHHH!" Dakota flails, holding on to the rope as we corner on two wheels.

(Not really, but that's what it feels like.)

"Mother of Jesus, what hellish labyrinth are we in?" I yell out the window as another car passes us.

"We're circling the devil's teat," Dakota whimpers. "That's what we're doing."

"We drive in Los Angeles, for fuck's sake. We can do this."

"The rope is slipping!" Dakota calls out.

"For the love of God, don't let go. Hang tight, Dakota. We can do this." On a scream, I turn on my blinker and hope for the best.

Ten minutes later . . .

"Let me know when you're ready," I say, gripping both ropes while Dakota heaves out the side of the car. "Roundabouts were made to destroy the hearts of tourists." I glare up at the cloudy gray sky. "I see you, Scotland. I see your witchy ways."

"So . . ." I break through the silence that's fallen over our car as we peacefully make our way down the winding back roads of Scotland. The scenery has become increasingly green—found those trees—and instead of troublesome buildings to navigate through, we're delighted with the tumbling mountains with the occasional sheep dotting the meadows. "That was fun."

"Why were you honking so much?" Dakota asks, weak and most likely dehydrated.

"It felt like it was my only defense mechanism."

"I've never seen your jaw unhinge like that before." She stares blankly out the windshield. "The swear words you said. Very . . . colorful."

"Seems like roundabouts bring out the trucker in me." I clear my throat, feeling hoarse from the banshee-like screaming I did while trying to cut across the three-lane death trap.

"I don't think I can ever unsee what happened back there."

"That's fair," I say quietly. "I understand. That was a side of me I don't think anyone was expecting to see, myself included. But, hell, we did it. We are taking Scotland by the whisky and lochs."

"That doesn't make sense," Dakota says, staring out at the stunning nature and rugged mountains. Dark shadows from the looming clouds above add a mythical feel you can't find in smoggy California.

"It does—you know, like 'taking the bull by the horns,' but . . . forget it. So, about that whole Penis Stone thing. I thought he was asking for . . . payment by tapping his crotch like that."

"The Scots aren't Neanderthals, Bonnie. They speak English."

"That was *not* English back there."

"Some people have thicker accents than others. When I spoke to Finella on the phone yesterday, she had a very pretty accent, easy to understand. I had no problem speaking with her."

"Well, that's a relief. Was she the one who told you about the Penis Stone?"

"No, I read about it when I was researching Corsekelly." The green shade that once was Dakota's face has now dimmed to a normal skin color, thankfully. "Apparently that's what the town is known for. That and a goat."

"Oh-kay. Want to elaborate on the Penis Stone?"

"You know the show *Iron Crowns*?"

"The one with all the incest and rape?" I ask.

"Yeah, the one you couldn't stomach anymore, so we switched over to watching *Jane the Virgin*."

"I would marry Rojelio in a heartbeat. Give me some of that Latin love."

"Even I would consider marrying Rojelio." Dakota chuckles.

"It's the Rojelio gift baskets, isn't it?"

She clutches her heart with her free hand. "He puts so much thought into them. Anyway, *Iron Crowns* made TV history when they had the Serpent Queen—"

"Ugh, she was creepy. I'm all for women's empowerment—own that crown, baby—but then she'd flick her serpent tongue out at people, and it just didn't sit right with me."

"And castrate her soon-to-be betrothed."

"Wait . . . what?"

"Listening now?" I nod. "Apparently he cheated on her with a chambermaid, and to make sure he learned his lesson, the Serpent Queen took him to this cave that has a flat stone slab in the middle of it. She had him pinned down, with his willy out, and then . . . *poof*, the boaby was gone."

I chuckle. "Oh, I see what you did there, and I like it. 'Boaby.' Do you think Scottish girls tickle the tip and talk to the boaby like it's an animal? 'Who's been a good boaby today? You have, yes, you have.'"

"Why are you the way you are?"

"Can't be sure." We both laugh. "So, Penis Stone, huh? Fascinating. Our new home is famous for a castration rock. I'm kind of digging it. *Iron Crowns* was filmed in Scotland, then?"

"All over. I saw that Corsekelly has a plaque in town dedicated to the Penis Stone."

"I'd be shocked if they didn't." I grip the steering wheel a little tighter. "My Instagram is about to be lit."

CHAPTER THREE
BONNIE

Roundabouts stuck in: One . . . for ten minutes.

Number of times Dakota has thrown up: Not enough fingers to count.

Number of Scotsman interactions: One, and I'm still trying to figure out what he was trying to say to us.

If a Scotsman taps his crotch, he might just be trying to tell you that boaby *means "penis," not that he wants sexual payment for his kind favor.*

◆ ◆ ◆

WELCOME TO CORSEKELLY—HOME OF FERGUS
RESIDENCE OF THE GREAT BOABY STONE
POPULATION 360

"What a sign," I say as we hop back into the car after taking a picture in front of Corsekelly's sign, which is rather large for such a small town. "'Boaby Stone' has a much better ring to it than 'Penis Stone.' Almost sounds like it's a lucky rock or something, and if you rub your cheek on it, you'll be granted good luck for years to come."

"You're referring to the Blarney Stone, and that's if you kiss it," Dakota says, buckling up and holding on to the rope, which has now permanently indented our palms. "If you kissed this stone, you might get herpes."

"What, do you think people actually put their penises on it?"

"Uh . . . yeah. There are pictures all over the internet of people in the cave, reenacting the scene with their wives, boaby out and everything."

"Ew, who wants to see that?"

Dakota shrugs. "*Iron Crowns* has the largest fan base in the world. People do crazy things."

"Yeah, but to act like your penis is going to be chopped off, you have to have some serious trust in your wife, and you'd better make sure not to piss her off before the photo opportunity. One 'oops' moment and your ding-a-ling is gone forever."

I start up the car and pull onto the narrow paved road that takes us past slate-covered cliffs and down into the valley of Corsekelly.

Oh my God.

The trees lining the road part, and we are greeted by a vast expanse of glittering water, framed by gorgeous mountains, dusted in green, and sprinkled with large slate stones. It's positively gorgeous here.

A new chapter rests right in front of us.

New opportunities.

New people—hopefully nice people.

New adventures.

I can feel it already: the change I'm making, the confidence this decision is instilling in me. This very well might be exactly what we both need.

"There's the town," Dakota says, pointing to a smattering of white clay buildings.

"And where's the rest of it?" I ask as we approach.

"That's it. It's really small."

I don't think I've ever seen a town this small. No more than twenty buildings border the town's main thoroughfare, which runs along the lakeshore and is aptly named Corsekelly Lane.

All facing out toward Loch Duich, the buildings are constructed of white clay, decorated with rock walls, and enhanced by colorful displays of seasonal flowers hanging from cast-iron plant hooks. Compared to the houses in America, they aren't grand by any means, and the windows and doors look far too small for an adult, but they're charming, picturesque, and make me feel like I've just entered a fantasy.

Compact and charismatic.

"You know, the town feels more like a pit stop rather than a place to live," I say to Dakota, who's busy staring out the window, taking in Corsekelly just as much as I am.

"But there is nothing touristy about it besides that tour bus parked in front of . . . I think that's a hotel. That's kind of nice. It will feel like we're tucked away."

"True." I nod. "And I love the wooden signs hanging above every door." Driving extra slow, I read them out loud. "FERGIE'S CASTLE. THE ADMIRAL. UNDER THE GOAT'S KILT INN—bet that doesn't smell very good." We both laugh, and I steer us down the stone-paved road. "THE MILL MARKET, BUBBLES LINEN BASKET, PARLAN'S PUMP PETROL, MURDACH'S WEE BAKESHOP, COFFEE . . . wait, *coffee*? Is that . . . that 'coffee house'?" I ask, grimacing as we draw even with a lackluster building.

Framed in white clay like the rest of the town, its only distinguishing features are a red door and a sign above it that spells out **COFFEE**. Two weathered picnic tables rest under each red-framed window, but that's as far as the charm goes.

Uh, we left Los Angeles for this?

It looks like the door is one gust of wind away from being torn off its hinges.

Where's the charm?

Where's the cute wooden sign?

Where's the plaid? Shouldn't there be plaid somewhere?

For heaven's sake, where is the plaid?

"Yes, it is," Dakota says, not even fazed.

"Wow, they sure know how to advertise their wares." I chuckle. "Where's the cute name?"

"They're direct. That has to be admired. Finella said there's parking around the corner, where we'll be staying."

"Okay." I round the corner and follow a gravel driveway that takes us under a canopy of trees. "Are we going the right way?" I ask as the road gets tighter and tighter.

"I think so. She said the cottage is just past the trees."

Driving no more than ten miles per hour, we bump along the road and finally reach a tiny white clay cottage with a thatched roof.

"Umm, did we just drive into a Disney movie and I didn't notice?" I ask.

A thatched roof . . . a legit, real, thatched roof. I think the last time I saw one of those was in *Snow White and the Seven Dwarfs*.

And . . . is that a . . . ?

"Oh hell no." I shake my head, pointing to the well that's right next to the house. "Does this place not have plumbing? I did not sign up to fetch the water for the bath."

"It has all the amenities we need," Dakota says, opening her car door.

I grip her arm and keep her in place. "When you say 'amenities,' does that include running water?"

"Yes," she says, exasperated. "You act like our plane was a time machine and I brought you back to the Middle Ages."

"Sorry if I'm startled by a thatched roof and a well, but that's a legit concern. Did you see the gas station back there? I'm not sure it even works."

"It's called a petrol pump, and it works. This isn't LA, Bonnie, something you should keep in mind. This is a simpler way of living. Relax and enjoy the slower pace."

She's right. Before making assumptions, I should really get to know the place first.

I'm here for adventure.

I'm here to figure out what I want to do with my life.

And making prejudgments is not going to do me any good.

"You're right. I'm sorry." I let out a deep breath. "The road trip was long, and my hand is sore from holding the rope. I promise once we get some food, I'll be much better."

Just as we exit the car, the front door to the cottage opens, and a short lady who looks to be in her sixties steps out. She has dark-brown hair, peppered with silver streaks, and an apron cinched around her waist.

"You must be Dakota," she says, walking over with a welcoming smile.

Dakota was right—a very pretty accent, and one I can easily understand.

Thank God.

"Finella, it's so great to finally meet you." Dakota hugs the woman and then beckons me over. "This is my best friend, Bonnie."

"Aye, Bonnie, 'tis a beautiful name. Means 'pretty' here in Scotland, and it seems to fit you perfectly." She looks me up and down with a kind smile.

"Oh, thank you. I've been told I'm one-sixteenth Scottish." I smile.

"Is that so?" She raises an eyebrow. "How lovely."

I feel a surge of pride to be standing in the lands of my ancestors. "It's good to be home, where my ancestors once walked. I can truly feel their presence." When I glance at Finella, I catch the smallest of smirks on her lips. Okay, sure, I'm only one-sixteenth Scottish, but that means something. I take in a deep breath. "It's nice to meet you, Finella. I can't get over how green it is here. Coming from a dry environment, it's refreshing to have nature all around us."

"'Tis beautiful here." She rests her hands on her hips, a wry smile tugging on her lips. "We'll miss it, but we're excited to go on a much-needed holibags."

Holibags?

What the hell does that mean?

"Come, come," she says. "We'll talk more inside. You two must be hungry. I've fried up some haggis for you with some tatties and neeps." She grabs both of us by the hands and guides us into the cottage. As we step inside our new home, I'm shocked at just how spacious it is. Off to the right is a stone fireplace and wood-framed hearth with a cast-iron stove in the middle. Two red couches sit on either side of the white-walled room, facing each other, with an oak coffee table in the middle.

To the left is a tiny kitchenette equipped with a two-burner stove, minifridge, and sink. Minimal cabinets, and instead of doors under the sink, the nook is blocked off with a white-and-red-checkered curtain. *Okay, that's kind of adorable.* To the back is an open door leading to a narrow set of stairs. No pictures adorn the walls, and there are no decorations to speak of. The rest of the space is dominated by a two-person dining table, laden with dishes of food. Quaint, but just enough.

A hell of a step up from our one-bedroom, window-barred, cracked-ceiling apartment in Los Angeles, that's for damn sure.

"Hope you enjoy the space," Finella says, pride puffing her chest.

"It's lovely," I say.

"Perfect," Dakota adds.

"Now, there's one bedroom on the ground floor and one upstairs. Bathroom around the corner. We keep a bucket next to the toilet, and if you go number two, we ask that you use the bucket to help flush it down."

I glance at Dakota, whose eyes widen with humor. I hold back my snicker, not wanting to be rude. But come on . . . a toilet bucket?

Yup . . . *lovely.*

"The fridge has some food in it," Finella continues. "Not too sure what ya girls like, but it has the basics. The Mill Market is down the street. Shona knows you're coming, so she can help show you around and order you anything you might need."

"Shona is the owner?" I ask.

"Aye." Finella sits us both down at the table and ladles out food. Balls of fried something that must be the haggis—whatever that is—and two mashed-up-looking things. The tatties and neeps, I suppose. "Everyone in Corsekelly knows you're coming. The town is quite welcoming to newcomers, and they've already promised me and Stuart they'll take good care of you while we're gone."

"Thank you," Dakota says, picking up a fork and digging right in. I pick up my fork as well but wait for her to taste the food first. When she doesn't seem to balk, I give myself the green light to eat up. "This is delicious, Finella." The tatties and neeps are mashed with a hint of nutmeg flavoring. Interesting but delightful. And the haggis has an oaty texture with a hint of pepper and a crumbly sausage feel.

I think I can get used to this.

"Thank ye. 'Tis an old family recipe. My Rowan's favorite."

Rowan. Is that someone's name?

"You won't see much of him," Finella continues. "Quite busy being the handyman around town."

So it *is* someone's name.

"Is Rowan your son?" I ask.

"Aye, he is. Strapping lad, though a tad grumpy, and keeps to himself. He does fancy himself a blonde, though. Especially a bonny one." She wiggles her brows, and I feel my face flush.

"Hear that, Bonnie? *Strapping*," Dakota says with a smile.

"Are either of ya attached?" Finella asks.

"Both single," Dakota answers.

"Is that so." She smiles widely.

"I'm not ready to date, though," Dakota quickly says. "I had a bad breakup with my girlfriend about a year ago. Still nursing those wounds."

"Och, ya fancy the lasses? You should meet Isla Murdach—she runs Murdach's Wee Bakeshop. I'd think she'd take kindly to you."

Now it's Dakota's turn to blush. I nudge her under the table with my foot. "Hear that? She'd fancy you."

"Not looking for a relationship," she says.

"Me neither," I say quickly. Who knows who this Rowan guy is— I'm almost certain I don't want anything to do with him. The whole grumpy thing doesn't work for me.

"So what brings you to the Highlands, then? On your application, you said adventure." Finella studies us both. "But I see darkness in your pretty eyes. There's more to it."

"A break," Dakota confesses. "A break from it all." And I know exactly what she means. She needs a break from the memories, from the chance of running into her ex. She needs to clear her head.

Just like me.

"A moment to breathe," I say. "To figure out what I'm doing with my life."

Finella smiles and clasps her hands together. "Then Corsekelly is the perfect place for the both of you."

Gravel crunches under our shoes as Dakota and I follow Finella down the tree-lined lane to the coffee house. A light sprinkle of rain starts up, and I pull up the hood of my sweatshirt.

"Nay, not to worry about the rain, lass," Finella says. "It's a given here in Scotland. Embrace it."

Well, if that's the case, I lower my hood and let the droplets of water scatter over my head and face. If I'm going to be here for six months, then I really should live like the locals.

"Here she is," Finella says as we round the bend and approach the coffee shop. "She might not be pretty on the outside, but she's warm on the inside." She opens the door, and to my surprise, the shop is completely empty—no one working, not a single soul in the building.

Even more shocking: the place is practically barren.

Two tables, each with two chairs, sit haphazardly in the middle of the room, looking like they were carved by a ten-year-old. Nothing decorates the walls, and the old wooden floors are coated in dirt and goo. To the left is an empty pastry case, and behind the counter are two coffee thermoses.

No espresso machine.

No fancy menu.

Just . . . coffee.

Umm . . .

"We open at ten and close at four."

"You open at ten?" How on earth do they open at ten when I was ordered to get coffee at six in the morning?

"Aye, not much activity in the area until ten. Most businesses around here open at nine and close no later than six, besides Fergie's Castle, the pub. The Admiral, our local eatery, will close at six on the weekdays and seven on the weekends, so if you're craving—what do you Americans call it, 'dinner'?—be sure to plan ahead. Fergie's will have some generic pub food, but it can get rowdy once the town shuts down and everyone gathers for a whisky."

"Wow, okay. Good to know," I say, just as my stomach does a weird somersault at the mention of food. *Oof.* That didn't feel good.

"We're closed on Sundays—almost the whole town is. The tour buses don't drive through here on Sundays, so we all take the day off, besides the pub. Hamish always has the pub open."

"Tour buses come through here?" I ask as Dakota walks around the small space, arms crossed, surveying our new job. There's no doubt she'll be able to keep up with her graphic design work while we're here. From the looks of the two coffee thermoses, it seems like I might have some spare time on my hands as well.

"Aye. For the Boaby Stone. We are quite proud of it, actually. Shona down at the market screen prints Boaby Stone T-shirts. 'I kissed the Boaby Stone,' they say. Quite clever. Stuart and I have a matching set."

Yeah, I'm going to need one of those. "I love a good penis shirt." Dakota elbows me in the side. I glance at her and shrug. "What? I do."

"Have you watched *Iron Crowns*?" Finella asks.

I'm about to answer when my intestines gurgle. An instant sweat breaks out on the back of my neck.

Uh, that doesn't feel right.

Not at all.

We might have a situation brewing.

"I have," Dakota says. "Haven't gotten to the Boaby Stone part yet. Can't wait for it."

"Thrilling. They show his actual boaby, ya know. The actor didn't have a stand-in. Sir Richard MacLain is quite endowed, I must say. Such a shame they pretended to castrate him." Finella sighs and goes to the counter. "Really simple here. Dark roast and decaf. We also have some hot chocolate packets if the kids want any. We haven't had food here in a while. Stuart used to bake, but he's slowed down a bit." Finella grows quiet just as my gut churns, the sound deafening in the small coffee shop.

Both Dakota and Finella turn to me, brows raised.

I smile uncomfortably. "You know, I don't think something is settling right."

"Don't sound like it." Finella eyes me up and down. "Are ya allergic to sheep lungs?"

"Uh . . . not that I know of."

33

"Heart? Liver? Stomach?"

"No . . . why?" I swallow hard, fear itching up the back of my neck.

"Och, that's haggis, lass."

Bile rises in my throat, and I pray I don't lose it all right here, in the middle of this dirty, unswept floor.

"Sheep stomach?" I ask, quietly.

"Aye, and liver, heart, and lungs. Quite good."

Oh *GOD*.

Smiling politely, I take a step back. "You know, I think I'm going to head back to the cottage and, um—" I burp and I pray to the holy heavens I can keep it together. "I'm going to go take a shower. Wash the airplane off."

Finella sees right through me.

"Aye, remember to use the water bucket." She gives me a wink.

"Dakota, learn the ropes," I say, wafting my finger around the room before taking off at a brisk power walk to the cottage.

"Ask what's in it before you eat it from now on," I say to myself in the mirror.

I'll spare you the details. Let's just say I've made my mark here in Scotland.

Jet-lagged, freshly showered, and ready for a pillow, I brush out my long blonde hair and run some wave serum through the strands to capture my natural curl. After brushing my teeth—twice—I've wrapped the plain white towel provided in the bathroom around my chest and have taken a deep breath just as the front door opens and closes.

Dakota.

She's in big trouble.

She's the one who did all the research—she should have warned me about the haggis.

With what little fight I have left in me, I toss the bathroom door open and stomp into the kitchen, only to find a towering man leaning against the sink, eating one of the haggis balls.

"Oh my God!" I shout, securing my towel even tighter around my torso. From the corner of my eye, I spot a broom and snatch it up, pointing the brush end at him. "Don't you dare come any closer."

He's unfazed.

Still leaning against the counter, haggis ball in hand, he stares me down. "Who the hell are you?"

Well, kick me in the crotch and lay me down to rest. He has to have the most delicious voice I've ever heard.

Full of timbre, with rolling *r*'s and a heavy dose of masculinity. It's odd to say, but his voice basically says, *I work with my hands and know how to use them as well.*

I'm tempted to rest my head against his chest and ask him to speak, just so I can feel the rumble of his voice over my body, but realize that's the exhaustion talking.

I snap myself out of my Scot-induced daydream and hold up the broom. "That's none of your concern. You're trespassing. If you don't leave in three seconds, I'm calling Finella."

"Aye, when you do, tell her the haggis is dry." He pops the rest of his ball in his mouth and chews. No smile, no humor in his face, just overall surliness.

"That's awfully rude."

"'Tis the truth." He dusts off his hands. "You a tourist?"

"Like I said, that's none of your concern. I suggest you leave before I put this broom to good use."

"Ya going to sweep me away? I'd like to see ya try with those scrawny arms."

Well, isn't he terribly unpleasant.

"Don't be too quick to judge. I pack a heavy punch. I could blow you right out of your shoes." I raise my fist in the air, but I quickly retract it when I notice it's shaking slightly.

I may act tough, but I also know when I'm beaten in size and stature.

The stranger crosses his arms over his brawny chest and studies me, his devilish green gaze roaming my body. It feels like his eyes are a sponge, soaking up every last inch of me until I'm completely dry.

Uneasy and exposed, though never one to back down, I attempt to provide him the same treatment, but it just makes me weak in the knees.

He's wearing dark-wash jeans, cuffed right above the top of his brown boots. The denim is stretched tight around his thick thighs, and his forest-green T-shirt does nothing to hide the rippling muscles underneath the fabric. Nor do the sleeves even attempt to disguise the boulders in his biceps or his sculpted shoulders. But what's really catching my eyes is the intricately woven tattoo that encircles his wrist like a watch and travels up his arm, all the way under his sleeve. And that's just his body. His face is a whole other story. Thick scruff lines his square jaw, and his brown hair is buzzed on the sides, with the slightest wave to the longer strands on top. His deep mossy eyes penetrate me better than Harry did the last time we had sex.

My, my, my . . .

"Get your fill?" he asks, startling me out of my swoon and right back into defense mode.

"I should ask the same of you," I say, stepping closer and brandishing my broom.

"Nothing I haven't seen before," he answers with such boredom in his voice that I'm mildly insulted.

"You're rude," I snap.

"I know."

Okay . . . well, at least we're on the same page about that . . .

"It would behoove you to leave the premises before I call the cops."

"Aye, and what's the phone number for the cops?" he challenges with a triumphant glint in his eyes, though his lips remain flat, unaffected.

I roll my top teeth over my lip, my stomach dropping. I really didn't do any research before I came here—that was not smart on my end.

"Uh, 911?"

"Eejit tourists," he mumbles, shaking his head. He pushes off the counter, and his chest meets the bristles of the broom. "Get dressed and leave. I'm sure Finella doesn't want you staying longer than you're supposed to."

"I'm supposed to stay for six months," I shoot back.

One brow crooks to the sky. "What?"

"Six months," I repeat, holding my chest high, glad my towel has yet to even loosen. "I'll be staying here, in this cottage, so if you would please leave, that would be—"

"What the hell are you doing here for six months?"

"Why are you so nosy?"

His chest presses deeper into the bristles. *Stand tall, Bonnie, don't let him intimidate you.* "Because Finella is my maw, and I want to know why you're staying in her cottage."

Oh.

My.

God.

This is Rowan?

Well, Finella wasn't spinning any Scottish fables about her son. Strapping *indeed*.

And a tad grumpy.

Ehh . . . a whole lot grumpy, from the way his eyebrows sharpen as he stares at me.

"You must be Rowan," I say, still keeping the broom between us. Less for protection and more out of pride—and to ensure I don't try to lick his biceps or anything.

Because yowser, those biceps.

Yup, strapping . . . very, very strapping.

No, doesn't matter if he's "climb me like a tree" kind of hot; he's being a jerk. *Stand your ground.*

"And you are . . ."

"Bonnie," I answer. "Bonnie St. James. I'm one-sixteenth Scottish."

"Aye." He looks me up and down with annoyance, eyes blazing across my skin. "And why are you here for six months?"

"My best friend and I are here to take care of the coffee shop while your parents are on vacation. Honestly, don't you communicate with them? Or do you just criticize your mom's cooking?"

His brow lifts but then quickly returns to neutral as he steps away from the broom and brings his hand to his jaw, studying me some more.

Wait . . . did he really not know his parents were about to go on vacation? It seems odd to me. Wouldn't that be something they'd tell him?

"Didn't you see the advert?" I ask.

"I did," he answers calmly, almost too calmly. "Wasn't aware the position was filled."

"Well, it was. By me and Dakota."

"Mm-hmm." He gives me another once-over, as if sizing me up for a fight.

I have my pride, but I'm almost positive if he flicked me with his thumb and index finger, he could shoot me all the way to the loch, towel flapping in the wind like a white signal of surrender.

"Stop that." I poke him with the broom.

Stagnant. Unwavering. He doesn't even blink an eye.

"Stop what?"

"Checking me out."

"Trust me, lass, if I was checking you out, you'd know it."

God, he's . . . rude.

"I heard Scotsmen are quite hospitable—seems that's not the case with you."

"Never been one to conform."

Irritated, I jab him with the broom again. "Unless you have anything else to say, you can leave now."

Running his hand over his jaw again, he steps away from the broom and, without a word, strides out of the cottage. The door clicks shut behind him. I lower the broom and let out a deep breath, catching through the kitchen window his tall frame walking away.

Well, isn't he what historical romances are made for?

The swoony Scot.

Hottie in the Highlands.

Killing Hearts in a Kilt.

Thankfully, according to Finella, he's not around much.

Hopefully that's the only interaction I'll have with him for the next six months, because I couldn't imagine dealing with that surly attitude for the duration of my visit. He was brimming with negativity—at least that's what it felt like—and I'm on a new path, a search for purpose. I can't be riddled with Scottish tempers.

Nope, this is the start of something new, and it won't involve Mr. Rowan McMuscleMan.

Chapter Four
ROWAN

I don't want to do this.

It's glaikit.

You can't force me.

You've got to be kidding me . . .

Fine.

Run-in with American: *One.*

Uncommunicative parents: *Two.*

Annoying author making me do pointless shite I don't want to do: *One.*

There . . . happy?

You've got to be fucking kidding me.

When were they planning on telling me they found people to look after the coffee house?

And what for?

I push my hand through my hair and round the bend where my parents' house is tucked away up against a mountain. When the white stone building comes into view, I throw my pickup into park and stare at it.

What the hell were they thinking?

Hamish down at the pub was the one who asked about the advert my parents submitted and the worldwide attention it had received. The advert I had no idea about. That was embarrassing enough, but to not be told that they'd actually found two lasses to take over the coffee shop? That's fucking ridiculous.

As anger settles over me, tensing my shoulders and neck, I push through the door of their quaint house. At the sound of my steps, both my parents startle on their black leather sofa in the living room, their bodies jostling against each other. The iPad they were holding tumbles to the floor with a thud.

"Jesus, Rowan, you startled us." Maw presses one hand to her heart and one to my da's thigh.

I slam the door shut. "When were you going to tell me?"

"Tell you what?" Maw asks, feigning innocence, but I know her sweet whisky-brown eyes conceal some severe calculation.

"The two Americans."

"Aye, did you meet them? Bonnie is quite the looker, isn't she?"

"When were you going to tell me?" I say, ignoring her.

My da lowers his glasses on his nose, his usually strong body looking withered under his tartan shirt. The past few months have been alarming, to say the least. There has been a distinct decrease in Da's muscle mass, in his energy levels and food consumption. Foods that he used to love he barely touches now. He even passed up some empire biscuits a few weeks ago, which first tipped me off that something might be going on. The other day I asked Maw if Da was okay, and she said he was fine, just eating healthy, which was why he'd lost so much weight. But he doesn't look like he's just lost weight—he looks frail.

"Tomorrow, when we leave," he says in his authoritative voice.

41

I grew up with that voice, constantly chattering in my ear, molding me into the man he wanted me to become, a man he could be proud of. Strong.

A man who takes care of his home.

A man who's proud of his heritage and his family name.

And yes, I do take pride in where I've come from, my heritage and the family name, but I want so much more from this life. I *need* so much more from this life, and I haven't been able to consider an alternate route from what my da has planned for me.

"You're leaving tomorrow? So . . . what, you were just going to pack your bags and take off with barely a goodbye?"

"We were going to say goodbye," Maw says, rising from the sofa and walking over to the entryway, where I'm still standing, my feet feeling like stone. She pats me on the cheek. "Did you eat?"

Is she kidding me right now? "Maw, I don't even know why you're leaving in the first place. You're being so goddamn secretive."

"No, we're not. We're going on holibags. That's all you need to know."

"No, I need to know where you're going. What if there's an emergency? Are you even going to take your phones with you, or are you going to go completely rogue?"

"Don't be silly—of course we'll bring our phones." Maw moves to the kitchen, where she starts fixing me a plate.

I turn to my da. "Was this your plan, to keep it all a secret?"

It's common knowledge in town that I don't necessarily get on well with my da. We have our grievances, our differences, and ideas of what my future should be. I wanted to focus on my craft, leave Corsekelly, find my own life, my own future. And Da . . . well, he said he wanted nothing to do with me leaving and claimed abandonment of my family and the town that played a huge part in my life.

Disrespectful.

Irresponsible.

Hurtful.

All words Da used when I confronted him about my decision. And as he spouted off his distaste for the mere notion of me leaving, I saw pain in his eyes. Raw and real.

I asked him for his truth, why he was so hurt about me leaving—truly hurt.

He masked up, shut down, and reminded me of what we'd lost already as a family.

Guess who won out regarding what I did with my life? All I can say is, it's not my idea to stay in Corsekelly as the town's repairman, going from house to house replacing faucets, cleaning gutters, and even cutting the grass. But that's what Da wanted. And after everything that happened . . . well, let's just say I owe him. I'll leave it at that.

"Don't you raise your voice with me," he says, shifting on the sofa and wincing at the same time.

A few months ago, Da stopped working at the coffee shop, leaving all the work to Maw. He insisted on taking a much-deserved break after thirty years of serving coffee to the locals and tourists. But Maw couldn't keep up with the demand of baking and serving customers. The coffee shop has languished without him.

"I'm not raising my voice," I say, my voice rising. "I'm just trying to understand all of this." I look my da dead in the eyes. "Are you sick and you're not telling me?"

"No," he says gruffly, standing from the sofa and making his way to the kitchen, where Maw hands him a plate. "We just want to take some time off, and we don't need to clear that decision with you."

I run my tongue over my teeth, corralling my anger. "That's fair, but I'd appreciate you respecting me enough to inform me about your plans. I'm your son, after all."

As the tension builds between me and Da, Maw hurries over and presses a plate into my hand. "Sit, eat, and we'll tell you all about the trip."

Keeping my eyes on Da, I take the plate and find a seat at the table in the kitchenette.

Shaky hands.

Unhealthy skin.

Sunken eyes.

Whatever they're about to tell me, I know there's so much more that they're not going to give away.

"About damn time," Lachlan, one of my two best friends, says as I push through the semicrowded pub. "Leith and I are starting to get sick of staring at each other."

"Surprising, given how narcissistic you both are." I take a seat at the high-top table they're sharing.

Leith and Lachlan Murdach.

Identical twins and proud owners of Bubbles Linen Basket, the town's launderette. They're also becoming incredibly famous online for the personal-training videos they post every Sunday. Decked out in their kilts and nothing else, they use Scotland's terrain to work out. Logs for bench pressing, stones for push-ups, hurdling fences for cardio—blurred under the kilts, of course. I saw the unedited version and nearly threw up in my mouth. They thought it would be funny to skip the underwear that day.

Another man's jiggling boaby is something you can't unsee.

"You seem extra irritated today," Leith says, handing me a tumbler of whisky. "Does this have to do with the two Americans who came strolling into town today?"

I down my whisky and set the glass on the table, not giving them the satisfaction of my answer.

"I think it does," Lachlan says. "Word on the street is they're blonde and bonny."

"Bonny" doesn't even begin to describe it.

Bonnie.

Ice-blue eyes, unlike any I'd ever seen before, studied me, devoured me in one slow perusal. Platinum-blonde hair fell over her shoulders and past her plump breasts, which were barely secured by a towel.

And the arrogance she exuded—the woman was half-naked and using a broom as a weapon, but she was still proud, stubborn, determined. I wasn't prepared for the wave of interest that wrapped around my limbs and sank into my bones. Nor was I ready for the headiness that flushed through my body when her eyes connected with mine.

But then she mentioned my parents' imminent departure. I was quickly distracted from her beauty and was put on high alert. How could she know more about them than I did?

A stranger.

"Have you met them?" Leith asks, looking far too excited.

"One," I say, wishing I hadn't gulped all my whisky down.

"And . . ."

I shrug. "She wasn't bad."

Throwing his head back, Leith lets out an obnoxious laugh and shoves my shoulder. "Don't buy it."

Yeah, neither do I.

Ignoring him, I drag my hand over my face. "Did you know my parents are going to be gone for six months?"

"Figured as much," Lachlan says. "That's what was in the advert—didn't you read it?"

Apparently not well enough.

"They're headed to Europe," I say. "Traveling around from country to country by train." At least, that's what they told me. I twist the empty tumbler between my hands, recalling the vague details I dragged out of them.

I can still feel the palpable silence in my parents' house as we all ate together, the forks clanging on crockery plates, the heavy weight hovering above all of us, the unspoken truth of what's really going on in our family. We're falling apart. We've been falling apart for years, and no one is willing to step up and fix things.

After this whole holibags shite, I'm sure as hell not.

"Sour you're not going with them?" Lachlan asks.

"No," I shoot back. "Irritated they didn't tell me until the night before they were planning on leaving." I look around the pub, making sure no one is paying our conversation any attention before I lower my voice. "Have you heard anything around town about my da's health?"

"No," Lachlan answers.

"Why?" Leith asks, turning serious. "You worried about him?"

"Just doesn't seem like his full self. He's weak, frail looking. Maw says he's on a diet, but I don't buy it. He never walks around town anymore. God forbid he'd talk to me about it, though. The man would rather die puffing his chest than let me in on any fault he might have."

"He seems like he's lost weight," Lachlan says. "But I thought he was just eating healthier, like your maw said. Haven't seen him in the pub at all, or at the Admiral."

Aye. Another warning sign.

Da loves this town, loves everyone who lives here, and thrives off talking to as many locals as he can.

I'm the exact opposite.

"Christ," I sigh just as Isla, Lachlan and Leith's younger sister, steps up to the table. "Hey, Isla."

She hands out another round of drinks and takes a seat at the table with us. "Saw your maw today, Rowan. She told me all about the new lesbian in town."

Hell.

Thank God Isla is smirking. My maw is blunt as fuck and has no boundaries to speak of. Makes living in a small town difficult.

"Said I should go make her acquaintance. Ask her out on a date."

"One of the Americans is a lesbian?" Leith asks.

"Yes, well, according to Finella. She said Dakota—that's her name—is recovering from a bad breakup."

"How uncomfortable was that conversation?" I say, shaking my head.

"Not as uncomfortable as the conversation we had after she found out I was gay. Progress." She winks.

"Is the other one a lesbian?" Leith asks, seeming far too eager at the prospect.

"Bonnie," I say, staring down at my glass. "Her name is Bonnie St. James."

The table falls silent as all three Murdachs stare me down.

"Och, do we know this Bonnie?" Isla asks.

I tip back my glass of whisky, though I barely let the liquid wet my lips. "Ran into her at the cottage."

"And . . . ?" Leith asks. "Care to elaborate?"

I take another sip. "She tried to attack me with a broom but barely even tapped me. Tiny thing."

"Everyone is tiny compared to you," Isla points out.

"Thinking on asking her out?" Lachlan asks.

"No," I answer, and I mean it. Yeah, her eyes are unlike anything I've ever seen, and behind her angry, furrowed brow, I spotted the softest of smiles, but I have zero interest in getting involved with an American, let alone one who's only here temporarily. "She's running the coffee shop—I don't foresee us crossing paths."

"Have you forgotten where you live?" Lachlan asks. "I'd be shocked if you don't run into her at least once a day."

"Trust me. I stay out of this town's way."

"Uh-huh." Leith laughs. "Ten pounds says you see her first thing tomorrow morning."

Chapter Five
BONNIE

Cake consumed: Zero, and I'm going through withdrawal.

New job: One—not what I want to do for life, but it will do for now.

Days since last male-induced orgasm: Seventy-two, but my dreams were pretty naughty last night.

Attractive but surly Scotsman: One, and he was unfortunately the star of my naughty dreams.

Tasks: One—make cake today.

◆ ◆ ◆

"Is Scotland on the surface of the sun?" I lift my hands to my eyes. "Dakota, are we on the sun?" I shout.

"I have coffee," she calls, her voice traveling upstairs to my bedroom, which feels more like a loft since there is no door and the ceiling is slanted on either side, barely giving me enough room to stand.

The prospect of caffeine gets me out of bed.

Last night, after Dakota got home from going over all the details of the coffee shop with Finella, I told her all about Rowan and his rudeness.

Was he cute? she asked.

Did he have big muscles?

Was he as strapping as Finella said he was?

Pfft, barely, I told her. *Sure, if you're into the rugged Scot type.*

After Dakota filled me in on some details about our stay, we decided I would take the upstairs room. Dakota took the downstairs room. It has a little more space than mine, but that's because she has to sleep on a twin bed, whereas I have a full.

There is no doubt my eyes are bloodshot right now from exhaustion. I didn't sleep too well last night, even though I attempted to go to bed early—I only found myself tossing and turning, trying to get comfortable in a strange bed, in a strange cottage, in a strange country.

Might be feeling a hair homesick.

I shield my eyes as I trudge down the stairs and head to the coffeepot. "Why is it so freaking bright—?" I pause, my eyes landing on the time on the coffee maker. "What the hell? Is it really four fifteen in the morning?"

"Yup," Dakota mumbles from one of the red couches.

"What kind of game is the sun trying to pull right now?" I fill up a cup and swirl some sugar around in it.

"Summer in Scotland means longer days. Didn't you notice it was still light out when we went to sleep?"

"I just assumed we were going to bed early."

"We went to bed at ten last night," Dakota says, staring out the window.

"What?" I groan. "Good God, where the hell did you take me? Accents, sheep stomach, water buckets for toilets, and endless sun. I don't think my body is ready for this."

"It'll get better, once we're here for a bit. It's just a bit of a culture shock at first."

"A bit?" I ask, sitting on the sofa across from her. "A Scotsman saw me in my towel yesterday and was unfazed when I pushed him with a broom. There is something fishy about the people out here."

"He's probably thinking the same about Americans, since you tried to defend yourself with a broom."

"That's not being weird—that's being innovative." I sip my coffee. "What the hell are we supposed to do for six hours before we open the coffee shop?"

"Explore? Get some food?"

"Uh, earth to Dakota, nothing opens up around here until nine."

"Oh yeah." She scratches the side of her head. "Man, I forgot about that. Uh, we could go look at the Penis Stone."

"Ah yes, six a.m. adventures to go look at a penis stone—that's exactly what I want to do."

"There's food here—I saw some muffins in a cupboard. We can pack them up and go for a walk along the loch, have a picnic breakfast."

The internet is shoddy at best, there's no TV in the cottage, and our only mode of entertainment is a bookshelf full of romance novels that I plan on tackling while I'm here, but my eyes are too busted for reading at the moment.

So a picnic by the loch sounds like a plan.

"Okay, let me go change."

"Yeah?" Dakota asks, looking surprised.

"Yeah." I nod and stand, taking another sip of my coffee.

I head upstairs, where I unpack a pair of leggings and a long-sleeve shirt. I toss them on quickly before I put my long hair up into a messy bun—a look I'm sure I'll adopt with the ever-changing weather. No use doing my hair if it's just going to get rained on all the time. I slip on my workout shoes and then head downstairs, where Dakota is pouring our coffee into to-go cups.

"Did you pack the muffins?" I ask.

"Not yet. They're in the cupboard above the fridge. I think there are some apples in the fridge too."

"Perfect." Dakota brought her hiking backpack, so we load it up and head out the door into the crisp morning air.

Calm greets us. The air doesn't seem to shift, but it carries a fresh weight that seeps into my bones and wakes me faster than the coffee. Birdsong surrounds us as a light haze lifts off the ground and dewdrops cling to each blade of grass from last night's rain.

Peaceful.

Serene.

Exactly what I need.

"It's beautiful," I whisper, feeling like if I talk any louder I might wake the entire town, though we're tucked away in our little grove of trees.

"I don't think I've ever experienced anything like it," Dakota whispers back. She reaches over, grabs my hand, and presses our palms together. "Thank you for coming with me, Bonnie."

Turning toward her, I match her grateful smile and pull her into a hug. "Thank you for drunkenly applying to the job for both of us."

She chuckles and pulls away. "From the look of it, we're not going to have any problem with coffee." We start down the gravel path as the sun peeks through the leaves, truly making this entire experience feel like a dream. "I did ask for help when it came to the currency here. Finella made a little chart for us so we understand the worth of each bill and coin."

"Oh crap, I totally forgot about money. Does it seem hard?"

Dakota shakes her head. "Finella did a good job laying it all out. I can show you later."

"They leave today?"

"Yeah," Dakota says as we near town. "As we were saying goodbye yesterday, she said the shop was in our hands and she trusts us."

"Well, that's a good thing, I guess." As we hit Corsekelly Lane, we both look left, then right. The stone dwellings are quiet, the street empty. A complete ghost town. Not a soul awake besides us. A stark contrast with LA, where time doesn't seem to stand still but moves past you at light speed.

In front of us is Loch Duich, the sun glistening off miniscule ripples of water. Off in the distance are the pointy peaks of the Highlands, decorated in green and peppered with evergreens, the perfect view for a deathly-early morning.

"Want to go down to the bank over there?" Dakota asks, pointing. "We can sit on the rocks so our butts don't get wet from the grass."

"That's a great idea. It's so wet here—completely different from California. I'm going to have to remember that when walking around."

We find two flat rocks that sit right at the water's edge and take a seat. Dakota divvies out our breakfast, and together we watch the water rippling in the sun, lapping just below our feet.

We're silent for a while, just enjoying our muffins and nature, until my mind starts to turn, reflecting on the last few years of my life.

I was never the best student, and it wasn't from a lack of trying. I just didn't . . . get it. I never truly excelled in any topic, and I settled with solid Cs my entire high school career, which didn't translate over into college.

Higher academics weren't looking for average.

They were looking for someone like Dakota. Perfect grades. President of the art club and the chess club—quite the brainiac. The girl took online college classes during high school, for crying out loud. And funnily enough, she quickly realized college was going to be a waste of her time once she found a niche in the social media marketing community. She's paid well, constantly has work flowing in, has built a phenomenal portfolio, and continues to grow.

I was the one who wanted to go to college. My parents didn't know that. They never knew about the applications, and I was sure to always grab the mail before them. I wanted it to be a surprise. To show them that even though they were constantly on me about getting my grades up, I could do things on my own and go to college, major in business, be my own event planner. But every time I picked up the mail, I was greeted with rejection after rejection.

With every pass, every apology letter from a university, it became blatantly clear that my parents were right—I couldn't do it.

I had to get out of their house, away from their disappointed faces. Once again, I'd let them down.

Los Angeles held promise, but I was still just average. Never truly excelling.

"This isn't how I expected things to go for us," I say quietly.

"You mean bouncing off to Scotland out of the blue?"

I chuckle and shake my head. "Well, I wasn't expecting that, but I also wasn't expecting to be put in a situation where bouncing off to Scotland was really my only chance at repairing myself." I sigh and lean back on one hand as I tilt my head up to the sky. "I'm twenty-four and don't have much to show for it. I was so sure I knew what I wanted to do. Move to Los Angeles, make connections, get into the party-planning scene . . ." What a joke that was. Three-time personal assistant with nothing to show for it besides knowing where every Starbucks is in Hollywood. Pathetic. "At least you know you're good at graphic design—you can easily do that wherever you go. But I don't really know who I am." Tears well up in my eyes. My throat grows tight as hopelessness overtakes me, a dark cloud ready to pour down.

"Your job doesn't define you as a person, Bonnie."

"But it gives you purpose. I haven't felt purpose in a while, not since . . . hell, I don't think I've ever felt purpose. I haven't felt genuinely needed. Even with Harry, he never truly needed me. And I know I didn't need him, but that breakup was painful because it was another blow to my self-esteem, another thing that made me wonder if maybe . . . maybe I'm not important enough."

"Stop it," Dakota says, reaching over and taking my hand. "You're important to me. Ever since you helped me take down Tijuana and Theresa on the handball court." I snort. "I'm serious, though, Bonnie. You are very important. I need you. If it weren't for you, I don't know how I would have made it through my breakup with Isabella. And even before that, you were . . . you are my other half. We complete each other, and you might not feel important, but you are vastly important to me."

And that does it to me. My tears spill over, and I let out a low sob. Dakota scoots closer as she wraps her arm around my shoulders and squeezes tight.

"Do you realize how valuable you are to me?" Dakota asks as I try to gain control of my emotions. "Like I said, I never would have made it through my breakup with Isabella without you. You have been my confidante, my rock, my laughter, my entertainment. I don't just choose you as a best friend because you've been in my life for what seems like forever—I choose you because I rely on you, because I need you . . . I always have."

And cue more tears.

Damn it, Dakota.

"You know I value our friendship, right?" I ask, wiping away my tears.

"I know."

"It's also gotten me through all the tough times, and I'm proud we've made it through all the ups and downs."

"But . . . ?" Dakota says with a chuckle.

"It doesn't feel like enough, and I don't want that to sound mean—"

"I understand what you're trying to say. You need more in your life. There's purpose behind our friendship, but you want that individual purpose too. You want to feel like you're accomplishing something."

"Exactly. And I have no idea what that is. I thought moving to Los Angeles and working closely with celebrities would spark something within me, but looking back over those years, nothing grabbed me, nothing made me feel excited. And the personal-assistant jobs I had weren't all mundane tasks—I did do some fun things, but those small moments never amounted to what I thought I wanted to do."

"Event planning?" Dakota asks.

I nod. "Yeah, even thinking about it now . . . do I really want to throw parties? Or was I just good at attending them in high school?"

"You were the life of the party," Dakota says with a smirk when I glance at her.

"And look where that got me." I bring my knees to my chest and wrap my arms around my shins. "By now, people our age at least have a direction they want to take their life. I'm still lost."

"Not true. They might have adult jobs and degrees, but a lot of people our age aren't really doing what they want to do. They're working to pay the bills. You have a unique opportunity to truly reflect and figure out who you want to become."

"I don't know where to start," I say. "My self-worth is pretty low. I know I've tried to laugh everything off, make jokes about my situation, but after just a day here, I already see that our fast-paced life was a distraction. We're surrounded by peace and beauty, and all it's doing is bringing all my fears to the forefront of my mind. What if I truly never amount to anything? What if I never live up to my full potential?"

Dakota shifts on her rock while picking a piece of lint off her pants. She's taking her time responding. Dakota is always thoughtful and insightful. She doesn't spew nonsense, and when she has to be real with me, she is. There is no fluff in our friendship, just pure love for each other, and honesty.

"What would you define as a successful life? Does a job really matter that much to you? Is that how you think you're going to find purpose?"

"It will give me something to strive for, something to challenge me."

She slowly nods. "You know, sometimes I think we get caught up in the idea that our jobs make or break us as humans, when that's not the case at all. A job is a means to make money and provide for yourself. I think it's the relationships we cultivate, the energy we put out into the world, that define us. You could be a billionaire with all the riches in the world, but that wouldn't mean your life was truly rich. I think we're both lucky, because we have each other—a true friendship that has stood the test of time, especially through the teenager hormone years." We both chuckle. "We're an example of women lifting each other up, and to me, that's powerful."

"Yeah, it is," I say, feeling a little lighter. "But why do I still feel like I'm missing something?"

"Because you are, and it will take some time to figure out what that is, but while you're here, with all this beauty in your backyard, you should try to find that missing puzzle piece."

"You're right." I sigh and again lean back on my hands, stretching my legs out. "Do you think this trip is going to change us?"

"Us, as in our friendship? Never. But us as in individuals? I hope so."

She rests her head on my shoulder and I rest my head on hers, letting the birds fill the silence with their morning songs.

I truly hope Dakota is right.

"Aye, they're dead," a voice says as something stiff and hard pokes me in the shoulder.

"Should we call the police? Look for a medic?"

Poke.

Poke.

Poke.

"What are you doing?" I mumble, shifting, only to feel a million needles pierce my back.

Oh dear God, my ass is numb.

"Och, she's alive," someone calls out. "What about t'other one?"

The sun is blazing on me as I try to open my eyes. Lifting one hand in front of my face, I block out the intense rays and squint them open. Dakota is lying near me, her head resting on my lap.

"Dakota." I sit up and give her a gentle shake.

"Hmm . . ."

"Wake up. We fell asleep on the rocks."

"What?" She tries to open her eyes as well but must realize—like I did—that Scotland resides on the surface of the sun. "Oh God, why is it so bright?" She sits up and blinks at our surroundings.

I do the same.

Our backpack's contents are strewn about the rocks, along with our bodies. Our thermoses of coffee have been tossed to the side, and our feet dangle above the lapping water, just begging to be dragged in.

"What time is it?"

"Half ten," the voices above us answer.

"Half ten?" I ask, my mind mush. "What is that? Half of ten? So, five in the morning? Good God, it's this bright out at five in the morning?"

"Nay. Half ten."

I finally turn and spot two older-looking women standing over us. They both have red hair and matching concerned expressions. "I'm sorry, I don't know what 'half ten' means."

"The Americans," one of the women scoffs.

"Aye, they are bonny, aren't they?"

"Yes, that's me, Bonnie—and you are?"

"Full of themselves too." They chuckle together and reach out, giving us a helping hand. "I'm Innis, and I run the inn here. This is Shona—she owns the Mill Market."

"It's nice to meet you," I say, straightening up as much as I can, even though I can't feel the entire back side of my body. "This is Dakota, and I'm Bonnie."

"Oh, Bonnie is your name?" Innis asks. "Aye. Nice to meet you. Are ye Scottish?"

"One-sixteenth," I say, puffing my chest. I watch Innis and Shona exchange a quick look of amusement.

"Well, then, the coffee shop is in good hands, even if you are tardy to open."

"What?" Dakota and I say at the same time.

"It's half ten," Shona says. "We went to get a cup but noticed it was closed, and then we saw two lifeless bodies down here by the rocks and decided to investigate. We thought you were dead."

"What does 'half ten' mean?" Dakota asks, looking panicked.

"Ten thirty."

"Oh my God," we both say. Quickly, we gather our things and take off toward the coffee shop, but not before thanking the ladies. They just laugh at us as we sprint up the gray brick road and straight to the coffee house, where . . .

Oh crap.

Standing tall, his arms crossed over a red-and-black-plaid shirt, is none other than Rowan MacGregor, as I've learned is his last name.

His eyes narrow and we run toward him, and I know I'm about to be met with a whole storm of grumpy.

"Taking it light on the job?" he asks.

I take a moment to catch my breath as he glowers down at me. "We were eating breakfast by the loch and fell asleep on the rocks." I clutch my aching back. "It was an accident."

"My parents trusted you to take care of their shop while they're gone, and this is how you act on the first day?"

"We're so sorry," Dakota says, jogging to my side. "It was not our intention to slack. We're just tired and jet-lagged, and the birdsong and lapping water were so peaceful, and we just couldn't help ourselves." There she goes, rambling. She gets that from me.

Rowan looks Dakota up and down, but it doesn't feel like the same intense perusal he gave me yesterday while I wielded my broom.

"And you are?"

"Dakota." She holds out her hand, but he doesn't take it. Ugh, he's so freaking rude. "You must be Rowan."

"Aye. And you must be the responsible one."

"What is that supposed to mean?" I ask, hands on my hips. "I'm responsible."

His intimidating eyes flash toward me for a brief second before he focuses back on Dakota. "Me maw and da asked me to stop over at the shop today to make sure you two were all set with everything you need. To my surprise, you weren't here."

"Not on purpose. We would never disregard your parents like that," I say.

His eyes remain trained on Dakota. "I don't babysit. I told my parents I won't be babysitting you two, but it looks like I might have to, judging by how day one is going."

"No, you won't," Dakota says, using her best mom voice. "This is all an honest mistake. I promise, we will be better."

"We don't have to prove anything to him." I fold my arms over my chest.

"Bonnie," Dakota says, chastising me.

Rowan shifts in front of us, hands falling to his hips. Challenging.

"What? He's being rude. It was an honest mistake. He doesn't have to be so mean about it. I see his intimidation tactics. The way he towers over the 'wee lasses,'" I say in my best Scottish accent. "I see right through you, Rowan." I move two fingers between my eyes and his, but he doesn't flinch, not even a blink. "I won't stand here and let you attempt to intimidate us. No, sir." I push past him, my shoulder brushing his, the stone of his arm sending my shoulder back as I continue forward. "Now, if you'll excuse us, we have some coffee to make. Come on, Dakota."

From behind me, I hear Dakota say, "I'm so sorry. It won't happen again."

I watch through the front window as Rowan angrily walks away. "You don't have to suck up to him," I say as Dakota steps inside and the door swings shut behind her.

"He's Stuart and Finella's son. I think it would be helpful if we were nice."

"Why? He's not being nice to us."

"Because what if we need help with something? He's the handyman, isn't he?"

"We'll be fine. What could possibly go wrong?"

Dakota strides behind the counter and starts scooping ground coffee into the coffee maker. "These are centuries-old buildings—pretty sure anything can go wrong, especially when you put words like that out into the universe. You're just asking to be jinxed."

"Please. We have all the luck on our side, remember? We're going to go rub our faces on the Penis Stone. That's all the luck we need."

"Once again, it's not the Blarney Stone. It's where a man's dick was chopped off."

"In the name of *women*," I declare, raising my fist. "Trust me, we are going to be completely fine."

◆ ◆ ◆

"Why do I let you talk?" Dakota asks, pressing her hand to her face as we stare at the kitchen faucet—which is turned on and completely dry.

"Are you alluding to me jinxing us?" I ask, hoping to the high heavens that I didn't.

"I don't know. You go and piss off the handyman, then after a long, boring day at the coffee shop, we come home to no running water when the water was just fine earlier today and yesterday."

I gasp and spin toward Dakota. "Oh my God, do you think this is sabotage?" I start moving around the cottage, sniffing the air, running my fingers over the surfaces. "I can smell him. He was here."

"You can't possibly smell him."

"I can," I insist.

"Then what does he smell like?"

60

"A kilt," I answer, not even thinking about it.

"You've never smelled a kilt in your entire life."

"False," I say, running my nose over the back of the couch . . . oof, musty. "Last fall, Bath and Body Works sold a candle called Scottish Kilt. That's what Rowan smells like."

"You've lost your mind."

"Have I?" I ask. "Or have I cracked the code on this man?"

"You've lost it." Sighing, Dakota grabs her phone and pulls up her contacts.

"I don't think calling your dad is going to be helpful right now. Not sure he knows much about Scottish plumbing."

"I'm not calling my dad." She holds the phone up to her ear. "I'm calling Rowan."

"You have his number?" When the hell did she get that?

"Finella gave it to me in case we needed anything," Dakota says. Ahh, that makes sense.

Wait . . . she's actually calling him.

"No, you can't call him. That's exactly what he wants you to do. We can figure this out on our own." Hurrying to the bathroom, I grab the toilet-water bucket and charge out of the cottage to the well.

Now, to be honest, I've never seen a well in person, but I've seen them being used on many a TV show and movie, and when I say "many," I'm pretty sure it's only been Disney movies, but that's beside the point. Those badass bitches knew exactly what they were doing when they were fetching water.

Squatting down beside the short stone well, I lean my head under the well's little thatched roof and peer down the hole.

Pitch black.

"Hello?" I call down, just to check that there aren't any trolls or gremlins lurking below. The Scottish are known for their fables and storytelling so, you know, just have to make sure. "Anyone home?" I ask, laughing to myself.

When there is no response, I take that as my cue to use the bucket.

"See, we don't need him," I mutter to myself. "We can just get our own water." Not ideal, and yes, I swore I would need modern plumbing when we first pulled up to the cottage, but I've become one with Scotland today. Sleeping on the rocks by a loch—*ha!*—will do that to you.

I pull down the rope that's attached to a pulley system and tie it securely around the handle of the bucket. I make sure to yank it a few times to test that it's completely secure. Don't need to lose our toilet-water bucket.

Once I feel it's ready, I let the bucket dangle over the well before grabbing the pulley's handle and turning it. The bucket lowers a few inches.

"Aha!" I yell, looking behind me to the cottage and spotting Dakota in the front window, phone still held up to her ear. "Look, Dakota, I'm fetching us water. Get a picture for the Gram."

I turn the handle a little bit more and marvel at how smoothly it's lowering the bucket. It's as if I was born to fetch water.

"We'll be taking baths in no time," I call out, even though the thought of doing this multiple times to fill the tub isn't at all appealing.

Ugh, and to think families used to share the bathwater. I can't even begin to think of all the dead skin floating around.

Dakota and I are close . . . but we're not *that* close.

"Just got off the pho—Bonnie, what the hell are you doing?" Dakota asks from behind me.

I pause my work and crane my neck around, flashing her a grin. "Did you not hear me? I'm fetching us water. We don't need Kilty McGrumpyshire to come over here and save the day. We are survivalists—we can make it on our own."

"Your form of survival is Uber Eats."

"Takes a smart woman to know where to get the best food, still warm, and for a good price." I tap the side of my head. "Call Kilty back and tell him we're good."

"I'm not calling him back—and why are you calling him that? You haven't seen him in a kilt. You don't even know if he owns one."

"Okay, let's not be naive," I say, lowering the bucket even deeper. "He smells like a kilt, he's grumpy, and . . . I don't know, 'shire' has a nice ring to it. Kilty McGrumpy—huh." I frown, sensing a shift in the rope. "I think I just hit something."

"What do you mean you just—?"

An ear-piercing screech fills the air, and before I can look over the edge to assess what's knocked my bucket, a mass of blackness comes barreling out of the well, straight toward me.

I fling myself back on the ground as what must be hundreds of bats pour out of the well like a tidal wave of God's fury crashing down on us.

Now, there is only one way to describe the sound that flies out of my mouth as a bat's wing clips me across the forehead: the war cry of a pig in heat as the farmer steals its trough right out from under its nose.

It's feral.

It's disturbing.

It's unlike anything I've ever heard fall past my lips.

And it isn't just one scream.

It's several.

"Ahhh! . . . snuff snuff . . . ahhhhhh bababa ahhhh snuff."

Oink.

(Not really, but an oink wouldn't surprise me at this point.)

"They're eating me alive!" I cry out to Dakota, who is nowhere to be seen. "They want my brains; they're begging for the sweet juices of my intelligence." I swat at the air before trying to army crawl across the ground. This tactic fails miserably as bat after bat dive-bombs me. "I just wanted water. Don't kill me for wanting to stay hydrated. Ahhhh!"

Still screaming, I cover my face with my hands, deciding that this is how I die. Then, to my horror, a giant bat scoops me up by the pants and lifts me off the ground.

"Don't take me to your lair. Please, I'm not ready for Dracula. I have the devil's blood—it'll make you sick. Blood infused with garlic. So much garlic. Please spare me. Spare my life."

"Shut the fuck up," a deep Scottish voice demands.

I lift my hands from my eyes and look up to find Rowan carrying me to the house and then tossing me through the door, which he quickly slams behind him as he, too, enters. I scramble off the floor and to my feet. My blonde hair is a windblown—or bat-blown—mess, scattered across my forehead, whipping against my face and tangled into knots.

I stand up straight and lift my chin before I slowly push a chunk of hair out of my eyes. "I had it handled out there."

Dakota is standing to the side, covering her mouth and chuckling so much that I can see her shoulders shake with suppressed laughter.

She will hear about my displeasure at her reaction later. Right now, I have to deal with a Scot.

"No, you didn't," he retorts. "You sounded like a horse getting its leg chopped off."

Huh . . . that would be another accurate way to describe the sounds coming from my mouth.

"Well, pardon me for expressing my discomfort as a million bats tried to bury themselves in my hair and take me to their master. Next time I'll be sure to giggle and act more ladylike."

"Wouldn't hurt," he says, and his reply makes me really, *really* want to kick him in the shin.

"Why are you so surly all the time? Got your kilt all twisted in your crack?"

He looks down at his jeans and back up at me. "I'm not wearing a kilt."

"Metaphorically."

"Aye, so would it be metaphorically the same if I asked whether or not your cowboy hat was screwed on a little too tight?"

"Not all Americans wear cowboy hats."

"Which proves his point," Dakota says from the side of her mouth. I glance at her with narrowed eyes—she seems to be having too much fun watching this interaction.

"That's neither here nor there," I say, straightening my shirt. "We don't need your assistance. We are perfectly fine using the well water. Now, if you would please scurry—"

"That well has been dried up for years."

Huffing, I fling my arm toward the well in frustration. "Then why have it there? Collecting bats? For unsuspecting people who think they're providing a service by fetching water?"

"It's decorative. Maw says it adds charm for tourists like yourself."

Well, Finella is correct about that. Definitely completes the look of the thatch-roofed, fairy-tale cottage in the woods.

But in terms of convenience, it's quite confusing.

"It's also written in the guest book, if you read it." He nods toward a binder on the coffee table.

"I fell asleep on jagged rocks in the middle of a strange town this morning," I say, cocking my hand on my hip. "Do you really think I have the stamina to power through a house manual?"

"It'd be the responsible thing to do, but och, you're not the responsible one, now, are ya?"

I turn to Dakota and jab a finger toward Rowan. "I told you he was rude. Rude and grumpy and mean and . . . smells like a kilt. Seriously, go smell him."

"What does a kilt smell like, per se?" he asks, arms still crossed over his barrel of a chest.

"Like a freaking Bath and Body Works candle. Honestly, who are you people?" Walking toward the sitting area, I throw my hands up to the sky and then fling my body onto the couch, where I sit petulantly.

"Uh, she's tired and needs a bath," Dakota says, stepping up as the peacemaker. "We'd be grateful if you could check out the water for us."

"Aye," Rowan says. I can feel his gaze on me, but I don't give him the time of day. No, sir, you can stare all you want. I'll keep my eyes trained on this tiny piece of black lint that has fallen on my pants. I pick at it and roll it between my fingers.

The lint here is hard.

There are so many little differences between Scotland and the US. I'm sure that's what it will be like for the next six months: discovering all these delightful cultural differences.

"You're rolling bat poo between your fingers," Rowan says as he walks toward the door.

"What?" I squeal, tossing it to the ground.

"Aye, it's all over your clothes. I'd change if I were you."

"Oh my God!" I yell as I scurry up the stairs to my bedroom.

CHAPTER SIX
ROWAN

Number of unruly Americans saved from bats: One.
Seeing Bonnie flail about on the ground: Day made.

◆ ◆ ◆

"Wh-why are you still here?" Bonnie says, coming out of the bathroom with a towel wrapped around her head.

In all my years, I've never seen anything quite as comical as Bonnie being attacked by bats in front of the cottage. I was just around the corner when Dakota called, and then I heard the bats' telltale screeching. I knew trouble was waiting just beyond the trees.

Sure enough, there was Bonnie, rolling around the ground, screaming and spewing off things like *Don't drink my blood, it's American—you'll think it's too sour.*

Humor beating through me, I lifted her up by her pants and brought her into the house. Light little thing that she is, she thought I was a goddamn bat carrying her away. Jesus, this lass.

"Clog in the pipes," Dakota answers from the couch. "According to Kilty McGrumpyshire, the cottage hasn't had a resident in a few months, which means the pipes are still getting acclimated to people using them again."

Kilty McGrumpyshire?

"Dakota," Bonnie hisses. "Don't call him that to his face. That's a behind-the-scenes nickname."

"Well, now it really isn't," Dakota says on a chuckle. She's pretty cool. Relaxed. Doesn't seem to get her hairs standing on all ends like her friend. While I've been working on the pipes, Dakota has been working on her computer. She told me she's a graphic designer, which I thought was pretty cool. I've always had a fondness for using the creative bone in your body.

I stand from my squatted position under the sink and dust off my hands. "You should be all set."

Dakota sets her computer to the side. "Thank you. We really appreciate it. Don't we, Bonnie?"

"Yeah, sure, whatever." Bonnie rolls her eyes.

I grumble a slew of Scottish curses under my breath while packing up my things. Stubborn. She's so fucking stubborn.

"Do you want to stay for dinner?" Dakota asks.

"Dakota," Bonnie hiss-whispers.

"What?" she snaps as if I'm not in the room. "He fixed our plumbing so you didn't have to smell like loch and batshit anymore."

"A wee tip—in Scotland we call our evening meal 'tea.'" I catch Bonnie rolling her eyes before I focus back on Dakota. "But anyway, what are ye serving?" I ask, just to push Bonnie's buttons.

"Uh . . ." Dakota stands from the couch and goes to the kitchen, where she paws through the barren pantry. "We can order something."

"Aye, you think so?" I ask. "Where ye ordering from at eight at night?"

"Ugh, I forgot everything closes around here. Well, we can go to the market quick and—"

"Closed," I say.

"Well . . . we . . . uh . . . Bonnie, grab the box cake you brought with you. We'll bake that quickly, and we can all share that."

"Oh hell no. He's not worthy of my box cake."

I hold back the chuckle that bubbles up inside me. Eyes trained on her lower half, I say, "Definitely not interested in your box . . . cake."

"Did you hear that?" Bonnie asks Dakota, pointing at me again. "He was referencing my vagina."

"Good God, Bonnie, he wasn't!"

"Nah, I wasn't. I was talking about your fud."

"Gah, even worse." She stomps her foot.

"Do you even know what a fud is?" I ask.

She goes to open her mouth, but she pauses, closing it. Then, "What is a fud?"

"A vagina."

"Ahh," she huffs. "You're infuriating." She flips her head over, unravels her towel, and drapes it over a chair before wrapping her wet hair up in her hands, twisting it around, and securing it with a hair band. To the room, she announces, "I'm going to the pub. I assume that's the only thing open right now?"

"Are you asking me?"

"Unfortunately."

"Aye, Fergie's is open."

"Then it's settled." She grabs her wallet and walks up to the door, which she cracks open. Most likely to see if the bats are still around. She pauses for a few seconds before heading out the door, closing it behind her.

Dakota sighs loudly and turns to me. "She's usually much more pleasant."

"Hard to believe."

"I think you just rub her the wrong way, but that could be because she thinks you're hot."

"She say that to you?" I ask, a little shocked.

"No." Dakota shakes her head. "But I know my friend, and based on the way she eats you up with her eyes, she at least finds you attractive, even if she can't stand your personality."

I let out a wee chuckle and push my hand through my hair. Could you imagine?

Shacking up with the ornery American?

Never.

◆ ◆ ◆

"How did I know he'd be tagging along?" Bonnie asks, clutching a beer as she glowers at me from a high top.

I'll give the girl a little respect: she's drinking a dark beer. Can't be sure exactly which one, but it takes a special kind of palate to drink an ale from a Scottish pub.

"Be nice," Dakota says, taking a seat.

For some reason, I do the same. Maybe because Dakota insisted, or maybe because I'm a glutton for punishment. Either way, I can foresee this being an uncomfortable meal. That's for damn sure.

"How does this work?" Dakota asks, picking up a menu from the table. "Wow, three choices. Okay." She chuckles. "What do you suggest?"

"Go with the fish and chips," I say. "Never can go wrong with them."

"Perfect. Is there a waiter . . . ?"

"I'll order at the bar. What do you want to drink?"

"Water is good for me. I don't need to drown in my sorrows like Bonnie over here."

At that moment, Bonnie tips her drink back and takes a large gulp, leaving a mustache of froth along her upper lip.

With a smirk, I hop off the chair and go up to the bar, where Hamish is filling up a pint. I've known the man since I was a wee lad. Younger than my father but older than me, he took over Fergie's Castle when his father retired and handed over the establishment. Now

Hamish and his wife take care of the place, keeping the menu simple every day and the locals happy with never-ending drinks.

"Three orders of fish, a Wolf for me, and a water."

He nods at me and starts pouring. He spots the girls over my shoulder, and his eyes widen in interest. "The Americans?"

"Aye."

"Leith and Lachlan called it."

"Called what?" I ask.

He hands me my beer and works on the water. "That you wouldn't be able to stay away."

"Their plumbing wasn't working. What was I supposed to do? Not answer the call?"

"Nay, you help." He hands me the water. "But eatin' with the lasses, now, *that* wasn't necessary." He winks and flashes a knowing smile as he turns away. "I'll put in your order."

Ignoring him, I head back to the table and hand Dakota her water, debating if I should sit down or not. It would be weird if I didn't at this point. Hamish had a point, though: I didn't have to join them, but I wanted to see how many of Bonnie's buttons I could push.

"Thank you," Dakota says, holding up her water and taking a drink. She eyes my beer. "What did you get?"

"The Wolf." I take a sip and let the malty flavors sit on my tongue. "It's going to be really good with the fish and chips."

"Isn't that what you got?" Dakota asks Bonnie.

"Aye, 'tis the name that caught me wee eye," Bonnie replies in an over-the-top Scottish accent.

"Poor impersonation."

"I don't know, I thought it was pretty spot on." She sips her beer, and for a second, I think I catch a humorous glint in her eye, but she looks away before I can assess it.

"Awright, me lad!" I hear Leith's voice call out behind my back right before his hand lands on my shoulder.

Fucking great.

"Isla and I thought we'd find you here, but I didn't think I'd see you with two lovely lasses." Leaning to Bonnie and Dakota, he whispers, "The big guy is kind of a loner."

Bonnie stretches out her hand immediately. "I'm Bonnie, and I can already tell we're going to be best friends. Come sit right next to me."

Leith takes her hand in his. "Leith, and it's nice to meet you. This is me sister, Isla." He takes a seat next to Bonnie, who looks far too happy, and Isla sits next to me. I can see she's feeling shy, from the way she leans a little closer to me and hunches her shoulders.

So I decide to do the intros for her. "Isla, this is Bonnie and Dakota. They're both watching over the coffee house while my parents are on holibags."

She smiles. "Nice to meet you." When she makes eye contact with Dakota, they both quickly turn to their respective drinks and bring them to their mouths.

"So, Leith, tell me all the dirty details about Rowan." Bonnie jabs a thumb toward me. "How do you know each other?"

"Best mates since we were wee lads," Leith says. He smirks at me, and I know that grin. He's about to take the piss out of me like any other good friend would. Though taking the piss can go both ways, and I have way more dirt on him.

"Oh, so you know a lot. Has he always been this grumpy?"

"Aye." He points his fingers at my brow. "See that crinkle between his eyes? It's been there since he was five."

"Don't let him fool you." Isla speaks up, giving my shoulder a squeeze. "Rowan might be grumpy, but he has a heart of gold."

"Is that so?" Bonnie asks. "I have yet to see this heart of gold."

"Nay, you saw it when I picked you up by your breeks and hauled you into the cottage."

"You tossed me on the floor."

"Where's this story going?" Leith asks, rubbing his hands together.

"The numpty thought she could get water out of the well, but instead she summoned a wave of bats. I arrived just as they were—Bonnie, how did you put it? Trying to suck her blood?"

"They were. I felt fangs."

I roll my eyes. "I took care of it."

"Tossed me around like a wet rag."

"You're welcome." I tip my beer in her direction.

Leith looks between us. "Is it just me, or am I sensing some sexual tension between the two of you?"

"Nope"—Dakota raises a hand—"I've been feeling it for the past two hours."

Isla smiles over at her. "I feel it too. It's practically bouncing off them."

With a sly grin, Bonnie tilts her head to the side. "Do you find me attractive, Kilty?"

Without skipping a beat, I say, "If I found the Loch Ness Monster attractive, then yes."

Bonnie's eyes narrow.

Leith claps his hands and laughs, while Dakota and Isla both chuckle and sip their drinks.

"Well, in case you were wondering, you're pretty revolting yourself," she snaps.

"I wasn't wondering," I say, only pissing her off even more, though I couldn't really care less what she thinks.

"So far, what have been the biggest culture shocks for you?" Isla asks Dakota and Bonnie, though she's really looking at Dakota.

Among the five of us, we've all split three large plates of fish and chips while the band's been striking up a folksy tune in the back of the pub, setting the mood. And hell, I'm in a good mood. I'm not sure if it's because I'm on my fourth beer, the fiddle is upbeat in the background, or I'm surrounded by friends, but I'm having a hell of a time. It has nothing to do with the blonde sitting across from me and the way she's poking her fingers in the air in a dance move she claims is all-American, or how she swapped seats with Dakota when Leith was asking about graphic design, so now I can smell her flowery scent as she sits right next to me.

None of that.

Nope.

It's the beer.

Most definitely the beer.

Her shoulder sways against mine, and I swallow hard as I catch a whiff of her shampoo.

God, it smells amazing.

"Biggest culture shock?" Dakota asks, nursing a beer now, her glass of water long forgotten. "Probably nothing being open. We're so used to having everything at the tips of our fingers. Stores are open twenty-four seven, food delivery is always available, and in LA there are so many different food choices that it's hard to make a decision."

"That and the daylight," Bonnie says, swaying to the music now. "I was not expecting it to be so sunny all the time. Four in the morning felt like nine."

"Our summer days are long, but it's nice, since we all shut down at five—at least most of us," Isla says. "We get to enjoy the summer weather."

"Are there any hiking trails around here?"

"Lots," Leith answers. "Plenty of outdoor activities. Sunday, when everything is closed, we can plan a hike up to Corsekelly Castle. It's half in ruins, but it's a great place for a picnic."

"We love it up there," Isla adds.

"Up where?" I hear Lachlan say as he comes up to the table and stands behind Leith.

Bonnie grips my arm and sways. "Holy shit, how many beers have I had?" She blinks. "Is anyone else seeing two Leiths?"

"'Tis my twin brother, Lachlan," Leith says, laughing.

"Two of you?" Bonnie looks me up and down. "Are there two of *you*? Is the other one nicer?"

"Just one." I sip my beer. "You wouldn't be able to handle two of me."

"Aye, this must be Bonnie and Dakota," Lachlan says, grinning. "I can already tell Rowan's smitten with Bonnie."

Jesus Christ.

"I recall him comparing my attraction level to the Loch Ness Monster," Bonnie says. "I don't think 'smitten' is the right word."

"That's Rowan for ya—truly knows the way to a lass's heart."

Fucking bawbag, doesn't know how to keep his mouth shut.

I stand from the table and push my stool in. "Off to the cludgie."

Without another word, I walk toward the back of the pub and pass some of the locals, who give me nods, and straight to the back, where the stall is vacant. I make quick work of relieving myself and wash my hands. By the time I exit, I catch Lachlan dancing near the band with Bonnie.

I pause for a moment, taking her in. Her long blonde hair flies about her shoulders, released from her hair band about an hour ago. Music from our local band fills the small confines of the pub, the fiddle taking center stage. Her contagious smile stretches from ear to ear as she shakes with the beat, using those pointy fingers to guide her movements.

She looks happy.

Relaxed . . .

Everything I'm not as I stand here staring at her, realizing very quickly that the girl in front of me is catching my attention.

Hell, not just catching my attention, but making me think stupid things like *What do her lips taste like?*

She gives Lachlan's chest a playful push, and they both laugh. He takes her hands in his, spinning her around the floor. All eyes are on them, and if I didn't know any better, I would say Lachlan is trying to goad me with the smirk he shoots my way when he's done spinning her.

Well, it's not going to work.

Not interested.

But even as I think that, jealousy pricks at the back of my neck.

Jealousy of what, though?

That they're having a good time?

Or that Lachlan has his hands all over Bonnie and I don't?

Either way, it shouldn't matter—this is my opportunity to leave.

I head toward the table just as Bonnie is flung in my direction, spinning away from Lachlan, laughter falling past her lips. She twists and trips toward the ground. Dread fills me as she flails her arms, still laughing, and on instinct, I reach out, catching her right before her head hits a table.

Light in my arms, she looks up at me in surprise, and then the maddest thing happens.

She smiles at me.

And before I know it, she's straightening up and taking my hands in hers and pulling me toward the dance floor.

"What are you doing?" I ask, my body feeling as stiff as a board.

"Dancing. Don't you dance, Kilty?"

"No."

"I don't buy it." Keeping my hand in hers, she coerces me into dancing by spinning under my arm and moving me back and forth.

I feel all eyes on me. Every local in the pub knows I'm so far out of my comfort zone that I'm surprised they're not all pulling out their phones to record the rare sight of me on a dance floor.

"Bonnie, I don't—"

She grips my hips, and my face burns as she sways them back and forth. "Sheesh, your pelvis is as hard as a rock. Are you hiding the real Boaby Stone in your pants?"

Move your hands a little bit more inward, and you'll know exactly what hard is.

"Loosen up. Maybe that's why you're always so grumpy—you're not loose. You'd think with some beer in your system, you'd be more willing to shake your booty." She turns me to the side and pokes me just as I move to the side, and she accidentally pokes me directly on the arse. "Oh dear Lord, I poked your behind." Laughing, she cups her mouth and says, "Pardon me, dear sir, but . . . did it at least make things come to life?"

Annnd, she's sloshed.

There is no way in hell sober Bonnie would be asking me if things were "coming to life," let alone dancing with me.

Bending down, I pick her up and toss her over my shoulder.

"What the—put me down at once. I demand it!"

"Your time here is up," I say, bringing her to the table, where Dakota's just finished paying the bill.

"You aren't the boss of me. I'm a grown woman. I make my own decisions."

Dakota quickly says goodbye to everyone before following me out the door.

"Dakota, tell this Highland beast to put me down at once."

"It's time for bed, Bonnie," Dakota says, and I'm grateful she's on the same page as me.

"I was just starting to have fun," she whines.

"You were poking Rowan's ass."

"Accidentally," she complains, still draped over my shoulder as I trudge down the road, the sun finally starting to set in the west. She's not heavy, but I'm still grateful Fergie's is close to the coffee shop, and we're soon turning down the gravel driveway. "You saw the way he was dancing. There was no sway in his hips at all. I was simply waking them up."

"You're going to be hurting tomorrow if you don't get some sleep," Dakota says. "We can't be late again."

I pause. "Och, do you want me to drop you off on your sleeping rocks to pass out? Seems like you sleep well there."

"You're an asshole," Bonnie mutters while Dakota chuckles.

That puts a smile on my face.

I pull my shirt over my head and toss it into the hamper. Slipping my boots off, I tuck them away where they belong and then remove my socks. As I walk out of my bedroom, I take one quick glance in the mirror and notice how rumpled my hair is.

It wasn't from me pushing my hand through it.

No, it was a little gift from Bonnie. Once it became clear I wouldn't put her down until she was in her bed, she decided she'd mess with my hair, sticking it on all ends.

"Take that and that and that," she said, over and over again while digging her fingers through the thick strands.

Hell, it felt fucking good.

She thought she was annoying me, but in reality I was hoping she'd keep doing it. And that's how I knew I might be a bit sloshed too.

I walk into my kitchen, grab the glass that I keep next to the sink, fill it up with some tap water, and guzzle it down, only to fill it up again.

Too wired to even consider going to sleep, I push through my front door, the evening air putting life into my chest while I walk over to my shed. Crickets chirp in the distance, and my front door light illuminates my path as my bare feet close the distance.

Slowly, I unlock the shed door and slide it open. I flip on the light I installed a few months ago when I realized I do my best work at night.

My small but comforting space comes to life from the overhanging light, instantly relaxing me. Shelves of drying projects, half-glazed pots,

78

and finished products line the walls. My kiln, which I replaced last year after my first one broke down, sits in the corner. And then there's my wheel, my place of solace.

It's been a long fucking day of repairing things here and there before giving my parents a quick send-off. I didn't get much more than a hug from my maw and a grunt from my da. After that, I helped some of our older residents with menial tasks, and then, of course, assisted Bonnie and Dakota. I'm exhausted but exhilarated at the same time.

I take a seat, set my glass down, dip my hands in water, and then grab a chunk of clay. I set it on the potter's wheel in front of me, where I spiral wedge it, letting out the air bubbles. The feel of the clay beneath my fingers soothes my busy soul, giving me the chance to clear my mind and just breathe. I turn on the wheel and slowly start to move my hands over the clay. Normally I listen to music while throwing, but the sounds of the night filter through my shed instead, and I get lost.

My annoyance at my parents and their evasiveness washes away.

The irritation of doing a job I hate, to appease my duty-driven father, disappears.

The anguish of not living the life I want slowly vanishes.

The horror of my past fades.

All that's left are my hands and my clay . . . and Bonnie.

Fuck.

Those eyes, that attitude, that smile.

I dip my fingers into the center of the clay, forming a hole.

Her brazenness, her quick wit, her eagerness to dance with me.

My teeth pull on the corner of my mouth as I round the clay back together.

She's proud, like me. Defensive like me. Stubborn . . . like me.

I press my thumb down, savoring the feel of the clay gliding under my skin and forming another bowl shape.

I think I might have met my match—and she's wrapped up in a tiny, feisty, all-American package.

CHAPTER SEVEN
BONNIE

Cake consumed today: *None, but that's about to change.*
    Days since last male-induced orgasm: *Seventy-three? Seventy-four?*
It's getting up there.
    Hangovers: *One massive head-cracking hangover.*
    Annoying Scottish men who treat women like potato sacks: *One,*
but God does he smell good. Like a really sexy pheromone-filled kilt.
    I don't know what they put in their beer over here, but golly is it strong.
Did I poke an ass last night?

"You're walking too fast, and my retinas are bleeding." I shield the sun from my eyes as Dakota drags me along the stone-paved street, away from the coffee shop. "I demand to know where you're taking me." Instead of answering, Dakota comes to an abrupt stop before a teal door.

I blink at the door, struggling to truly see anything in this god-forsaken sunlight—I thought Scotland was all rain and clouds; bunch of turd wash *that* is—before Dakota opens it and pushes me inside. I stumble into the sweetest-smelling room I've ever been in.

Two bakery cases rest next to the intricately carved counter—a Murdach clan crest shaved into the middle. On the other side of the beautifully wood-paneled space is a high bar attached to the wall with accompanying seats for those who want to eat in the bakery. There isn't much decor, but there doesn't need to be, given the wood-stained corbels in the corners and the wood-slatted ceilings.

Adorable.

"Hey, ladies." I look up to find Isla walking toward us, an apron around her waist and a towel in her hands. "How are you feeling?"

Isla is adorable too. Really freaking adorable. Vibrant red hair brushes her shoulders, and she has these steely eyes that she barely highlights with a touch of mascara. A light splattering of freckles decorates her nose, and the smallest of nose rings glimmers in the light.

When she walked up last night and Rowan introduced us, I gauged Dakota's reaction—blushing cheeks and light smirk—and I knew my best friend was a little smitten.

I don't blame her. Isla is a bombshell with a sweet accent. Every word that comes out of her mouth is like a melody.

And, most importantly, she owns a bakery, which means . . .

"Caaaaake," I groan like a woman looking for water in a desert.

Isla chuckles. "That good, huh?"

Dakota places her hand on my back. "We need a little pick-me-up for this girl before we head over to the coffee shop."

Why the bakery is open before the coffee house, I have no idea, but right now this is working in my favor.

"I think I can help you out with that." She works her way behind the counter near the bakery cases. "You're looking for cake? Or breakfast."

"Both," Dakota answers as I slink over to the food display. One side is full of what look like Hot Pockets, and the other contains a plethora of pastries and yumminess. I float over to that side.

"Well, we have some breakfast pies. All have egg in them, and then we add different things like spinach, bacon, haggis."

I hold my hand up. "No haggis, please . . . no haggis."

Isla chuckles. "Aye, it's an acquired taste."

"What's that cake?" I ask, pointing to a round loaf with almonds decorating the top.

"That's Dundee cake. A Scottish specialty. I actually won second place at the Highland Games for mine. It was the first time they had a Dundee cake competition—it's usually just shortbread, which I placed third in."

"Wow, that's incredible," Dakota says. "If that's the case, we're going to have to try both."

"Not so fast," I say and raise a brow at Isla. "What's in the Dundee cake?"

She smiles. "It's a much tastier version of America's fruitcake. But this is made with currants, sultanas—which are white grapes—and almonds."

I tap my chin. "Yeah, I feel like I would like that. Wrap it up."

"And the shortbread?"

Dakota nods. "And two breakfast pies, egg and spinach. We need protein too."

"I need cake first. I swear the withdrawal is real."

As she packs up everything, Isla asks, "Did you have fun last night?"

Dakota leans against the counter, taking over the conversation, and if I weren't so hungover I would make it hard on her, tease her like any other good friend, but I give the girl a break. Also, it's nice to see her stepping out of her comfort zone.

"We did. The music added to the whole mood."

"You should have danced."

"I didn't have enough drinks in me to get out on the dance floor."

"Hasn't stopped you before," I mumble. Dakota shoots me a look, and I slump against the counter. *Be nice,* I silently chastise myself. *She has the money to buy the cake.*

"Maybe another night, then," Isla says as Dakota hands her a credit card. "Nay, we'll open a tab for you."

"Ohh, a tab, I like the sound of that," I say, perking up while Isla hands Dakota a paper bag full of our treats.

"Do not let Bonnie add anything to the tab or start her own," Dakota says, looking Isla directly in the eyes. "Do you understand? If given access to such a privilege, she will run us into the ground. Her obsession with cake is borderline lunacy."

"Ha, as if you don't have the same problem." I point my thumb toward Dakota. "Loves cake . . . but obsessed with *muffins*." I wink, and Dakota knocks me in the stomach with her elbow.

Okay, I deserved that.

Isla smiles playfully and winks. "Pretty obsessed with *muffins* myself."

And oh my God, the way Isla stares my friend down . . . I swear on the Dundee cake, a wave of butterflies erupts in my stomach.

Dakota's cheeks redden, and she fumbles with the bag as she walks backward to the door. "Yeah, muffins . . . ahem," she says, clearing her throat, and *be still my heart* she's so nervous. "Muffins are good."

"Especially when licked, right?" I say, because why not, at this point? Already in the doghouse.

"Especially," Isla says, laughing as she starts wiping down the counter. "Have a good day, lasses."

"You too, Isla." I give her a wave and take Dakota by the arm, ushering her out the door and onto the street.

She's silent as we make our way to the coffee shop, but the minute we're inside and the door is shut, she pounces on me.

"What the hell was that back there?"

"What was what?" I snag the bag from her and set it on one of the shop's two tables as I sit down in one of the matching chairs. Not even bothering with any kind of finesse, I dive into the bag and pull out the Dundee cake. I tear off a piece and stuff it in my mouth. "Holy

Highlands, that is delicious." Almond flavoring washes over my tongue, followed by hints of orange and sweet raisin. "Want a piece?" I hold up the round cake to her, but she just stares me down.

"Bonnie, that was humiliating back there. *Licking* muffins? Could you be any more obvious?"

"I could have said licking vaginas, but I kept it classy." I take another bite as I melt into my seat. I think I'll be having a love affair with Dundee cake while I'm here.

"That was not classy." She presses her hand to her forehead and starts pacing. "God, what she must think of me."

"She's probably thinking, 'When can I take the stiff blonde out on a date?'"

"She was not thinking that."

"Uh, she totally is. From the way she was eyeing you last night and the playful banter this morning, oh yes, ma'am, she's definitely wondering when she can ask you out."

Dakota pauses and sets her hands on her hips. "You really think so?" The smallest of smirks plays on her lips. And God, I've missed that mischievous smile, the one that shows just how excited she is despite her best efforts to hide it. I haven't seen it in a while, not since Isabella broke her heart.

"Yup. Only a matter of time before she comes over here and asks out my beautiful best friend." I hold out a piece of the Dundee cake, and this time she takes it. "Honestly, Isla is a hot piece of Scottish ass."

Dakota's cheeks redden, and she sits down next to me. "She's really pretty, isn't she?"

"Totally. Her freckles are cute."

"I really like her freckles," Dakota says with excitement. "And her voice."

"Oh, look at you—you're so smitten."

"Not smitten, just . . ." She shrugs, and I push her shoulder.

"You're smitten, and I like it. This is a good thing."

"What if she does ask me out?"

"Uh, you say yes and go out with her. Are you kidding me, Dakota? You need this. Even if it's a vacation fling. You've put yourself in this nondating box ever since Isabella broke up with you, but now it's time to get out and open up to new possibilities. This is important, the first date after the breakup. If anything, it gets you back in the game, and that's what I want to see—my girl happy."

"Yeah, I know." She sighs and takes a bite of the cake. "She really is pretty."

"Total smoke show," I say, dropping crumbs into my mouth as I tilt my head back.

"You know I'm going to make your life a living hell whenever Rowan is around, though, after that whole bakeshop scene."

"What? Why? The circumstances are completely different." I stand up from the table, walk over to the two coffee thermoses, and start making coffee. How this place is still open with only two options, I have no idea. "I don't like Rowan, but you like Isla."

"Oh, please," Dakota scoffs. "You can't tell me you don't find him attractive."

"I mean, yeah, is he all brawny and beautiful to look at? Sure. But that only takes you so far. You need a connection, and the only thing connecting us is stubbornness."

"Mark my words, I think you two are going to hook up . . . multiple times before we leave Scotland."

"Ha! Never. Not interested. Plus, I'm not here to hook up—I'm here to find my passion."

"Maybe your passion is Kilty McGrumpyshire, and you don't even know it."

Doubtful.

"Is that the third tour bus that's come into Corsekelly today?" I ask, standing from my chair. I walk over to the propped-open door and stare down the tourists, who don't even look our way. "Why aren't they coming in to get some coffee? Are they really just here for the Penis Stone?"

"It is odd that we haven't seen one person today besides a few locals," Dakota says, furrowing her brow. "Just like yesterday. Makes me feel uneasy. The sign blatantly says COFFEE. It's been a drizzly day—why don't they want anything to warm up with?"

"Exactly what I'm saying." I toss my hands up in the air and head back into the shop, where I sit at one of the uneven tables. "I don't think I can take six months of this boredom. At least you're getting work done. I'm just sitting here on my ass taking career assessment quizzes that have turned out to be more depressing than anything."

"What are they saying?" Dakota asks, shutting her computer.

"That I have great organizational skills and should be an assistant."

"Oof, that's harsh."

"Tell me about it. Last thing I wanted to hear today." Groaning, I slouch in the chair and glance around the bleak space. "Finella is a nice lady and all, but could she add some charm to this place? Anything to liven up these serial killer–white walls. Look at these tables: it's like they were constructed by someone just learning to use a hammer. And the floors, I mean—"

"Ahhhhhhhhhhh!"

"Mother of Jesus!" I scream, clutching my heart, my eyes snapping to the open door. I gasp. A goat stands on the threshold. *What the ever-loving—*

"Ahhhhhhhhhhh!" it screams again, startling me right out of my chair and onto the floor with a thump.

"Satan's beast," I say, scrambling to my feet and holding one of the dilapidated chairs in front of me. "Why does it sound like a human?" I brandish the chair in the goat's direction. "Back, you. Back. Hee-ah, hee-ah."

But the goat doesn't move. It just screams again, this time with a bit of a moan to it, and I'll be honest—the sound makes me 90 percent scared for my life and 10 percent horny.

It steps into the shop, and I back up against the wall, chair out in front of me, ready for any sudden movements.

"Dakota, do something. It clearly wants to communicate with us."

Dakota is up on the counter, arms wrapped around her tucked-in legs. "What do you want me to do?"

"Talk to him, see what he's come for."

"Do you think I developed magical goat-speaking powers overnight?"

"Maybe," I say, clucking at him now, but he just steps deeper into the shop. "Oh God, he's going to make this a thing. Scaring the Americans with his screeches. I can sense it."

"I wonder if this is Fergus," Dakota says.

"Who's Fergus?"

"The town goat. Centuries ago, during one of the Scottish uprisings, Corsekelly was about to be attacked when a goat came screaming into town, waking everyone up. They were able to escape before they were killed and then rebuild Corsekelly after the enemies burned down their homes. Fergus is a direct descendent of that hero goat. Didn't you see the goat statue out in the town square?"

"No, I was trying to drive on the wrong side of the road when we arrived. Wasn't really sightseeing." I slowly start inching closer to Dakota, keeping the chair held up as a barrier. "So you're telling me this goat is idolized by the town?"

"Given that a lot of the businesses are named after a goat, I would say yes."

"Which means we need to handle this extraction delicately. Got it. Well, I volunteer you. Animals like you more; they can sense your ability to connect with them."

"Since when?"

"Since that goldfish at the pet store followed your finger."

"It was trying to *eat* my finger."

"Doesn't matter, the goldfish thought you were good enough to eat. So go ahead; don't be nervous. I'm sure—"

"Fergus, old lad, there you are," Lachlan says, striding into the coffee house, followed closely by Leith. Shirtless and wearing matching kilts, they both give him a pat and then take in the horrified looks on our faces. "Awright, lasses. Everything okay?"

"They seem to be scared of Fergus," Leith says, stroking the now-silent goat on the back of the neck.

"Scared of a wee goat?"

Carefully I set the chair down, not wanting to provoke the beast. "He startled us with his boisterous hello."

Lachlan and Leith both laugh, and I shamelessly watch as their thick pecs and defined abs bounce up and down. The Murdachs have good genes, that's for damn sure.

"Aye, he sure knows how to announce himself," Leith says, patting Fergus on the back. "But he comes from an impeccable lineage that saved this very town. We would be lost without him. Back in 2001, his father's life was threatened by the outbreak of foot-and-mouth disease, but it didn't spread to the Highlands, thankfully. We were nervous, though—it wreaked havoc on England's agriculture."

"Well, thank goodness for that," I say as Dakota hops off the counter.

"Want some coffee?" she asks, acting as if she wasn't just terrorized by a farm animal.

Leith holds up his hand. "We're about to go do a training video for our followers. But thank you. We were just stopping by to grab Fergus—he's a celebrity on our videos—and to see if you lasses wanted to go on a hike with us on Sunday. Picnic up at Corsekelly Castle, like I mentioned in the pub."

"Training video?" I ask.

"Aye, personal training. The Training Kilts," Lachlan says. "If you ever see us hopping around town carrying logs and acting like fools, it's for a training video. We sell training packages with accompanying kilts—and we're building quite the fan base. Which reminds me, Dakota, would we be able to pick your brain about some new graphics for our website?"

"Of course. Anytime. We're, uh, not very busy here."

"The coffee shop is never too busy. Shame," Leith sighs. "Stuart put his heart into this store."

"Was it different before Stuart left?" I ask, surprised.

"Aye. Stuart used to sell these delicious butteries with homemade jam. He would sell out by noon. That's all it was—simple coffee, butteries, and his classic storytelling. Word got round, and tour buses would clear him out. He built quite the happy life. Then he retired, and Finella couldn't keep up. I'm glad they're on holibags. They need it."

"Butteries? What are those?" I ask.

"Ehm, like a flattened croissant," Leith answers. "Traditional butteries are hard to come by. They're supposed to be made with butter and lard, but the mass producers started using palm oil, and they're just not the same."

"They sound good."

"They look like hell. Lot of Scots call them the 'roadkill pastry,' because they look like they've been run over by a car, but have one toasted with some jeely, and I'll tell ya, you're in heaven."

"I'm sad he doesn't make them anymore."

Leith sighs and gives the coffee house another look. "Remember when this place used to be full? Maybe when Finella gets back, she'll have a renewed spirit."

"Hopefully," Lachlan agrees and then claps his hands together—prompting Fergus to scream again. The boys laugh, while Dakota and I clutch our hearts. "So, Sunday . . . are you lasses up for a hike?"

I glance at Dakota, who smiles and shrugs. "Sure," I say. "We really don't have any plans. Should we bring something?"

"Isla is packing the food. Just bring some water for yourself. Meet you at half ten at the bakeshop." Lachlan gives us a wave, and then both boys take off.

Once they're out of earshot, I turn to Dakota and give her a playful grin. "Hear that? *Isla* is packing us food. Maybe she'll let you taste her muffin."

"Grow up." Dakota chucks a rolled-up napkin at me.

"What on earth are you doing?" Dakota says as she shuts the door to the cottage.

"Damn you, dough!" I scream. I flop back on the kitchen floor and sit cross-legged, my hands extended so I don't get any of the butter-lard mixture that's caked on my hands anywhere.

"Uh . . . what is happening?"

"I'm trying to make butteries," I say, just about ready to throw a fit.

"Is that why you wanted to leave the shop early?"

"Yes," I answer, exasperated. "I found a simple recipe online, went to the Mill Market, where Shona helped me collect the ingredients, and then I came back here, confident that you'd be coming home to fresh, warm butteries." I toss my arm toward the pile of melting dough on the counter. "But that is my third attempt, and I honestly think I might throw it down the well."

"Why are you trying to make butteries?"

"I don't know. The way Lachlan and Leith were talking about them, I thought it would be fun to get domestic, you know? I make boxed cake all the time; why not try something new?"

"Bonnie." She walks over and squats down so we're eye to eye. "You know I love you, but boxed cake is completely different from a homemade pastry."

"Uh, I do two-tiered boxed cakes. That's special *and* challenging."

"Yes, but it also only requires you to measure correctly and stir. It doesn't call for yeast and whatever goop is all over your hands."

I glance down. "It has been slightly more difficult."

"I can tell." She sweetly rubs her hand over my shoulder. "It's so nice that you were trying something new, though."

"Yeah, I guess it's something new." I start to perk up. "Hey, look at me stepping out of my comfort zone."

"I'm very proud of you."

I rise to my feet and stare at the mess on the counter.

"You know, I think I'm going to make this my mission. I'm going to master the buttery while I'm here. And I'm going to bring it back to America and open a buttery food truck, with homemade currant jam. And people from all over the country are going to come to my food truck and ask me to butter their buttery, and then movie sets will catch wind of my butteries and hire my truck to come feed their team, and when the assholes who fired me come to the truck, I'll tell them I just ran out and that maybe if they hadn't been so rude to me, I would be able to find some extras in the back for them."

"Wow, spent some time thinking about this?" Dakota chuckles.

"No, it all just flashed in front of me."

"You're ridiculous, but I love you."

I go to my dough on the counter and poke it. "It just keeps melting and I don't know why, but I'm going to figure it out. Who knows, maybe I can bring some to the picnic this Sunday. Surprise everyone."

"I'm sure they'd appreciate it."

"Okay," I say, feeling renewed. I can do this. I've got to channel my inner baking skills.

This time Sunday, I'm going to have quite the surprise for our new friends.

"How's it coming?" Dakota asks, stepping out of her room, empty bowl in hand.

"Butteries can go to hell."

"That well, huh?"

"No wonder the Scots call them the 'roadkill pastry'—that's where they belong, next to all the other lonely carcasses. I'm a failure."

I stare down at my creation. Flat as a pancake, with butter oozing out the sides, it is very displeasing to the eyes.

"Don't give up, Bonnie. I know you can do this."

"Your enthusiasm is only irritating me."

"Fine. You suck at life."

I look up at my best friend, my brow furrowed. "Hey, now, that was just mean."

"Tough love, baby."

"Oh my God, Bonnie, is the cottage burning down?" Dakota says as she flies through the front door, still holding her keys from closing up the coffee shop. She waves a hand in front of her face, clearing out the smoke.

"No," I groan, feeling defeated as I sit on the floor with my back against the fridge, an oven mitt on one hand. "Just the butteries going up in flames."

She coughs and picks up a book, then tries to wave the smoke out of the cottage with it. "What happened?"

"I think too much lard. Something dripped and burned in the oven, and now it's smoking me out. I think it's a sign. Butter and lard don't want me anywhere near them."

"How did they come out?"

I stand and bring the baking sheet over to her. Congealed into one giant liquid mess, the "butteries" are once again melted and burned. They definitely look like roadkill, but not in the charming way I'm sure Lachlan and Leith meant.

"Huh . . . well, those don't look appetizing."

"Thank you for pointing out the obvious."

"Keep trying." She gives my shoulder a pat. "Make butteries your bitch."

Hmm . . .

"Think they'd respond to some good old-fashioned tying up and whipping? Haven't tried that yet."

"You never know until you try," Dakota says on a laugh.

"I'm about to become their madam. Safe word . . . 'boaby stone.'"

Chapter Eight
ROWAN

Authors I can't stand who are making me do this: One.

Looking forward to a much-needed break from the blonde tornado who spun into my life. Also, waiting desperately for Shona to restock Curly Wurlys at the market.

"What are we waiting for?" I ask, glancing around the group and adjusting the rucksack on my back. "Everyone's here."

Lachlan, Leith, and Isla exchange glances. Within a second, I know the Murdachs have planned something and they're trying to decide who should break the news to me.

"Your turn," Leith says to Lachlan. "I told him about Hamish and the electric outlet near the sink he needed to fix."

Lachlan looks at Isla. "I told him about Fergus pooping in his shoes."

"This wasn't my idea," Isla says, crossing her arms over her chest.

Leith grumbles and turns to Lachlan. "Rock, paper, scissors. Seven out of nine, loser tells him."

"Seven out of nine? That's absurd," Isla says. "Do three out of five."

"Do sudden death, or I kick all of your asses," I say, growing irritated.

"Even mine?" Isla asks, innocence in her usually steely eyes.

"Aye, even you."

"Fine." Leith and Lachlan hold out their hands. They count off and Leith wins with rock.

Lachlan groans and is opening his mouth to make his confession when a voice behind me calls out, "We're here."

I turn to find Dakota and Bonnie walking up to us, each of them carrying a water bottle at their side. When Bonnie locks eyes with me, I see my thoughts mirrored in her expression.

What is she doing here?

What is he doing here?

"Sorry we're late," Dakota says. "Bonnie lost her other shoe, and we couldn't find it. Somehow it ended up in her bed." She flashes a smile at Isla.

"You're right on time," Isla says, walking up to Dakota and giving her a hug. I watch the surprised expression on Dakota's face soften into happiness. Isla quickly hugs Bonnie as well and clears her throat. "The boys and I were talking, and since you lasses are new to the route, we're going to buddy up."

Uh, we did not discuss that.

"Leith and Lachlan are going to lead the way," Isla continues. "Dakota, you can buddy up with me and we'll go second, since the terrain is a little rocky. And, Bonnie, you can walk with Rowan. He's sturdy, so if you slip, just grab any of his muscles."

"Including the one in his pants," Leith says, and Isla slaps him on the back of the head.

"Ignore him." Leaning against the bakeshop are two hiking sticks. Isla hands one to each girl. "These should help during the steep parts. It will be challenging, but I promise it'll totally be worth it, especially since I packed some fresh shortbread for us for when we get to the castle."

"Sounds great," Dakota says, looking far more excited than Bonnie, who's staring daggers at me as she grips her hiking stick.

How convenient that I get matched up with Bonnie. This situation smells of meddling friends who think they know better than me.

Isla waves a hand at her brothers. "Leith and Lachlan, lead the way."

They take off, and we all file in line through an alley between the stone buildings, two by two by two, like a herd of hairy coos making our way up toward the castle.

At first, Bonnie and I don't say anything to each other.

It's awkward.

Uncomfortable.

And this is not how I planned on spending my Sunday.

Meanwhile, Leith and Lachlan are laughing up ahead, while Dakota and Isla seem to be deep in conversation.

Once we make it out of town and start onto the footpath that leads to the castle, I start to feel Bonnie brushing against me and grumbling something under her breath. Ignoring her, I continue to walk, trying to at least enjoy the silence. That's until . . .

"Can you stop hogging the trail with your mammoth body?" Bonnie says, shoving me with her shoulder, but given our size difference, she doesn't move me an inch.

"I'm just walking."

"You're manspreading."

"How is that possible?"

"I don't know—you tell me. You're the one walking like a Neanderthal with his arms all puffed out, knocking me into the bushes."

"I'm not manspreading; this is just the size of my body."

"You're too big."

I snort. "I've never had that complaint before."

"Ugh, I should have seen that coming."

"For someone who's in a foreign country with a plush job, you seem to be cranky all the time."

"I'm not cranky, just . . . irritated." She blows out a long breath.

"You get irritated that easily?"

"Well, yes, but your manspreading is not the only reason I'm irritated."

"I'm not manspreading," I repeat, glancing down at her. Her ponytail sways from side to side with each of her steps, and she looks cute in her leggings and tank top, a jacket tied around her waist. I half expected her to be one of those girls who shows up for a hike in heels, but she's not. When she doesn't say anything after that, I figure I might as well pry. This is a long hike, and walking it with someone who is silent is going to be painfully awkward. I hate to admit it, but . . . even though I enjoy silence, I also hate when I can feel people are mad. Takes away from the peace I'm trying to capture while hiking. "Why are you irritated?"

"Do you really care?" The hostility is clear in her voice, but I can also sense she wants to get this off her chest. Contrary to what she must think about me, I'm not a complete asshole.

"Try me."

She doesn't answer right away but instead falls silent, the crunch of the ground beneath our feet the only sound either of us is making.

Finally she says, "I was trying to make something to bring to the picnic today. You know, contribute to the group, since the Murdachs were so kind to invite us."

"Okay . . ."

"It didn't go as planned."

"Mess up?"

"Six times." She sighs heavily. "Six freaking times, and I swear, on the sixth I almost burned down the cottage. Dakota came home to smoke filtering out the front door and windows."

"What were you trying to make?"

"Butteries."

"Butteries?" I ask. Haven't had those since . . . well, since Da stopped working at the shop. "Why were you trying to make those?"

"Lachlan and Leith came to the coffee shop the other day to invite us on the hike. They were also looking for Fergus, who announced himself with an ear-piercing scream minutes before they arrived."

"Fergus has a set of pipes on him."

She chuckles, and the sound actually puts me at ease. For a moment, I feel the tension dissipating between us. "He sounds like an actual human, and it's startling. I thought some psychopathic Boaby Stone–loving tourist was coming to murder us."

That makes me grin. "We're used to him by now."

"Not sure I'll ever get used to that." She trips over a rock, and I grab her arm, steadying her. She glances up at me, and those eyes nearly gut me as she says, "Thanks."

Clearing my throat, I quickly look away. "Sure."

"Anyway, they were telling us about what the shop was like before your dad retired—how it was always full of customers, thanks to the butteries he'd bake."

"Aye," I say. And it could still be full if Da wasn't so stubborn. "He'd sell out by noon, thanks to all the tourists. He started making a special batch for the locals and opening an hour earlier, just so they could get their fill before the buses started rolling through." I run my hand over my jaw. "I can't tell you the last time I had a buttery." I lift up a tree branch for us to duck under as the path starts to become more cumbersome. The others are farther up ahead, spaced evenly, and it doesn't bother me. It's kind of nice hanging back and walking with Bonnie, though I'd never tell her that. She'd gloat too much—I know I would.

"Well, I was hoping to have some for today, but it's been an absolute disaster trying to make them." Her voice is full of defeat, and it makes me wonder if there's more to her failed attempts at making butteries, something adding to her melancholy. "Just add it to the list of things I can't do."

"How bad was it?"

"Bad."

"Were you using my da's recipe?" I ask.

"No, I found one on the internet."

"Mistake number one, lass. Online recipes don't have the special touch."

"Well, I wasn't about to call up your dad while he's on holi-boobies."

"Holibags." I let out the smallest of chuckles. I feel her glance my way, but I keep my gaze on the path, not wanting to show her that I actually thought that was funny. "Maw keeps a recipe book in the cottage for guests who want to try some traditional Scottish recipes while they're here. Butteries and red current jam are on the first page, I believe."

"That's good to know. Although, given my track record, I think I would screw up your dad's recipe too."

"The hardest part is folding in all the butter. But once you have the technique down, you get used to it."

"Have you made them?" she asks.

A large rock about two feet high blocks our path, and I lift myself onto it first, ducking out of the way of another branch. I turn to assist Bonnie, but she already has one foot up on the rock, hoisting herself up. When she stands, she sets her hands on her hips and glances around. We're still under heavy tree cover at this point, but it will clear out soon, and I'll be interested to see her reaction when the pristine valley comes into view. "Yeah, I used to help me da make 'em early in the morning." I let out a heavy breath, remembering those mornings.

Take pride in everything you do, son.

The menial tasks, the ones no one wants to do, those are the tasks you should always take on to help the town.

Remember who you are. You're a MacGregor, and we take care of our own.

99

Throwing pottery isn't helping this town—it's a waste of time better spent somewhere else.

Those early mornings held some good moments, but most of them sit sour in my gut—especially since he retired quickly and left Maw in the lurch with the shop, essentially turning away tourists and going against everything he'd ever instilled in me.

Not to mention the fact that he wouldn't let me anywhere near the kitchen to help out Maw.

Hell . . . I can't even think about that now.

Not when I'm trying to wash away those painful memories as I hike up this hill . . .

"Wow, I had no clue. You must have a good relationship with your dad, then." If only she knew. "My parents wanted me to go to college; I told them I didn't need to and that I would find what I was looking for in Los Angeles. Funny thing is, I wanted to go to college." She pauses, her voice a little shaky, and I wonder if she's going to cry. *Please don't cry.* I wouldn't know what to do. Hold her? Comfort her? Before I can make a decision, she continues. "I wanted to surprise my parents and tell them I actually was accepted into college, but the rejection letters rolled in, one right after the other. I could have gone to community college, but I was too proud for that. I decided I didn't need college and moved to Los Angeles with Dakota." She sighs. "I barely speak with my parents now. If I truly needed them, they'd be there for me, but I know they're ashamed of me."

"I know shame well," I say before I can stop myself.

"Really? But it seems like you get along so well with your parents."

Well, that just goes to show—you can never judge a family from the outside. When you dive deep, you might find years upon years of pain.

Wanting to avoid any serious conversation about my parents, I stay silent and continue to push back branches as we make our way up the hill. We're starting to get to the steep part, where the path narrows and we'll need to file together into a line. It's the most grueling part of the hike, but well worth it.

"Might want to drink some water. It's going to get tough in a few," I say.

"Oh . . . okay."

And just like that, silence falls upon us once again.

"Take my hand," I say, leaning over the last boulder Bonnie has to climb.

She doesn't even second-guess it this time. Instead, she slips her small hand into mine, and I help pull her up. When she makes it over the rock, she lets out a big breath and drops my hand.

"Thanks," she says and then turns to look out over the hill we've just climbed.

Green surrounds the panoramic landscape, peaks and valleys covered in freshly bloomed purple heather. The rich blue sky is dotted with puffy white clouds, though darker ones lurk in the distance, indicating an impending storm. I'll need to keep an eye on that. A light wind picks up, swirling around us, causing her ponytail to whip in front of me and offering a brief cool-off from our steep ascent.

"Wow, it's gorgeous," she says, hands on her hips as she peers down the hill. "I can't believe we climbed that."

I'm fascinated with her reaction as she takes in the rolling scenery sprawled out in front of us. There's something to be said about catching someone's reaction when they experience my homeland for the first time.

Awe.

Complete awe.

I glance out toward the loch and the valley, and I have to be grateful in this moment. I've trained myself to climb this hill and to be grateful rather than resentful. I might not be on the path I planned for myself, but I have to appreciate the air I breathe, the heartbeat in my chest, and the chance to keep taking one step at a time.

When Bonnie turns around, her brow knits together. "Where did everyone go?"

I look behind me, only to find our friends gone. "My guess, exploring." I nod toward the castle ruins, about one hundred feet from the actual footpath. "Want to check it out?"

"Yeah, I do."

I lead her toward the front of the castle, where most of the stone is still intact. Three of the four walls are partially standing, the crumbling stone now halfway buried under the grass and soil around the base. Any wood that was used for the door or architecture is long gone, and in its place is a faint resemblance of a castle with an arch in the front, moss climbing up the sides, and a ceiling open to the sky.

"Did a king and queen use to live here?"

I chuckle and shake my head. "Nay, laird and lady. They occupied the castle, but when the South came to attack Corsekelly, they fled and never returned."

"Was that when Fergus's ancestor alerted the town?"

I nod. "Yes. The town was burned down as well as the castle. The southerners didn't find the land worthy of their time and moved on. Neither did the laird and the lady, and they abandoned the place after seeing the ruined town. But to the townspeople, this was home, so they came back and rebuilt."

We walk through the stone-arch entrance and past a few fallen stones covered by grass and moss. Dakota and Isla are off to the right, their voices trailing softly, while Lachlan and Leith are performing their typical routine whenever we come up here. A boulder sits behind the ruins, about five feet wide and six feet tall. They compete to see who can scale it the fastest. They've shot an entire video on it.

Fucking eejits.

The clouds overhead block the sun as the wind picks up. Just as I thought: a storm is coming. I glance over my shoulder and take in the distance, trying to calculate the kind of time we have left up here. A shiver of fear climbs up the back of my neck at those dark clouds. Memories flash before me.

Painful memories.

Life-altering memories.

"I can't imagine how they wouldn't want to come back to this. It's beautiful," Bonnie says, knocking me out of my reverie.

"Sometimes people can't see the value in what's standing right in front of them," I say, and her eyes flash to mine.

The smallest of smirks pulls on the corner of her lips. "Are you saying I don't value you, Rowan?"

"Nay." I shake my head.

"Hmm, I think you are. And you know, it's been nice not fighting with you."

"It's been okay," I tease, and she bumps her shoulder against mine, pulling me all the way back into the present.

"Admit it, I'm not as bad as you thought I was."

"I never thought you were bad—just stubborn and far too talkative."

"Not all of us want to communicate like cavemen," she counters, working her way through the ruins. I take a moment to admire her. Her hand trails over the mossy stone, and a smile lifts up the corners of her mouth. Hell, she truly is beautiful, and that smile, when it's directed at me, makes my stomach dance with nerves. I can't remember the last time I had that feeling. If ever.

"I save my words—makes a bigger impact."

"Makes you seem like an asshole." I just shrug in response, and she rolls her eyes. "Tell me, how many times have you been up here?"

"More than I can count. Sometimes we'll hike up here, all four of us, and not say a single thing—we just get lost in our own thoughts." *Many times, dangerous thoughts.*

"I could see how that would be soothing." She moves past a stack of stone that's piled in the center of what I imagine was once the castle's main living space. I once heard the stack was from the turret where the lady would hide from the laird. Apparently, they weren't the kind of couple who were deeply in love. Maybe that's why they didn't stay. "So you've known the Murdachs since you were young, I'm assuming." I nod. "Have you ever had a crush on Isla?"

I rub the side of my jaw. "Aye. We dated for a few months."

"Seriously?" she asks, eyes wide. "Were you her last boyfriend?"

I shake my head. "No, that was an unfortunate man in a town twenty miles north. After a few months of dating him, she came up to Leith, Lachlan, and me and announced that she was more interested in dating Mac's sister than him."

Bonnie laughs. "I wish Dakota'd had a realization like that. Instead, she met Isabella, her ex, through a job I had. Isabella and I would have to work together a lot when our bosses were collaborating on a makeup line. She was very open about her sexuality, and she flirted shamelessly with Dakota. It took Dakota a hot second to understand it, but she was developing feelings for her. Isabella was not only her first but also the girl who made Dakota realize she's gay." Bonnie picks up a rock from the ground and tosses it in her hand. "If I ever run into Isabella on the street, I'd give her a piece of her mind. She played games, manipulated Dakota, and really messed her up."

Not sure what to say, I stay silent.

Bonnie keeps talking, and I'm not surprised—she seems to be a person who, once she starts talking, doesn't stop.

"I've had my fair share of boyfriends, but they never mentally messed with me. Mostly, they were just idiots. Immature, not ready for a relationship. Then again, not sure I was either." She sighs. "You don't need to hear this." She pats her stomach and looks around the ruins. It seems like she'd do anything to avoid eye contact with me. "Where's the food? This girl is hungry."

I'm about to call out to Isla when I see her come through an arch, Dakota at her side. "Did I hear someone's hungry?" she asks.

"Starving," Bonnie says.

Isla lowers her backpack and unzips it. She and Dakota unfold a blanket, and we're all taking seats just as Leith and Lachlan join us. Isla passes around some ham sandwiches, and Leith hands out drinks. Together, we feast, and by the companionable silence that settles over us, I can tell the hike has worked up everyone's appetite.

"Dakota was telling me you were trying to bake some butteries," Isla finally says, turning to Bonnie.

"You were?" Leith asks, looking far too eager.

"Yeah, I was going to make some to bring on the hike to surprise you guys, but I failed miserably. Six attempts, and they were all epic fails."

"You should have Rowan help you," Lachlan suggests with a sly grin.

"I heard he knows how to make a tasty buttery," Bonnie says.

"You actually *spoke* to her?" Leith asks, the fucking eejit.

"He spoke a lot," Bonnie says. "A total chatterbox. Smoke was coming out of his ears from all the overthinking. Fascinating spectacle, actually." She smirks at me, and hell . . . I like the teasing.

"I've seen the smoke before," Leith says. "But that's only been when he's trying to solve a simple math problem. Really takes it out of the big guy."

"What's eight times six?" I ask Leith right before taking a bite of my sandwich.

Leith's eyes narrow, his smarmy smile turning into a frown. "Och, you know I failed miserably with my times tables. Way to hit me where it hurts."

"It's true," Lachlan joins in. "He always got his sixes, sevens, and eights mixed up."

"They are entirely too close together."

"So are the other numbers," I say, and our little circle laughs.

I feel lighter at that collective laugh. I didn't realize how much I needed this reprieve, this camaraderie, until just now. Things have been heavy with my parents. I've felt angry, frustrated . . . hell, embarrassed, since I didn't even know they were leaving. And being out here, with my friends—old and new—eases the ache in my chest. Gives me a fresh breath of air to my lungs. I glance over at Bonnie, and our eyes meet for a brief second before she turns away and takes a bite of her sandwich. I'll admit that one little glance did a lot for me as well. Just in the last ten minutes, it feels like something has shifted between us: the anger seems to have dissipated, and a bond is forming. A bond that might develop into something more. My stomach dips. I don't know—I could be wrong.

"Get the fuck down from there. The storm is rolling in!" I yell, my patience wearing thin as I look up at Bonnie, standing on top of an outer wall that overlooks the valley. A few pebbles have crumbled under her feet already.

"Where do you get off telling me what to do?" Bonnie shouts down at me.

"I'm not carrying your body down this damn hill. That's where I get off."

"Who said you're going to have to carry me?"

Fucking irritating woman.

A crack of thunder rumbles through the hills, sending my heartbeat into a frenzy.

Fuck . . .

Panic starts to overtake me.

The rest of the group decided to head down the mountain a half hour ago. We stayed longer because Bonnie wanted to explore some more. She's spent the last fifteen minutes trying to distinguish where the bedrooms, the kitchen, and the living quarters were. I've spent that time trailing behind her as she climbs wall after wall. Knowing how bad the storms can be up here, I volunteered to stay back with her, even though Leith, Lachlan, and Isla all second-guessed my choice, each one of them saying they could stay with her while I headed down first.

I was wrong.

Terribly wrong.

Standing on top of the ruins, arms spread, looking out toward the town below us, she's speaking to Mother Nature, asking for forgiveness for the time she threw out an ice cream wrapper, missed the trash can, and watched it tumble down the street instead of chasing after it.

Litter, basically.

She's apologizing for littering while panic grips my body, harder and harder, with every rumble of thunder in the distance.

The wind whips through the trees viciously, the storm moving faster than expected, and I watch her sway backward, teetering on the edge of the weathered stone.

"Jesus Christ, get down!" I yell as my palms break out in a sweat, ready to catch her.

"Sheesh, fine, all right." She maneuvers herself down the ruins and lands perfectly on two feet before turning toward me, a grin on her face. "See, I'm fine. No need to—"

CRACK. BOOM.

Thunder erupts above and nearly shakes me to my core. A sheet of rain splits through the clouds and descends upon us. As water pours down, I stare at her, angry and irritated, my patience hanging on by a thread.

"Huh . . . who would have known it was going to storm?"

"I did," I snap. "I knew, and you wouldn't listen. Did you really think apologizing about littering years ago was necessary?"

She wipes the rain from her face. "Clearly Mother Nature didn't accept my apology. That, or she's making me pay my penance." She throws out her arms and tilts her head back. "I receive your punishment with open arms."

Thunder booms around us, and I grab her arm, pulling her deeper into the ruins and into a small alcove where we'll be protected. I hold her close, hoping to avoid any lightning strikes.

"Uh, what are you doing?" she asks, her chin pressed against my chest.

"Making sure you don't get electrocuted."

"Look who's overreacting about—"

CRACK. BOOM.

A sharp snap of light hits a pile of stones a few feet away. Bonnie yelps, burying her head in my chest and wrapping her arms around my body.

"Okay, okay, I'll admit it—ignoring you was a bad idea. I should have gotten down when you told me. Hell, maybe we should have gone back with the others."

I blink a few times, shocked that she's folded so quickly. I was expecting a little more pushback. "Can I get that in writing, please?"

"No."

She snuggles in closer, and I feel her tremble beneath me. I just hope she can't feel me trembling against her.

"Are you cold?"

"Shaken," she says. "My bones shake when I'm startled or scared."

"You're scared?" I ask, feeling a little sorry for her. *That's right, put all your energy into her, not yourself.*

Focus. On. Her.

"Aren't you?" She looks up at me, and God, she truly is bonny. Droplets of water coat her long eyelashes, and rain runs down her perfectly plump lips, which I'm sure do wicked things.

But then her words register.

Aren't you?

Fucking terrified.

It was a storm, just like this. Years ago. Came out of nowhere and changed everything.

But she doesn't need to know that.

I shake my head. "Nay. The storm will pass." And that's something I have to keep reminding myself. It will pass.

"Will it be harder to get down the hill?"

"Aye. Much harder," I say through a clenched jaw.

"So do you offer piggyback rides?"

I raise a brow. "No."

"Ugh, what kind of burly, strapping young lad are you?"

"Not the kind that carries stubborn, eejit tourists down the side of a hill."

"What if I injured myself?"

"You didn't, but if you did, I'd drag you down—the mud will be slippery enough."

She huffs against me and rests her cheek on my chest. "You're infuriating."

"Get used to it."

She sighs and then hugs me a little tighter, her arms still shaking, her body still trembling. I squeeze her a little tighter, and even though it's technically her fault we are still up here, I move my hand up and down her back, trying to soothe the shivers out of her.

Keep my hands busy. Keep my mind from wandering.

Briefly, she glances up and gives me a soft smile before then returning her cheek to my chest and gripping me even tighter.

I want to believe that we're standing like this to avoid the rain and lightning. I want to believe this position is just self-preservation.

But with every stroke down her back, I feel her melt farther and farther against me. And the scary thing of it all is that I like it.

I really fucking like it.

And she's helping me forget . . .

◆ ◆ ◆

The sun glitters through the wet leaves above us as we make our way to the bottom of the footpath.

"Watch it," I say as she slips down a steep, muddy patch on the edge of the hill. I quickly grab her hand and steady her for the final few feet.

"Thank you," she says as we step off the path and onto the gravel car park, which sits on the edge of town.

We're both drenched. Head to toe. Mud sloshes in our shoes from falling multiple times down the hill, and our hair is slicked down. Bonnie's falls over her eyes occasionally. Every time she's pushed it away, a new swipe of mud has decorated her face, making it look like she's wearing camouflage. Thanks to all the low-hanging branches, we both have twigs and leaves sticking out of our clothing. Basically we're a sight to behold, and the trip down has left me exhausted. Mentally and physically.

We stood beneath the ruins for a good twenty minutes, our arms laced around each other, until I felt it was safe to venture down. Well, as safe as it could be. The rain continued halfway through our journey, though it finally let up as we grew closer and closer to town. But the damage was done.

We resemble something that would come out of Loch Duich in the middle of the night to feast on children.

"So, that was fun." She laughs nervously.

I don't respond. Instead, I turn away and start walking into town, irritated and completely beat. Carrying worry on your shoulders while hiking dangerous terrain is tiring. I was nervous she was going to hurt herself, that another storm might roll around—or hell, that I was going to take a bad fall and she was going to have to make it down the hill without me to get help.

"So you're just not going to talk to me now?" She jogs up next to me.

Yup.

I keep walking . . . well, more like stalking, my footsteps echoing against the paved road and through the silent Sunday town. Everyone's tucked away in their houses, besides the odd local out on a stroll.

"After everything we've been through today, that's it? We make it to town, and now you're just going to walk away?"

I spin on her. "You're safe, and you know how to get back to your cottage. I did my job."

"You did your job?" she asks. "What is this? Some historical romance where the hero saves the damsel in distress and then takes off? I could have made it down the hill myself."

I push my hand through my wet hair. "You're unbelievable."

"Thank you." She smiles, and Jesus Christ, it makes me want to push her up against the wall of the Mill Market and tame that sassy mouth.

"You realize you could have really been hurt up there?"

"Aww, Rowan, you care about me." Her voice is teasing, but all it does is grate on my nerves. She has no fucking idea the kind of trouble we could have been in.

What a fucking emotional roller coaster today has been. One minute I tolerate her company, the next I feel myself craving conversation, and then I want to tear a tree down bare handed and chuck it across the mountaintop because she drives me so goddamn mad.

"This isn't funny, Bonnie."

Her smile slowly fades, and her head tilts to the side as she studies me. "You really were worried."

"Yes," I growl in frustration. "We're lucky something more serious didn't happen. If you'd just listened to me, we wouldn't be covered in mud and drenched to our core."

"But we're fine."

"We could have been hurt."

"'Could have' being the key phrase." She presses her hand to my shoulder. "No need to get so upset."

111

"Yeah, that's easy for you to say—you weren't the one responsible for another life."

"You don't have to be responsible for me, Rowan. I can take care of myself."

"Okay, then, take care of yourself," I say, pushing past her and heading toward my cottage.

Jesus Christ.

What the hell happened today? I was supposed to go on a leisurely hike with my friends, and I spent most of it arguing with a smart-mouthed blonde, getting stuck in a torrential downpour, and then letting that smart-mouthed blonde get under my skin.

Hours later, after a long shower and a hearty helping of beef stew, I lean back in my chair and stare up at the ceiling, my eyes focused on its arched wooden beams. Bonnie weighs heavily on my mind.

She drives me crazy.

She makes me want to scream, throw things, and then kiss her all in the same moment.

I shake my head. There is no way I'm developing feelings for her. No way in hell.

Yes, she's attractive, but feelings . . . no.

I need to go back to my initial plan: stay as far away from the lass as possible. In the week she's been here, my life has never felt more chaotic, and the last thing I need is to be out of control whenever she's around.

Distance. I need solid distance from her, and everything will be fine.

CHAPTER NINE
BONNIE

Cake consumed today: Three slices of Dundee cake.

Days since last male-induced orgasm: Eighty-one.

Boredom: Massive amounts, too much to count.

Rainstorms since arrival to Scotland: Fourteen. No wonder it's so green here.

Serving coffee to invisible humans is frankly borderline lunacy. At least Fergus is still showing up unannounced. Last time, he screamed so loud that I piddled. A goat made me piddle. But then I petted him, and now I think we're starting to build a strong bond. This is my life now.

◆　◆　◆

"Coffee? Yeah, you—I know you want coffee." I wave a cup in the air. "It's tasty—true Scottish flavors. Ever taste a kilt? We squeeze them right into the brew. We actually use kilts as coffee filters. Delivers the true essence of the land's ancestors." The tourist I'm verbally accosting puts his hand up over his face and walks right on by.

Sheesh, he's rude.

"A simple 'No, thank you' would suffice!" I shout out before walking back into the shop.

"Why are you saying everything smells or tastes like a kilt?" Dakota asks. She's standing behind the counter, hovering over her computer and drawing pad. "You know there's so much more to Scotland than just kilts."

I tap my chin and lean against the wall. "Think I should have said we stir each cup of coffee with bagpipes?"

"You're losing it."

"I am, Dakota," I say as I walk over to the counter, where I hoist myself up, letting my feet dangle down. "What the hell are we doing here day in and day out? We're wasting away." I motion to her computer, which she's been parked behind since we got here. "You're at least doing something." I squint at her screen. "Is that a soup can with an inspirational quote on it?" I wave my hand, dismissing the new freelance job she received from an up-and-coming influencer who specializes in dishing out "inspirational soup." Dakota was telling me about it last night. I swear, marketing is getting cornier and cornier. "I'm so bored here. I'm just staring at the wall."

"Then do something."

"Okay, so what do you suppose I do? Play some music and come up with a tap dance routine that might bring in more customers?"

"Nooo," she drags out and then motions to the space. "Fix things up."

"Pardon?"

She sighs and lifts herself away from her computer. "If you want more customers, figure out how to get them. Catcalling them from the doorway about kilt-flavored coffee is not the way to do it. You want to keep busy, and, well, here's a project sitting right in front of you. Take advantage of it."

"You mean . . . fix up the coffee shop?"

"Why not? I told you Finella left us with her credit card when you were taking care of your haggis situation—remember? She told us to use it however we need to make the store shine."

"I vaguely recall this." I tap my chin and look over the space as ideas start to trickle into my mind. "You really think she meant it? To help make this place shine?"

"Yeah." Dakota shrugs and goes back to work.

"Dakota." I reach over and shut her laptop, something I know she hates, but I need her complete attention. "Do you think . . . do you think Finella was alluding to us actually making something of the coffee shop again? Like, did she hire us to bring it back to life?"

"Maybe. She did mention that she created the ad to bring some fun attention to the coffee shop. Wasn't expecting it to bring two Americans to Corsekelly to run it, but she said Americans know their coffee houses, and maybe we could put our touch on it."

"And you're just telling me this now? After over a week of absolute boredom? What is wrong with you?"

"Why on earth would you try to fix something if you don't have a baseline?" Dakota asks, and her simple reasoning is far too annoying to appreciate. "You can't possibly fix something without finding out what's wrong with it first."

She's right about that . . . unfortunately.

Just then, another tour bus pulls away. I glance at the time on my phone—they were here for half an hour. Half an hour in Corsekelly, and not one of them came into the coffee shop.

The only visitor was Fergus, and frankly that's just sad. But we did have a riveting conversation about hooves. Even though his look like little vaginas, I told him not to be self-conscious—and if he really wanted to spice things up, I could paint them in a pretty plaid pattern with nail polish. He said he would consider it. Between you and me, I'm pretty sure he's going to pass.

But Fergus as our lone visitor isn't going to cut it.

"Do you know how much business we miss out on because we're offering plain coffee and hot chocolate packets?" I ask. "This place has the potential for more—much more. We could offer so many other drinks, baked goods, specials that go hand in hand. Coffee and a buttery. We can have Penis Stone souvenirs. There aren't many here in town. And what about Fergus? I mean, he's a town treasure, and no one is selling anything Fergus themed. Think of all the money we could make for Finella and Stuart. We could jump-start this entire coffee shop and give it a new life."

For the first time in I don't know how long, excitement bubbles up inside me. My mind whirs with all the possibilities, all the potential the coffee house has.

"You can design a new sign. Create a logo for the shop. Design all the shirts and merch. The *menus*—oh my God, this could be huge, Dakota." I push at her shoulder. "Doesn't this excite you?"

"Sure," she says, so casually that it makes me want to scream.

"What do you mean, 'sure'? Done right, we could capitalize on those tour buses and create something special here. And according to all the career assessments I've taken, organizational skills are my best attribute. This is right up my alley."

Dakota smiles and opens her laptop back up. "I can see you really creating something special."

"Really? Do you mean that?"

"Of course. I say go for it."

"Yeah?" I ask, nearly bouncing up and down.

"Yeah, but whatever you do, you have to run it by Rowan first."

Poof!

Did you see that splatter of hope? That was all my excitement drying up like a string bean in the desert.

Shriveled up and morphed into dust, only to be picked up by a gust of wind and carried off into the land where dreams don't come true.

"What do you mean, run it by Rowan?"

"Did you not pay attention to a thing I told you our first night?"

"Oh, excuse me." I hold up my hands. "I was jet-lagged, had a Scottish man try to speak to me while tapping his crotch, thought I was going to die on a roundabout in a MINI Cooper, was fed sheep intestines—and then quickly disposed of those intestines—only to be accosted by a grumpy Scot who found my broom wielding more comical than threatening. I apologize for not remembering the smallest of details."

"Maybe that was why you were fired three times," Dakota says with a huge smirk.

I point a finger at her. "You're an asshole."

We both laugh, and Dakota turns back to her screen. "Seriously, though, Finella said whatever we do, just to run it by him first." She shrugs. "Seems fair. She doesn't want two strangers coming in and destroying the integrity of their coffee shop."

"But . . . I haven't seen or spoken to him since he stormed off after the hike."

"About that . . . according to Isla, it seemed like you really pissed him off—which is not the story you gave me."

My eyes narrow. "What do you mean, according to Isla? When did you speak to her?"

"Yesterday." The smallest of smirks pulls at the corners of Dakota's mouth. "I was stocking up on your Dundee cake supply."

"Oh, don't you dare use me as an excuse to go into the bakeshop. We all know why you were there. And you didn't even come home with Dundee cake. You came home with shortbread."

"Which you ate all of." She lifts a brow.

"Boredom eating is a real thing," I say, folding my arms over my chest. "But that's beside the point. You were talking about me?"

"No," Dakota sighs. "Isla asked how you were doing after being stuck up on the mountain with Rowan during the rainstorm. Ever since he lost his brother—"

"Wait, what?" I ask, sitting taller. "Rowan has a brother?"

"Had," Dakota says quietly. "Isla didn't get into it, and I didn't pry. All I know is that he doesn't like serious rainstorms. She wanted to make sure he wasn't too harsh on you. Last time they were stuck on a mountain together when it was storming, Rowan apparently lost his mind. It took some time to calm him down."

"Oh my God," I just about whisper as I think back to our hike, how I carelessly disregarded his warnings and his persistent need to make it down the hill before the rain became too strong. The tension in his back every time I slipped, his stern grip as we walked through mud. His demeanor after we stepped off the trail.

Anger.

Distress.

Relief.

Wow, I don't think I've ever felt more like an ass.

"I had no idea," I say softly.

"Apparently he holds it all in—which explains why he's so grumpy and standoffish. From what Isla alluded to, there seems to be some darkness in Rowan's family. So yeah, even if you two aren't getting along right now, maybe cut him some slack. Don't go full Bonnie on him."

"Too late." I cringe.

Begging for forgiveness from Mother Nature over littering . . . yup, I went full Bonnie on him . . . while he was in the midst of panicking.

Really great, Bonnie. Just perfect.

"Hey, Shona," I say, walking into the Mill Market.

The quaint shop can best be described as what would happen if someone blasted Target with a shrink gun and then redecorated with Scottish charm. Its baskets overflow with fruits and vegetables. Its wooden shelves are perfectly stocked. And its beautiful plank wood floors wave and roll with the earth beneath it. Just like Target, the Mill Market has almost everything you could need. Unlike Target, it all comes in small quantities.

"Hello, Dakota."

"I'm Bonnie, actually," I chuckle.

"Och. I'm sorry." She shakes her head. "Blame it on the old-lady brain."

"Not a problem at all."

"Anything I can help you find?"

I walk past a display of haggis and mushy peas and feel my bones shiver from the inside out. I know other countries probably balk at the idea of putting peanut butter and jelly on a sandwich, but at least it isn't a can of harvested sheep innards.

"Looking for a notepad and fun pens."

"Aye, right this way."

She walks out from behind the counter and guides me down a small aisle, past the fruits and vegetables, past the meat and dairy cases, and into a small section stocked full of household items.

Pots, pans, kitchen utensils, greeting cards, wrapping paper, toys, and school supplies.

"Here ya go, lass. We have a few notebooks that might tickle yer fancy." She lifts one up from the little stack on the shelf. "This has a goat on it—reminds me of Fergie, the old man. Take this one—it will bring good luck."

"Okay," I say, glancing at the others and noticing they all have goats on them. Gives me something to share with Fergus. I'm sure he'll appreciate it.

"And fun pens . . . well, all we have are these Flair pens. A pack of black, red, and blue. I can put in an order for some other ones if you'd like."

I take the familiar pens along with the notebook. "These will be just fine, thank you."

"Of course. Do you need anything else? We just got a fresh shipment of Curly Wurlys, and they're quite divine, if you've never tried one before."

119

"Is that a pig's tail?" I ask, the only thing coming to mind at those words.

She chuckles and shakes her head. "Nay, it's Cadbury chocolate with caramel. Everyone in town loves them, so I always stock up. Best you get some now before those Murdach boys find them. And MacGregor too—he's been known to buy a handful at a time."

"Rowan likes them?"

"Aye. How those boys all stay in shape despite their massive Curly Wurly intake is beyond me. Here." She pulls me up to the sugar shelf and grabs a few long, white-and-purple-wrapped treats and sets them in my hand. "You won't be sorry."

"Okay, yeah." I stare down at the candy. "I'm going to have to start running if I keep eating the way I have since I've been here."

"Isla's shortbread?" she asks as we head to the counter.

"That and the Dundee cake. Although I ate a dozen shortbread cookies without even realizing—so I think that's more dangerous than the cake. At least that I know how to pace."

"'Tis all right to indulge, just keep up on your fitness. Take the Hairy Coo Footpath every morn. That'll do ye just fine."

"The Hairy Coo Footpath?" I ask. What an adorable name.

She rings up my purchases and puts it all on my tab. *Thank God.* I still don't have the hang of the whole foreign-money thing yet.

"No one tell you about the hairy coos? They're our Highland cattle. They roam about the grasslands. Cute fellas, if you ask me. There's a two-mile path that loops around their feeding area. A few years ago we laid down a dirt path to help with tourism. Give visitors more to see than just Fergus and the Boaby Stone."

"Oh, that's a good idea. Do a lot of people hike it?"

She shakes her head. "Only locals. Not many people know about it."

"Oh, well, that's a shame." Another potential attraction for tourists that's not living up to its potential. There is so much charm in this town, and it's all overshadowed by a penis rock.

"'Tis pretty, though, and a bonny morning walk. The path starts right past the Boaby Stone entrance, tucked into the hills. Can't miss it. Marked well too."

"Thank you. I'll walk it tomorrow morning."

"Enjoy." She hands me a paper bag of my items and gives me a small wave.

I came in for a notepad and some pens. I'm leaving with a bribery tool—the Curly Wurlys—and a new way to curb all the calories. A successful trip to the Mill Market, indeed.

"Are you sure you don't want me to go with you?" Dakota asks as she jogs in place in front of me.

Yes, Dakota has been running every day since she got here. She found a challenging trail she really enjoys and has been tracking her times to watch for improvement. Besides her brilliantly creative mind, she's also very math oriented. She loves data and solving problems. So this behavior doesn't surprise me in the least. I'm also not surprised that her slowest time so far happened on the day we shared half a Dundee cake.

I was also sluggish that day, but I wasn't sorry about it.

"Positive. You go train for the Olympics, while I take a leisurely walk with the cows."

"Okay, have fun. You remember where the trail is, right?"

"Yes, I do."

"And you have your cow-poop barometer ready?"

I nod. "Yup. Going to sniff it out to see if it's a suitable running trail for you."

"You're the best. Meet you back at the cottage." She takes off, and I watch her set the time on her watch before she heads into a run.

I walk up to the entrance and marvel at the stick arch that marks the start of the footpath. It reminds me of what you see at the end of a driveway in Texas, welcoming you to a ranch. Straight ahead are rolling green hills spotted with heather and gray slate rocks. Behind the hills are even taller mountains, jagged and peaked to points, which I heard from a local the other day usually have snow on the caps during the winter. Unfortunately, no snow for this walk, but it's still breathtaking.

I'm already excited about the possibility of this being my morning routine. Water in hand, shoes tied tight, I walk through the arch and down the trail. The dirt crunches under my shoes while early birds chirp off in the distance.

Yes, I could get very used to this.

The greenery, the crystal-clear brook that runs by the trail and into the loch, the soothing sound of trickling water, and oh look, a hairy coo.

Isn't he *adorable*.

Picture a cow with a seventies hairstyle. Long brown locks sweep over his face, and massive horns come out the side of his head. Isn't he darling? I could just stare at him all—

SMACK.

My cheek connects with what feels like a stone wall, and I fall back on my ass with a thump.

What on earth?

"Ah hell." A deep, accented voice rolls through my entire body.

Blinking and trying to get ahold of my bearings, I slowly take in the wall before me. Except it's not a wall. Toned, tanned legs, running shorts . . . bulge . . . deep, muscular V, followed by defined abs, massive pecs . . . oh sweet Jesus, those nipples. So proportionate and pretty. My eyes keep running, following a path of dark, twisted ink that stains one pec and travels over his shoulder and down his arm.

And then his face comes into view as he squats down. Dark scruff, wet lips, mossy-green eyes.

"What the hell are you doing?" Rowan asks, pulling me to my feet.

I blink some more, my face level with his beautifully sculpted chest. My oh my, do they breed them well in Scotland.

"Hello? Are you okay?"

"You're shirtless."

He glances down at his wet, glistening chest. "Aye. And you have a shirt on."

I glance down at my chest and nod. "Aye."

The smallest of smirks appears on his lips before it disappears. "Glad we established who's wearing a shirt and who's not."

"'Tis quite the accomplishment this fine morn," I say in a horrible Scottish accent. Maybe that knock did something to my brain.

"Okay, well . . ." He frowns. "If you're not concussed, I'm going to take off."

"I don't think I'm concussed. Although I don't know what a concussion feels like."

"Are you dizzy?"

I do feel slightly dizzy, but I'm not sure if it's from being knocked down or from the combination of my lack of male-induced orgasms and seeing Rowan with his shirt off.

"Maybe?"

His brow knits together. "Do you feel like you're going to throw up?"

I didn't eat breakfast, so that could be why I'm feeling slightly faint.

"Maybe?"

"Jesus." He drags his hand down his face and exhales heavily. Taking me by my upper arm, he spins me around and starts walking me back toward town.

"Hey, what do you think you're doing?"

"Taking you to your cottage."

"But I planned on seeing more hairy coos."

"Not if you're feeling dizzy and nauseous," he grumbles. "We didn't even run into each other that hard."

"Says the guy built like a rock wall." I swat at his hand. "And I would appreciate it if you didn't manhandle me like this. I am a lady, after all."

"I'm holding you up so you don't fall again."

I swat at him a second time, but he doesn't budge. Sheesh, he's strong. "I'm more than capable of walking—" I trip over a tree root and nearly fall forward, but Mr. Muscles pulls me back.

Muscles McGrumpyshire.

"You were saying?" he asks drily.

"That was an unfortunate coincidence."

He silently walks me all the way back to the cottage, his grip tight, unwavering.

"Mornin', Rowan," a man calls out, tipping his pageboy hat in our direction.

"Mornin', Alasdair," Rowan says, his voice sounding chipper, so different from when he speaks with me.

"Morning," I shout, waiving obnoxiously.

Alasdair chuckles. "Morning, lass. Good luck with the beast—he looks like he's on a war path."

"Oh, you know, just a caveman trying to control every aspect of my life," I shout back as Rowan walks us away. Have never spoken to the man in my life, but I like his jolly smile. Can you guess? Rowan doesn't appreciate my tiny conversation with Alasdair. He indicated this by tightening his grip. Impossible man.

"You know," I say as he marches me down the gravel driveway to the cottage, "I think I can make it from here."

Nothing.

Not a single word.

When we reach the cottage, he pushes through the door and walks me to the couch. While I sit down, he goes to the kitchen and digs through a drawer before pulling out a flashlight. Striding back over, he squats in front of me and flashes it in front of my eyes.

"What are you doing?"

"Making sure your pupils aren't dilated. That's a sign of concussion."

"Are they?"

"No." He turns off the flashlight and heads back to the kitchen, where he puts it back in the drawer and fills up a glass of water. He stalks back and hands it over. Planting his hands on his hips, he stares down at me.

"Can I help you?" I ask.

His strong jaw twitches as his chest rises. "Drink the water."

"Why? Did you bewitch it with special healing powers?"

"Jesus . . . fuck." He pushes both hands through his hair. "Fine, do whatever ye want." He turns on his heel and storms toward the door.

"Wait. I think . . . uh, can you get me a bowl? I think I might throw up."

With lightning speed, he grabs the kitchen trash can and brings it to me before sitting on the arm of the couch and placing his hand on my back. I lean my face over the trash can for a grand total of five seconds. Then I turn my head toward him and smile.

"Just kidding."

Annnd ohhh boy, if I thought that storm was bad the other day, the one that's brewing right in front of me might be even worse. Yes, maybe I should take it a little easy on him after what I learned about his brother, but there's something about the clench in his jaw that makes me want to keep pushing his buttons.

Before he can erupt, I place my hand on his thigh. "Settle down, Grumps. I'm fine."

He tears the trash can away and shoves it back in the kitchen. "Good to know." With that, he charges to the front door, rips it open, and strides outside.

Yikes. Someone doesn't like to joke in the morning.

Feeling guilty and remembering why I need to be nice to this guy, I chase after him. When I move past the front door of the cottage, I spot him, both hands on the back of his head, his back tensing with anger.

I'm about to say something when he turns around. His eyes widen in surprise as they meet mine, but that surprise is short lived, and he closes the distance between us.

Body vibrating with fury, he gets right in my face. "Don't joke about being injured. Got it?"

"Rowan, you can't be serious. I was knocked down, and you're acting like I cracked my head open."

His eyes darken, and his jaw clenches so tightly that I'm afraid he might break a tooth. His eyes search mine, and I can feel him wanting to say something. But he doesn't open his mouth—instead he just stares at me. I wonder what he's holding back.

Does this have anything to do with his brother? This innate need to constantly protect, to make sure everyone is okay? I think back to what Dakota said about Rowan and rainstorms, the way he tensed every time I slipped. Was that . . . ?

I take stock of the situation: his breathing is heavy, his fists are clenched at his sides. So much anger. So much hurt. It's all bottled up, ready to be released, and if I don't defuse the situation, it's going to blow up right on me.

And then . . . get ready for it, ladies . . .

His eyes fall to my lips.

Yup. They fall right to my lips, which means we have clearance for the one thing that I know will defuse any situation with a man this angry.

Might not be smart.

Might be a little on the dangerous side.

But it's guaranteed to work . . .

In one swift motion, I grip both his cheeks, pull him down, and crash my lips against his.

Just like that.

Kissing the beast in front of the cottage.

And boy oh boy is it the most uncomfortable thing I've ever done in my life.

Butterflies do not erupt.

There is no sign of hearts flying out of my head.

Nor is there a distant harpist playing romantic background music.

The only things present during this torturous moment are his stiff lips and flailing arms, as if his lips got stuck in a bear trap and he doesn't quite comprehend how to release himself.

Dramatic much, Rowan?

Deciding to end his apparent misery, I release him, and he quickly steps back, putting distance between us. He runs the back of his hand over his lips while staring at me . . . appalled.

I set my hands on my hips. "Did you just wipe my kiss away?" I can't help but feel a tad insulted.

"What the hell was that?"

"I asked you a question." I stand taller.

"What did it look like?" he asks, giving his lips one more wipe while looking me dead in the eyes.

The bastard.

"I'll have you know, I'm a lovely kisser." He doesn't say anything. "And you looked at my lips. I saw it. That's the universal sign for 'trespassers welcome.' And if you didn't approach me with cod mouth, I could have demonstrated that, but there is only so much a person can do when your lips are puckered up like an ass—"

"Don't be fucking kissing me," he says, taking another step back.

"I'm not diseased."

"Don't kiss me," he repeats.

"Why? Do you have a girlfriend? A wife?"

"Nay." Another step back, his eyes still on mine.

"Do you not find me attractive?"

"Doesn't matter."

"Sure does," I say, pressing him. "Now you opened up a box you shouldn't have opened. Why don't you want to kiss me? I brushed my teeth this morning."

"Because I don't want to. There doesn't need to be a reason other than that."

"Well, it's rude."

He scoffs. "It's rude to kiss someone when they don't want to be kissed."

"Oh my God, it's not like I licked the side of your face and then shoved the tip of my tongue up your nose. I kissed you. Grow up."

"You grow up," he shoots back.

"Gah." I point at him. "You grow up."

"You're the one kissing random people. You grow up."

"Maybe you both should grow up," Dakota says, jogging up the driveway.

Rowan rolls his eyes in response and takes off jogging himself. Wait, no. He can't jog off—we have things to discuss. Chasing after this man does not sit well with me, but . . .

"Hey!" I call out to him. "I need to talk to you." No response. "You can't run from me—I'll find you!" I shout. And then he's gone, disappearing past the trees. "Damn it," I mutter.

I walk back into the cottage, where Dakota is stretching. "What was that all about?"

"I kissed him."

"What?" she asks, the shock clear in her voice as I make my way toward the shower.

"Don't worry, he kissed me back with his codfish mouth. I think I would have found more of a love connection with Fergus."

"Why did you kiss him?"

"Read the room, Dakota," I say, slamming the bathroom door shut.

◆ ◆ ◆

Why the hell did I kiss him?

I tap my pen on my empty notebook paper, chin propped in hand as I lean over the coffee shop counter. Dakota ran to get us lunch at the Admiral—there's a scotch beefsteak sandwich they serve there that is *kisses fingers* to die for.

While Dakota has been working on her soup-can images—the current one features a dancing chicken on the top waving a flag; I don't ask, I just smile and say it looks nice—I've been trying to drum up ideas for the shop. But I keep falling short, because all I can think about is this morning.

Honestly, I'm hosting a bunch of emotions right now, and I'm ready to kick some of them out.

Anger because he's infuriating. That one will probably stay—not going anywhere soon.

Embarrassment because I kissed him, hoping it would calm him down—but he acted as if I was a hairy coo lapping at his lips. Positively disgusted. Yup, humiliation will probably hang out for a bit too.

And then I have these . . . how do I put it . . . uh, adoration-type feelings. I adore his thick pecs, his furious green eyes, his bristly voice, and the repartee we have. I like it maybe a little too much. So . . . looks like those feelings will stay as well.

Ugh.

I'm lifting up and pressing my palm to my eye just as Dakota walks into the coffee shop with a bagful of the goods.

Okay, there is one thing that will distract me, and that's food.

Especially that steak sandwich.

"Are the tatties hot?" I ask, clapping my hands as I meet Dakota at one of the tables.

"Fresh, still steaming."

"God, my mouth is a-gusher right now."

"Attractive," Dakota says, laughing. "Ran into Rowan, by the way."

"Is that so?" I ask coyly, popping open the to-go containers and letting the delicious onion and garlic smells fill me with joy.

"Yup, told me to tell you that when he got home, he washed his face with bleach."

My eyes snap to hers. "He did not."

Dakota chuckles and takes a seat, a salmon sandwich in front of her. "That's what he said; just relaying the message."

What an ass.

As if I would feel bad now.

Oh no . . . he'd better watch out because I very well might kiss him again. Except this time, I'll use tongue.

◆　◆　◆

"Was the Penis Stone everything you imagined?"

"*Boaby* Stone," Meredith, a tourist in a bright-green shirt that reads MAKING SCOTLAND MY BITCH, says.

"Ah, yes, sorry. The slang word around here is 'penis.'" Not true at all, but whatever. She's from the States—she doesn't know any better. "So, the Boaby Stone, was it everything you dreamed of?"

We're standing outside the entrance to the Boaby Stone cave, a pack of tourists filtering in and out, either completely satisfied or vastly disappointed by the sight before them. I've spent all morning pulling tourists to the side before they hop back on their buses to conduct a little survey I put together.

"It was beautiful. I really felt the *Iron Crowns* energy in there, and I swear I could hear Sir Armaden's screams when his penis was cut off."

Oh-kay, not a real thing that happened, lady, but whatever. She's making Scotland her bitch, so I'm going with it.

"Fascinating." I pretend to write something down. "Did you take a picture in front of it?"

"Oh yes. I'm here with a group of my friends, and we pretended to chop each other's boobs off."

How . . . pleasant.

"You guys are a gas," I say, pushing her arm playfully. "Wish I got in on that action."

"We can go back if you want. Add you to the group picture."

"Oh no, no, that's okay. You don't want a stranger in those memories, anyway." I clear my throat and add, "Did you get a chance to walk through town? Corsekelly is quite lovely."

"We did," she says. "We petted Fergus and took a few pictures with him."

"Did he scream for you?" I ask.

"No, does he do that?"

"I guess only for the lucky souls," I answer. Even though Fergus and I have started a little love affair, he still screams to make himself known. Not sure I'll ever get over it. "So, did you visit any places of business?"

"Stopped into the Mill Market for a boaby shirt and got a funny-looking candy. Curly Wurly—never heard of it."

"Oh, they're good," I say, knowing full well I have only one left. I purchased them as a bribery tool for Rowan, but somehow they ended up in my belly. Jury is still out on how that exactly happened.

"Can't wait to try them."

"So that's it? No other places?"

"Nope, that's it."

"Uh-huh, no . . . coffee?"

"Oh, well, we were craving some coffee, and this would be a great time for a pick-me-up, but from the reviews online, we knew this wasn't the place to get it. So we're waiting for two more stops."

"On-online?" I stutter, trying not to blow my cover.

"Yes, the bus company has a forum for tourists where we can review places on the route and talk about all the *musts* to stop into. The Mill Market was one of them. So was Murdach's Wee Bakeshop. My friend

Kacee grabbed us some haggis pies for the road." Meredith points to her chest. "Making Ireland our bitch."

"Scotland."

"What?" she asks.

"Scotland." I motion to her shirt. "You're making Scotland your bitch."

"What did I say?"

"Ireland."

"Ohh." She laughs. "That's next."

The bus driver honks the horn, and she looks back at her friends, who are waving for her to join them.

"Well, I'd best be going."

"Yes, don't want to miss out on any of the other stops. Thank you so much for your time. I really appreciate it."

"Of course." She gives me an awkward high five and then takes off.

I tap my pen against my chin as I watch the bus pull away. Once it's out of sight, I make a beeline for the coffee shop.

I need to see this online forum.

"Not worth your time. Barely any seating, coffee leaves much to be desired. Nice owners, but horrible selection, there is none at all. What's with the chairs? Were they made in the 1800s? I was served a hot chocolate packet, and I had to stir it on my own." I look up from Dakota's computer. "These are all comments on the tour bus forum, clear as day, right under the Corsekelly stop. No wonder no one comes in here. And this is just one tour bus company. How many others do you think are like this?"

Dakota is sitting in the chair across from me, legs crossed. "Uh-huh." She stares off into the distance.

"Hello," I say, snapping my fingers in front of her face. "Did you hear me? These reviews are awful."

"What? Oh yeah, they're bad. Totally killing business."

"Were you even paying attention?"

"For the first ten minutes of reviews, I was."

"Dakota, what the hell? You've been drifting off all freaking day. What's going on?"

"Nothing," she says, her cheeks reddening.

"Uh . . . I don't buy it."

I look over at the coffee counter and notice a familiar box. My head snaps back to her. "Oh my God, you went to the bakeshop again."

"You were out of shortbread."

"Because I have no ability to control myself, which means you need to be the one cutting me off, not feeding into the madness."

"I'm a good friend."

"No, you're using me as an excuse to go see Isla."

She grins. "Maybe."

I push the computer away and fold my arms over my chest. "Okay, tell me what happened."

"Well, she said hi."

"Oh yes, wow. Be still my heart, a greeting," I deadpan. Dakota flicks her pen at me in response.

Chuckling, I say, "What else happened?"

"We talked a little about the weather, simple things, and then, when I was leaving, she asked what I was doing Friday night."

"What?" I sit up. "Uh, this is something you should have told me the minute I walked into the coffee shop. She asked you out?"

"You were all hyped up on the research you conducted—I was letting you have your moment."

"Moment had, now tell me about yours."

She's smiling so hard that my cheeks actually hurt for her. "Well, it might be a little lame, but I consider it a step in the right direction. She asked what I was doing Friday, and when I said nothing, she said I should bring you and meet up at the pub, to hang out and have some drinks."

"Ohhh, she did ask you out."

"And you," Dakota says, a little defeated.

"I'm just a buffer for you. She did that to be nice."

"Maybe. So . . . will you go?"

"Of course. I'm one hell of a wing-woman. I got you—boo." I wink. "God, how exciting."

"Don't make it a thing."

I give her a side-eye. "You should already know I'm going to make it a thing."

"I'm asking you, please . . . don't make it a thing."

"But I love making it a thing."

"Please, Bonnie."

"Ugh," I groan. "This is painful."

"Bonnie . . ."

"Fine." I lean back in my chair. "I won't make it a thing."

"Thank you. So, about the reviews—"

"Oh my God, you're going on a date." I clap my hands excitedly.

Dakota puts her head in her hand. "You're making it a thing . . ."

Chapter Ten
ROWAN

Curly Wurlys consumed: Seven.
Curly Wurlys left in stash: One.
Awkward, unexpected kisses: One.
Missed opportunity to kiss back: One.
A certain blonde has pushed me to blowing through my stash quicker than I care for, and I'm not fucking happy about it. And she's made me consider why I didn't kiss her back. Maybe because she drives me insane? Maybe because I have no idea how I really feel about her? Maybe because I'm out of my mind with my parents, her, the changes that are happening at a rapid pace.

Can't blame a guy, right?

"Rowan, are you there? It's your mother."

"Yes, Maw. I know. I can see that from the caller ID."

"Well, I can barely hear you!" she yells into the phone.

"Because you don't have the phone on speaker," I hear my da say.

"I pressed the button."

"You didn't press the button. It's not lit up."

"How do you know it has to be lit up?" Maw asks.

"That's how the phone works. Press the button."

"I did."

"You clearly didn't."

"Jesus Christ, just someone press the button!" I shout.

"Fine, I'll press the button again—oh look, it's lit up."

"I told you, you bawbag," Da says, making me chuckle.

"You watch your tone, Stuart," Maw snaps. "Or I won't fetch you that cola like you asked."

"Sorry," he mumbles.

Da and his cola.

"Rowan, are you there?"

"Yes, I'm still here," I answer while kicking my feet up on my coffee table.

"How are you?" Maw shouts, nearly breaking my eardrum.

"You don't have to shout, Maw, I can hear you just fine."

"Och, sorry." She chuckles. "You'd think I've never used a phone before. How are you?"

It's rare when she does use a phone, though. If she wants to talk to someone, she usually just walks over to them. The only person she talks to on the phone is her sister, and that's pretty much it.

"I'm doing fine." I twist my water bottle in hand, staring down at the fizz tablet that's reacting to the water. "How's holibags?"

"Lovely, lovely. We had the most wonderful chicken today. I asked the waitress for the recipe, and she said they didn't do that."

"Yeah, Maw." I push my hand through my hair. "It's not like the Admiral, where you can go up to Alasdair and ask him for his piecrust recipe."

"Well, it should be. We paid enough. You would think they'd allow you to take home the recipe."

"Where exactly are you?" I ask.

"Oh now, now, none of that business."

"Don't you think it's well mad that you're in another country and I don't know about it? It's not settling well with me, Maw. I'm worried, ye ken?"

"You have nothing to worry about, Rowan. We're safe."

Yeah, well, easy for her to say.

I take a deep breath, trying not to grow frustrated with my parents and stress them out. "Given what's happened in the past, I'd assume you would be more sensitive to me fretting about the well-being of my family members."

A sigh. "Rowan, I promise you, you have nothing to worry about."

"Why won't you tell me?" I ask, sounding harsher than I wanted.

"Just drop it, Rowan," Da chimes in with his stern voice.

And now that he's spoken up, it's done. But I don't think it's *nothing* to worry about. They're not saying where they are. Da sounds weaker. Something is going on, and it's really starting to concern me that they aren't involving me in their lives.

I press my fingers to the bridge of my nose. "Fine, but you're being smart? Taking all precautions? You know how people can treat tourists, especially older ones. They take advantage."

"We're not that old," Maw scoffs. Old enough. "And yes, we're being safe. Now, let's talk about you. Shona was telling me how you've become familiar with Bonnie. She couldn't remember who was who at first, but she described her as the long-haired blonde."

Fucking Shona.

"I'm not *familiar* with Bonnie, whatever the hell that means."

"Well, that's not what I've heard. Seems like you've been carrying her all around town. Going on hikes. Apparently, you appeared from the trees all muddy and wet. Care to explain? She assumed you two were rolling around together."

"Shona shouldn't assume and just keep to herself. We were stuck in a rainstorm, got wet and muddy. That is all."

"You two danced together."

Jesus Christ, does she have a camera crew following me around?

"You know, you don't want to talk about where you are, and I don't want to talk about Bonnie—got it?"

"Watch your tone, lad," Da cuts in again.

"You know, I have to go. I have some things to do." I stare down at my fizzy water.

"Oh, okay, dear. Well, stay in touch, and make sure the lasses are taken care of. Anything they need, lend a helping hand."

"Uh-huh."

"We love you, Rowan."

Exasperated, I blow out a low breath. "Love you too."

I hang up my phone and take a look at the time. Little past six thirty. I could use more than just an electrolyte water at this point. I could use an entire bucket of beer.

I stand from the sofa, head to my bedroom, and pick out some fresh clothes before turning on the shower. I'm heading to the pub.

Friday night at Fergie's Castle is always packed, but Hamish opens up the doors and allows outdoor seating during the summer. Makes the space less crowded, and having a few pints with the loch lapping at the shore across the way is soothing.

Because everyone is at the pub on Friday, I put on a nice pair of jeans and a simple white button-up shirt, making sure to roll the sleeves up to my elbows. I've styled my hair for once and am about to leave when I quickly spray a bit of cologne that I never wear. My friends might appreciate some cologne.

This has nothing to do with possibly seeing Bonnie.

Not even a little.

When I make my way into town, I can already tell that Fergie's has a little bit of a crowd, based on the noise emanating from the building.

A few summers ago, Hamish spent a great deal of time working on the pub's outdoor courtyard and repairing the stone wall that borders Loch Duich. He added planters that hold flowers during the summer and sprigs of spruce during the winter. He evenly spaced out picnic tables with large red umbrellas securely fastened in the middle, providing protection from what sun we do get. And then, toward the wall, he built a ladder ball court for those drunken nights when you think your ability to throw balls on a string is on point, when it's really not. I suppress a smile at a few rowdier memories as I step onto the courtyard. To my surprise, a few picnic tables are still available.

Excited to be able to sit outside and enjoy a pint, I'm making my way past the picnic tables—just as someone grabs my hand.

"Rowan, you look nice."

I glance down to find Isla, looking nice as well in a summer dress, her red hair gathered high on her head in a ponytail.

"Hey, Isla. You look good yourself. I didn't even recognize you."

"Oh really? Am I that squirrely day to day?" She smirks at me.

"You know what I mean."

She tugs on my hand. "Join me. I ordered a pitcher and two plates of nachos. They're the special tonight, and you know I'm not going to pass up some nachos."

"Two plates' worth?" I chuckle. "And a pitcher—you're going to need someone to carry you home."

"No, it's not all for me. I'm expecting company."

"Who . . . ?"

"Hey, Isla." I don't have to turn around to know who just excitedly greeted her, but I do anyway. "Who's your friend—?"

Bonnie is standing next to Dakota, and they're both dressed up as well and . . . hell, Bonnie, uh . . . fuck, she looks drop-dead gorgeous.

Her long blonde hair is styled in waves and is pinned back half up, half down. Heavy black mascara highlights those mesmerizing eyes, and a light shade of pink paints her plump lips. And that dress. Hell. Light blue, it's tight around her waist and breasts and flairs out at her hips. Mouthwatering, that's the only way to describe her.

"Oh, Rowan." She chuckles. "I didn't recognize you in a button-up shirt."

"Should say the same about the dress," I say, and her eyes narrow.

"You both look really nice," Isla says sweetly before clearing her throat and turning to Dakota. "I love your hair."

Dakota blushes. "Thank you. You look great too."

And oh my God, they're on a date . . . with a third wheel.

Bonnie is the dead giveaway—she's stepped off to the side and is twiddling her fingers together in front of her chest, looking far too excited.

We both stare at Dakota and Isla, who are staring at each other and smiling. I don't know much about Dakota, but from what I've seen, she could be a good match for Isla. They're both calm, thoughtful, and take good care of their friends.

Hence the reason I've been asked to become this date's fourth wheel.

Normally I would quickly bow out and grab a pint to myself, sit on the stone wall, and stare out at the loch, but I have a feeling—from the way they're staring at each other—that they're going to want some alone time, but there is no way they would dingy Bonnie. They're not that kind of people.

So . . . looks like I'm on Bonnie patrol tonight. *Great.*

"I ordered us the beer you two said you liked and some nachos. I hope that's all right," Isla says with a nervous smile.

"I love nachos," Bonnie says, taking a seat at the picnic table. Dakota sits next to her, and Isla takes a seat across from Dakota, which leaves me with sitting across from Bonnie.

When I take a seat, Bonnie's eyes widen.

"What are you doing?" she asks.

"Isla invited me." I smirk.

"I hope that's okay," Isla says, always the people pleaser. "I can kick him out right now, and he could get his own nachos." I know she's not serious, but I'd allow it if she was.

"Please kick him—"

"The more the merrier," Dakota says, elbowing Bonnie.

Just then Hamish delivers the beer and the nachos, something he never does, but then again, he's always had a soft spot for Isla. Who doesn't here? She owns a bakeshop, is incredibly sweet, and is always one of the first locals to volunteer to help out wherever it's needed.

"Thank you, Hamish," she says.

"Of course, darling. Enjoy." He nods at me quickly and then takes off.

"Wow, these look amazing," Bonnie says while Isla starts pouring everyone a glass of beer.

Clearing her throat, Isla meets Dakota's gaze. "How was your day?"

Dakota smiles, her whole face flushed. "It was productive."

"Oh? What did you do?"

Shifting in place, she glances at Bonnie and me—Bonnie chowing down on a nacho, completely oblivious to Dakota's discomfort. "Uh, you know, just some stuff on the computer."

Heat slides up the back of my neck as I realize just how much the girls want privacy.

"I've never been a super fan of jalapeños," Bonnie says, staring down at one that's pinched between her fingers. "Which is weird, given that I'm from Southern California. You would think Mexican food is in my bloodstream, but then I had one a few months ago by accident and I couldn't help but think, 'spicy, but delightful.'" She pops it in her mouth and looks around the table. "Really good."

Dakota clears her throat. "Do you, uh, like jalapeños, Isla?"

"I do," she answers awkwardly.

"Now, olives. Ooo-eee, there's something I've never been able to get enough of," Bonnie says, picking one up and plopping it in her mouth.

"Do you like olives, Isla?" Dakota asks, and holy hell, I'm dying a slow, slow death.

"I do," Isla responds. "Do you?"

Dakota is about to answer when Bonnie says, "Oh, she loves them. When we were kids, she used to buy five cans at the store, and we'd sit under my trampoline with a can opener eating them all. It was a weird addiction, but our parents were glad we weren't doing drugs. Oh, these chips are amazing. Crunchy and holding the cheese just like—"

"Bonnie, I need to show you something," I say, standing from the table.

"What?" she asks, appearing completely confused. She looks me up and down. "What do you need to show me?"

"It's over there." I point to the stone wall.

"Uh . . . I'm good." She picks up another nacho, and I glance down at Dakota, who shoots me a pleading look.

That's it—she wants her friend gone so she can relax with Isla. I get that. If I was trying to go on a date and my mate was with me, it would be hard to relax.

I round the picnic table. "It'll just take a second. It's important."

"You're being weird," she says. "Why are you talking like your jaw is clenched tight?"

Dear Jesus, this woman.

"Just go see what he wants," Dakota says, nudging Bonnie in the back.

"What if it's his penis or something? Last time a guy said he wanted to show me something, he stretched his nutsac over his pants and said, 'Look, it's gum.'"

Who the hell is she hanging out with?

"Do you really think I would do that?"

Bonnie gives me a smooth once-over, her eyes resting a second too long on my chest. Finally, she answers, "Maybe."

Christ.

"I've never met a more infuriating woman," I say before I can stop myself.

"Oh yeah, now I really want to leave with you." Bonnie rolls her eyes.

Dakota shoves Bonnie this time, and they exchange a look. In that one look, I can see Dakota secretly telling her friend to get the hell up. Luckily, it works. Bonnie stands and smooths her dress. "Fine, but if he shows me his 'gum,' you owe me some more shortbread." She sighs and turns toward me. "Okay, show me whatever it is you want to show me."

The girl really is clueless sometimes.

I grab her by the upper arm and walk her over to the wall, far enough away from the table that no one can hear us.

She looks around, examining the area, and then turns to me. "What? Is there some kind of special rock that will give you luck if you rub it? Is there another Boaby Stone here?"

"You're really fucking clueless."

"Excuse me?" she asks, hands on her hips, and hell, the position only lifts her breasts more.

I clear my throat. "They're on a date."

"Uh . . . duh. I'm her wing-woman."

"Yeah, pretty sure Dakota doesn't need a wing-woman at this point."

"You don't even know her. She asked me to go because she's shy. Dakota has been through a lot, and she leans on me, especially when it comes to her love life. This is important to her, and there is no way I'm going to let her down, not when I know I'm needed. Don't believe me? Just look at . . ." Bonnie's voice fades as she turns to the table—Dakota and Isla are deep in conversation now. "Huh, would you look at that."

"I don't think she needs you. What they need is space, away from someone blabbing on about the history of their jalapeño and olive consumption."

"Uh, that was a smooth icebreaker. Not all of us can just huff our way through a conversation."

"I don't huff through a conversation."

"Practically." She folds her arms, and that just makes things even worse for me.

Christ, it's as if I've never seen a pair of boobs before. *Eyes up, Rowan.*

"Well, I guess if she doesn't need me, I'll just go home," Bonnie says.

"Okay," I answer nonchalantly. I'm turning to walk away when she pulls on my arm.

"You're supposed to say, 'You can have dinner with me,'" she says, and her defensive tone almost makes me laugh.

"Why would you even want to when I huff through a conversation?"

Her lips twist to the side, and the smallest of smiles appears on her beautiful face. "Touché," she says. She tugs on my arm again. "Don't make me eat alone." She bats her eyelashes. "Pleeeease, Rowan, I feel bad about the other day—"

"You feel bad?" I scoff. "You feel bad about driving me batshit."

"Funny that you mention batshit . . ."

I roll my eyes and drag my hand over my face. Fuck, this woman has me feeling all kinds of emotions that I can't quite seem to process. It doesn't help that she's looking damn beautiful tonight, those brilliant eyes of hers pleading for me to give this a chance.

I'd be lying if I said I didn't want to eat with her. Despite our tension-filled moments, I still want to be around her, see how far she can push me before she turns around, a complete one-eighty, and makes me laugh.

She tugs on my hand. "Please, Rowan. We can keep an eye on the girls from here and jump in if they need help—and we can keep each other company." She smiles and . . . damn it.

That smile lowers my defenses in seconds. It's sweet and loaded with promises of friendship and good times.

Hell . . .

"Fine." I point at her. "But don't give me the story behind any other food preferences."

"Oh darn, I was planning on going into the history of my life and cake." She smirks.

"Save it for someone else." I nod toward an empty table near the stone wall that's far enough away from Dakota and Isla. "Grab that table. I'll snag a plate of nachos and some beers from Isla."

"Sounds good."

I approach the table, and Isla glances up at me, gratefulness in her eyes. "Everything okay?" she asks.

"Yeah." I scratch the back of my neck. "Figured you two might want a break from all the jalapeño and olive talk. Bonnie and I are going to hang at the table over there." I point to where Bonnie is, and she gives them an enthusiastic wave. "Figured we could grab beer and some nachos."

"Yes, please. We won't be able to eat and drink all of this," Isla says.

I'm filling up a pint for each of us and grabbing the plates when Dakota says, "She hides it well, Rowan, but she's struggling. Be kind."

"Of course," I say, wishing I could read between the lines. Struggling with what?

Honestly, given Bonnie's personality, I never would have guessed that she was struggling with something. She's always so full of life . . . and saucy behavior.

I hold up the plate and beer. "Thanks. Have fun, lasses."

"Thank you," Isla mouths to me before I take off.

I really hope they find a connection. They both seem like they're searching for something, and I'm hoping they've just found it.

As I walk toward her, Bonnie hops up from her bench and helps me with the nachos while I set the beers down on the table. I take a seat across from her and pick up my beer, bringing it to my lips and taking a small sip.

An IPA. Not my first choice but still good. Probably Deuchars. It's a go-to for a lot of locals at Fergie's Castle.

"Oh, this beer is really good," Bonnie says, setting her pint down. "Might be my favorite I've had so far. Is it yours?"

I shake my head. "Prefer an ale."

"Ohhh, you like to chew your beer. I do too, on occasion, but I have to be in the mood. Like when we had fish and chips, the maltiness of that beer with the oil and vinegar . . ." She kisses her fingertips like a chef. "Perfect. But this IPA goes great with the nachos."

I pick up a chip full of cheese and beans. "Yeah, it does." Bonnie rests her chin in her hand and stares at me. I pull some cheese off my finger with my mouth and ask, "What?"

"You're rather dressed up for the evening, Rowan. It's a Friday night. Were you expecting to find a lass to take home tonight?"

"No."

"Please, a man with your kind of virility—I'm sure you must go on the prowl often."

"I know everyone in town."

"Doesn't mean you don't have a little sidepiece around here." She perks up and looks around while absentmindedly picking up a chip and stuffing it in her mouth. "What about Shona? Cougar, but still a looker."

"Shona is my maw's best friend. She changed my diapers."

"So she's familiar with your nakedness, then."

My brow shoots up. "You realize how disturbing that is?"

"You know, when I said it out loud, it felt disturbing." She looks around again. "Okay, what about that girl over there?" She points to a brunette wearing a bright-red shirt.

"That's Alana."

"Ohhh, Alana. She sounds lovely."

"She's also married to Alasdair, who owns the Admiral."

"Hmm . . . are they interested in threesomes?"

I take another sip of my beer. "Want me to ask them for you? I'm sure they'd be open to a blonde joining their marriage."

"Not for me, for you."

Leaning back, I call out, "Alana, come here."

"What are you doing?" Bonnie hisses as Alana approaches our table.

"All right, you two." She holds her hand out to Bonnie. "I'm Alana. I don't think we've met yet."

"Alana, this is Bonnie. Bonnie, meet Alana."

"Pleasure," Bonnie says, tacking on a smile and shaking her hand. "Rowan here said you're married to Alasdair."

"Aye, we've known each other since we were wee ones. Parents swore we would get married one day, and we did."

"Ah, that's sweet," Bonnie says, dreamy eyed.

But that look quickly vanishes when I open my mouth. "Bonnie here was wondering if you have room in your marriage for one more. She's looking to hop on for a threesome."

"Rowan!" Bonnie gasps. "No, I did not say that. There was no mention of threesomes at all."

"You just said you wanted a threesome."

"Rowan," she says through clenched teeth, her eyes screaming murder.

"We're taking applications," Alana cuts in, always ready for a laugh. "We're looking for someone adventurous. Would you say you're adventurous, Bonnie?"

Her eyes widen, and she sits back, hands twisting her beer. "I, uh . . . I mean, I've dabbled in things here and there, but—"

"Have you ever kissed another woman?"

"Well, there was this one time I kissed Dakota, but that wasn't really sexual."

"Experience in the bedroom—how many years?"

Completely shell shocked, Bonnie fidgets nervously. "Uh . . ." She looks up in an apparent effort to calculate in her head. "Carry the five . . . I'm sorry, math is hard under pressure."

"Have you ever used a feather? Alasdair likes a good feathering," Alana says, and I nearly lose it.

"Not per se," Bonnie says, really twisting her beer now. "But, you know, I could always—"

Alana and I both laugh out loud, and Bonnie stares, pressing her hand to her heart.

"What's going on here?" she asks. "Are you . . . are you teasing me?"

Alana nods. "Aye, but I do enjoy that you dabble in things here and there."

"So . . . you're not looking for a third to your marriage?"

Alana shakes her head. "Does that disappoint you?"

"No, I mean . . . no." She takes a deep breath and directs her attention to me. "I hate you."

I chuckle and sip my beer as Alana pats me on the back and wishes me luck. Eyes trained on Bonnie, I wait for the onslaught of whatever she's going to do to retaliate, but she stays silent instead, stewing.

Which, let's be honest, is worse. Because she's planning something vindictive—I can feel it.

She leans back, beer in hand. "Did you get a good chuckle out of that?"

"Aye."

"I see." She slowly stands, eyes still on me.

"What are you doing?"

"Wouldn't you like to know." With one hand on the picnic table, she hops up on her bench and faces the crowd congregated outside the pub. "Ahoy!" she yells, grabbing everyone's attention. The crowd quiets down, all eyes trained on her. She clears her throat. "I would like it to be known that I kissed Rowan McGrumpyshire"—she points to me—"and he has cod lips. Dead cod lips. Worst kiss I've ever experienced in my life. Total and utter disaster. Be warned, all lasses . . . and lads, for that matter: if you're looking to pucker up with the crotchety beast, be prepared to be disappointed. Dead . . . fish . . . lips." She holds up her beer in a toast. "Slangevar."

And just like the good Scottish people they are, they all hold their beers up and say, "Slangevar!" before taking a drink.

She sits down and smirks at me.

"Feel better?" I ask. She nods, looking completely and utterly happy with herself. "Good." I stand as well and step up on the bench.

"What the hell are you doing?" she snaps. "Get down."

I put my hand up. "Just need to clarify some things." Copying her, I turn to the pub's patrons and call out, "Ahoy!" A few people laugh and cheer. I give a small wave before clearing my throat as well. "Aye, it's true, I had dead codfish mouth when she spelled me with her witchy ways."

"They were not witchy!" Bonnie shouts.

"But I tightened my mouth tight because, according to local lore, women with long blonde hair and ice-blue eyes could be the Serpent Queen. And I saw it"—I lean forward, getting into the story—"one evening, I saw her lick her lips . . ."

"Serpent tongue," Lyall says from the side.

"Derived from a basilisk," Baird calls out from the back.

"Exactly. The elusive serpent tongue. The myth is true, lads— she's upon us. Slithery, scaly, ready to pop off your boabies, and I'd be damned if I let it touch my tongue. Kiss of death."

"And then off to the Boaby Stone," Lyall adds.

I point at him. "Precisely. Beware, lads . . . and lasses, for that matter. The Serpent Queen is among us, and she's ravenous for her next victim." I hold up my pint. "Slangevar."

"Slangevar!" everyone says. With that, they take another sip of their drinks and go back to their conversations.

I hop down and sit back on my bench, looking expectantly at Bonnie. She runs her tongue over her teeth and doesn't flinch, or even blink. Just stares.

"Aren't you pleasant company?" she finally says.

I down the rest of my beer and grin. "I think so."

◆ ◆ ◆

"Oh, I so have you."

"No, you don't," I scoff.

"Yes, I do." Bonnie taps the side of her head. "I'm three steps ahead of you, son."

"That's what you said the last three times you lost."

"I mean it this time." She rubs her hands together and reaches for a glass. She takes a sip and then moves it across the three men's morris board we borrowed from the pub.

After a rousing stare-down from Bonnie while I finished off the nachos, we glanced over at Dakota and Isla to see how they were doing, and it was as if they were the only ones on the planet. Talking intimately close, hands reaching out across the table to push hair out of their faces, intention in their eyes, never a lull in conversation. Nothing fazed them. Bonnie and I could have both whipped off our clothes and performed a naked jig, and they wouldn't have noticed.

So, I offered a pub game to Bonnie—one I know I excel at—and she jumped on it.

Three men's morris, the Scottish way.

Like tic-tac-toe on a wooden grid, but the pieces we move are pint glasses. Every time we move them, we take a sip . . . a small one. Whoever loses has to chug one pint.

Bonnie is swaying to the music filtering from the pub, and she's starting to show signs of being drunk. It's kind of funny, because the more she drinks, the more she develops a fake bravado, like she can take on the world and do it one handed.

"Oh, you are going down, Grumpyshire."

I move my glass and take a sip.

"Aha!" she yells. "Bam. Drink up, sucker."

She moves her glass, and I stare down at the board.

"Uh, you didn't win."

"Yes, I did." She motions to the line of glasses. "One, two, three. In a row. Suck it."

"That's my glass." I point to the one in the corner.

"No, it's not."

"Yes, it is. I've been drinking out of it this entire time."

"Then you've been moving my glass." She gasps and reels back, a hand to her chest. "Oh my God, sabotage!" She points at me. "Sabotage. Right here, in broad daylight."

Technically not broad daylight. It's nine at night and the sun is still up, but I'm not about to argue with her.

"I'm not sabotaging you—that's my glass."

"You know damn well it's not. You're just trying to mess with my drunk mind. Well, I'm not taking it. I won—drink up."

"It's my glass."

"God." She shakes her head. "I knew you'd be a sore loser, but really, Rowan, acting like I'm cheating? Isn't that beneath you?" She leans over the table, her cleavage in full display. "Drink up, lad."

I gulp, telling my eyes to look up, but hell . . . I must be feeling my drink too, because I can't seem to stop looking at her boobs.

"And while you drink, learn some manners. It isn't polite to stare at a lady's bosom."

"Call it a 'bosom' and I won't stare at it," I say, picking up a glass and chugging. That's a lie—I'll still stare.

◆ ◆ ◆

"I don't understand what we're doing here."

"I think we roll the dice," I say, studying the backgammon board.

"What are the dice for?"

"Uh . . ." I scratch the side of my head. "To tell us how many spaces to move."

"Where are the spaces?"

I squint at the board some more. "Can't be sure. I think it's missing pieces."

She runs her finger over the felt of the board and strokes the triangle sections. She starts with one finger, and then adds two . . .

"What are you doing?" I ask, shifting on the bench.

"Stroking the triangles."

"Why?"

She shrugs. "Drunk, and I haven't stroked anything in a long time."

"Stop it."

She glances up at me, eyebrow raised. "Is this turning you on, Rowan?"

"No."

Yes.

"Are you . . . sure?" she asks in a seductive voice.

"You know, two can play at that game." I bring my finger to one of the triangles and start to slowly massage it.

Her eyes zero in on my finger, and her tongue peeks out, wetting her lips. "That's a nice cadence you've got going on there. Looks like good pressure."

"Aye. Really good pressure," I say, dropping my voice.

Really getting into it, she strokes her triangle harder, faster.

Jesus. I swallow hard, watching as her tongue pokes out and wets the top of her lip. That tongue, what I could do with it . . .

This can't be one sided.

So I pick up the pace, eyeing her, and when her gaze lands on my finger, I slow it down, really dragging out the "pleasure."

"Oh God," she says, her free hand traveling up her chest to her neck.

"Uh . . . do you two need a second?" Hamish asks as he steps up to our table.

We both jump and snap away from the board, hands going to our laps.

I clear my throat. "Just playing backgammon."

"I've never seen it played like that."

"American way," Bonnie says.

"Aye, well, if you're done playing, another table would like it."

"Sure, yup, all done." Bonnie folds the board and shoves it toward Hamish. He thanks us and takes off. Bonnie glances at me. "Were we just . . . jerking each other off with a board game?"

"I wasn't . . . were you?"

"No." She shakes her head quickly. "Nope . . . not even a little."

"Good, because my dick is way bigger than that felt triangle."

Her mouth falls open as I smirk and finish off another pint.

"You're not so bad when you're drunk," Bonnie says, tossing a ladder ball clear across the playing area and missing the playing ladder completely. The sun is setting, the cast-iron lights that surround the courtyard are flickering on, and we're currently battling a couple of tourists—Jim and Yolanda—who are on their second honeymoon. They're staying at Under the Goat's Kilt Inn and decided to extend their visit one more night because they've loved their time in Corsekelly.

They're also destroying us in ladder ball.

"You're tolerable," I say as I toss a ball as well, which whacks Jim in the shin. "Sorry," I call out. He just waves in response. Third time I've done that—you'd think he'd have faster reflexes by now.

"I'm more than tolerable." She whips her arm back and flings a ball. "Tallyho." It wallops Yolanda in the arm. "Oof, sorry, Yolly!" Bonnie calls out. "They must think we're aiming for them."

"I did on the last one," I admit. "Wanted to see if he would move."

Bonnie chuckles and grabs my arm. "I just aimed at Yolly. Thought maybe if I aimed at her rather than at the ladder, I would hit the ladder. Didn't work."

"Solid logic, though."

"Thank you."

From across the court, Jim says, "I think we're going to call it a night."

"Ahh, well, make sure you ice that welt." Bonnie waves. "Enjoy Corsekelly, and stop in the coffee shop for subpar coffee tomorrow morning."

They take off and Bonnie sighs, leaning against me.

"I think I should get home too," I say, my brain feeling sluggish, the effects of way too much beer.

"Me too." Bonnie wobbles as she starts to walk away. "Hey, where did Dakota and Isla go?" I glance over at their table, which is now vacant. Hell, almost the entire pub is vacant. When did that happen? She reaches for her phone and scans a text. "Oh, they went for a walk. Gah, do you think they're holding hands? Oh my God, what if they kiss?" She grabs my shirt and shakes me. "Do you think they'll kiss?"

"I don't know," I say. "Maybe?"

"Oh, what I wouldn't give to see that. Dakota has the softest lips—she is constantly moisturizing them. I bet Isla will be immediately delighted by them. And the passion behind the kiss—think there'll be passion?"

I shrug. "Maybe?"

"Ugh, you're so . . . boring."

"Is that so?" I hold her up by her arm and guide her away from the pub and toward her cottage. "If I'm so boring, then how the hell did I entertain you all night?"

"Duh, I entertained you."

"You wish. I was entertained *because* I entertained you."

Her nose scrunches up. "That makes no sense."

"Sounded right in my head."

She glances around, seeming to catch up to the fact that we're walking. "Where are you taking me?"

"To the cottage, where else?"

"You could be taking me to your sex dungeon."

"Nah, you're not sex-dungeon material."

"What is that supposed to mean?" Her voice rises in defense. "You saw me stroking that triangle. I was really good at it."

"Really good is a stretch."

"As if your finger digging was any good."

"I wasn't digging. Jesus."

She stumbles over a rock when we get to the driveway, and I hold her up. Seems like I've been doing a lot of that lately. "Why are you taking me to the cottage? I wasn't done drinking."

"You were done. Just seconds ago you said you should go home."

"Who made you the boss?"

"God?" I ask, really unsure who made me the boss at this point.

"Oh no, there is no way God would make you the boss."

"Do you like to disagree with me just to fight?"

"No." She smirks just as we reach the cottage.

That smirk is dangerous.

That single smirk could make me do something stupid.

Something really stupid . . . like kiss her. Because she's the kind of girl who can dig under your skin, make you want more, and I'm not sure I'm mentally ready for that kind of battle.

So, to avoid any poor decisions, I throw the door open and push her inside. "There. Now, good night."

I'm turning to walk away when she calls out, "The minute you're gone, I'm going back to the pub."

I pause, and my back stiffens as I turn around to face her. "The hell you are . . ."

CHAPTER ELEVEN
BONNIE

Beers consumed: *Feels like at least twenty-five.*
> **Days since last male-induced orgasm:** *Who's counting anymore?*
> **Hairy chests hand is playing with:** *One.*
> *Uhh . . . why is my hand on a hairy chest?*

What is that delightful smell?

Why am I so warm?

Am I petting a chinchilla?

I squint my eyes open. The sun is too bright, and my head is try-ing to crack itself open. But despite the scrambled eggs my brain is transforming into, I notice one thing that isn't right . . . there is a man in my bed.

Not just any man . . .

Whispers

Kilty McGrumpyshire.

Gasp

My hands quickly fall to my body—I feel my breasts first.

Exposed.

Oh my God, why am I naked?

"Why am I naked?" I shout, sitting up in bed and startling the hell out of Rowan. He rolls off the bed, just as I realize I'm not naked—I'm still wearing my dress. My boobs have just fallen out of it like little escapees.

Just as Rowan pops his head up, I clap my hands over my boobs and turn toward him. His shirt is unbuttoned, but the rest of him is covered.

Did I unbutton his shirt?

Ugh. I forgot about his tattoo.

And his perfectly proportioned nipples.

Even in the morning, fresh off the booze train, he's gorgeous.

"What the hell are you doing?" he asks, pressing a palm to his eye.

"Why are you in my bed?"

He glances around. "Hell if I know." He blinks a few times. "Why are your tits out of your dress?"

"They went rogue last night. It has nothing to do with you." I turn away and stuff the stubborn ladies back in. Dignity and all. Once I'm tucked away, I turn back around to find the smallest of smirks on his lips, and good God, my loins practically throw themselves at him.

Deadly. He is positively deadly with a smirk.

Trying to control myself, I say, "Your chest hair is really soft. What little chest hair you have, that is."

He glances down at the small patch between his pecs and then back up at me. "I put leave-in conditioner in it."

"Really?" I didn't take him for a leave-in conditioner kind of guy, although his hair is luscious.

"No." He stands, and that's when I see his jeans are unbuttoned, revealing a peek of his black underwear.

Of course he'd have black underwear. I don't know why that's a turn-on for me, but it is. So are the abs carved into his taut stomach and the little patch of hair right above his waistline.

"Checking me out, Bonnie?"

I cross my arms over my chest and look away. "I'd rather burn my eyes out with acid."

He chuckles, and just like that . . . my nipples are hard.

"Good to know." He grabs his shoes and moves around the bed, through the cramped room, and down the stairs.

"Where are you going?" I ask, chasing after him—for God knows what reason.

"Home. I need to wash your stink off me."

"I don't stink," I scoff as we make it into the living room. He sits down on the couch and puts his boots on, his fingers flying through the laces. I don't think I've ever seen someone tie their boots that fast.

Why is that something I'm noticing?

I blame the hangover.

When he stands, he tilts his head to the side, studying me as he slowly buttons up his shirt—a total detriment to society. He might drive me crazy, but his body was made to be naked at all times.

"You look sad. Do you not want me to leave?" he asks in a teasing tone.

"Oh, I def—"

"Uh . . . good morning," I hear Dakota say behind me.

I quickly spin around to find her standing in her bedroom doorway, a sly smile turning up her lips.

Oof, how could I forget Dakota was here? I probably assumed she went home with Isla. Although not everyone works like I do—bringing an orgasm producer home but failing to receive said orgasm.

Not that I would want him to give me one.

Yeah, I know, I didn't believe that last sentence either, but I figured, you know . . . to save face and all.

"Morning, lass," Rowan says casually, as if standing in our house with his shirt half-undone and jeans open is completely and utterly normal. "How was your date with Isla?"

Dakota frowns and glances cautiously between us. "It was nice."

"Did you kiss?" I ask, clasping my hands together at my chest, momentarily forgetting my predicament.

"No." Dakota's face brightens. "We did hold hands, though, while we went for a walk."

"Oh, be still my heart," I gush. Turning to Rowan, I grab the lapels of his shirt and shake him—or at least attempt to. "Did you hear that? They held hands."

"Which pales in comparison to whatever you two did last night," Dakota says.

I wave my hand at her. "Nothing happened." To Rowan, I whisper, "Nothing happened, right?"

"Her tits threw themselves at me, and she told me my chest felt like a chinchilla."

"I said that out loud?"

"Mumbled it," he says, awkwardly patting me on the back.

"What a . . . thrilling night," Dakota says, still looking confused. "So is this . . ." She wags her finger between us. "A thing?"

"What? No." I shake my head. "Nope. No . . . no."

"If you didn't get that, it's a solid no," Rowan chimes in.

"Okay." Dakota rocks on her heels. "Would you like to stay for breakfast, Rowan?"

"Oh, he has to get going—"

"Would love to." He pats me on the back again and then makes his way to the kitchen, shirt and jeans still undone. "Shall I cook us up some eggs and toast?"

"That would be great," Dakota says, smirking at me.

Why does it feel like they're on the same team—one I am forbidden to join?

◆ ◆ ◆

"So, tell us about your date," I say, sitting down at the dining table with Dakota while Rowan moves around in the kitchen.

"It was really good." Dakota plays with a napkin on the table. "She's pretty awesome, but Rowan already knows this."

"I do," he says, his perfectly deep voice adding to the conversation. "She's quite the catch."

"What did you talk about?"

"Everything. Our childhoods, how different they were. Spoke about our friendship, and how even though I don't have siblings, you've always been a sister to me."

"True. I have no problem fighting you for the last piece of cake."

"Claws out and everything," she says, and we both laugh. "But it was also nice to have someone actually look me in the eye while I spoke. It felt like she cared about what I had to say. Isabella was never like that. Maybe a little at first, but then . . . I don't know. I felt more like a puppet to her than anything."

I nod, remembering just how toxic that entire relationship was. "Tell me about the hand holding."

"Well, she asked if I wanted to go for a walk, and of course I wanted to since you and Rowan were starting to get rowdy and loud."

"Were we?"

Dakota laughs. "Uh, yeah. It was quite the sight to behold."

I cringe. "Sorry."

"It's okay, you were having fun. You need fun."

Rowan glances over his shoulder at me from the stove, and I quickly look away. I don't want him to see any ounce of vulnerability, because yeah, I did have fun last night—at least from what I can remember.

I had one of the best times I've had in a long time that didn't involve Dakota. He helped take my mind off my nagging need to prove something to myself, to find anything that shows I'm on the right track, that I'm worthy. It's a feeling that's been plaguing me for what feels like every second of the day, and he erased that. He helped me relax, chill, just enjoy life for a moment rather than focus on what I could have done differently the last few years.

Yes, we might bicker and pick on each other, but I know it's all in good spirit. I like a guy who doesn't hold back, and Rowan doesn't. He says whatever is on his mind. It can be terrifying at times, but also thrilling. And that realization is startling because I think . . . oh God . . . I think I might be having some sort of affectionate feelings toward the man.

No . . .

Right?

It must just be indigestion from the beer last night.

At least, that's what I'm going to tell myself, because there is no way I want to face these feelings right now. I'd rather lay down the denial card, thank you very much.

"So, the hand holding." I nudge her under the table, a sign I want her to move on.

"Yes, well, we started walking through town, along the loch. I was telling her about LA when she slipped her hand into mine."

"Smooth," Rowan says, and I detect a hint of pride in his voice.

"I was a little surprised at first, but then it felt so right, and we wove our fingers together. It was perfect. I had so many butterflies take off in my stomach that it almost felt like I couldn't breathe."

"Gah, my heart can't take this." I reach over and take Dakota's hand. "I'm so excited for you. So, does this mean you'll go out again?"

"If she asks, I will."

"Why don't you ask her?" Rowan chimes in, bringing two plates of food to the table. He sets them in front of us with silverware and then returns to the counter, leaning against it and picking up a plate for himself. He grabs a fork and starts to dig in, and I realize something—he might drive me crazy and he might be the grumpiest person I've ever met, but underneath it all, he's a very kind and caring man.

A protector.

The Highland Fling

Someone who likes to serve others.

I don't think I've ever met a man like him. It's scary, yet refreshing.

"I've never asked someone out before," Dakota admits. "What would I even say?"

"Simple," Rowan says. "Just say, 'Hey, I had a great time Friday night. Would you want to do it again sometime?'"

"That's a great way to put it," I say, though it feels odd to agree with Rowan.

"You think?" Dakota pushes some eggs around. "It makes me so nervous."

"Think about how nervous Isla was to ask you out in the first place," Rowan points out. "Being the only lesbian—or gay person—in a small town means that dating has had its challenges, and when she has ventured out, she's been burned every time. Asking you out was a big deal . . . and probably why she invited the third wheel too." Rowan nods toward me.

"I was a very charming third wheel."

"'Charming' is a stretch." I'm about to protest when he winks and then shoves a forkful of eggs into his mouth.

Good God, if he winks like that again, I'll pop my breasts back out of this dress and shimmy them in front of his face. No shame.

"You think she'd appreciate it if I asked her out? We didn't kiss or anything—maybe she didn't think it was a good date."

"If she held your hand, it was a good date. Trust me, Isla works slow. Ask her out, Dakota. I bet it'll really make her day."

"Yeah?"

Rowan nods. "Yeah."

"Okay, then I'll do it." Dakota puffs her chest. "I'll ask her out. Thanks, Rowan."

"Anytime."

❖ ❖ ❖

Dakota is in the bathroom, getting ready for her big day, while I laze about at the dining table, watching Rowan finish up with the dishes that he insisted upon washing.

He's so hot and cold all the time. I honestly don't know how to read him. All I know is that last night and this morning—especially this morning—he's put a dent in the armor I wear when I'm around him.

He switches off the water, dries his hands, and then turns around, gripping the counter and leaning against it, eyes trained on me. His shirt and jeans are buttoned now, but he still has a fresh-from-bed look, which is doing crazy things to whatever resolve I have left.

"Thank you," I say before he can open his mouth.

"What for?"

"Well, for breakfast and the dishes, but mainly for giving Dakota the confidence she needed to take that next step—one I'm not sure she'd have made without some insider encouragement."

"Dakota reminds me a lot of Isla—soft spoken, sweet, and shy when it comes to relationships. They both need a push, a bit of help to make those steps toward creating something they want."

I rest my chin in my hand and give him a long look. "You're very thoughtful, Rowan."

"Not the arsehole you think I am, huh?"

"Never thought you were. Just . . . I don't know. You know how to press my buttons."

"Same, lass." He pushes off the counter and stuffs his hands in his pockets. "I'm going to take off. I'll see you around."

He's started to the door when I call out, "Hold on." I get out of my chair and close the distance between us.

I don't know what I'm about to do, but I know I need to do something, because there are about a hundred different emotions buzzing through me, bubbling up and needing release.

Feeling awkward and hoping he doesn't push me away, I reach out and wrap my arms around his waist. I pause for a moment, waiting for a reaction, and when he doesn't move, I take that as a good sign and give him a hug.

Holding my breath, I wait for what feels like minutes, but is only seconds, before his arms encircle me as well and he pulls me in tight. I press my cheek to his chest, remembering how good this felt when we were up at Corsekelly Castle. And it feels so good now that our hug lasts, stretching on and on.

When I finally pull away, he fixes me with a stare. "What was that for?"

I shrug. "Thought maybe you needed a hug."

He slowly nods. "Didn't think I did . . . until you gave me one."

The air stills between us, despite the fresh breeze wafting in from the open kitchen window. The prolonged anticipation that's been building between us—the hate, the fights, the curiosity, the attraction—it feels like it's colliding all at once, in this moment, and it's almost unbearable.

Boldly, his eyes rake over me, resting a little longer on my breasts and then climbing to my eyes. They flare, entranced, as I lick my lips. The smoldering flame flickering in his eyes, the rise and fall of his thick chest, the clench of his jaw—all signs that maybe, just maybe, the pull I'm feeling toward this man isn't just me. That he very well might be experiencing the same thing.

He takes a step forward, his hand slides around my waist, and I swear to God I can feel my knees weaken as his strong hand grips my side. His other hand lifts my chin as he wets his lips. I hold my breath.

Waiting, anticipating . . . hoping that his mouth descends on mine. Hoping that, even though we might be at each other's throats, he finds it as exciting as I do.

His thumb pulls on my lip, and he lowers just a little bit more—until Dakota opens the bathroom door and walks out, whistling a Taylor Swift song.

Rowan quickly steps away and pushes his hand through his hair, turning his back to me.

God damn it, Dakota. She doesn't even come into the living room— she walks straight into her bedroom without giving us a glance.

"I should go," Rowan says, not looking at me but instead ducking his head and moving toward the door.

"Wait!" I call out, desperate. "I . . . uh . . . can you, um . . ." *Jesus, spit it out, Bonnie.* "Can you help me with something?"

He looks over his shoulder. "Right now?"

"No," I say, even though I want to say yes. I want to ask him if he can help me with the ache between my legs. *Hey-o.* "Later, can you stop by the coffee shop?"

"Sure." His brow furrows. "Everything okay?"

"Yeah." Not really. I'm nervous, excited. I want to stay in his arms. And I want to talk through my thoughts about the shop, but I'm scared he might think they're stupid, not worthy of consideration.

"Okay." He takes a step away, and I hear him exhale harshly before he turns around, grabs me by the hand, and pulls me into another tight hug. With his chin resting on my head, he says, "I had fun last night."

"I did too," I admit, feeling those butterflies Dakota was talking about.

He squeezes me and then takes off, giving me a brief wave before exiting the cottage.

A large smile erupts over my face as I watch him walk away.

Oh no . . . this isn't good at all.

It's happening. I think I'm crushing on Kilty McGrumpyshire.

"Hey, lasses," Isla says, walking into the coffee house with a basket of shortbread and Dundee cake. God bless Dakota for snagging the baker in town. "I brought you some replenishments."

"You didn't have to do—"

"You're a doll," I say, cutting Dakota off and taking the basket. "I was craving shortbread this morning after my walk."

"Did you do the Hairy Coo Footpath?" Isla asks, leaning against the counter near Dakota.

"I did, and I love it so much. Those hairy coos are adorable. Might be my favorite part of Scotland."

"Oh, Rowan isn't?" Isla teases with a wink, making Dakota laugh out loud.

"Did you hear he stayed the night?" Dakota says.

Isla nods. "I did. Caught him doin' the walk of shame on the way to the bakery."

"There's no walk of shame. Nothing happened. We just passed out in my bed. Trust me, if something happened, my lady parts would know about it. Let's just say it's been quite a long time since I've done the walk of shame."

"Interesting. He looked like he got some last night," Isla says, which piques my interest.

"Is that so?" I lean my chin into my hand and bat my eyelashes at her from over the counter. "Please, tell me more."

She chuckles. "He was smiling, and it's not very often Rowan smiles."

I press my hand to my chest, and I can't help but feel a sense of accomplishment. "I did that to him. I made him smile."

"Aye, something did, and I'm guessing if he spent the night at your place, you played a role."

"He made us breakfast *and* did the dishes," Dakota says. "He was actually really sweet. Didn't even ask, just started taking care of us."

"That's Rowan for you," Isla says wistfully. "He might have a hard exterior, but he's quite gentle, and he takes care of his own. I'm starting to guess that he's seeing you as part of his small inner circle. You two are lucky."

That's a good way to put it, because I feel lucky. Rowan seems like the kind of person who doesn't bring many people into his life, but when he does, he does everything he can to keep them in and take care of them. It's evident in the way he speaks of Isla and her need to be asked out for a change, or in how he steered me away so she and Dakota could have a night alone. He's considerate, and I'm wondering if my annoyance with him earlier blinded me to that.

"I can tell he's a good man. I think Bonnie should go for him," Dakota says with a knowing look.

"I think so too," Isla says as both of their gazes fall on me.

"Thank you for your opinion, ladies, but I think you two should just focus on yourselves for now. Which reminds me, Dakota, shouldn't you be asking Isla—?"

"Isla, why don't I walk you out?" Dakota cuts me off before I embarrass her.

"Oh aye." She gives me a wave. "Enjoy the basket. Don't eat it too fast."

I shove a shortbread cookie in my mouth. "I won't," I say as it melts on my tongue. "I know how to pace myself." I pick up another cookie and shove it in my mouth. So good.

So freaking good.

Together, they walk out of the coffee shop, and, being the nosy friend that I am, I tiptoe up to the door, ready to eavesdrop. Just as I reach the threshold and lean an ear out, a large body blocks me.

My mouth still full of shortbread, I slowly move my eyes up the broad frame and find a curious pair of green eyes looking down at me.

"Care to tell me what you're doing?"

"Eavesdropping," I say as crumbs fall from my mouth. "Care to join me?"

Rowan nudges my shoulder, moving me out of the way. "No. Give them space."

"But what if she's doing it wrong?"

"She won't."

"But—"

"Give them space," he says a little more sternly.

"Ugh." I back away. "You're taking all the fun out of my friendship. We intrude on each other's lives. That's what we do—it's what keeps us alive."

"Aye, well, not this time." He runs a hand down my shoulder, and his large palm connects with mine—which distracts me just long enough for him to pull me deeper into the coffee shop, where we both take a seat at one of the tables. "What do you need help with?" He releases my hand, and I kind of want to ask him if he'd hold it again.

"I need help listening in on my friend."

"Bonnie."

"What?" I smile widely at him.

"Let them be."

"You're really annoying."

"So you've told me. Now, unless you actually need help with something, I'm going to leave." He starts to stand, but I quickly grab his hand and tug him back down.

"No, I do need your help." I nod toward the coffee maker. "Can I get you some ordinary coffee?"

He shakes his head. "I'm good."

"Okay." I cross one leg over the other. I catch his gaze land on my freshly shaved legs for a brief moment before they travel up to my face, sending a shiver of lust straight up my spine.

One look—that's all it takes where this man is concerned.

One look, and I'm ready to bounce up and down on his lap.

I clear my throat. "Have you seen the reviews for the coffee shop on the tour bus websites?"

"There are reviews?" he asks, looking confused.

"Yes. All the tour bus companies provide information for each stop, and in Corsekelly, almost all the reviews say not to bother with the coffee shop because there's nothing special about it."

"That's not . . ." His voice fades as he looks around the empty space. "Well, it wasn't always like this."

"But it is now, and something needs to be done. We've been here for over two weeks, and I think I've served coffee a dozen times. We've had days where the only visitor was Fergus."

"My maw couldn't take it all on. It was too much." He runs his hand down his face. "Still don't understand why my da retired. I really think . . ." Rowan bites the side of his mouth. "Hell, I think my da might be sick, and he's not telling me. He insisted he was just tired and they had enough in savings and retirement for him to be done. But it was too hard for my maw to let go. She loves being in town, talking to everyone, but she doesn't know how to keep up or how to create any grand ideas to actually improve the shop." He chuckles to himself. "The only grand idea she had was to blast the job advert on social media, and look what that did." He nods at me. "Brought two nosy and irritating Americans into town."

"I'm going to take that as a compliment, because I know for a fact that I'm growing on you." I fluff my hair.

"Aye, and how do you know that?" he says, nudging my leg playfully.

"Uh, do you not remember the hug before you left the cottage, confessing you had fun with me?"

"I think I was still drunk." He smirks, and I melt.

"Nice try, Grumpyshire. You're totally into this." I motion my hand up and down my body and watch his teeth tug on his lower lip while he takes me in.

Dear Jesus, please help me keep my shirt on right now.

His eyes return to mine. "So, what's your idea?" he asks. "I know you have one brewing in that head of yours."

"I was hoping we could overhaul the coffee house. Freshen it up, bring back the butteries, and add more coffee choices—real ones. Make it cozy in here, a place where tourists want to stop in. We could sell merchandise that centers on the Boaby Stone and Fergus, the things that make this town unique. Even the hairy coos. We don't even have any pamphlets that direct tourists where to go. You could do so much—like a town bingo. You'd distribute the cards to the tour buses ahead of time, and in the half hour they're here, there'd be a few things the tourists have to do, have to visit, and then they'd get a free shirt or something. I don't know, I'm just spitballing here, but there's so much potential, especially with the popularity of *Iron Crowns*, which I saw online—just signed on for three more seasons."

He scratches the side of his jaw. "What happens when you go back home? You'll be leaving my maw to handle it all on her own?"

"Who says I'm leaving? Maybe I like Corsekelly and want to live here. Maybe I'll find a strapping lad who sweeps me off my feet. Someone like Leith or Lachlan. Or maybe both of them. I don't mind shacking up with two hot twins who prance around town in kilts and lift logs as their workout."

"They couldn't handle you."

"Oh?" I cross my arms over my chest. "And you think you're the authority on who can handle me?"

"Aye." The intensity of his gaze nearly overwhelms me.

I sigh. Now is not the time to get into another heated battle. "If I do end up leaving, I'll be sure to help your mom find a reliable employee. Hell, she brought in two Americans—I'm pretty sure we could find someone who wouldn't mind staying in a storybook cottage in Scotland's cutest town. Not a hard sell, Rowy."

"Don't call me that," he says quickly, and I chuckle.

"Come on." I nudge his foot. "Think about how this would help your mom, your parents. Maybe there's something they always wanted when it came to the coffee house. We could make it happen."

He mulls it over as he takes in the shop, really giving it a good look. "It is shite in here," he admits, which makes me laugh again. "I remember when this place was full of life." He looks at me. "Why do you want to do this?"

"Truth?"

"Aye."

"I relate to this coffee house more than I care to admit. Once had all the potential in the world, but over time, lost its luster . . . its purpose. Making it shine will give me something to do, something that actually makes me feel like I'm contributing rather than just living a mundane life."

"You have purpose, Bonnie," he says, and even though it's a sweet statement, it rings false.

"I thought I did." I shake my head. "It's been hard to find lately. I feel like this will give me purpose, something to focus on and a way to apply myself. I need . . ." I let out a heavy breath. "I need to feel like I'm useful, Rowan. Right now, I couldn't think any less of myself."

"Hey." He lifts my chin so I see the crinkle in his brow. "We all have our low moments. Trust me. Not all of us are living our truth. Not completely."

"Are you talking about yourself?" I ask, and it feels like some barrier between us just broke from this one confession.

"Aye." He looks away and stands from his chair, pulling on the back of his neck. "The plan was to leave Corsekelly, to do something better, something I really wanted, but that plan changed in an instant."

"What happened?" I ask.

He's opening his mouth to answer just as Dakota comes barreling through the door. "Isla said yes!" She tosses her arms up in the air and dances in place. "Oh my God, she said yes."

Terrible, terrible timing, Dakota.

But, oh, I'm happy for my friend. Really excited, actually.

"That's great," Rowan says, giving me a quick look before patting Dakota on the shoulder.

"Thank you for encouraging me." Dakota wraps him up in a hug and squeezes him tight. When she pulls away, she turns to me with a grin. "I see what you're talking about, all those muscles."

Dear God, Dakota. A filter, please.

Rowan steps away and turns toward the door. "I'm sure you two have a lot to talk about. I'll leave you to it."

"Wait, Rowan, we weren't done."

"Just do whatever, Bonnie." Before I can answer, he takes off, the door shutting behind him.

Dakota shoots me a confused look. "Did I interrupt something?"

Normally my response would be sarcastic, but I don't want to take away from her big moment. I shake my head. "So she said yes, huh? Tell me all about it."

Smiling brightly, she recounts the entire conversation, and even though I'm dying to know what Rowan was going to say, I could not be happier in this moment.

"Hey, Leith," I say, walking up to the high-top table he's occupying in the pub.

"Bonnie, you're looking beautiful tonight." He pulls me into a tight hug, enveloping me in his woodsy cologne. It's nice.

"Thank you. You're very handsome yourself."

I take a step back as he adjusts the collar of his shirt. "I ironed this myself."

"Well, you did a superior job."

"Thank you. Now, what can I help you with? I know you're looking for something, because you have a little crinkle between your eyes." He pokes my forehead and chuckles.

"Am I that obvious?"

"Aye." He nods.

"I was looking for Rowan. I was hoping he'd be here. We have some unfinished business."

"Does this have to do with him walking out of your cottage this morning? Isla told me she spotted the old scoundrel."

Wow, news spreads even quicker here than in Los Angeles, where people live and breathe by gossip websites.

"Nothing happened."

"So I've been told." He shakes his head. "If it were me, *something* would have happened. You're a fine lass, quite the catch."

I chuckle and tip his chin. "And you're quite the ladies' man."

"Try to be, but I ken it's the broody one you're after."

I shake my head. "Not after him; just need to talk to him."

"So you're telling me there's still a chance?"

I shrug. "Never say never."

He fist pumps the air playfully. "I'll take it."

"Now, would you be able to tell me where Rowan is?"

"Most likely hunkered down in his cottage."

Well, that's not helpful. I purse my lips and look to the side, trying to figure out what to do next.

"I can tell you how to get there if you want. About a five-minute walk from here."

Look at Leith being a good friend. He very well might be my favorite Murdach now.

"You don't think he'd get mad?"

Leith gives me a good once-over. "If you showed up at my door, I definitely wouldn't be mad."

"Okay, okay, enough with the flirting—you're going to make me blush."

He chuckles. "We Scots are quite the charmers. Now, come here." He stands from his seat and guides me out the front door and around the corner. "See that road over there, Loch Lane?" He points to a street just around the petrol station. "Take that all the way to the end. You'll come to a cottage on the right—can't miss it. Navy-blue door. That's Rowan's place."

"That seems pretty easy."

"Can't get lost. Good luck, lass."

With a quick goodbye, I take off down Loch Lane, admiring all the little cottages I pass on the way. I can't imagine how anyone would want to live somewhere else. It truly feels like an entirely made-up world out here, a world you only see in movies and storybooks. As I come to the end of the lane, I spot a cottage on the right, tucked behind some trees. Its door is painted navy blue.

A stone wall circles the front of the cottage with an old iron gate, potted flowers hang off the house on hooks, and the white walls glisten in the sun. It's a beautiful little cottage, and I could easily see it serving as his oasis—a place to tuck himself away at night, an escape after a long day in a small town.

Just like where Dakota and I are staying.

Nerves bloom in my stomach as I walk through the gate, which creaks out my arrival. I hope this was a good idea. My determination to get to the bottom of what Rowan was starting to say at the coffee shop wanes, and regret creeps in. What if he truly wants to be alone and I'm barging in on that time?

I look behind me, down Loch Lane. The rooftops of town peek out beyond a grove of trees. I could run away undetected—

The door to the cottage suddenly opens, revealing Rowan, standing in a pair of low-hanging sweatpants and nothing else.

Uh, I don't think someone could get me to flee even if there was a fire. I don't mind the prospect of staring at this man all night.

His hand grips the edge of the door, his knuckles whitening from how hard he's squeezing the wood. I catch a ripple in his forearm as my eyes travel over his intricate tattoo to his clenched jaw and narrowed eyes.

God, angry looks so sexy on him.

"Can I come in?" I ask.

I'm met with silence as his eyes do a slow once-over, traveling up my leggings and plain T-shirt. And just when I think he's about to say no, he pushes the door open a little more. I duck under his arm and walk into his cottage.

It's simple, clean, and everything I would expect from him. To the right sits a black leather couch facing a small fireplace. There's no TV in sight, but instead, an open book is turned facedown on the coffee table. To the left is a small kitchen and a two-person dining table. It's just like our cottage, but Rowan's is better organized, with newer wood cabinets and modern hardware. Above the coffee maker is a row of beautifully crafted mugs, hanging from hooks and bringing a sense of color to the white, rustic space.

When he shuts the door, I turn to face him, and his eyes rake over me one more time. He looks like a wolf on the prowl, and I'm the prey. It's equally terrifying and exhilarating.

"Uh . . . Leith told me where you live."

He doesn't say anything, so I keep on going, my pulse rising every second.

"I wanted to finish our conversation from earlier. I didn't think it had a proper conclusion."

Nothing. Not a quirk to the brow, not a tick in the jaw. Just arms crossed, staring at me.

"Were you, uh, interested in finishing that conversation?" I ask, twisting my hands together, a jittery sensation bouncing inside me.

Rowan is a private person. I know this. Did I just completely over-step my bounds?

Then again, if he didn't want me here, he wouldn't have let me in, right?

Motioning to his cottage, I say, "You've done a lovely job with the space. I like the subtle pops of color."

He runs a hand along the side of his jaw, and . . . can I just pause for a second and appreciate the specimen in front of me?

Chiseled, sculpted, a Scottish Adonis with a handsome face and the perfect amount of scruff on his jaw, which seems to never change in length. He's unlike any man I've ever seen in person but have always dreamed up. His carved V borders an extreme set of abs. His large pecs connect to boulder-like arms and large, sexy hands.

And when anger vibrates through him—like it is now—every one of his muscles fires off. It's quite the sight to behold.

"Are you going to say something?" I ask, feeling myself shrink in his presence, beneath his intimidating stare. "Because it's rude to invite someone in but not talk. You have company, Rowan—be a good host."

His jaw works side to side but remains clamped shut.

Well, this seems to have been a huge mistake.

Not in the mood for a blowup, I let out a heavy, defeated breath. I should probably leave—catch him on another day when he's ready to be human, not a Neanderthal.

"Okay, well, this was a lovely visit. Thank you for the hospitality."

I push past him, but he reaches out and gently takes my arm, halting me in place. We're standing side by side—he faces one direction, and I face the other. "Coffee?" he quietly asks.

"Uh . . . sure."

Slowly, he releases my arm, and his fingers trail over my skin like feathers, sending a shiver up my spine as he pulls away.

He strides to the kitchen, keeping his back toward me. I watch him prepare a simple pot of coffee and then pull two mugs from the hooks. While the coffee brews, he opens a cabinet that's next to the fridge and pulls out a Tupperware container full of . . . oh dear God.

It's cake.

Things are about to get embarrassing.

"Is that, uh . . . cake you've got over there?"

He doesn't answer.

"Because if so, you know I would love a piece, big guy."

He pulls two beautifully made plates off a shelf, the same style as the mugs. Then he cuts two pieces of cake, puts them on the plates with forks, and brings them to the coffee table, just as the coffee maker beeps.

He fills each mug. "Cream or sugar?"

"Both," I answer, standing awkwardly in the middle of his cottage, unsure of what to do with my hands—or my body, for that matter. Do I sit down? Do I wait for him? Do I snag the cake and sprint out the door?

Option three is looking pretty promising—that is, until he turns around with two mugs and I catch sight of him once more.

Yeah, there's no way I would be able to leave at this point. I'm dedicated to watching his pecs flex tonight.

He heads toward the couch, then takes a seat and sets everything down on the coffee table. When he looks up at me, he asks, "Are you going to sit down or stand there all night?"

"Well, you know, you've made things quite uncomfortable." I move around the couch and take a seat. "I'm not sure I'm even allowed to breathe in your space."

"You can breathe."

"Oh, look at that, you can talk." He slides a mug over to my side and then leans back on the couch, staring at me.

But he doesn't just stare. He practically looks into my soul as his arm casually drapes along the back of the couch.

"So." I pat my lap. "Are we just going to look at each other?" He doesn't answer, and I can't take it anymore. It's probably some sort of Scottish intimidation tactic that I'm unaware of, but there's only so much silence I can endure before I start to lose my mind.

I've hit that point.

I reach out and push against his leg. "What is wrong with you?" I scoot closer, poking him in the quad, determined to annoy him until he says something. "Talk to me. Say something—anything. Just stop sitting there in silence without a word or—"

"You look beautiful tonight, Bonnie." And just like that, he steals my breath from me. He looks away, clenching his fist and opening it, as if he's trying to control himself.

"Are you finally admitting you find me attractive?" I ask, hoping that lightens the mood.

The teasing falls short as he reaches out and lifts my chin. "Ye ken I do."

Okay, then.

Glad we established that.

Annnd . . . why did I come here, again?

My mind draws a blank as my heart rate picks up. My desire escalates to a body-pounding level that I've never experienced in my life.

Please, Bonnie, don't do something stupid.

Chapter Twelve
ROWAN

Americans making me talk way too much: One.
I knew she was going to be bad news the minute I saw her, but for some reason I'm holding on to that bad news and, apparently, trying to make it mine.

◆ ◆ ◆

I've thought about her all day.

Ever since I left her cottage, I've thought about her.

The way her hand felt moving over my chest, her warm body tucked up against mine in the morning, the hug before I left, her admission . . .

Hell, my admission.

And then later, in the coffee shop, I was ready to blurt out my sordid history in the middle of the day, as if I've known this lass forever. It was a reality check.

I've lost my damn mind.

When have I ever talked about the past? Let alone to someone I barely know?

Never.

And yet, when I heard the gate creak a few moments ago, the sign of someone coming, I knew it was going to be her. I felt her presence. Seeing her, those eyes . . . *fuck*, I couldn't turn her away if I wanted to, and all those emotions I felt in the coffee shop, all my confessions, came bubbling up again.

The only way I knew to keep myself from pouring everything out to her was to stay silent.

But it seems like that tactic has run its course.

Fidgeting with her hair, she looks off to the side. "So, you find me attractive, good to know. Not too bad yourself."

She's fucking adorable.

"And even though this conversation is quite riveting, I think we should eat some cake." She picks up her plate, scoops a giant bite, and plops it in her mouth. As if she's forgotten about the last minute, she moans against her fork and sinks back into the sofa. "Where the hell has *this* been since I've arrived? Dundee cake is good and all, but this . . . this . . . what is this?" She pokes the cake with her fork.

"Iced cherry cake."

"Well, hold my boobs and slap my ass because *ooooeeee* is this a delight in my mouth." She takes another forkful and closes her eyes. "The flavors are magnificent. And it's so moist. Oh man do I love a moist cake. Moist . . . moist, moist, moist." She shoves the last bite in her mouth and leans over, poking at the cake on my plate. "Are you going to eat this?" She snags a forkful and picks up the plate, holding it in front of her as she chews. "Is this from Isla's shop? Because she's been holding out on me."

"I made it," I say.

Silence.

Slowly, she turns and looks me in the eyes. Her mouth carefully chews. Swallows. And then . . . "You made this?" she asks in such awe that, hell, my calm exterior cracks.

A smirk tugs at my lips and I nod. "Aye, I made it."

"For yourself?"

"Aye . . . ," I reply, confused.

"You mean to tell me that you came home one day and thought, 'You know, I think I'm going to make myself a cherry cake.'"

"Is there something wrong with that?"

She sets her fork down, cake still on it, and folds her hands carefully on her lap. "I'm going to be honest with you, Rowan. Never in my life have I ever wanted to jump a man's bones as much as I want to right now."

All of this over cake?

She clears her throat and lifts her chin. "But I am a lady, and even though I showed animalistic eating habits just a few moments ago, I refuse to jump any man at this age."

"Aren't you twenty-four?" I ask.

"A respectable twenty-four. I'm not a twenty-two-year-old floozy anymore. I mean business. So, I will say thank you for the cake, kind sir, and then be on my way."

"Do whatever ye want," I say, calling her bluff and picking up my plate of cake, which still has her fork on it. I lift the fork to my mouth, watching her hands—itching, ready to pounce in three, two, one . . .

"On second thought, you look like you need company." She takes the fork and shoves the cake in her mouth. "Oh, sweet sugary nectar, you're giving me life."

I chuckle. She's so fucking ridiculous.

"Help yourself," I tease.

"Don't mind if I do." She takes another bite and then picks up her coffee. She takes a sip, and her eyes widen. "Oh my God, what kind of coffee is this?"

"Special blend I order in. Cherry coffee with cherry cake—my favorite combo."

Her hand falls to my thigh, and she gives it a good squeeze. A bolt of lust shoots straight to my cock. I take a deep breath.

Keep it together, lad.

"Rowan, do you realize the kind of flavor combination you've created here? This could easily sell in the shop as a special."

"Who's going to make the cherry cake?"

"Uh . . . you?"

"Not interested," I say, finishing the rest of the cake and setting the plate down.

"Don't you want to help your parents?"

"I've given up enough for them," I say, my throat feeling tight all of a sudden. To an outsider, my comment must sound selfish, but if she knew what I've been through, she'd understand exactly where the feelings are coming from, where my need to help falls flat.

From the sympathetic look on Bonnie's face, it's a safe guess that no one has told her exactly what happened to my brother.

"What have you given up?"

"Not something I want to talk about."

"Is that what you were alluding to back at the coffee shop?"

I blow out a heavy breath. "Bonnie—"

"Fine, we don't have to talk about that. I can tell you're getting angry. Let's talk about something else."

"Why are you here?"

"Isn't it obvious?" she asks, batting her eyelashes. "Came for the cake and compliments."

"You didn't know I had cake."

"Lucky guess." She shakes my leg. "Come on, Rowan, relax. Stop being so stiff."

Keep touching my leg like that, and the "stiffness" won't go away.

"Be real, Bonnie," I say. "Why are you here?"

Her smile fades and she leans back, removing her hand from my leg.

"Honestly?" I nod. "I wanted to see you. Make sure you were okay. Talk to you." She shrugs. "Spend an evening with you without alcohol. I got the impression that you might be hurting in one way or another, and I thought it would be nice to talk to someone who might truly understand what I'm going through as well."

When she lifts her eyes to mine, I immediately see vulnerability. She might love to joke and tease, but behind that facade is a broken heart, a damaged spirit, and that's what makes her real.

I nod toward her feet. "Take your shoes off and get comfortable."

She takes her shoes off and shoots me a beaming smile that hits me in the gut. This might have been a bad idea. That single smile tells me that this girl very well might own me by the end of the night.

"Favorite thing about Corsekelly?" Bonnie asks, curled up on my sofa. She looks good in my house—comfortable, relaxed.

"I like that it's tucked away in the Highlands. Makes me feel like we have our own little clan here."

"I can feel that. I grew up in a smallish town—well, small for California—but it didn't have the same kind of feel that Corsekelly has. Just feels magical here."

"We get that a lot."

A smile crosses her face. "Ever have a one-night stand with a tourist?"

I roll my eyes. "What do you think?"

"Easily."

I just lift my brow and look away.

"Oooh, there are some stories there. Listen, I'm all for getting it when you can. No judgment here." She holds up her hands.

"What about you?" I ask. "Doesn't Los Angeles have a bunch of tourists?"

"Not the kind of tourists I'm sure you get here. A lot of families go on vacation to LA, strutting down the Walk of Fame and taking pictures with their favorite actors' and actresses' handprints. I've never found a tourist who was single and looking for a good time. But have I had the odd one-night stand? Yes. Sadly disappointing the three times it happened."

"Shame," I say, sipping from my mug.

"Tell me about it." She groans. "Ugh, it's been so long since I've copulated. I've almost lost count at this point. What about you? When was the last time you had sex?"

Not quite what I had in mind for conversation topics.

"Uh, not sure. Not recently."

"Look at you, not counting the days. Good for you." She gives me an approving nod.

"Well, in a small town like Corsekelly, not many opportunities present themselves."

"Understandable." She taps her chin. "Have you ever taken a picture with your boaby on the Boaby Stone?"

"No."

"Have you set your naked boaby on the Boaby Stone?"

"No."

"Why not? Ladies put their breasts on it and take pictures."

"Because there are crazy fans out there who will lick the Boaby Stone. Not exactly hygienic. And I don't even have a TV—never seen the show."

"Why don't you have a TV?"

"Never wanted one. I like to read, listen to podcasts, do puzzles."

"Oh my God, you're a cute old man."

"I'm not old."

She leans over and touches my temple. "There are a few gray hairs in here."

"I'm thirty-two."

"Is that so?" She gives me a slow once-over. "Eight years my senior and in impeccable shape—must be all those runs with the hairy coos."

"And the ability to pace myself with cake," I say with a pointed look.

She whips out her index finger. "Don't you dare cake shame me! I enjoyed every last bite of that cake, and if you weren't sitting in front of me, being the cake guard, I would have helped myself to more already. So I've been showing some restraint, if you must know."

"Shocking," I tease, which only makes her grin. "What's your favorite thing about Corsekelly?" I ask her this time, playing along with her little game.

"Besides the bakeshop, I truly do enjoy the people here. I like how everyone is so nice and welcoming and willing to help. They knew we were coming, and instead of pointing and saying, 'There are the Americans,' they welcomed us into their little world."

"Scots get a bad reputation about attitude. We're usually portrayed in the media as angry brutes, shouting constantly, but in reality we're quite passionate, but kind, human beings."

"I could see that. It's clear in the way Dakota and I have been welcomed." She picks up her mug, takes a sip, and then sets it back down. "What's the juiciest gossip you've heard since we arrived?"

"Juiciest?" I ask, rubbing my jaw. "Probably that you were caught coming out of the pub bathroom with Lachlan."

"What?" Her eyes widen. "Who's been saying that?"

"Everyone." I chuckle.

"Everyone? Who's everyone? That . . . that's—" She eyes me. "Are you lying?"

"Aye." I laugh some more.

"Not funny, Rowan."

"I thought it was."

"Think you can make one of these for me?" Bonnie asks, finishing off her second serving of cake.

"Not sure you're worth it just yet."

186

"Oh, I'm worth it." She winks. "I know how to thank people quite kindly."

"Keep saying things like that, and the Lachlan story could very well be true."

"Please, if I walked out of the pub bathroom with anyone, it would be Leith. He actually hit on me before I came over here."

"Not surprised."

She nudges me with her foot. "Aren't you going to act all jealous and rage-y and demand an apology on my behalf?"

"Why? You're not mine to claim."

"Not yet." She winks again.

Hell, that wink was full of promises.

Promises I hope she intends to keep.

"Move your hand—you're doing that on purpose." She swats at my hand, which is holding the pen. We're sitting side by side on the sofa, and with every second that passes, she somehow inches closer.

"Stop distracting me."

"You're distracting me with your hand."

"Found it," I call out, circling the word *flannel* in the word search we're working on together.

"Damn it!" Bonnie slaps the sofa. "You have a distinct advantage because you're holding the book and the pen."

"Fine, here." I hand her everything and then rest my arm over the back of the sofa, scooting in close to her and taking in her sweet scent, a mix of floral and vanilla. "Next word."

She snuggles in close. "'Loch Ness Monster'—go."

"Found it," I say, seconds later, and point to it.

"What? You're cheating."

"Or I'm really good."

She shakes her head. "No way, you're cheating."

Maybe I saw it earlier, but she doesn't need to know that.

◆ ◆ ◆

"I'm not hurting you, am I?" Bonnie asks as she leans into me, her feet tucked up under her. My arm is still on the back of the sofa, but now I'm playing with the long strands of her hair.

"No." In reality, I don't think I've ever felt this comfortable. This content. Outside, rain pelts the ground, and my cottage fills with that fresh rain smell I always look forward to as thunder and lightning crash through the sky. And for once, the storm doesn't unsettle me. Instead, as I gaze at Bonnie, I decide it provides the perfect soundtrack for the end of our evening.

I have no idea when Bonnie plans on leaving, but I'm not going to force her out, even though it's past ten and sleep starts to knock at me with yawn after yawn. I'm not ending this night—she's going to have to call it.

When I sat down to read my book earlier, I never expected the evening to end up like this: Bonnie leaning against me, talking quietly while we play game after game of word search and lose ourselves in conversation . . . and don't forget those two servings of cake and coffee.

"You're warm," she says, nuzzling her head against my chest, her voice soft, almost sleepy. "You're so comfortable. And you smell good."

Not sure what to say, I stay quiet and twirl a long blonde strand around my finger.

"Can I ask you something that might make you mad?"

"Sure," I say, feeling so relaxed that I actually mean it. Maybe that was her intention all along. Either way, she can ask me anything at this point.

"Someone told me you had a brother."

Hell.

Maybe not everything.

I blow out a long breath and lean back, slouching so my head is tilted up against the cushion and my gaze is fixed on the ceiling.

"I did," I answer honestly.

"What happened to him?"

I swallow hard. "Passed away from a head injury." Bonnie turns and faces me, her hand falling on my chest, her eyes intent on my face. "Callum was twenty. I was twenty-two. We were hiking with Leith and Lachlan, all of us drunk and being eejits. We got caught up in a rainstorm and didn't think much of it until Callum slipped in a pile of mud and slammed his head against a rock. He was unresponsive." Bonnie's hand slowly rubs over my chest, easing the tension that's building over my heart. "Somehow we got him down the mountain and called an ambulance. We shouldn't have moved him, but we didn't want to leave him up there in the rain either. His brain swelled, and there was no recovering after that."

"Oh my God," Bonnie says. "The hike up to the castle, your anger . . . it was because of Callum."

"Aye. I swore I'd never stop hiking, because it was one of his favorite things to do, but I use loads of caution now. The rucksack I was carrying when we went to the castle was full of first aid supplies, and I keep track of the weather pretty constantly."

"I'm so sorry. I wish I had known. I feel terrible that I put you in that position."

"It's not something you need to worry about." I push my hand through her hair, a sense of understanding passing through us. "But he was the reason I was harsh with you—probably why I'm harsh with everybody."

"You haven't gotten over his death."

"Does anyone ever get over losing someone they love?"

"No, I suppose not," she answers softly.

Gently, she rests her cheek on my bare chest and wraps her arm around my waist, pressing tight against my body, almost as if she's trying to fuse us together. I welcome it—the warmth, the comfort.

Hell, when was the last time I actually felt another person try to comfort me like this? I honestly can't recall . . . maybe never.

"Was that the change you were talking about in the coffee shop? Why you never left town?"

"How did I know you were going to ask that?"

She lifts up. "I'm sorry if I'm being nosy."

"You are. But it's okay." I yawn, covering my mouth. "Maybe we save it for another day."

Understanding softens her eyes as she sits up and looks over at the clock on the oven. "Jeez, I didn't realize how late it was. I'm sorry. I should head home." A loud crack of thunder rattles the cottage, and she winces. "Or, you know, this couch is pretty comfortable."

Chuckling, I stand as I bring her to her feet, and we link our hands together for a brief moment. I give her a squeeze, pulling a small smile from her lips right before I move around the cottage, taking care of the dishes and locking up. I lead her to my bedroom, which is off the back, and then rummage through my dresser for a shirt.

"To sleep in," I say, handing it to her. "There's toothpaste and an extra toothbrush in the cabinet in the bathroom."

"Okay. Thank you. Let me text Dakota to let her know I'm staying so she doesn't worry. I'll probably just need a blanket and a pillow for the couch."

I walk up to her and pinch her chin with my forefinger and thumb. "You're sleeping in my bed tonight . . . with me."

Her mouth drops open, forming a bonny little O. I take off to the bathroom, where I get ready quickly, mentally preparing myself for a long night of yearning and no touching.

CHAPTER THIRTEEN
BONNIE

Cake consumed today: Happily, two and a half pieces.

Days since last male-induced orgasm: Uh . . . ninety? Ninety-nine? Hopefully zero soon.

Number of hot Scots who said I'd be sleeping with them: One . . . THE one and only.

Men I'm crushing on hard: One. See above.

His shirt smells like heaven. His toothpaste tastes like heaven. His face is pure heaven. I think I may have passed out and gone to heaven.

And I'm not leaving.

"So should I just hop in?" I ask, standing at the foot of Rowan's large bed, in his shirt, staring at the way he's casually lying under the covers, his torso uncovered and his hands behind his head.

"Not going to bite, lass."

Yeah . . . but I might.

Slowly I make my way to my side of the bed. "You know, this was easier when I was drunk."

"Do you even remember it?"

"No, which made it easier, because I will for sure remember how awkward I am right now."

He flips the covers over for me, welcoming me in. How can he be so cool about it? As if this isn't monumental? As if we haven't had this on-again, off-again, fun-yet-tumultuous relationship ever since I got here? As if me climbing into bed next to him is the most natural thing in the world?

And maybe it is for him.

Once settled, I lie stiffly next to him, keeping all my limbs to myself and staring straight up at the ceiling. He flips the nightstand light off and then turns toward me, his hand scooping me around the waist and pulling me close so we're facing each other.

His minty breath floats between us as his wide palm keeps hold on my back. My hand falls to his chest, and my fingers lightly stroke the dark ink on his pec.

"Does your tattoo hold any meaning?"

"Aye. It's the MacGregor clan crest woven into a Celtic knot—a tribute to my brother."

"That's . . . that's beautiful, Rowan."

"It's how I can keep him close to my heart," he answers, his grip growing tighter.

I smooth my hand up his neck, to his jaw, trying to calm my rattling nerves. I've never been this nervous when it comes to a man. I'm usually so confident, but Rowan has me out of sorts. I'm not sure if what I'm doing is okay, or if he wants me touching him at all.

I bite my bottom lip. "I feel like I should tell you something."

"What's that?" he asks, his voice husky, like a soft rumble of thunder in the distance.

"I'm starting to like you."

He chuckles, the sound rattling the bed ever so slightly. "Is that so?"

"Don't make a big deal about it."

"How could I not, when I've been nothing but grumpy and awful to be around?"

"I never said it's awful to be around you. Grumpy, yes, but Kilty McGrumpyshire has grown on me."

"Yeah, well . . . the stubborn and saucy American has grown on me as well."

I smile. "Does that mean . . . you like me back?"

Growing serious, he replies, "I think I have for a while."

His hand travels up my back to the nape of my neck. Butterflies erupt in my chest as he pulls me a few more inches closer, cutting what little distance there is between us.

Forehead to forehead, he's silent for a few breaths. "The first time you kissed me," he murmurs, "it was torture to not kiss you back, but I had to stand my stubborn ground. I felt the imprint of your lips on mine for days. I smelled your perfume on me for hours after, and your badgering made me laugh minutes later. It was the worst, best first kiss I've ever had with someone."

"You consider *that* a first kiss?"

"Aye. I do."

"But it wasn't a pretty one."

"Doesn't need to be."

"So what does all of this mean? Are you going to kiss me now?" I ask, feeling breathless and excited.

"Nay." He shakes his head against mine. "I'm going to hold you, though."

Disappointment falls, and I realize just how much I really wanted him to kiss me—just how much I actually want this man. But cuddling into him, letting him hold me during a thunderstorm, that should be good enough . . . right?

"Come here," he says, rolling onto his back and pulling me into his embrace. I rest my head against his chest, and his protective arm clamps around me as he kisses the top of my head. "Thank you for tonight," he says quietly.

"You don't have to thank me."

"I don't talk about my brother very often, Bonnie. You listened, and that meant something to me."

"I know you would have done the same for me." I move my hands slowly across his chest. "Rowan?"

"Hmm?"

"Does this mean . . . we're starting something?"

"Are you fishing for a date, lass?"

"Wouldn't hurt you to ask, you know."

"Okay."

And I wait . . . and wait . . . and wait.

"Uh, are you going to ask?"

"On my terms, Bonnie. Now just go to sleep."

"On your terms—what does that even mean?"

"Means I'll ask when I ask."

"Well, I can't wait around forever, you know. I'm fresh meat in a Scottish meat market. I might be asked out tomorrow, and because you never asked me out, I would take that date."

"Then take it," he says casually.

I pinch his side, and he barely flinches. "You're not supposed to say that."

"I know you wouldn't take it. You're too infatuated with me."

"Oh, now you did it," I exclaim. "Now I'm going to go ask Leith out just to spite you."

He chuckles. "Good luck. I heard he likes to lick necks on first dates."

"Well, then he's the perfect man for me."

◆　◆　◆

A burst of light sears through my eyelids as thunder booms outside. I startle awake, my heart rate surging as I try to grasp where I am. The room is swathed in darkness, and the warm body that held me as I fell asleep is nowhere to be found. I sit up in bed and search the room, but I don't see him anywhere.

Folding down the covers, I slowly get out of bed and make my way through the open bedroom door. I pad into the main living space, where I spot him in the kitchen, wearing just a pair of black boxer briefs. His back is turned to me, and tension rolls through it as he grips the counter in front of him, his head tilted down. Lightning flashes and another boom of thunder rattles the house, but he remains still, unaffected.

Carefully, I walk up behind him and run my hand along his bare back to let him know I'm here. His muscles tense under my touch, but he quickly relaxes beneath my hand.

"Are you okay?" I ask.

He shakes his head. "Nightmare," he answers honestly. "About Callum."

"Oh, Rowan, I'm so sorry." I move under his arm, positioning myself between him and the counter. I lift up his head and catch a glimpse of his distraught eyes as lightning flashes outside. "It's because you talked about what happened, isn't it?"

He nods. "Yeah, always happens when I bring him up. Haunts me. I relive it. Every sound, smell, and then . . . silence." He swallows hard. "I was hoping it wasn't going to hit me as hard as it usually does, but it felt more intense tonight."

"I'm sorry. I'm so sorry I made you talk about it."

"You didn't make me do anything." He wraps his hands around my waist and carefully lifts me up onto the counter, pressing his body against the cabinets so he's between my legs. I savor the ease, the intimacy of this moment, as my hands float up to his shoulders.

"Still, I feel awful for bringing it up." One of my hands climbs up to his jaw, and I stroke his sandpaper scruff. What would this feel like between my legs? Probably amazing. Beard burn is a guilty pleasure of mine.

"Don't, no need to feel bad, lass," he says. His hands move over the shirt I borrowed and slowly inch beneath the hemline, where his palms scorch my already-warmed thighs. "Did the thunder wake you?"

I nod as his hands climb higher. "It's probably the loudest I've ever heard," I say just as another crash sounds. "I can feel it in my bones."

"I used to love the storms here. Now, well . . . it's truly the one thing I'd change about Scotland, if I could."

"Because they remind you of your brother."

He nods.

"Is that why you stayed in last night? You knew it was going to storm?"

He shakes his head. "No, I stayed in because I knew you were going to find me and finish the conversation from the coffee shop."

"You did *not* know that."

He nods. "Aye, I did, and you proved me right."

I chuckle. "Am I that transparent?"

"I wish." He sighs and moves his hands up until they reach my hips. His brow rises, and his eyes meet mine. "Are you wearing knickers?"

It was only a matter of time before he figured it out. "No, I'm not. I was wearing a thong and didn't feel like sleeping in it."

"So you climbed into my bed bare-arsed?"

I laugh and poke at him. "Wishing you kissed me now, huh?"

"Wishing I did a whole lot more."

"Then, what was the holdup?"

"Wasn't in a good headspace," he admits, and everything clicks into place.

"You don't want our first time to be clouded by memories of your brother."

He nods. "Aye." One hand comes up to my cheek, and his thumb pulls on my bottom lip. "You're special, Bonnie. Annoying and irritating and stubborn—"

"Uh, is this going to take a turn down Niceville? Because those aren't compliments."

"If you'd let me finish," he snaps, making me laugh and rest my head on his chest. *Still grumpy, will probably always be grumpy.* "As I was saying . . . irritating, stubborn, sassy, but you also have a warm heart, and I hate to admit it, but you're funny too. You deserve a kiss that isn't just something to do on a rainy night, but because it's backed up by a special moment."

"Like right now?" I ask, wrapping my legs around him and pulling him in even closer.

His eyes search mine, indecision weighing heavily.

Right now could be perfect.

Middle of the night.

Confessions falling past both of our lips.

The need to be close.

The air seems to stand still.

His eyes caress mine.

His breaths are short . . . yearning.

And right when I think he's about to pull away, he lowers his head, drawing closer, making my heart lurch in my chest.

Please don't let this be fake, please let this be a moment—the perfect moment.

Lightning flashes, and there is only a breath between us.

Thunder booms, shaking everything beneath us.

Then, his lips press against mine.

I suck in a sharp breath and instantly run my hands up his neck to his cheeks, where I hold him, not wanting him to pull away but to stay locked like this, his soft lips moving gently over mine, exploring, testing . . . tasting.

For such a brute of a man, he kisses with impressive intention. There is no sloppiness or driving need to prove something. Instead, he's careful but intense.

Hunger sears through his lips as they move against mine, and his grip on my cheek and the soft press of his body against mine belie his outward calm. His tongue swipes across my lower lip, asking for more, and I oblige, opening wide for him. When his tongue meets mine, I groan against his mouth and grip him tighter.

Achingly incomplete until this moment, I get lost in our fervent passion, in his heavy breaths, in the low and sensual groans floating past our mouths.

Kissing this man is everything I hoped it would be.

Ardent.

Needy.

Consuming.

Overpowering.

World changing.

Another flash of lighting illuminates the room, but this time the thunder takes seconds longer to boom, heralding the storm's retreat.

His kisses slow, his grip loosens, and with one final press to my mouth, he pulls away and rests his forehead on mine.

"Hell," he mumbles.

"Yeah . . . agreed."

His eyes connect with mine, and a lopsided smile tugs on his lips. "I think you're trouble."

"I think you might be right."

Picking me up again, he lowers me to the ground and says, "Let's head to bed." He takes my hand in his and guides me to his bedroom. I slip into bed, and he lies down on the other side, flat on his back. He sticks one hand behind his head and wraps the other around me, pulling me in close to his side.

I settle into him, and as my hand travels to his chest, the tension that had laced his muscles is gone—he's relaxed.

The storm quiets outside, and Rowan does too, his breathing evening out. He's drifting off to sleep, but I'm buzzing. Desire pumps through me, need consumes me, and before I can stop myself, I allow my hand to roam his bare torso, lightly dragging my fingers over his abs, taking in every perfect indent, every curve. His stomach is carved as if from granite, and it's such a huge turn-on that I find the ache between my legs increasing with every swipe.

I need to stop.

Right now.

But instead, my hand travels down to the waistband of his boxer briefs. I glide my fingertips over the elastic, wondering what he'd do if I just moved my hand a little farther.

What would I find?

Would he be hard?

He hasn't shifted or moved since I started touching him.

His breathing hasn't altered.

What would happen if I just . . . slowly . . . moved . . .

His hand that's wrapped around me tugs at my shirt, exposing my skin as his large palm slowly grips my rear end.

Oh . . . dear . . . God.

I bite my bottom lip as my arousal spikes.

I don't move.

My breath is held captive.

My pulse feels like a jackhammer in my throat.

And then he glides over my backside, feeling, exploring, his palm rough and calloused, making the pass of his hand that much more heady . . . luxurious.

Taking a deep breath, I lower my hand an inch, and my fingertips connect with his thick girth. My eyes nearly roll to the back of my head, and for the first time since I started my exploration, I feel his breathing hitch and grow shallow. Quickly in, quickly out.

His reaction grants me more courage as I cover his erection with my hand.

Big.

He's so big.

I wouldn't expect anything less from such a mammoth of a man, but it's still a little shocking and intimidating.

My hand fully grips his girth, and he sucks in a sharp breath as his hips jut forward.

I need more. I want to feel him without a barrier. So without giving it a second thought, I slip my hand under his briefs and circle his entirety in my palm. A contradiction of soft, velvet skin and stone, he feels amazing.

"Fuck," he grumbles softly as I start to ever so slowly pump up and down.

I drag my hand to the tip and pass my thumb over the head a few times. His grip on my ass tightens, and his legs spread. I take that as my cue.

He wants more.

I want more.

So much more.

I sit up and push the covers down, my body buzzing with anticipation. I grip the waistband of his briefs and drag them down his legs, discarding them on the floor. In the dim light, I take in the gloriously delicious outline of his cock jutting up against his stomach. I shift my hair to the side so it's out of my way but so he can still see my face as I lower myself, lifting his shaft and bringing it to my lips.

I start at the tip and slowly suck him into my mouth.

"Jesus," he mumbles with a sigh, his hand finding the hem of my shirt again, his fingers gliding up and under the fabric. The connection brings a level of intimacy to what I'm doing, a touch I never realized I needed.

Slowly, I lower my mouth around him while my other hand grips his base tightly. With every descent, I spend a few seconds sucking hard, enough time to get him breathing harder and harder, until I open all the way and take him to the back of my throat.

"Fuck," he hisses as I swallow. I do this a few more times until I pull all the way off and release my hold, barely keeping his cock held in my hand. He tightens under my touch, and precum forms at the tip. His cock is so hard, so ready, that I know he's only moments away. "Bonnie, lass . . . ," he gasps.

Oh, he's really close.

His eyes are squeezed shut and his chest rises and falls so rapidly that it would be impossible to count how many breaths he takes in a minute. But I hold still.

He thrashes.

His cock juts up.

His hand grips the sheets.

His teeth pull on his bottom lip.

And then . . . a feral groan.

With that, my mouth descends again, and I maneuver him all the way back before I pull up hard, sucking the entire time.

"Fuck, I'm coming!" he shouts as his hips drive up. I take him easily, reveling in his pleasure until he's completely sated. He's breathing heavily, disbelief morphing his face as he gazes down at me. He lifts a hand and strokes it tenderly through my hair as he slowly comes back to life.

And then . . . determination laces his features.

He lifts up, his abs tightening, contracting, before he flips me to my back and spreads my legs wide enough for his large body to fit between them.

"Rowan," I breathe out heavily. "You don't have to—"

"The fuck I don't." He pushes the hem of my shirt past my belly button but doesn't go any farther. It makes me lose my mind—until he hooks one of my legs over his shoulder and lowers his head.

Giving pleasure is just as much of a turn-on for me as receiving, so I'm ready for him as his lips meet my inner thigh. My body is already sensitive, thrumming with need as all feeling focuses down to my core, lighting me up with anticipation.

He trails scratchy, luscious kisses along my sensitive skin, moving closer and closer to my center before he pulls away and moves to my other leg. He pays tribute to each side, worshipping with his mouth and driving me crazy.

My pelvis lifts up, seeking any kind of connection, and when his mouth pulls away, excitement booms deep in the pit of my stomach—until he turns to the other leg.

"Oh my God, Rowan," I say, the ache so strong that I feel like I might cry. "Please."

"No," he says and then goes back to trailing kisses along my thigh, drawing so close, right to where I need him, then pulling away and moving back toward my knee.

Devil of a man.

I shift beneath him, angling to get him to touch me, but he's strong and holds me down, drawing out this delicious torture until the throb is so intense I cry out.

"Please," I beg. "Please, Rowan."

He draws his tongue out and laps it down my leg, closer and closer, until his tongue meets my hip. He circles it over my hipbone and runs it down to my pubic bone, right above my slit. There he plays with me, teases me, drawing circles over and over again. I feel my arousal pool, my need so great that I might come without him even touching me.

"I want to come on your tongue," I say, not holding back.

"Are you close?" he asks.

"Yes," I breathe out. "Don't you feel me shaking for you?"

"Aye," he says, his voice such a deep rumble that I nearly come right there.

His eyes find mine as he lowers his tongue an inch, just to the very top, and he slips it in and out, making the ache grow more intense.

"Rowan," I say in desperation just as his hand spreads me and his tongue presses against my clit. "Oh God," I cry out, my chest heaving up toward the ceiling, my hands falling to my sides, gripping the sheets.

His tongue stills for a few breaths, and then he starts flicking it along my clit, using just enough pressure to build me up hard and fast.

An intense calm washes over me as a pulse beats through my veins, stiffening my muscles, pulling toward my center.

Every thought, every feeling, every emotion, they all pool together, sending a wave of numbness through my limbs.

My body tenses.

My stomach bottoms out.

Nothing exists besides Rowan's tongue and the way he's moving it along my clit, until he presses down hard and flicks over me so fast that my orgasm bursts through me, powerful and satisfying all at once.

"Oh my God!" I yell as he continues to move his tongue, my hips gliding up and down, drawing out every last ounce of pleasure until there is absolutely nothing left.

When he moves away, I reach for him, pulling him up along my body and pressing a kiss to his mouth. "You have no idea what you just did to me," I whisper, gazing at him in the near darkness.

"I'm pretty sure I have a good guess."

"No . . . you just ruined me."

"Lass, your mouth on my cock—*that* ruined me."

◆ ◆ ◆

"Why does it smell so good in here?" I ask, walking into Rowan's kitchen with one palm pressed against my eye, trying to wipe away the sleep. Waking up alone to a chilly, foggy morning was not exactly what I wanted after last night's activities, but that's all washed away when I catch Rowan, shirtless, standing at the stove, making me breakfast.

"Made some tattie scones," he says, flipping off the stovetop and putting a pan of eggs on a trivet. He turns toward me and beckons me with a finger. I shamelessly walk over to him, unable to suppress the grin tugging at my lips. He loops one arm around my waist and quietly says, "Mornin', lass," while pressing a kiss to the top of my head.

Be still my heart.

"Good morning." I trail my hand up his chest and then lift up on my toes and kiss his jaw. His hand falls to my ass, gripping it tightly through my shirt. And if it weren't for the amazing-smelling breakfast, I would be climbing this man like a tree right now. "Do you always make breakfast for the ladies you have over?"

"Nay, I kick them out of bed once they're pleasured. Consider yourself lucky." He smirks and releases me before serving up two plates of food.

The table is charmingly set with a butter crock and jam jar, mugs of coffee, and a beautiful hand-thrown vase of wildflowers. God, could he be any sweeter?

I take a seat at the table and marvel at the shirtless hunk of a man serving me a plate of delicious food.

"This looks amazing. I've never had a tattie scone. What should I do?"

He reaches over to my plate and picks up one of the flat, triangular pastries. "I prefer them with a light coat of Brodies butter—it's the best; don't let anyone tell you otherwise—and then a wee bit of homemade jam."

"You make your own jam?"

"Aye, me maw and I make quite a few batches every year."

"Do you sell them?"

He shakes his head as he hands me a scone. "'Tis for the town. We hand them out every summer."

I take a bite, and good God, where have these been my entire life? "Wow, Rowan." I give the scone a good inspection. "These are so freaking good. Does Isla sell these?"

"Nay, she focuses on shortbread, Dundee cakes, and savory pies—and occasionally empire cakes and puddings. Have you tried her sticky toffee pudding yet?"

"No, but I've been trying to steer clear of the bakeshop. I'm in danger of gaining another solid two pounds on my hips alone."

His gaze meets mine over the rim of his coffee mug. "Shouldn't be worried about that, lass. I like something to grip onto."

My face reddens, and memories of last night flash through my mind. His tender teasing. His grunts. My moans. Our explosive orgasms. I don't think I've ever had a night like that, and we didn't even go all the way.

"Thinking about last night?" he asks before shoving a forkful of eggs into his mouth.

"Maybe." I take another bite of the scone, savoring its soft texture, perfectly combined with the tart jam and subtle butter. "Does this mean you're going to ask me out on a date?"

He eyes me but doesn't say anything. Those eyes—so intense, but playful at the same time. "Not sure yet."

"Rowan." I nudge him under the table, making him laugh. "After everything that happened, you're really not going to ask me out?"

"Didn't say I wasn't." His smirk is almost unbearable.

"But you're not confirming that you are."

"Like to keep you on your toes." He pushes at my plate. "Eat up, lass."

"You're infuriating."

"And you're beautiful when you're annoyed."

Well . . . damn.

I point my fork at him. "Don't try to butter me up with compliments."

"Fine. Your hair is a damn mess."

I pat down my head. "Really?"

He chuckles. "Nay. You're still beautiful."

"You don't have to walk me all the way," I say when we reach the driveway leading to the cottage.

"Wasn't planning on it. This is where I send you on your way."

I study him, my hand still clutching his. "You know, you're a strange man. Sweet and passionate and protective one minute and then a grumpy, sarcastic ass the next."

"Take what you can get, lass." He leans forward, lifts my chin, and presses a sweet kiss to my lips. "See you around."

He lets go of my hand and starts to walk away.

"Uh, excuse me." He pauses and looks over his shoulder. "'See you around'? That's all you've got? No 'I'll call you'?"

"Don't have your number." He winks and takes off, not turning around again, not even when I huff out in frustration.

"Infuriating man," I mumble, stomping down the driveway and straight into the cottage. Dakota is sitting at the table, enjoying her own breakfast of eggs. She's in her running gear, and a light sheen of sweat coats her skin. Man, I need to start working out more like her, or else the shortbread and tattie scones and cherry cake really will catch up to me.

"Good morning." She smirks, taking me in. I'm still wearing Rowan's shirt and no bra, though I did pull on my leggings before leaving his house. My shirt and undergarments are tucked into a bag Rowan gave me, which I'm clutching with one hand.

"It's not what it looks like."

"Looks like you slept over at Rowan's house. And from the goofy grin on your face, I'd say your dry spell's ended."

"I'm not sporting a goofy grin. I'm irritated with that man."

"You might be irritated on the inside, but you're glowing on the outside." She sits back and takes a large gulp from her water glass. "Care to share?"

I plop into the seat across from her. "I sucked his cock."

Dakota's eyes widen, and she spits her water back in her glass. "Jesus, Bonnie," she chuckles as water dribbles down her chin. "Warn a girl before you go and say something like that."

"You wanted me to share, and that's what happened. It was in the middle of the night too. At first he just held me, and then I woke up to find him in the kitchen by himself. That's where we kissed." I sigh at the memory of that moment. "It was so perfect, and then, when we went back to bed . . . well, I was a little handsy and then so was he, so I stripped him down and had my way with his body."

"Wow, you really went for it. I'm proud of you. Did he reciprocate?"

"Oh, did he." I shake my head in disbelief. "I don't think I've ever come that hard, Dakota. I was on a different planet. It was insane."

"Yeah?"

"Yeah," I sigh. "And then he made me breakfast, ruined me for all men, walked me home, and said . . . 'See you around.'"

Dakota tilts her head back and laughs. "Oh, that's perfect."

"It's not funny."

"No, it really is. He loves goading you, and that's exactly what he did."

"The devil of a man."

"Yeah, but you like it." She smirks.

I do.

I really freaking do.

CHAPTER FOURTEEN
BONNIE

Days since last male-induced orgasm: ZERO!
Need I really say more at this point?

"So that's it?" I ask Dakota as we both stare down at a flat piece of rock in a dank cave. Water glistens off the walls, and our feet are sinking half an inch into the muddy ground, something I wasn't expecting when I wore my cute tennis shoes.

"I believe so," Dakota says. "The Boaby Stone."

I lean toward her. "Is it as unimpressive to you as it is to me?"

"Frankly, the only thing impressive about it is that it's probably seen more dick than you have."

"Hey," I say on a laugh, shoving her to the side.

She chuckles and then pulls out her phone to take a picture. "Want to pretend your arm is a penis and take a picture?"

"Isn't it obvious that's why we're here?"

"Just making sure."

Squatting down to the height of the stone, which reaches just below my knees, I position my arm in front of my crotch and then hover it right above the slab. I don't want to make actual contact, because there has been real dick on it—lots of real dick—and touching a melting pot of penis is not on my to-do list today.

"Smile," Dakota says right before taking a picture.

I stand, and when she offers her screen, I quickly approve the picture. "Send that to me. Do you want one of yourself with a fake penis?"

"I'm good."

I pause and stare at her. "Soooo . . . you made me take a picture, but you're not going to take one?"

"I didn't make you—you did it of your own accord. It's Instagram worthy for you, but I keep it classy for my clients."

"Ugh, if you start talking about keeping your brand cohesive on social media again, I'm going to tour the Highlands without you," I say, striding away from the stone and toward the cave's entrance. I duck past the dripping water at the opening as I hear Dakota trail behind me.

"It's important, Bonnie. Influencers and companies find me through Instagram. I can't have a picture on there of me pretending my arm is a penis."

I whip around, halting her in place as I plant my hands on my hips. "It's because my arms are longer than yours, isn't it? You're too ashamed to have your fake penis next to my fake penis."

"Yes, Bonnie," she deadpans. "That's exactly right. I have fake-penis envy."

I snap my fingers and smile. "I knew it." I reach out and take her hand in mine. "Come on, now, we have much to see."

We decided to visit a few spots in the Highlands today. We have plans to go to Inverness and explore later on, and when we can really squeeze in some time together, we want to hit up Edinburgh. We aren't just here to work and find ourselves. We're also here to take in the country.

And that is what today is about: exploring with my best friend.

◆ ◆ ◆

My eleventh-grade English teacher was obsessed with England. A real lover of Shakespeare. He would drive us crazy with anecdotes and vacation pictures of him splashed around England.

Mr. Dorsey in a red phone booth.

Mr. Dorsey in front of Buckingham Palace.

Mr. Dorsey in the countryside.

Mr. Dorsey at Stonehenge.

At one point, Josh Flanders stood up in the middle of a slideshow of Mr. Dorsey prancing in an English field with sheep and told the man to get a life. Josh was sent to the principal, but mentally I applauded him. Who on earth would be so obsessed with another country?

Ahem

Slowly raises hand

Yeah, I get it now.

I so freaking get it.

Ugh, poor Mr. Dorsey. I want to write a letter to him and tell him . . . "I see you."

And then I want to write him a letter describing in intricate detail the way the heather on the hills sways rhythmically with the wind, almost like it's dancing.

To make my point: I'm obsessed with Scotland.

I came to that realization about five minutes ago, when Dakota slowly pulled around a bend on a narrow road that opens up to a valley. My heart caught in my throat as the landscape unfolded before us.

After pulling off onto a lookout with a bench, we sat in the car and quietly stared for a few good minutes before I got out of the car and breathed it all in.

The fresh air was the first thing to ignite my senses. So pure.

The second thing was the soft sound of a trickling brook winding and weaving through the valley. Not big enough to be a river, but powerful enough to set the soundtrack for the view in front of us.

The third thing was the contrast in bold colors Mother Nature has chosen to bless us with. A palette of whimsical childhood hues clashing together, making the soil pop, the clouds dance, and the peaks claim authority over the land.

The only word for it all: *breathtaking.*

"Wow," Dakota says as she pulls a travel cooler with our lunches out of the car.

"I know. I think we found the spot."

"We did." She chuckles, and we both take a seat on the wide bench.

Before we left Corsekelly, we stopped at the bakeshop for some savory pies—both opting for cheese and onion today—and of course some shortbread, because what's one more helping for my hips?

"Isla was right about this place," I say, taking a bite of my pie and enjoying the hearty and acidic flavors of the cooked onion. "I'm so glad she told us about it."

"Me too," Dakota says quietly.

I know that quiet.

That quiet is a result of her thinking heavily about something.

That quiet has been present through almost our entire drive.

Yes, we were taking in the views and listening to traditional Scottish music, but she usually comments on a few things, at the very least. There was no commenting this time.

I bump her with my shoulder. "What's going on in that head of yours? And don't tell me nothing. We've been friends since the fourth grade—I know when you're thinking too hard."

"Do I really give it away?"

"Smoke comes out of your ears. I like to think of it as sort of a Batsignal, but just for me." Cupping my hands around my mouth—pie balanced precariously on my lap—I say, "Alert, alert, Bonnie, help is needed. Help is needed."

"You are so stupid." Dakota laughs and then lets out a long sigh. "I'm scared."

"Scared?" I ask, turning to face her. *Sorry, scenery.* "Why are you scared?"

"I don't think I know how to navigate this thing with Isla. And I'm really starting to like her. I don't want to make a mistake."

"Dakota—"

"Isabella was always telling me that I was doing things wrong. I wasn't holding her hand enough. I wasn't giving her enough affection. I wasn't dressing the way she wanted me to dress. I wasn't posting enough about gay rights. I should be using my Instagram platform for the lesbian community, not for my business. I wasn't . . . gay enough." Shoulders slouched, she twists her hands in her lap. "Those words haunt me. I can still see her with that blonde, when I found them in bed together. She didn't even care I caught her cheating on me. She just shrugged and said, 'You're not gay enough for me; I moved on.' What if . . . what if it's the same with Isla?"

Anger eclipses me, and I have to take a brief pause before I say something that won't help the situation—only magnify it.

Once I'm feeling calm, I take Dakota's hand in mine. "I want to make one thing clear: being gay doesn't define you. Do you understand that? I think sometimes people fall under the impression that if you're gay, that's who you are. You're gay, and they leave it at that. But that's not fair. And just like a beautiful, nonsmelly onion"—she chuckles—"you have layers, and being gay isn't the outer ring; it isn't even the second or third. It's deep at your core, and you keep it there, close to your heart, because that's the way you choose to live your life. You choose to define yourself as a good friend. As a beautiful artist. As a savvy businesswoman who has used her platform to grow her freelance work. You are so much more than a lesbian. Yes, that's a piece of who you are, but it's not the definition."

She smiles softly and tilts her head, resting it on my shoulder. "I love you."

"I love you too." I kiss the top of her head. "Isabella put you through hell, and she's made you second-guess every piece of you that makes you special, unique, the best friend you are. Don't let one person's blinded opinion of you make you question the person you've grown to be."

"I loved her, though. She was my first . . . ever. She helped open my eyes to a part of me I was hiding for such a long time. She was right about my being gay, which was the biggest revelation of my life. It's hard not to trust her opinion on everything else, when she knew I was gay."

"I can understand that." I stroke her hair. "Yes, she might have opened your eyes, but that's all she did. And if it wasn't her, it was going to be another girl—you just happened to run into Isabella first. Don't give her all the credit for something that was bound to occur." I lift her chin up so she has to look me in the eyes. "This is your chance to grow, Dakota. Your chance to be yourself, not the person Isabella wanted you to be." I motion to the valley in front of us. "And what better place to do it than here, in Scotland."

She chuckles. "You're right."

"I know I am." I smile, picking up my pie. "Give yourself some grace when it comes to Isla. It will take a bit of time to get used to navigating a new relationship, but she seems patient, kind, and understanding. The best you can do for her, and for you, is be yourself." I take a bite of my pie and chew.

"When did you become so wise?"

"I think it's all the shortbread and Scottish air."

Dakota studies me, a smirk playing at her lips. "I think you're starting to find yourself here."

"Yeah?"

She nods. "I see a new spark in your eyes. There's excitement in your voice."

"I am excited. The entire drive here, while we were taking in the landscape, I kept writing down ideas for the coffee shop and my plan of attack. Want to hear them?"

"I would love to."

◆ ◆ ◆

"Enjoy," I say to an old man wearing a plaid shirt with SCOTLAND embroidered on the back as he leaves the shop, coffee in hand.

He told me he stopped in on this Monday morning because he heard the coffee was boring and that's what he likes—boring coffee.

Yay for the sale, but serving coffee to a small demographic of cantankerous crotches isn't really what I'm looking for.

Leaning against the counter, I pull out my goat notebook and look over my notes. There's so much I want to do, but I honestly don't know where to start. I really want to go over this stuff with Rowan, and that was the idea lurking in my head the other night, to maybe talk some things through. But then, when we started just getting to know each other and having fun, I didn't feel like bringing up the coffee shop.

Nope, I brought up his dead brother instead.

Smart, Bonnie. Really smart.

Exhaling, I press my forehead to my hand and start doodling on the side of my notebook.

Dakota is over at the bakeshop—no shock there—and through the open door, I spot Lachlan and Leith, in just their kilts, of course, doing jumping jacks and lifting a log over their heads while Fergus watches over them. Tourists from the current bus circle around, counting along with them and taking pictures.

Yup, quite the sight to behold.

I've checked out a few of their training videos online, and they really have something going for them. And Dakota has been helping them out with some graphics—I've seen the rough drafts, and they are going to *die* over them.

A large frame steps through the door, pulling me from my doodling. Rowan's face comes into focus as my eyes adjust to the light. I lift myself up off the counter, a smile stretching over my face.

"Hey."

"Hey, is Dakota here?" He glances around.

"No."

"Och, okay. Is she at the bakeshop?"

"Yeah, why?"

"Just wanted a chat." He turns to walk away, and I nearly trip over my own feet running after him.

"Wait a second. That's all?"

Chuckling, he turns back and pulls me close. "Just kidding, lass. Wanted to see how you were going to react."

"Pissing me off isn't doing you any favors."

"It has been since I met you." He gives me the smallest of kisses and then releases me before walking over to a table and bringing me with him. We both take a seat, and he leans back, casually sitting in the chair while my body hums, ready for anything he wants to give. "Saw a man leave here with some coffee."

"He said he liked boring coffee, so this was the place for him."

"Ouch." Rowan laughs and glances around the empty space. "So . . . what's the plan?"

"Plan?"

"For the shop. What are you going to do?"

"Oh, well, I mean . . . I have some ideas, but I haven't started anything."

"Why not?"

"Because I wanted to run them by you first. This is your family's shop, after all."

"Aye, true." He nods at me. "Then, run 'em by me."

Simple as that, huh?

Excited to share, I run to the counter, grab my notebook and pen, and sit down across from him. "Now, these are just ideas—nothing is concrete."

"Hit me."

"Well, we need to power wash these floors—they're grimy and need a new life."

He glances down. "Aye. I have a power washer."

"That's amazing, really? God, I love power washers. Unsung heroes of renovating. I can't wait to blow the dirt off these—"

"You're not using it," he says with finality. "I'll do it."

Uh, excuse me?

"Oh no. I'll have the pleasure of doing it. I've spent way too many bored hours in here watching power-washing compilations on YouTube to not have the pleasure of doing it myself."

"You've been watching power-washing videos on YouTube?"

Doesn't everybody?

"Yes, it's quite soothing. Like raking sand in one of those sand gardens people keep on desks. It's crazy satisfying to watch dirt be blasted away by water. I'm afraid to admit I've probably committed at least ten hours to watching compilations online. Paired with fun music, and you've got yourself a wonderful way to waste some time."

He blinks a few times. "You're serious."

"Do I need to show you my YouTube history? I don't even need to search them out anymore—they just show up on the suggested feed. But do you know what really chaps my ass?" I lean forward conspiratorially. "It's when these YouTube people compile some of the *same* power-washing videos. I've seen them already—we want new material." I shake my fist in the air.

"I think I'm going to take back the other night."

"Can't," I say with a smile. "Already had my mouth on your dick, and that means I claimed you." His eyes seductively narrow as he shifts in his chair. "Oh, you like that, huh? Me talking about having your c—"

"Watch it, Bonnie, this teasing can go both ways."

My mouth snaps shut. Based on past experience, I'm assuming he could do some real damage.

"Anyway." I clear my throat, tapping my pen on my notebook. "Power washing and then some fresh paint on the walls. I think we stick with the beautiful white in here, but freshen it up, and the red door as well. I love the colors in here, but they've dulled over time. And do you think we could add shutters to the windows and some window boxes? Is that something you know how to do?"

He nods. "Aye."

"Will it take you long?"

"Few hours."

"Really? Gah, okay. I think it will dress up the outside and make it more inviting. And as for the inside, we need some new tables. These"—I tap on the table—"are firewood. Is there a place around here where we can get some tables and chairs?"

"Kyle of Lochalsh."

"Uh, what?"

"Quick fifteen-minute drive to the west. Larger town, has a wood-worker there. Hamish and Alasdair both bought their tables and chairs from there, and reasonably priced. Maw's been wanting to purchase some, but Da said only once these tables fall apart."

"Well, looks like I'm taking an ax to them, because they need to fall apart." I make a note in my notebook. "Would you be willing to take me over there? I don't ever want to drive on these roads myself again."

"Aye, I can take you. We can go eat at the Waterside Restaurant after."

I pause, look up. "Are you . . . are you asking me out?"

With that devilish smirk, he leans over the table and pinches my chin. "Aye, lass. I am. Are you saying yes?"

"I don't know . . . ," I tease.

He chuckles, leans over, and plants a chaste kiss on my lips. "Offer stands for as long as it takes to be accepted."

My oh my, he's the charmer. He knows exactly how to make me weak in the knees.

"I would love to go out with you, Rowan."

"Good. Wednesday night."

"Okay. After we close tonight, I would like to power wash the floors. Can you bring over the machine?"

"You're not power washing."

"This is not up for discussion, Rowan." I stab my pen to the table. "I am power washing, and then tomorrow we can paint."

"We?" He lifts a brow.

"Yes. We. I'm going to ask Dakota to ask Isla as well. Think you can ask the Murdach twins?"

"What's in it for me?" He taps his fingers on the table, casual, looking as handsome as ever.

"Our date Wednesday night."

"You're the one who wanted a date."

"Don't act like you don't want to take me out," I scoff. "You're looking for a reprise of the other night."

"I'm looking for a lot more than that, and I'm not talking physically."

Oy. This man.

"When you say things like that, you give me chills and butterflies at the same time," I admit. "Makes me feel really special."

"'Cause you are, lass." He nods toward my paper. "What else you got?"

How he can just bounce around topics like that, unfazed, is impressive. My mind is still running through last night, and he's just chugging along through the conversation.

Gathering my wits, I ask, "Is that a yes to the Murdach twins?"

"Aye."

"Thank you." I slip my hand in his, and he holds it tight. "I found an espresso machine online that's for sale in Inverness. It's a year old, and the coffee house is going out of business—a Starbucks took over." Rowan rolls his eyes. "They're selling everything they can, and they said they're putting the machine on hold for me. Dakota was going to go pick it up with Isla, and then we're going to start testing new drinks. Nothing too fancy—just enough to entice more people into the shop. There's also a local tea brand I've seen around town that I would love to carry in the shop, to offer something to customers who don't drink coffee. They carry a Scottish breakfast, Earl Grey, and a Highland blend that is positively delightful."

"Good idea."

His approval sends a surge of confidence through me.

"As for food . . ." His jaw ticks, his eyes narrow. "Would you help me—?"

"No," he says, his voice stern. *What is the deal?*

"Rowan."

"I'm not baking for the shop."

"I wasn't asking you to—if you'd let me finish," I say, parroting his words from the other day. "Teach me how to make butteries—oh, and maybe that cherry cake and tattie scones? I'm pretty good at following directions, and since we open up at ten, I could wake up early—now that I'm used to the time difference—and start baking for the day." When he doesn't say anything, I squeeze his hand. "Please, Rowan. Food is going to make a huge difference, and it won't compete with Isla. I think if we have three solid options, we'll do just fine, especially since we'll be more of a stop for the tourists. We'd offer just enough for them."

He drags his hand over his face. "I haven't made butteries in years."

"I'll bake with my top off, or even completely naked . . . just an apron."

That piques his interest. He raises a brow. "You'll let me teach you, naked?"

"Yes. However you want me—that's how I'll stay the entire time. And if you want a break, to do . . . whatever," I say in a seductive voice, "then, we take a break."

"Sex and baking."

"Aye," I say with a wink, which makes him chuckle and then blow out a long breath.

"You drive a hard bargain, lass."

"Enticing, though, yeah?"

He slowly nods, wetting his lips. "Especially since I haven't seen you completely naked yet."

"Your fault, not mine. I stripped you down. You're the one who only pushed up my shirt."

"Regretting that mistake now." He scratches the side of his face, his nails scraping along his thick scruff. "Deal."

"Yeah?" I ask, excited.

"Aye, but you wear nothing but an apron."

"Done." *Eeep.* Excited—for many reasons—I make another note in my notebook. "That leaves us with merchandise. Dakota is going to design new signs, and we would love to come up with a fun name for the coffee shop, since everything else in town has one. Then we can make and sell merchandise based on what we call the shop. We can easily play off the Boaby Stone, Fergus, or the hairy coo . . ." An idea pops into my head. "Oh my God, what if we called the shop the Hairy Coo Coffee Company? We could hang cute black-and-white photos of the cows on the walls, make some hairy coo–themed merchandise, and then direct people to the footpath, so it gets more visitors than just locals."

He twists his lips to the side, considering the idea. "You know, I really think Maw and Da would like that. They've always loved the hairy coo, and they were a driving force behind the path being made in the first place."

"Really? Then it's meant to be. I bet Dakota could make an adorable sign with the 'Hairy Coo' front and center."

He nods slowly, a smile playing at his lips. "I really like the idea."

That little smile, the excitement in his voice. I don't think I've ever felt this much pride in my entire life, and for the first time in a very long time, I feel . . . useful.

◆ ◆ ◆

"What are you doing?"

I startle, dropping my phone on the counter. With a smirk, Rowan picks it up and glances at the screen. He raises a brow as he shows it to me, as if I don't know what's on it.

"Power-washing videos?"

"Don't judge!" I snatch my phone away and put it in my back pocket. Once we closed, I moved the tables and chairs outside. Earlier, Rowan said he would take care of them by literally chopping them into firewood. I told him I didn't care what he did with them, but if he did decide to chop them up, I was going to need a slo-mo video of that, of course with his shirt off. From the look in his eyes, I think he's going to deliver. We decided to close the shop for the next few days while we do small renovations. Pretty sure the public isn't going to miss us much.

"Did you bring it?" I ask, rubbing my hands together.

"Yes, but you're not—"

"Balderdash, I'm doing it." Pushing past him, I walk over to the door, where I spot the hefty machine. Beautiful in all its splendor, a knight of destroying grime. A fighter of fungus. A true champion of cleanliness. The one, the only . . . the power washer. "Ryobi 2300, nice choice," I say, taking in the robust beast. "Does it come with the bonus turbo nozzle?"

"It's disturbing how much you know about power washers."

"*Does* it?" I ask, needing to know the answer.

"The nozzle's attached," Rowan says, sounding slightly terrified.

"Beautiful. And you hooked it up to the hose already. This is a dream." I pick up the metal spray wand and test the weight.

"Whoa, whoa, whoa, Bonnie."

"From what I've read, you just press this button." The power washer turns on with a soothing hum. "And then—" I pull on the handle and blast water out of the nozzle. The small kickback startles me. I back into the doorframe of the shop, flinging my arm out—and spraying Rowan directly in the crotch.

Uh-oh.

Man.

Down.

"Oh God." I drop the spray handle and run over to his body, curled on the floor. "Rowan, are you okay?"

"Told you . . . not to," he says, breathing hard and cradling his crotch.

"Did it . . . did I . . . ?" *Oh God.* "Did I spray your balls off?"

He lets out a dry cough and shakes his head. "Nah, baws are in place, but you definitely took out a few of the cadets."

"Sperm?" I ask, rubbing his back.

"Yes, Bonnie . . . sperm."

"Hopefully they were going to be slow swimmers anyway." I pat his back, and my eyes stray to the power washer. Even in my guilt, I can't help a tug of longing. "I hope you know, I truly wish the best for your crotch at this moment, but I'm going to need you to get up so I can go to town on these floors."

He glances up at me from his fetal position. "Are you serious?"

"Dead serious. I can feel it in my bones that I'm a power-washing wizard." I tug on his arm. "Let's get you up on the counter, out of range, and you can watch over me while you nurse your boaby and baws."

"I don't think anything is out of range for you," he groans, slowly getting up.

I keep a steady grip on him as he hobbles to the counter and hoists himself up. "I wasn't prepared for the wand to jump like that. Knowing the kind of power that electric puppy is packing, I'll be in a properly prepared stance now." I pat him on the leg and am moving to walk away when he snags my arm and spins me toward him.

He kisses me quickly. "You might have destroyed any possible boners for today, but hearing your confidence . . . well, it very well might restore what you just destroyed."

"Is my confidence a turn-on?"

"Your confidence makes me happy, Bonnie," he says seriously. "Makes me believe you're starting to find that purpose, and that's what matters."

Taken aback, I say, "Wow, McGrumpyshire, you're about to get yourself laid."

He groans, shifting to the side. "Wait until tomorrow."

Chuckling, I give him one more kiss and then go back to the power washer and pick up the wand. "Should I start in the corner?"

"Aye, and then work all the dirt toward the door."

"Okay. I got this."

With a deep breath, I get into my stance, hold the wand with a good stiff arm, and then pull back on the trigger. I get a small kickback, but this time I'm prepared and hold strong, immediately blasting grime off the old wood floors. I perform a spot test, like all good power washers, no more than a few square inches, but as the water blasts against the hardwood floors, I immediately see how much this is going to change the look of the shop. When I release the trigger, letting the water slosh for a second and clear out, I lean forward and marvel at the stunning oak floor that's been here this whole time.

"Rowan, it's beautiful."

"Is it? I honestly can't remember at this point."

"It is, and the power washer doesn't seem to pull up any of the wood or stain. Shall I continue?"

"You're apparently the expert. Go ahead."

Excitement pulses through me. I get into position . . . and blast.

◆ ◆ ◆

"Bonnie, oh my gosh," Dakota says, walking into the coffee shop for the first time since I cleaned the floors. She had her date with Isla last night, so while she was out, I took care of business. Honestly, I don't know which was more satisfying: having Rowan between my legs or washing all the dirt off these floors.

Of course, I would never tell him that.

Don't want to give the man a complex.

He was amazing the other night and all . . . but . . . power washing . . .

"They look brand new."

"Right? I'm so pleased. I made Rowan take a few photos." I pull out my phone and show her the pictures Rowan reluctantly took of me wielding the washer while he nursed his manhood.

"You look like a total boss."

"Right? I made this one my Instagram profile pic."

"How could you not?"

Just then, Isla and the twins come into the coffee house. All three of them stop and take in the floors.

"Holy crap," Leith says first.

"Wow," Lachlan adds. "We need to do this to our floors."

Isla walks up to Dakota and slips her hand in hers. "You did a wonderful job, Bonnie."

"Thanks." I beam with pride. "It was pretty easy and extremely satisfying. I'm more than happy to do it for anyone else who might need something power washed. I think I've found a new hobby."

"Just keep your crotch covered," Rowan says, walking into the shop behind them.

"Yeah, Bonnie told me she blasted you in the balls," Dakota says. "Are you okay?"

"Nothing's been damaged, but I did feel like I took a classic football toss to the old lad."

"Rowan told us about it this morning," Leith says. "Glad I didn't follow through with asking you out, or else that could have been me."

"As if she would have said yes," Lachlan says.

"She showed interest."

"Sorry to tell ye, but she only had interest in me, lads," Rowan says, walking over and pressing his lips to mine. Soft, yet firm. Best kisser, hands down.

"Full of yourself much?" I ask, even though he's exactly right.

"Nay, I just know infatuation when I see it." He winks and then nods to the door. "Leith, Lachlan, grab the paint supplies while we lay down the paint cloths. We don't want anything to mess up these floors."

My oh my, look at Rowan taking action. The bossiness is kind of a turn-on.

Bossy McGrumpyshire . . . has a nice ring to it.

While the twins are out, the rest of us get to work on the cloth drapes, lining them up with the baseboards and taping them down. "Heard you two were snogging last night," Rowan says to Isla and Dakota with a grin.

What? I snap my head toward them.

They *snogged?*

As in, they had their first kiss?

Why wasn't I informed of this monumental occasion?

"Wait, you had your first kiss last night and you didn't tell me?" I try to hide the hurt, but it's heavy in my voice. Dakota and I tell each other everything, and a first kiss with a Scottish lass is definite must-need information.

"We technically kissed on Sunday." Isla winces.

"Sunday?" I shout. "When? I was with you the whole day, Dakota."

She glances around the shop, looking uncomfortable. "Uh, you know those flowers I picked when we were out exploring that field? I brought them over to Isla when I went on that walk after we got back. We kissed then."

"And you didn't tell me?" I roar.

"You've been a little occupied." She nods toward Rowan.

I push Rowan out of the way. "Uh, that's not a reason to not tell me. Your first kiss is way more important than that irritable doof." He grumbles something next to me, but I ignore him, turning my attention to Isla. "How was it? Did my girl win you over? I kissed her once, and she had the softest lips. Was it a good kiss?"

Isla smiles. "Aye, it was a very good kiss."

"God." I toss open a drop cloth. "And then you made out. Where did you make out?"

"Isla's place," Leith says, walking in with Lachlan, their arms full of paint cans, pans, and rollers.

"Can we not air out all the details?" Isla says.

"Why do they know all the details?" Dakota asks.

"Yeah"—I plant my hands on my hip—"why do they know all the details?"

Cautiously, Isla looks between her brothers and Dakota. "They were perverts and looked through the windows." Isla squeezes Dakota's hand. "I promise I didn't tell them."

"Okay," Dakota says quietly, and they exchange a look, the kind of look I'd exchange with my best friend. The kind of look that tells everyone around them that they are close enough to communicate without words.

And that's not something I like very much.

Is that why she didn't say something to me? Because they're not sharing their relationship with many people? Though, apparently, news gets around.

I get keeping it quiet, but why wouldn't she want to share with *me*?

"Looked like a good snogging session," Lachlan says, clearly not reading the room as he starts pouring paint into paint pans.

"Can you shut up?" Isla snaps.

"I mean, I can, but I don't want to."

"Enough with the snogging talk," Rowan cuts in. "We need to focus on the painting." Rowan to the rescue, like always. "We have to do the ceiling, moldings, and walls. The only things not getting painted in here are the wood beams on the ceiling and the wood floors. Please be careful to keep those clean. And pair up. Leith and Lachlan, take the ceiling. I'll work on the right side with Bonnie, and you girls cover the left. I'm buying drinks if we get this done by eight."

That encourages the boys, who quickly get to work, while Dakota and Isla start on their side. I watch from across the room as they murmur to each other, laughing and smiling. I feel a pang of jealousy.

When Dakota was with Isabella, I never saw her act the way she's acting now—content and carefree. That should have been clue number one that Isabella wasn't the girl for her. But seeing her with Isla, it almost feels like—and I know this might sound stupid—but it almost feels like my best friend is being stolen away from me. I know I encouraged her to go for it, but still . . . a girl can feel left out.

With Isabella, she told me everything. From every hand hold, every look, every kiss, I was there, step by step, helping her realize that it's okay to like a girl. It's okay to come out of your shell and realize exactly who you are.

And now, with Isla, I selfishly expected to be involved every step of the way as well. But, sadly, I'm starting to see Dakota grow wings and pull away. Going to talk to Isla alone, the double date that turned into a single one, and now this.

It's almost as if . . . she doesn't need me anymore, and that strikes me hard, because, if anything, Dakota gave me an ounce of purpose while fighting through these unknown feelings I've absorbed.

Now what?

Doubt and loneliness start to creep into the back of my mind.

I'm tempted to ask Rowan if I can switch partners, but that's just an overreaction. Right? I'm overreacting. I'm thrown off that everyone knew about their kiss and I didn't. I've known Dakota forever. We've known every little thing about each other's lives, and being left out of this important factoid—her kissing her second girl ever—stings, for sure, but I'll get over it. She looks happy, and I don't want to make a big deal over something that will probably seem so trivial to her.

In the grand scheme of things, it doesn't matter.

What matters is Dakota's happiness. And with one glance in their direction, I can tell she's truly finding her place here in Corsekelly.

Deep breaths, Bonnie. It's fine. You're fine.

"Hey, you all right?" Rowan asks.

"Huh? Oh yeah, sorry. Just, uh . . . thinking." I tack on a smile, but I think we both know it's fake.

It's fine. It will all be okay.

You're not losing your friend.

Stop overreacting and have fun.

I take a deep breath, grab a roller from Rowan, and head to the wall. Before we start, he leans in and kisses me on the side of the head. "Date tomorrow."

That brings a smile to my face. "Are you going to dress up?"

"Are you?"

"Naturally. I plan on dressing up under my clothes as well." I wiggle my brows, and he laughs.

"Dressin' down would be better." He wiggles his brows back.

"If you expect me to wear a dress with no underwear, you're out of your mind."

"Worth a shot." He dots my nose with some paint and then gets to work.

Chapter Fifteen

ROWAN

Power-washed balls: Check.
Date with power-washing queen: Check.
Nervous.
Excited.
Hopeful.
It's all I can say about my upcoming date with Bonnie.

◆ ◆ ◆

I couldn't sleep last night.

As rain pelted against my bedroom window, I kept thinking about Callum and what he would have thought of Bonnie. There's no doubt they would have become good friends. They both love driving me crazy, testing me, challenging me. They would most likely have become best friends within a week.

And that makes me fucking sad, which is why I'm out in my shed at four in the morning, doors wide open so I can watch the rain pepper the already-saturated ground.

Callum was keen on my pottery. Massively so, actually, and he was always badgering me to do something with my talent. I can still hear the awe in his voice when I showed him the very first bowl I made. It was wonky, uneven, and not much of a bowl, but damn it if Callum didn't use it almost every day when he was baking. He couldn't fathom how a piece of wet clay could be formed into something so beautiful.

Clay already prepped, I turn on my wheel. The hum of the motor fills my small space as I dip my wet fingers into the soggy clay, laying the groundwork for a mug.

You have a talent, Rowan, he said. *Use it. Why stay here where no one can appreciate it? Build up your stock and move to Edinburgh, where it's swimming in tourists looking to take home a piece of Scotland.*

And that was the plan.

I was going to help bake for a few more years until Callum was fully ready to take over the shop, and then I was going to do something for myself.

That's what I told my da I was going to do.

And that was the start of the rift between the two of us.

I'd thought he'd get over it with time, but he never did, and once Callum passed away . . . well, we haven't been able to recover. Da keeps pushing me further and further away.

The breeze gusts outside, sending a mist of rain in my direction. I welcome it as I sit under the single dim light in my shed. That's all I turned on. It's all I wanted.

With a sigh, I clear my head of the past. Needing to focus on something positive, I work on the clay in front of me, slowly raising the sides, hollowing it out into the shape I drew this morning.

Something that would fit Bonnie's small hands but also leave plenty of room for the coffee she needs to function in the morning.

After our conversation about the shop and all her ideas, I knew right away I needed to make her something to reflect this new journey she's on. The idea came to me this morning. A simple mug with a cinch in its waist, a flare at the top, and a hairy coo stamped on the side.

Turning toward the rain, feeling the weight of it pound against the ground, I smile to myself.

"What do you think, Callum? Think she'll like it?"

Another breeze picks up, and I smile, realizing just how content I feel in this moment. Clay between my fingers, my brother by my side, with thoughts of Bonnie dripping through my mind.

The pain and the anxiety over my parents all wash away with the rain, making me think that maybe things are about to change for me. Maybe this is the start of something new.

Something truly special . . .

I check my hair one last time in the rearview mirror of my pickup and then open the driver's side door. I don't have many fancy clothes, but I did find a pair of barely worn dark-washed jeans in my drawers and paired them with a light-green button-up shirt. I made sure to style my hair and spritz on some cologne. I know she likes my scruff, so I didn't shave, hoping to rub it against her soft skin later.

With a deep breath, I head to the cottage and knock on the front door. I know Dakota and Isla are walking around the loch right now. I caught them strolling and holding hands while I drove over here, so I'm not expecting to run into anyone but Bonnie.

I couldn't help but notice a glimmer of jealousy in Bonnie's eyes yesterday at Isla and Dakota's strong connection. I considered asking her about it but decided at the last minute not to. I didn't want to dive into anything that could make her uncomfortable, even though she seems to have no problem asking me all sorts of cringe-inducing questions.

But yesterday was different. Her usual confidence disappeared, and she seemed so fragile, almost embarrassed that she didn't know Dakota and Isla had kissed, and I didn't want to elevate that embarrassment. So I dropped it.

Hopefully, after we left the pub, they worked out whatever awkwardness they were going through.

Footsteps approach inside the cottage.

The door opens.

And fucking shite.

My breath is stolen at the sight of Bonnie.

Dressed in a pale-yellow dress that hugs her curves and highlights her breasts, she smiles brightly at me. Her hair hangs over her shoulders in curls, her eyes are devastatingly piercing, and her lips are painted glossy pink. I can honestly say I've never seen anyone more beautiful.

"Wow, lass." I smooth my hand over my mouth. "You look stunning."

She sways cutely. "You look quite handsome yourself."

I move in and loop my arms around her, my hands falling to the spot just above her ass. Thanks to the heels she's wearing, I don't have to bend down too far to kiss her. What I wouldn't give to just push her through this door and have my way with her—but based on the number of times she's asked me if I'd be taking her out, I need to make sure we actually leave this cottage.

Aye . . . my girl.

That's something I never expected. Before Bonnie came to Corsekelly, I was resigned to the idea that I was stuck in the town I grew up in, doing a job I hated to appease others. But now it feels like there might be possibility for something else. Something more.

That is, if she wants to stay in Scotland. Something I try to not think about. There's plenty of time to see if this goes anywhere, plenty of time to convince her to stay if it does.

"God, you smell amazing," she says, pressing her lips to mine one last time, her hands gripping my shirt tightly.

"Thank you." I find her hand and walk her to my pickup, where I open the door for her. When she's situated, I grab the seat belt and hand it to her. "Buckle up, lass." I wink and round the truck, hopping in on my side. "You haven't driven to the Inner Sound yet, right?"

She shakes her head. "No, Dakota and I went northeast on our exploration. Isla gave us directions to a beautiful spot looking over a river valley."

"Aye, well, you're in for a pretty drive." I turn the music up just enough so she can hear it. I've chosen one of my favorite Scottish bands, Tartanium, for our short road trip.

"Wow, really setting the mood, aren't you?" she says over the soft hum of a fiddle taking a solo right before the drumbeat kicks in.

I smile at her. "Just trying to give you the full Scottish experience. Is it working?"

"I think the *full* Scottish experience will come later. Don't you think?"

"Aye, if you're lucky," I say, laughing.

"I'm feeling lucky tonight."

We spent a good hour at Campbell's Carpentry picking out tables. There were two sets Bonnie couldn't decide on, so we opted to mix and match them, which will give the space a more eclectic feel. With the new tables and chairs ordered, a purchase I know Maw will be happy about, we walked through Kyle for a wee bit, spent some time around the waterfront, and now we're sitting in the Waterside Restaurant, our food ordered and drinks on the table. Smiles stretch over both of our faces as we stare at each other in the dim lighting.

"Who were the celebrities you assisted back in the States?" I ask, breaking the comfortable silence.

"My first job, I was assistant to an executive manager for a production company. The guy fired me because I wouldn't sit on his lap when he asked me to."

Anger rolls over me. "Seriously?"

"Yeah. He said he could really help further my career if I helped him out . . ."

"What the fuck is wrong with men?" I take a sip of my water. I didn't opt for a beer because I'm driving, but I'm coming down with the urge to drink. "I hope you told him to fuck off."

"I did. And then he screamed that I would never work in the industry again. Which wasn't true, because, as you can imagine, there are a lot of awful people who need assistants, and some of them don't care if you have a reference."

"I could see that." Growing serious, I reach across the table and take her hand in mine. "You're very strong for making sure he didn't take advantage of you."

"Thank you," she says quietly. "Looking back now, I think I grew to respect myself a bit more." She smiles to herself. "You know, I never looked at it that way until just now."

"That you grew to respect yourself?"

She nods. "Yeah." Her eyes connect with mine. "Thank you."

"No need to thank me, lass. You're the brave one."

Hell, the way she's looking at me right now, like I'm some goddamn hero, it puffs my chest while simultaneously twisting my stomach into nervous knots. Doesn't she realize how much strength and courage it takes to stand up to someone like her old boss? It's a horrible and far too common situation, but the fact that she recognized her worth in that moment makes me want to plant myself firmly by her side.

"Who were the other two?" I ask.

"The second person I assisted was a basketball player's wife, actually. She was pretty nice, but it was her rabid troll of a sister who was the problem. She accused me of hitting on the basketball player, which of course wasn't true. For starters, he wasn't my type—not much into the blonds." She winks. "But I'm also more professional than that. I valued my job too much, especially after losing the first one. But alas, the wife didn't believe me, so I was fired—yet again."

"Sounded like a toxic environment anyway."

"I did like Lisa, but . . . ugh, now that I think about it, she was the one who introduced us to Isabella, Dakota's ex. Isabella was working for one of Lisa's collaborators. So yeah, 'toxic' is the right way to put it. We did have some fun times, but the fun didn't outweigh the bad—not even close. Plus, Lisa was trying to launch her own makeup line and had me test the products. Oh boy, the number of times my lips swelled from her lipsticks is too high to count."

"Why was she starting her own makeup line?"

"She was on a reality TV show, *Wives of Basketball Players*, and she was trying to capitalize on her fame. She teamed up with a shitty company that didn't actually care about the product, just the sales, so of course it was awful. I don't think she sold many because of the whole lip-swelling issue. She tried to pass it off as a tingle, but it was done."

"Karma." I wink at her.

"Exactly, and the last person who fired me was the best by far. Daloria Day."

"Oh damn, I've heard of her. Isn't she in that popular TV drama?"

"Yup, portrayed as America's sweetheart, but she was a pill to work with. I knew that going in and I was prepared. I took notes on everything, made sure to never make a wrong step, and I didn't. But then a costar she was crushing on said hi to me. She was furious that he gave me the time of day and had never done the same to her. So, she said I didn't make her coffee right and fired me on the spot."

"Isn't that ironic," I say. "Given what you're doing now."

"Orders haven't been super complicated at the shop."

"Doesn't matter—you get it right every time."

She laughs, just as our food is delivered. "Oh wow, this looks amazing."

Together, we ordered the seafood platter, and it's just as big as I remembered, piled high with crab legs, lobster, smoked salmon, oysters, clams, tatties, and lemon wedges. Holy hell, my mouth is watering. I can't remember the last time I came to Kyle, or treated someone out to a nice meal, but I'm glad I asked Bonnie—for many reasons.

I hold up an oyster. "You should really eat all of these."

She quirks her brow. "Do you really think I need an aphrodisiac to get frisky tonight?"

"You tell me."

"I could have stayed in the minute you showed up to my door."

"Aye . . . me too, lass."

"This isn't going to work." Bonnie shakes her head and slaps her napkin on the table. "We're going to need to leave, actually. I'm going to ask Dakota to come pick me up so I don't have to ride back with you."

"Could ye be any more dramatic?"

"Dramatic?" Her voice rises before she leans in and whispers, "You've never seen one *Star Wars* movie. How is that even something? Is that a Scotland thing?"

"No, I just never felt the need to watch them. Not a sci-fi person."

"It's not—" She presses a hand to her forehead. "It's not really sci-fi. I mean, yeah, it's in space, but it's a space *opera*. There's drama and love and lasers and sassy droids and hairy seven-foot-tall beasts that speak a language everyone understands for some reason. And all the hidden identities, *ugh*, and the new ones, a little bitch of a supreme leader who might make you laugh when you're not supposed to because of how whiny he is. Talk about daddy issues. And strong females. I don't think people give Princess Leia enough credit, but she's one badass leader and, frankly, the glue that holds everyone together."

I stare at her blankly. "Sassy droids?"

"Ugh," she groans. "You're killing me, Rowan. Why are you like this?"

"Just to annoy you."

"Clearly." She tosses her hands in the air. "Well, you're going to have to watch them with me."

"Don't be that person."

"Oh, I'm going to be that person, and I'm not even sorry about it, because for every movie you watch, I'll bounce up and down on your lap."

That makes me laugh out loud. "The way you use your words—I've never heard someone express themselves the way you do."

"I aim to please." She claps her hands together. "Okay, so when is this movie marathon?"

"How about after we set up the coffee shop and you learn to bake?" She thinks on it. "I don't know, I was thinking tonight."

Fuck no.

"No."

"No?"

I shake my head. "No. You're mine tonight."

"Since we just passed the cottage, I'm assuming we're going back to your place?"

"You assumed right," I say, the buildup of the evening driving me to the brink.

Her little touches here and there, the stolen kisses, that dress, the conversation, the teasing—it's all added up to this phenomenal prospect of what's to come.

In silence, we drive up to my cottage. I hop out and round the pickup before opening the door for her, anticipation building in my veins. After tea, we walked to Kyle's ice cream shop, where we both got a cup of white chocolate raspberry ice cream with chocolate fudge on top. The entire drive home, all I could think about was the prospect of tasting the faint flavors of chocolate and raspberries on her lips.

I bring her inside the house and shut the door behind me. "Bedroom," I say, nodding down the hall.

"Not even going to offer a girl a drink?"

"Want a drink?" I ask quickly.

She shakes her head.

"Then get your sweet arse to the bedroom."

She takes my hand in hers and leads me to the back, which gives me a moment to appreciate her arse in this dress. Heart shaped and round, it's perfect. She complained that the dress felt tight thanks to all the shortbread she's been eating, but I think she looks like a goddamn knockout—and so did every lad who came across her tonight.

I saw the double takes, the way their eyes traveled over her body. And fine, they could look all they wanted, but there was only one Scot she was going home with.

Turning toward me, she goes straight to my shirt, where she starts to undo the buttons.

Wetting my lips, I let her and keep my eyes on hers the entire time. When my shirt is completely undone, she pushes it down my shoulders and lets it fall to the floor. From there, she moves to my jeans, unbuckles them, and unzips the zipper. I push them off along with my shoes and socks and stand in front of her in nothing but a pair of tented boxer briefs.

"Sit," she commands, and hell, her bossiness is fucking hot. I gladly comply. I sit on the bed as she turns her back to me and gathers her hair to the side. "Unzip me."

With fucking pleasure.

I reach up and grab the small zipper, letting it glide down her back until I find the end. Slowly, she pushes the dress off her shoulders and shimmies out of it, exposing her matching pale-yellow bra and thong.

Christ, her ass is perfect, but before I can get my hands on it, she turns around and straddles me. Her arms fall to my shoulders as she glides her pelvis against mine.

"Hell, Bonnie."

Her lips find mine, and they're hungry, demanding, searching for even more than we had the other night.

She pushes me back against the mattress and leans down, her hair floating to the side, her lips locked on mine as her hips start to slowly grind against mine.

Oh fucking hell.

"God, I love how big you are," she says against my lips, teasing my mouth open and plunging her tongue inside. There's a sense of urgency coming off her. Normally, I'd ask to slow down, to live in the goddamn moment, but hell, I'm urgent too.

I reach up behind her and unhook her bra. The straps fall quickly, and she lifts up, tossing it to the side.

"Jesus fuck, you're sexy." My hands travel up her torso to her ample breasts. I cup them and pass my thumbs over her nipples as she continues to grind against me. Her back arches, pressing her breasts farther into my hands, and I take that moment to squeeze a little harder. With a light moan, her mouth falls open. She doesn't hold back, doesn't stand for shyness. She's confident, she takes what she wants, and she's sexy as hell doing it.

"Rowan," she moans again when I pinch her nipples. Her hips move faster, her hands landing on my stomach now, and I swear I can sense her orgasm moving to its apex. Her fingers dig into my stomach, her breaths shorten, and her eyes squeeze shut as I roll her nipples between my fingers. "Yes, oh my God." She falls against me and her lips descend on mine, while her hips buck up and down, until finally . . .

"Oh fuck," she whispers, drawing out her orgasm, our underwear the only barrier.

When her hips slow down, I flip her to her back and yank off her thong, followed by my boxer briefs. My goddamn dick is painfully hard as I reach for a condom from my nightstand and roll it over. Bonnie is still lightly panting on the bed, her eyes shut.

"Lass." Her eyes open. "Are you okay?"

She smiles. "Perfect." Holding out her arms, she welcomes me into her embrace, and I hover above her, slowing down the evening just slightly so she can gather herself. With one elbow propping me up, I give myself a chance to glide my fingers over her soft skin, to her puckered nipples, and then all the way down to her pubic bone. I repeat the path over and over again, savoring the feel of her skin and watching how so easily she is turned on, how quickly she can recover and be ready all over again.

"I want you inside me," she whispers.

"I want inside you too, lass. Desperately."

Her hands cup my face, and as she spreads her legs, she presses her mouth to mine, letting her tongue tell me exactly what she wants. Positioning my cock at her entrance, I slowly push in and catch her exhale on my lips as I stretch her open.

"You all right?" I whisper.

"So good," she says, so I move a little bit deeper, ever so carefully, pumping in and out, easing in. "So, so good."

My hand cups her face, and I tenderly drag my thumb over her cheek as our kisses become fervent, much needier than before, but I'm not urgent with my thrusts—I keep those controlled and really focus on her mouth, on making that connection.

That is, until she wraps her legs around my hips and pulls me in all the way. She gasps while I grunt, my eyes nearly rolling to the back of my head.

Warm.

Tight.

Goddamn heaven.

That's what she feels like. Fucking heaven.

"More, Rowan," she begs. "I need more. I need you to move."

I need it too.

Keeping my mouth on hers, I lift up slightly for a better angle and start to thrust in and out of her. I take it slow at first, dragging out each pulse, making sure she can feel every inch of me. And with every second that passes, I pick up the pace until we're both breathing heavily and our bodies are slapping together, our movements becoming erratic, our pleasure mounting.

"God, I can't get deep enough," I say before moving my mouth to her neck, then down to her breasts.

"Flip me over."

Taking charge, I do just that and prop her ass up. I get up on my knees, position myself at her entrance, and drive forward.

"Oh my God," she cries out, squeezing tightly around me. "Yes, Rowan. Oh my God, yes. Just like that."

I grip her hips, my control starting to waver as I pump into her over and over again. Her moans tear through the silent night.

"Never been this good," I say. "Never."

"More. Harder."

I pick up the pace, really slamming into her. My heart rate feels out of control, my movements sloppy and out of sync, but it doesn't matter as my orgasm builds at the base of my spine and starts to spread through all my limbs. I'm about to come, and I'm about to come hard.

"Yes, Rowan. Yes. Oh my God." She clenches around my cock, her orgasm ripping through her, and in seconds, my balls tighten and a feral groan flies out of my mouth. I'm coming right along with her.

"Mother . . . fucker," I call out, blackness surrounding me, nothing in my entire life ever feeling this damn good.

I pump into her a few more times before we both collapse on the bed.

Sated.

Pleasured.

Fucking spent.

I kiss the spot between her shoulder blades and then the back of her neck. She turns her head, and I find her lips. I slowly kiss her for a few more seconds before I pull away and take care of my condom.

When I return to the bed, she's worked her way under the covers and has a corner pulled down for me to climb in. Once I'm situated, she's like a magnet to metal, quickly pressing herself to my side and resting her hand on my chest.

I gently run my hand through her hair and listen to the light rain that's started to pelt the roof.

"I love the rain," she says quietly. "We don't get much of it out in California, but when we do, I always make sure to open a window, sit back, and just listen. I feel spoiled that I get to hear it all the time here."

"For a while, I hated rainstorms, because of Callum. They just reminded me of him, but now I'm starting to think of them as more of a moment to connect with my brother. To remember the good times."

"Tell me one of them."

Smiling, I give it some thought, reaching back into my Rolodex of memories. "Da hates being startled. He freaks out every time and always says, 'Get tae! What're ye doin'?'" She chuckles along with me. "So, Callum and I used to try to come up with different ways to startle him and record it. This one time Callum thought it would be genius to hide in the fridge."

"What? How did he do that?"

"Maw always waits till we're almost out of food before she goes shopping, so it was the perfect moment. She was out at the market in Kyle. Da was watching rugby and knew he had a few beers left in the fridge. We removed all the shelves, and Callum snuck in when he heard Da coming to get a beer. I was acting as if I was looking for a snack in one of the cupboards, but secretly I was recording. Da opened the fridge, and Callum popped out. He scared the living daylights out of

Da, who was so startled he punched Callum dead in the face. Not on purpose, just out of a pure gut reaction to fend off what he said at the time was the 'feckin' Loch Ness Monster.'"

"Oh my God," Bonnie laughs at my side. "That's amazing."

"It was. Maw came home to a peeved husband, a son who couldn't stop laughing, and another son with a black eye. That was the end of the scaring, at least for a few weeks, until Callum thought popping a balloon near Da's ear was the next-greatest idea."

"Was it?"

I shake my head. "It wasn't. Callum found out quickly that Da's reflexes were even sharper in such close proximity."

"Another black eye?"

"Aye." I chuckle, reveling in the realization that I can talk about my brother with Bonnie and not feel pain—just happiness. "From then on out, it was always distance scares."

"Smart boys." She sighs. "I'm an only child. Dakota is too, and I think it's why we're so close—we truly only had each other growing up. She has always been my person, through thick and thin."

"I can see that. You two have a wonderful relationship."

"We do." I kiss the top of her head, and quietly she says, "Rowan?"

"Hmm?"

"You make me happy."

I sigh. "You make me happy too, lass."

CHAPTER SIXTEEN
BONNIE

Perfect date I'll never forget: One.
   How many times I felt cherished last night: *Too many to count.*
   Male-induced orgasms: *Five.*
   Hot Scot who's making me fall for him: *One.*
   Rowan was insatiable. He wanted me, every chance he got. And frankly, I think I wanted him more. Also, listening to him come is really freaking hot. There's a slight accent in his come noise: it's sex gold.

◆   ◆   ◆

"What do you think? Should I hang this one here?"

Dakota glances up from her computer. "It looks too big for the space."

"Yeah, maybe."

I glance down at all the black-and-white photos I had printed and framed of the local hairy coos. Thursday, Rowan and I went for a walk on the Hairy Coo Footpath and took a bunch of pictures of the long-haired cows. Lots of close-ups showing off their adorable snouts and soulful eyes. Dakota then edited and cropped them and sent them to a guy in Kyle who prints and frames pieces for their gallery. Rowan was supposed to go with me to pick them up, but Shona was having a plumbing issue at the Mill Market. I insisted I would be fine driving on my own.

I was . . . okay.

I hated every second of it, but at least I got the pictures, and they are so freaking good.

"Okay, what about this?" Dakota asks me now, turning her computer in my direction.

The logo.

And God, it's adorable. Dead center is an outlined picture of a hairy coo, all shaggy hair and curving horns, and around it in a circle is the name of the coffee house—the Hairy Coo Coffee Company.

"Dakota, this is . . . amazing." I squat down lower to get a better look. "This would be perfect on mugs and shirts. Oh my God, my nipples just got hard because I'm so excited."

"You really like it?"

"I love it."

"Think Finella and Stuart will?"

"Will they what?" Rowan asks, stepping into the shop, arms full of groceries. I haven't seen him since this morning. It was a few hours ago, and yet it feels like days. When we make eye contact, he winks, and I nearly fling my body at him and maul his face.

"Will they like the logo?" Dakota says, completely oblivious to my urges.

Rowan sets the groceries down on the counter and walks over to the new tables we bought—which look positively amazing in the space, by the way—and bends down to take a good look. A small smile starts to form on his lips, and when he stands up, he possessively presses his hand to the nape of my neck. "They're going to absolutely love it."

"You're not just saying that?" Dakota asks, eyes glinting with excitement.

"I don't bullshit. I always mean what I say."

"That's true," I add. "It's perfect, Dakota."

"Thank you. Okay, I'm going to send the file to the guy over in Inverness and then grab the signage with the espresso machine." She stands. "I'll see you tomorrow afternoon."

"Wait, what?" I ask, confused.

"Isla and I are staying in Inverness. The printer needs time for the menus and the sign. We decided to stay the night and sightsee a bit."

"Oh." I swallow down a pang of disappointment. "You're going sightseeing—that should be fun."

"I'm really excited, especially since we haven't been able to see much of Scotland." She leans in, gives me a hug, and then takes off out the door, computer tucked under her arm. "Bye."

"Are you all right?" Rowan asks as the door swings shut.

"Huh? Oh yeah, fine." I clear my throat and act like I'm studying the pictures, when in reality, I feel . . . sad. We were supposed to explore Inverness together. We joked about finding the rental car guy again and trying to see if we could understand him better now that we've been in Scotland for a while. We also wanted to visit Inverness Castle, and there were a few restaurants we wanted to try. Is she going to do those things without me?

"You don't seem fine." Rowan takes my shoulders and gently turns me toward him. "You seem really upset, actually."

"It's nothing," I say, looking out toward the front window, where I see Isla meet up with Dakota. They exchange a quick kiss on the lips before linking their hands together and heading toward the cottage.

"Hey." Rowan moves my head so I meet his eyes. "If it was nothing, you wouldn't look like you're about to cry."

"I'm not about to cry, I just . . . I thought Dakota and I were going to explore Inverness together, that's all."

"Och." He nods. "I see." He looks back. "Go with them, then. We can bake another day."

I shake my head. "No, clearly they have some romantic trip planned. I'm not about to be the third wheel."

"Isla's pretty understanding. If you were honest with them, I'm sure she'd welcome you along."

I shake my head and lean into his embrace as his strong arms wrap me up. "No, that's okay. Dakota was most likely looking forward to this trip. I'll get over it."

He kisses the top of my head and gives me a squeeze. "I know it won't be the same as going with your best friend, but I can take you some time, if you'd like."

Smiling, I look up at him and kiss his jaw. "I'd like that."

"Okay, once the butter is spread—wait, no, just two-thirds, stick to this side," Rowan says, his voice patient and calm despite my anxiously trying to predict what we do next. And it's not on purpose either. For some reason I feel flustered, like I need to impress him or something.

Before we started baking, Rowan took me over to the bakeshop, where Elsbeth, Isla's assistant, was filling in for her. We ordered some chicken curry pies, grabbed some fruit and drinks from the Mill Market, and had a quaint lunch in front of the loch, where Rowan regaled me with story after story of him and the Murdach twins getting into trouble. And funnily enough, as Rowan was telling those stories, they ran by us, shirtless, wearing their kilts and hoisting logs, with their "cameraman," a local boy named Dennis, following closely behind.

Once we packed up, we headed into the "wee" kitchen in the back of the coffee shop. It might be small, but there are multiple ovens, which is exactly what we need for our three types of baked goods.

While he spread out the groceries, I whipped open an apron and then reached for the hem of my shirt. As promised, I was ready to bake in the nude, but he quickly held my hands down and said he loved the idea of me naked, but not when anyone could walk in, especially with the way Fergus comes in and out of his own accord. Rowan claimed that being caught naked in front of a historically significant goat would read a little weird. I had to agree with him. Fergus feels like a brother at this point, and I'd never want my brother to catch me in the buff. So, the clothes stayed on.

"You don't spread it all over the dough?" I ask now, staring down at the butter combination gracing my latest attempt at butteries.

"No. Just this section. Then we'll fold the dough three times, roll it back out to the original starting size, and let it cool for forty minutes."

"You let it cool?" A light bulb goes on in my head. "Oh, I wasn't doing that when I tried to make them. I would just go into folding and rolling again. That's why it was melting, huh?"

He nods. "Aye, you have to let the butter cool before you start working it again."

"So then, these take forever to make."

"But they're worth it, and if you time it right, you can have multiple batches going at the same time, along with other items like the tattie scones. You could also make the dough the day before and bake them in the morning. That's what my da would do. When things started to get slow toward the end of the workday, he'd always get the dough ready."

"Oh, that's a really good idea."

Together we roll out the dough and then set it to the side to cool— as far away from the ovens as possible.

"Let's start on the tattie scones." He pulls out a large can of premade mashed potatoes, and I gasp out loud.

"You use premade mashed potatoes?"

He chuckles. "Old family secret. You can't tell the difference, and it cuts down the work significantly."

"Wow, the MacGregor clan, cutting corners. I kind of like it."

"You'll like it a lot, because the recipe calls for a pound of mashed potatoes, and I doubt you're going to want to peel, chop, and boil multiple batches of potatoes every day."

"I didn't even think about that."

He gives me a chaste peck on my cheek. "Stick with me, lass—I'll show you all the tricks."

He sets out everything we'll need for the tattie scones, and even though I know he's been weird about it, I still can't help the question that flies past my lips. "Why are you so reluctant about baking for the coffee shop?"

"I knew you were going to ask that today." He checks the recipe again. "Surprised it took you this long."

"You don't have to answer me if you don't want to. I was just curious. You seem to be so good at it."

"I am. Growing up, we always helped in the kitchen. But Callum had a passion for it. He had plans to grow the coffee shop with Da, possibly expand over into Kyle. The butteries were their bread and butter—no pun intended. Not many people will take the time to make them, but a lot of people want them."

"I can see that."

Turning around, Rowan folds his arms over his chest and leans against the counter, his eyes looking toward the open window that's letting in a nice, cool breeze. "Growing up, it was clear I wasn't set on working in the coffee shop. I wanted . . . other things. Da wasn't happy about that, but he accepted it because he had Callum. They were much closer than I've ever been with me da. But the day Callum died was the worst day of my life, and not just because I lost my brother. I also lost my father."

"What do you mean?" I ask, stepping in close to him and placing my hands on his folded arms.

"Our relationship was already a bit . . . strained, but then he blamed me for what happened. Blamed me for Callum drinking, for not being cautious, for us being a bunch of eejits."

"But it wasn't your fault—you couldn't have predicted what was going to happen."

"He didn't see it that way. I'm the older son, the protector, and that day, I didn't protect my brother. It caused a huge rift in the family. Da was broken, and working in the shop every day—without Callum—just about killed him. Slowly, his spirit started to fall, his willingness to try new things vanished, and he stuck to simple things, because simple was all his heart could handle. Finally, by the time he was ready to retire, he would only serve butteries, and mainly to the locals." He reaches out and pushes a strand of my hair out of my face and behind my ear. "I told Da I'd help him. That I would make it up to him, help him bake, make Callum's dreams a reality."

He chokes up, and my heart nearly breaks. I run my hand up to his chest and press my palm to his heart, letting him know I'm here.

"Da didn't want my help. Said he never wanted to see me in this kitchen again. *I* was the one who didn't want a part of this life, so I didn't get to have it. And when I set out to find my own path, he shut that down too, said I needed to stay close for Maw and take care of the town. Corsekelly thrives off its own, and losing two MacGregor boys could break it. So . . . I stayed."

"Oh, Rowan." I hold back the tears that threaten to fall. "I'm so sorry."

This man has sacrificed a lot in his life. From the outside, it wouldn't look that way—he'd look like just another grouchy curmudgeon with something against out-of-towners, but peel back the layers and you'll find a beautiful soul, with an equally beautiful heart, wanting to help. He's just struggling to do so.

"So, why change? If you're not allowed in the kitchen, why now?"

The corner of his lip tilts up. "Well, this stunning blonde walked into my life and begged me." He smooths his thumb over my cheek. "I also saw the worry in Maw's eyes before they left. She's not the type to do something so extreme, like try to make an advert go viral. She's always been the quiet one and speaks up when the time is right. Something must be going on for her to have brought you and Dakota in." He looks off to the side, a clench to his jaw. "Something is going on with them, and they're not telling me. So I figured, if they're not going to tell me, then at least I can help you make their life's work into something more. Restrictions be damned."

I take a second and move my finger up to his jaw, where I turn his head. "You're a good man, Rowan MacGregor," I say, gazing into his eyes.

"It means a lot to hear you say that, lass."

"I believe it wholeheartedly." I roll up onto my toes, grip the back of his neck, and bring his mouth to mine. I linger longer than I should, especially since we have a lot of baking to do, but I want him to know how important he is, how wonderful he is.

When I pull away, he lazily smiles. "I hope you don't plan on doing that a lot—I'm not sure we're going to get much accomplished if you do."

I chuckle. "I want more cherry cake, and since you saved that for last, I think we both know there will be no more kissing."

"Not *no* more," he says, looping his arms around my waist and pulling me in so I can't escape.

"Minimal."

He kisses the tip of my nose. "I can agree to minimal, as long as you come over tonight."

"As if I would be anywhere else."

One more kiss and he releases me. "Okay, tattie scones, let's get to it."

"Hey." I place my hand on his arm. "Thank you for sharing with me. It means a lot that you trust me with this part of your life."

"You make it easy, lass."

We turn back to the ingredients, and he shows me the next steps in preparing the dough—but the entire time, all I can think about is how much Corsekelly is starting to feel like home, how this man makes me feel more special, more important, than any person I've ever met, and being here, in the kitchen, with something to do, I feel . . . purpose.

Maybe this is what I was meant to do. Where I was meant to be all along.

◆ ◆ ◆

"I'm nervous," I say, wringing my hands together as we wait for a few select locals to arrive.

"Don't be nervous, lass."

We spent the entire day baking. I'm exhausted, but I'm invigorated as well. Rowan was very pleased with how everything was looking, especially the butteries, and now we're holding a small tasting party for a few close people who know the kind of quality Stuart would provide with his baked goods.

I haven't tasted anything yet—I wanted to taste with everyone else. I didn't trust myself to judge if my baking actually is any good. Rowan decided to wait with me as well.

Also, between you and me, I was too damn nervous. The possibility of failure hangs over me, ready to rain down on me like a brilliant Scottish storm, and I'm trying to prolong things, hoping and praying the clouds will part and the success of the sun will shine through.

We invited four people: the Murdach twins, Shona from the Mill Market, and Hamish, all of whom were avid patrons and buttery eaters before Stuart retired.

Rowan glances down at my fidgeting fingers and kisses the side of my head. "Relax."

"You didn't prep them, did you? They're not going to be nice, just to be nice, right?"

"Trust me, they would never do that. They're all excited about the changes being made, but they were most worried about the baking. If you're bringing the coffee shop back to life, they want it done right."

"Oh, not to add any pressure . . ."

He chuckles. "Lass, I was there the entire time you baked, and I know you followed every direction carefully. This is going to go really well."

"I hope so." I look out the window, wondering when they're going to get here. "I just kind of wish Dakota was here. She was supposed to be."

"Did you tell her about the tasting?"

"Yeah. I assumed she would be here to support me."

"Maybe she forgot." *Because she's wrapped up in Isla . . .*

"She probably did." Which doesn't make me feel any better. I finally find something that I might be good at—*might* being the key word at this point; we'll find out soon if I'm not—and she's not here. She knows how important this is to me. I even sent her a text a while ago with pictures of all my baked goods, but I haven't heard back from her.

I don't want to admit it because I think I might be acting like a dramatic teenager, but I'm starting to feel a little bitter.

I know, I know, she's fresh in a relationship—I should cut her some slack.

Deep breath, Bonnie.

You don't need your best friend for everything.

At least, that's what I'm trying to convince myself of.

"Here they come," Rowan says. "They're going to love it."

Leith and Lachlan walk in first and immediately stop at the threshold of the shop. Leith presses his hand to Lachlan's chest. "Holy shite, it smells good in here."

Lachlan sniffs around and then grasps Leith's hand. "Hell, I was just brought back to secondary school, when we used to sneak in here and steal butteries with Rowan."

"Told you, lass," Rowan whispers to me before turning to Leith and Lachlan. "Take a seat, lads."

Hamish and Shona walk in next, and since they haven't seen the changes we've made to the shop, I giddily watch the awe in their eyes as they take it all in.

"Wow," Shona says, "it looks great in here."

"Thank you," I say, stepping up next to them. "We have some pictures of the hairy coo we still need to hang, and Rowan still needs to install the inside shutters that match the outside ones. And he needs to make some shelving for merchandise, but that's last."

"It's quite lovely," Hamish says, taking a seat and running his hand over the new tables. "Are these from Campbell's?"

"Aye," Rowan says. "He let us do some mix-matching."

Shona takes a seat as well. "I love it. Och, darling, Finella and Stuart are going to love these changes."

Pride surges through me as Rowan places a plate of our baked goods in front of everyone, as well as a small cup of tea and a small cup of coffee.

"Bonnie made classic butteries, tattie scones, and then cherry cake. On the table there is jam and butter, and the tea and coffee, whichever you prefer."

"We hope to offer five varieties of tea and ten different coffee drinks," I add. "We don't want to do more than that. We'll keep it simple, but with a little bit of flair."

"Good choices," Hamish says, looking over the little mock-up menu we have on each table as well. "These will work well for the tourists coming in and out. Now, you're just sticking with these three baked goods?"

I nod. "Yes, we figured if they want more they can go to the bakeshop. We also didn't want to step on Isla's toes."

"Aye," Hamish says.

"Dig in," Rowan says as he takes my hand and sits me down at one of the other tables, facing away from everyone. "Time to taste test, lass." He hands me a plate, and I gaze down at all the hard work I put into today. Never in a million years would I have thought I'd be living in Scotland, baking traditional treats with a hunky Scotsman, but here I am, living out the wildest dream I never knew I had.

I'm about to pick up my buttery when a long, loud moan erupts from behind me. I turn around to see Leith slouched in his chair, buttery in one hand, his eyes nearly rolling to the back of his head. "Sweet Jesus, these are outstanding." He takes another bite. "God bless America and Bonnie."

I chuckle just as Lachlan has the same reaction. "Hell's bells, these are phenomenal." He takes a huge bite, nearly stuffing it all in his mouth.

The nerves I was feeling quickly vanish as pleased sounds fill the coffee shop. Rowan winks at me and takes a bite of his buttery. As he chews, a smile plays at his lips.

"Bonnie, these are really fucking good."

"Yeah?"

He slowly nods. "Aye. They're perfect, lass."

They're perfect, lass. I don't believe anything I've ever done has been perfect. I've never found that something that has made me special. I've never uncovered a hidden talent that set me apart from everyone else. Never once have I exceeded expectations. I've been average. Average my entire life.

But to hear Rowan say something I created is perfect?

255

It brings tears to my eyes. For the first time in my adult life, I actually feel accomplished. I feel like I'm contributing to something bigger than myself, and I'm not just running errands and making sure there is a certain kind of candy in someone's dressing room. I'm actually providing a service with my very own hands—and it makes people happy.

And even though this moment feels monumental to me, one person is missing, and I want her approval more than anything. I wish she could have seen Leith's and Lachlan's reactions, could have heard Shona's kind words.

My best friend's—the one opinion I truly care about.

I might have done a good job, but it feels bittersweet.

"Bonnie, you okay?" Rowan asks. "You haven't taken a bite yet."

"Oh, yeah . . . fine." I try to push back my thoughts of my floundering relationship with Dakota and enjoy this moment. I lift up the buttery and smile. "Here goes nothing."

I glance at the clock one more time.

Nine at night.

Where the hell are they?

I told Rowan I wanted to spend some time with Dakota when she got home from Inverness, so I skipped out on going to his place, even though I desperately wanted to. After the emotional drain of yesterday's tasting, we both snuggled into his bed last night, and most of today, just holding each other. But now that I'm waiting for Dakota to show up, frustration washes over me—frustration that could easily be fixed by what Rowan hides under his kilt. I say that without ever having seen him in a kilt. Trust me, though, I have had fantasies of it.

Tapping my finger on the table, I stand from one of the red couches and start to pace the quaint living space.

I'm wearing one of Rowan's shirts, and I can still smell his cologne on the fabric, the subtle scent occasionally calming my boiling anger.

Well, I'm not boiling—just simmering at this point.

Lights flash down the driveway, and I quickly run to the door and look out the window. Isla's car moves down the gravel, and because I've reached a borderline psychotic level of "Is my friend dead or is she being rude and not letting me know her whereabouts?" I fling the door open and stand on the threshold.

Isla turns off the car, and the lights fade into the darkening evening. Dakota opens the passenger door and says, "Bonnie, is everything okay?"

Now, be calm. She might have a good explanation as to why she said she would be home around dinnertime and then shows up around bedtime.

There could be a very reasonable explanation. *Whatever you do, do not snap at her—that will put her on the defensive.*

"Where the hell have you been?" I ask, hands on my hips.

Good job, Bonnie.

She frowns and shuts the door to the car as Isla comes around with Dakota's bag.

"I'll, uh, leave you two alone." Isla tilts Dakota's face toward her and places a hand on her hip before leaning in and pressing a kiss to her lips. Like the angry voyeur I am, I stand there, staring at their sweet goodbye, not even bothering to look away and give them privacy. When they step apart, I hear Isla murmur, "Thank you for last night."

Then she turns to me and waves. "Have a good night, Bonnie."

"Yeah, you too," I say awkwardly as anger boils inside me. When I turn to look at my friend, the same anger is mirrored in her as she stalks toward the cottage, bag in hand. She doesn't even wait for me to move, bumping my shoulder as she enters.

I shut the door behind me and slip on my metaphorical boxing gloves.

But Dakota doesn't say anything. Instead, she goes straight to her room.

"Uh, care to talk to me?" I call out.

"No."

She shuts her bedroom door.

Why the hell is she mad?

She doesn't get to be mad.

I'm the mad one right now.

Storming toward her door, I fling it open to find her texting on her phone, most likely to Isla about her psycho best friend.

"Where have you been?" I feel like the mother of a teenager right now, demanding answers, and from the annoyed look I get from her, I really am feeling the teenage vibes.

"With Isla."

Duh.

"You said you were going to be here by dinnertime."

"Yeah, well, we stopped somewhere and had dinner."

"You could have told me."

"Why? You're not my mother."

"Uh, excuse me?" I say, nearly blown over by her attitude. "First of all, where is this sass coming from? Second of all, pardon me for caring if you're dead or alive."

Dakota flings her arm to the side. "That was embarrassing back there, and you made Isla uncomfortable."

"I was worried."

"Worried about what? Your espresso machine and signage? Don't worry, we dropped it off at the shop. You can go check if you want."

"What? Are you serious? Dakota, I was worried about *you.*"

"So is that why you kept texting me all day yesterday and today about the sign but never thought to ask how our trip was?"

She stands, grabs her bag, and pushes past me.

"Where are you going?"

"Isla's."

"The hell you are." I charge toward the door and stand in front of it, barring her escape. "We're still talking, and I'll have you know, I didn't ask about your trip because I was hurt."

"Hurt? About what?"

"We were supposed to go to Inverness together."

Dakota opens her mouth and then closes it. The tension in her shoulders drops. "I thought that was a joke."

"You might have thought it was, but I thought we were going to sightsee together."

"We did. We went through the Highlands."

"A portion, but there is so much more of Scotland, and Inverness is a day trip."

"I didn't know," she says calmly, the steam quickly fading. "Isla was excited to show me around, and I didn't want to say no. I was thrilled she even asked me, you know, since Isabella never wanted to take me anywhere. I'm sorry, Bonnie."

Two words, that's all it takes. Two words to break me down into a bubbling mess.

Tears well up in my eyes.

Throat constricts.

And then I'm a pile of emotions, sitting on the floor.

Dakota sits next to me and wraps her arm around my shoulder. "Hey, I didn't know it meant that much to you. I really am sorry."

"It's not that." I take a deep breath and consider telling her how I've been feeling lately.

Left out.

Forgotten.

Like I'm losing my best friend to someone else.

Like I'm no longer needed or important to my person.

But in the grand scheme of things, it seems so juvenile and not something that needs to drag down this moment. Dakota is here now, and we have a little more time before we truly have to go to bed. We should make the most of it.

"Then, what is it?"

"Stressed," I answer. "I've just been really stressed lately, and not knowing where you were only added to that. I'm sorry if I embarrassed you."

"No, you're right, I should have texted. It was just a good day, and I got lost in the moment. But I don't want to talk about that." She pulls me to my feet. "Did you sleep over at Rowan's again?"

I smile. "I did."

"Mmm-hmm." Dakota wiggles her eyebrows like a dork.

"I'm going to break the news to you right now—anytime I'm over at Rowan's, you can count on us having sex. No need to wiggle your eyebrows."

She chuckles and then yawns. "Figured as much. Hey, I'm super tired from the last two days. I think I'm going to head to bed, okay?"

"Oh . . . okay, sure," I say, a little caught off guard.

"Was there something you wanted to talk to me about?" Dakota asks, sensing my hesitancy.

"No, I just thought we could catch up, but I get it." I fake yawn. "Long day over here too."

"Bonnie, we can catch up tomorrow, at the shop."

"True. Doye." I playfully hit my forehead, knowing for damn certain that I've never said the word *doye* out loud in my entire life. "Okay, then. I guess I'll catch you on the flippity-flop."

Dakota's eyes narrow. "You're being weird."

"Too much sugar. You know how I get." I twirl my finger next to my ear. "Crazy. Anyhoo." I pat my stomach for some reason and then jab my thumb toward the stairs. "Guess I'll be on my way."

"Oh-kay," she drags out, watching me moonwalk to the stairs. "Good night."

"Good night."

When I reach my bedroom, I fling myself onto my bed and stare up at the ceiling. What the hell was that?

For certain, it was the most awkward interaction I've ever had with Dakota, even worse than the time I thought I got my period when we were playing in her backyard and she hadn't gotten hers yet, so I knew she wouldn't understand the severity of not being prepared. What just happened was way worse than that.

With a sigh, I roll to my side and pick up my phone to set an alarm for my morning hairy coo walk. That's when I catch a text from Rowan.

I quickly open it, ready to cling to anything that might possibly take away this heavy buildup that's sitting on my lungs like a ten-ton weight.

Rowan: Hope you're having fun with Dakota. Wanted to quickly say I was very impressed with you yesterday. Proud to call you me girl. Night, lass.

I press my lips together as they tremble. A single tear falls down the side of my face.

How did he know I needed that text more than anything right now?

Through blurred vision, I text him back.

Bonnie: Thank you, Rowan, that means a lot. Must be that one-sixteenth Scottish in me that makes me such a good baker, huh?

He texts back right away.

Rowan: Sorry to break it to you, lass. One sixteenth is barely a blip in the gene pool.

Bonnie: Don't you belittle my heritage.

Rowan: Not belittling, just helping you understand, your one-sixteenth has nothing on this one hundred percenter.

Bonnie: If you were one hundred percent Scottish, then I would have seen you in a kilt already.

Rowan: All in good time, lass. Good night. Wish you were here.

Bonnie: Wish I was there too. Good night, Rowan.

I clutch my phone to my chest and stare up at the ceiling as a long sigh flows out of my lungs. Oh God . . . I like the man. A lot.

I like how he cares for me.

How he teases me.

How he's protective and can sense when something is bothering me.

I like his smile and his deep voice that rattles me to my very core when he whispers in my ear.

I like that he's proud of me . . .

I like . . . oh God . . . I think I love him.

"Bonnie, hey, wait up."

I turn to find Isla jogging up to me just as I step onto the Hairy Coo Footpath. It's early, the fog still lifting off the grass as the sun barely peeks over the horizon. I had a hard time falling asleep last night and wound up waking early, my mind whirring over all the changes in my life.

Rowan.

The coffee shop.

Dakota.

It's weighing heavily on me.

"Good morning, Isla," I say, slowing down so she can catch up.

"Morning to ye. Are you open to having a walking partner?"

"Sure," I answer, right before giving her a hug hello.

Together, we walk down the path and around the bend where I ran smack into a shirtless Rowan, though he's absent from this go-around. Unfortunately. Wouldn't mind another sweaty stone wall to the face right about now, especially after not seeing him last night.

"Sorry about getting Dakota back late. If I knew you were worried, I would have never suggested we go out for a bite."

"Oh, no need to apologize. It's fine," I say as the back of my neck heats up with embarrassment. "I'm sorry if I was rude to you."

She chuckles. "Look at us, apologizing for something so small."

"Typical ladies," I joke.

"I do want to make sure you like me, though, because I really like Dakota."

Shocked, I turn toward her and stop her with a hand to her arm. "Isla, I do like you. Have I given off the vibe that I don't?"

"No, not really. I mean, maybe a little, and when I asked Dakota about it, she said you've just been busy—but I wasn't sure if that was a cover-up."

Confrontation—with someone other than Dakota—is not something I'm comfortable with. When it comes to my friendship with Dakota, I can tell her anything, talk to her about anything, and truly express my feelings. But with anyone else, I just turn into an apologetic mess and try to smooth things over quickly so I can be done with the awkward tornado that just blew in and blew out.

"It wasn't a cover-up." We start walking again. "I've been stressed and maybe . . . a little jealous of the two of you. I know that sounds stupid and I shouldn't be jealous. *I* was the one encouraging Dakota to start dating again, but I just felt her pulling away, and it made me a little crazy. If that makes sense."

"Aye, I understand. You two have such a strong bond."

"Yes, and after things ended with Isabella, I had Dakota all to myself again, and I soaked that up. Isabella took a lot of Dakota time away from me, and it was painful. Maybe I was having some flashbacks, I don't know. Either way, I really do like you, Isla. I think you're lovely and sweet, and I know your intentions are honest. Plus, Rowan has nothing but the best to say about you. He once told me if I should trust my best friend with anyone, it should be you."

"Thank you. I think very highly of Rowan myself. You two are the perfect balance for each other."

"We can drive each other mad at the drop of a hat, but we also make each other very happy."

"And that's what matters." We pass the first cattle pasture, but unluckily for us, the cute shaggy beasts are too far away to try to pet, so we keep walking. "Can I ask you something?"

"Sure, anything," I answer.

"Isabella . . . what did she *do* to Dakota? I had a lot of fun this past weekend, but I felt Dakota shutting down on me at some points, especially when it came to going to bed. She was very stiff. I ended up holding her to try to get her to relax, and once she did, we were able to have a . . . er . . . a really good evening."

"When you say 'really good,' do you mean you two got frisky?" I laugh, and so does Isla.

"I mean, I don't kiss and tell."

"But you sure do blush when you mention it."

"Damn these Scottish cheeks." She presses her hands to her red face.

"Spare me the details, but if we're being serious, yeah, Isabella did a number on Dakota. It's taken her a year to get back into dating."

"What did she do?"

"What didn't she do?" I ask, rolling my eyes. "She was Dakota's first girlfriend ever, which is a revelation on its own, but pair that with someone who is vindictive and manipulative, and you have a recipe for disaster. Dakota started to equate her gayness to everything Isabella didn't like about her. So she thought if she dressed in a way that Isabella didn't like, she wasn't being a proper lesbian. If she didn't kiss a certain way, talk a certain way, publicly display her affection a certain way, that it was all wrong."

"Och, that's awful."

"It was really bad. Dakota felt broken for a very long time. She would second-guess herself, wonder if she was actually gay or if it was Isabella. She was completely mind-fucked."

"Well, that would explain why she apologizes or second-guesses every move she makes and everything she says. When we kissed for the first time, she pulled away and apologized right before she tried to flee the scene. I had to reassure her I desperately wanted her to kiss me. And I feel like I do that more often than not."

"Reassure her?"

"Aye," Isla sighs. "I'm not irritated with having to tell her how beautiful she is or talented or thoughtful. It's that I wish she saw it herself, ye ken?"

"I know exactly what you're talking about, and I think it will all come in time. She needs to be with the right person, and once she starts seeing the value in herself, it will shine through. Trust me, Dakota can't be knocked down for that long. She's strong willed and has always been bound and determined to make something of herself. Keep working on her, don't let her apologize for something she shouldn't be apologizing for, and show her what it's like to be in a healthy, normal relationship."

"That's really good advice. Thank ye, Bonnie."

"Of course. Always feel free to come to me with questions. I'm the Dakota whisperer."

"I'll hold you to that." She bumps my shoulder, and even though I haven't spoken to Dakota yet today, deep down I feel just a little bit closer to her after talking to Isla.

See, Bonnie, everything is going to be okay.

Chapter Seventeen
ROWAN

Days since I realized I'm falling for Bonnie: One.
Hours spent thinking about Bonnie: Every single goddamn hour.
I'm toast.
Roasted.
Charred and served.
Bonnie has planted herself in my headspace, and nothing can remove her.
Nothing.

◆ ◆ ◆

"You're gorgeous," I say as Bonnie sinks down on my length until she bottoms out.

The minute she got to my place, she stripped down, pushed me into my bedroom, and relieved me of my clothes. She then spent a good ten minutes worshipping my body until I couldn't take it anymore. She sheathed me with a condom and is now slowly rocking up and down my shaft.

"I missed you," she says, looking down at me, her hair like a golden curtain pushed to the side. "Is it desperate that I missed you?"

I chuckle and grip her hips, trying to entice her to pick up the pace, but instead she draws it out some more. "Nay, lass. I missed you too."

"Missed me, or missed sex?"

"Missed you more, but I did miss this with you."

She smirks. "Good answer." Her hands fall to my torso and drag up to my pecs, where she grips and shifts her body, giving us a different angle. It must really work for her, because her mouth falls open and a low moan erupts from her.

"Just like that," I say, pushing my pelvis up into her. "Fuck, you feel perfect."

She grips my cheek and presses her mouth to mine, begging for entrance with her tongue. I don't give it at first—instead, I let her live off closed but powerful kisses. She does everything she can to pry open my mouth, even bite my bottom lip, but I hold still as my hands travel down her back and grip her ass. I spread her cheeks and push up into her hard and fast. Her mouth pops off mine, and she cries out in pleasure.

"Yes, Rowan. Yes, please don't stop." She lifts up, one hand planted against my chest, the other pushing her hair back as her tits bounce right in front of me . . .

Hell.

"Bonnie," I choke out. "Lass, you there?"

Her eyes squeeze shut, her hips move faster, and I feel her start to clench around my cock instantaneously. "Oh . . . fuck," she whispers as her teeth pull on her bottom lip and she comes.

The feel of her tight warmth, wrapped around me, does me in. My balls tighten, pleasure rips through every limb, and my cock swells inside of her as I come harder than I can ever remember.

Together, we pulse out every last ounce of pleasure until we are completely spent.

After I clean us both up, I lean against the headboard and pull her close. She sighs against me, and I don't think I've ever been this fucking happy in my entire life.

"I'm hungry," she says as I play with her hair.

"Want some cake?"

She lifts up and looks me in the eyes. "You have cake?"

"I made some earlier today. Since you were coming over."

"If I didn't just have sex with you, I would be jumping on that Scottish sausage of yours."

"Eloquent." I reach over the bed and toss my shirt at her. "Put that on so I don't have to stare at your gorgeous body all night."

"What a travesty."

I throw on a pair of athletic shorts and then head to the kitchen, where I take down two of my hand-thrown plates that I fired up in the kiln the other day. They came out just the way I wanted, the glaze a beautiful mixture of blues and greens to represent the green of the Highlands and the blue of the lochs. My goal is to handmake all my plates and serving ware, but with how little free time I have, it's been taking me longer than I've wanted.

Not to mention, I was in a creative drought before Bonnie showed up. Now, it's as if the potter's wheel is in my head, constantly turning with new ideas, techniques I want to try. Just need to find more time.

From the fridge, I take out the chocolate cake with chocolate frosting I made earlier and cut two large slices. I know my girl, and she's not shy about her portions of cake. Might as well give her the amount she's actually going to eat so she doesn't have to ask for another helping.

When I turn around, I find her curled up on the sofa, hair piled on top of her head, looking fresh, with a little bit of beard burn on her cheeks.

I walk over to her and drag my finger over her reddened cheek. "Does this hurt?"

She shakes her head. "No, I like knowing you've claimed me."

Smiling, I lean down and lift her to a sitting position. "Good, because you're mine." I press a quick kiss to her lips and then head to the kitchen, where I grab our plates.

"Why are you so amazing?" she asks when I hand her the plate. "Did you make this from scratch?"

"How else do you make a cake?"

She takes a bite and moans. "God, that's so good. So much better than when I make a cake from a box."

"Me da would have a coronary if you ever gave him a boxed cake."

"Scottish snobs," she scoffs with a grin. "So, I was thinking about putting the menus up this Friday, after making a few more batches of the butteries and scones. See how the Friday and Saturday tour buses react, then assess and make adjustments for Monday. What do you think?"

"Do you feel comfortable with the espresso machine?"

She nods, her mouth full of cake. When she swallows, she says, "I spent a year using this exact machine when I worked with Lisa. She preferred a certain coffee bean combination, freshly ground, and then made on the spot. I got exceptionally good at some pretty fancy drinks. Caramel macchiatos, americanos, and cappuccinos were my go-tos. I was nervous to come to this job because I didn't know the kind of experience needed, but when I saw the extent of drink choices in the shop, I knew my skills were more than adequate. I'm comfortable making what we have on the menu, and I can nail those drinks."

"And baking, how do you feel about taking on that part of the job?"

"Good. I want to stock up a little this week on the butteries and store them like you told me. I'll save the fresh ones for the locals—"

"Smart."

"Want to keep them on my good side. I don't think the cake will go as fast as the other two, but we'll see. I'll have a few of those ready to cut into slices. I ordered recyclable takeout containers. Even though the Styrofoam was cheaper, I couldn't save the extra penny knowing the kind of waste they are."

"Maw would be happy with that choice, especially since we always find discarded takeaway containers whenever we go on Highland walks. Probably thrown there by tourists."

"I don't understand how someone can do that. Just toss trash into the wild as if it's their own personal dumpster."

"Me neither, but you can't fix everyone. We can only do our best, and making conscious decisions like that helps."

"Why, McGrumpyshire, are you an earth lover?"

"When you live in a place like Corsekelly, how could you not be?"

"True." She sinks her fork into the cake and picks up another bite. "So, you think Friday, a tiny grand opening?"

"Aye. I think that's a great idea."

"Great. I'll also email the tour bus companies about our changes."

"Well, I'll be first in line when you open up."

"Yeah?" She leans over and presses a chocolatey kiss to my lips. "You'll really show up?"

"Aye."

"Promise?"

"Promise. You're my girl, aren't you?" I ask.

"You tell me . . . am I?" she asks coyly.

I lean over this time and cup her chin. "You know you are."

"Soo, does *girl* mean 'girlfriend' in Scottish? Are you going to introduce me like this . . ." She clears her throat and impersonates a terrible Scottish accent. "Aye, ye bawbag, 'tis here me lass. She owns me boaby."

I don't answer right away. Instead, I just stare at her, and she wilts under my gaze, fidgeting, trying to smile, trying everything to avoid eye contact.

Finally she asks, "Can you not stare at me like that? It makes me horny."

"What?" I ask, laughing.

"Aha! Broke the silence." She snaps her fingers in victory. "Knew that was going to work."

Shaking my head, I lean back in my chair and stare at her some more. Fucking crazy, unpredictable woman, but even in all her unpredictability, she excites me.

"Question," she says, mouth full. "When your parents get back, do you think you're going to have a conversation with them?"

I feel my brows draw together. "Talk to them about what?"

"The whole 'not doing what you want to do with your life' thing. It just seemed like you had fun in the kitchen with me. Wasn't sure if you would cross that bridge with your parents again."

"No." I keep my answer short and concise, hoping she'll move on from the topic.

"Rowan, you can't possibly walk around here unhappy for the rest of your life."

"I'm not unhappy."

"Could have fooled me," she mumbles, avoiding eye contact.

"How the hell am I not happy? You make me happy, Bonnie."

That grants me a smile, but when she reaches over to take my hand in hers, I know it's not enough. "I know a lost soul when I see one. We recognize ourselves in others. You're lost, Rowan."

"Where the hell is this all coming from?" Talk about the night making a fucking one-eighty.

Sex.

Cake.

Now a serious conversation about how I'm not living my life?

Color me fucking confused.

"I don't know—you seemed so happy baking with me."

"Because I was with *you*," I say.

"Then, what is it that will make you happy?"

I slide my empty plate to the side. "Ending this conversation."

"Why won't you tell me what it is you want to do in life?"

"Why does it matter? It's never going to fucking happen, so there's no use talking about it." I push out of my chair and grab my plate, setting it in the sink before striding back to my bedroom. Then, sinking down on the edge of the bed, I push my hands through my hair. Annoyed, frustrated, wishing she'd never brought this topic up to begin with.

It doesn't take her much time to follow me, and when she enters the room, she climbs up on the bed, drops the shirt she was wearing on the floor, and presses her body against my back. Her hands float to my front, and she kisses my shoulder blades.

"I'm sorry," she whispers. "I didn't mean to make you upset."

Hell, I shouldn't have snapped at her. There's no excuse. I'm just not ready to share that part of my life, not when she's striving to succeed at something. I don't want her to see my failure and think what she's doing isn't possible.

"Just drop it, okay?"

"Okay," she says, smoothing her hands down to my stomach. She slips a hand under the waistband of my shorts and grips me tightly.

Fuck.

From that one touch, I'm hard.

She scoots away from my back and lays me down on the bed. "Push your shorts down for me."

Desperate to forget those last few minutes, I do just that and free myself, letting my erection spring forward.

And then she straddles me, sitting on my chest and leaning forward to take me into her mouth. Her bottom half is in perfect reach, and I bring her to my mouth, where I quickly find her clit and start kissing her, licking her, letting her know that even when I snap at her, I want her just the same.

◆ ◆ ◆

"Stay for breakfast," I say, tugging on Bonnie's arm.

"You said I *was* breakfast," she counters, brushing the wet tangles out of her hair. "Or were you lying just to get in the shower with me?"

"I was lying," I admit, feeling hungry for her again.

"Can't fault a guy for being honest, even after the fact. What's for breakfast?"

"Yogurt parfaits."

"Really?" she asks, eyebrows rising.

"What's wrong with that?"

"Nothing. Just surprised, I guess. Are you going to layer the fruit?"

"That's what a parfait is, isn't it?" I stand from the bed and gently pat her on the arse on the way out to the kitchen.

"What kind of yogurt?"

"Vanilla," I call out just as my phone rings in my jeans pocket. I pull it out and see my maw's name flash across the screen. "Hello?"

"Rowan, good morning."

"Good morning, Maw," I say, already on edge from the weary tone in her voice. "Everything okay?"

Bonnie comes into the room, looking concerned.

"I have your da here with me. Say hello, Stuart."

"Hello," my da's gruff voice sounds through the phone.

"Morning, Da."

"Do you have a moment to chat?" Maw asks. "We need to talk to you about something important."

"Er, something important," I say, glancing at Bonnie. She motions to the door, and I shake my head. "Hold on, Maw." I put the phone on mute and say, "Can you give me a few minutes? Don't leave. This won't take long."

"Sure, I'll go for a quick walk and be back. I'm going to need to see those yogurt parfait skills."

I wink. "You got it." She slips her sandals on and then lets herself out of the cottage. Taking the phone off mute, I say, "Okay, sorry about that. Is this about some of the expenses on the credit card for the shop?" I had a wee feeling they might question those. Maw encouraged Dakota and Bonnie to make some changes if they saw fit, but I can understand if they're concerned.

"Nay," Maw says. "It's about your da."

The hairs on the back of my neck rise, and I take a seat at my dining table. Silence falls on the other end of the line as well, and an uncertain feeling of impending bad news creeps into my stomach.

"Everything okay, Da?" I ask, swallowing hard.

"We hate to do this over the phone, but we won't see you in person for a few more months, and we've been told you need to know."

My hands start to shake, my lungs tighten, and that uncertain feeling turns into pure fear. "What's wrong?"

There's a pregnant pause, and the only thing I can hear is my own heartbeat, pounding desperately for good news but knowing that's not going to be the case.

"Your da's sick, Rowan."

Fuck.

I knew something was going on. I fucking knew it.

My hand goes to my hair, and I pull on the short strands. "How sick?"

"It started a few months ago, right before he retired from the coffee shop. He wasn't feeling himself, and we assumed it was his arthritis kicking in, making daily tasks around the shop harder. We have plenty saved for retirement, so we figured it would be okay—that was, until we went to the doctor. We were devastated to find out he, er . . . he has bone cancer."

"What?" I whisper, my heart pounding so hard I think for a moment that I misheard her. "Bone cancer?"

"Aye," Maw confirms. "To be truthful, we aren't really on holibags right now. We're in London, talking with a specialist and going through treatments."

What the fucking shite?

"Why the fuck didn't you tell me?"

"Watch your tone," Da says, and even though his voice is weakened, it still packs a heavy punch.

"We didn't want to worry you," Maw speaks up. "We weren't quite sure about the severity of your da's cancer. We thought that if we shielded you from the truth, maybe we wouldn't have to worry you at all. We heard Dr. Irvine was very good at coming up with a treatment plan, but we knew he was expensive, since it's a private treatment. That's why I ran the advert for the coffee shop, hopefully to create some fun buzz, hire two strangers who might want to take on a project, bring it back to life so there's something to support us when we get back to Corsekelly."

"Jesus Christ," I mutter.

"But things haven't gone as we'd hoped here. Your da has quite a few tumors. Dr. Irvine took biopsies of all of them, and some are treatable, but there's one on his hip that is quite large and has spread to other parts of his body. Dr. Irvine . . . he . . ." Maw's voice breaks.

Her quiet weeping chokes me up as my mind whirls with confusion.

"I'm dying," Da finishes for her as she lets out a sob.

Dying.

My heart shatters into a million pieces.

Bone cancer.

Tumors.

Dying.

I can't seem to wrap my head around the actual facts; all I can focus on is why I'm just finding out about this now.

"You should have told me sooner," I choke out.

"It wasn't your right to know. We knew what we were doing," Da says, and that sets the spark that lights the raging fire inside me.

"To hell it's not!" I shout, standing now. "You're my goddamn father, and it's not only my right but my responsibility to know when you're sick, when you need help . . . when you're fucking dying!" I roar into the phone as every emotion I've ever had about my da bubbles up and pours out of me.

"Rowan," Da snaps, but I don't care—I keep pushing forward.

"You've known you've had cancer for the past few months and didn't tell me. When I asked you if you were sick before you left, you lied to my face."

"We didn't want to worry you," Maw repeats, always trying to play the peacemaker. Well, which is it? I didn't deserve to know, or they didn't want to worry me? It's always like this with them—Maw trying to smooth things over while Da and I light up the room with our anger.

"Ever care to think that I could have helped you? That's what family is for. And if you needed help with the coffee shop, Maw, I could have helped. I've already been helping—"

"You made it quite clear you wanted nothing to do with the shop," Da says, the stubborn arsehole throwing that in my face once again.

"People change," I say with a clenched jaw. "But you're too stubborn to see that. You can't possibly look past the history that clogs your wee brain and see that people change. People try to make their lives better, to make something of themselves."

"How's that going for you?" Da asks. "Haven't seen that pottery for sale anywhere. Haven't seen you live out the dream you wanted, that you threw your family away for."

What?

Where the hell did that come from?

"I didn't throw you away," I say, knowing we shouldn't be having this conversation right now. Da has cancer, a realization I'm sure he's having a hard time accepting. And knowing him, he's twisting and turning that confusion and fear into anger. He did the same thing when Callum passed—he directed all his anger at me. "I'm still here, taking care of the town's business like you wanted me to. Isn't that enough?"

"Not when you disrespect the MacGregor clan. We might be simple, but we're good people."

"You think I don't know that?"

"You don't show it."

Jesus fucking Christ. I don't think I've been this angry in my entire life. It feels like my soul is physically being stolen from my body with every passing breath, replaced with a darkness that's spreading through every limb, every muscle, every goddamn bone.

None of this matters—none of the history between my da and me matters right now, not when he's dying. He might want to continue our age-old argument, but I don't have time for that.

"Where are you?"

"Rowan, you don't need—"

"I swear to God, if you don't tell me, I'll track you down. I can look at your credit card statements. I can figure it out, so make it easy on both of us and tell me where the fuck you are."

Maw rattles off an address that I write down on a piece of paper. She tells me they still have another conversation with the doctor and not to worry, but it doesn't matter. Nothing they say will matter at this point. My mind is made up.

"We don't need you to come here," Da barks into the phone.

"Seems like you'd rather die than admit it, but you need me more than you think."

I hang up and toss my phone on the table. My knuckles turn white as I grip my dining table, and before I can even register what I'm doing, I pick it up and chuck it against the wall. Wood splinters from the crash as I roar, "Fuck!" and then dig my hands through my hair.

He's dying.

My da is dying and—

My gaze strays to the window, and I narrow my eyes. The doors to my pottery shed are wide open, and I catch a lock of blonde hair floating out of the entrance.

What the actual fuck?

Fury blazes inside me. I can feel my face turn red as I rage through the cottage, fling the door open, and stomp to the open shed.

Sure enough, Bonnie is standing inside, holding up a recently fired mug.

"What the hell are you doing in here?"

A frightened yelp escapes her lips as she jumps. The mug slips from her hands and shatters to the ground.

She turns toward me, and those crystal eyes widen, feigning innocence. "You see—"

"Don't fucking lie to me, Bonnie." She goes quiet, her shoulders sagging. I could see it before she even started talking: the telltale sign of her coming up with some elaborate explanation for invading my privacy.

"Well . . . ?" I press, folding my arms over my chest.

"Honestly"—she fidgets—"I wanted to see if this was where you kept your power washer. I thought maybe I would steal it and clean some of the algae off the cottage. But, oh my God, Rowan, you're a potter. How come you didn't—?"

"You had no right coming in here!" I yell, pointing at the shed.

Her body shifts backward from the power of my voice, and her eyes grow wider, more frightened. "I didn't . . ." She swallows hard. "I didn't think it was a big deal. I'm sorry, but Rowan, you're really good. You could sell this—"

"Out."

"Rowan, please, let me—"

"I said, fucking out!" I scream, my chest vibrating, my hands shaking, emotions surging through me. A breakdown is imminent.

Bonnie startles and hurries out of the shed. Once she's outside, I slam the doors shut and then spin on her. "Don't fucking go in there, do you hear me?"

She nods, tears brimming in her eyes.

"I . . . I'm sorry."

When I see the tears roll down her cheek, a wee voice in the back of my head tells me I need to apologize, but it's quickly drowned out by the uncontrollable rage that's piercing through me.

Fuck.

Bonnie . . . I'm . . . I'm sorry.

The thoughts ring through my head, but my mouth can't seem to form the words.

"Rowan, please say something," she begs, her beautiful eyes pleading, but a wave of numbness falls over me. Bonnie's distraught, and it's my fault, but I can't find it within me to care.

Turning away, I stride back to the cottage and flee to my room before slamming the door shut.

Sinking onto my bed, I bury my head in my hands and think about what the hell I'm going to do.

It takes about two seconds to decide.

London.

I'm going to London.

CHAPTER EIGHTEEN
BONNIE

Broken heart: *One.*
Nausea is in full force. What the hell just happened?

◆ ◆ ◆

I've seen Rowan grumpy.

I've even seen him angry.

But I've never seen him like that.

It was as if a completely different person took over his body and lashed out.

After he stormed back inside, I stood in front of the shed for a few moments until I found enough courage to go back to the cottage, but when I entered, he was locked in his room. His message was loud and clear: he didn't want me near him. After that, I didn't waste any time in leaving. I gathered my things and practically ran back to my cottage.

Now, sitting in my unmade bed, I wait for Dakota to get home.

When I was delirious and striding back to the cottage, I sent her a few panicked texts. When I got to my bedroom, a few more. And two minutes ago I tried calling, and after two rings, the phone went to voice mail.

No response.

No best friend when I need her the most.

Anxiety at an all-time high, I try to steady my breathing, knowing I have a lot to get done today.

I can do this. Everything will be okay.

God, I wish Dakota was here.

Shakily, I stand and change my clothes, feeling like I need a fresh start. Once my shoes are on, I stick my phone in the back pocket of my jean shorts and head to the coffee shop, where I find Fergus standing by the door.

Trusty, dependable—

"Ahhhhhh."

Screaming Fergus.

At the sight of what seems to be my only friend these days, I swallow down a flood of emotions and give him a pat on the head. "Good morning, Fergie. I see you're clearing the lungs out already. Getting ready to startle some tourists, I hope."

With a small back kick of his legs, he lifts his nose and clops away.

I'm going to take that as a morning greeting and not as another person screaming at me.

Making quick work of the lock, I let myself into the shop, flip on the lights, and take in the clean, white-walled space. We hung up the inside shutters and the pictures, giving the room a much more homey feeling. I'm still waiting on installing shelves, because we haven't settled on merchandise. Before we go all in, we want to make sure the baked goods and new coffee choices attract more business.

At least, that was the general consensus. Now I have no idea.

I make my way from table to table, setting the chairs on the floor and putting out the little vases Rowan brought in the other day. I pause, realization dawning on me as I look down at the vase in my hand. He made these. He said he had them lying around. But what he meant was they were lying around his shed.

I look at the bottom of the vase. No signature, no indication that he was the one who made them, and yet they're pristine. Beautifully shaped, with a red glaze that adds the perfect pop of color the space needs.

I should have asked him where they were from. I should have complimented them more. Then again, he probably wouldn't have admitted he made them. Is that what he's been hiding this whole time? The life he wanted to live but never got to?

Just as I set the vase down, the door to the shop opens and Dakota steps inside.

"Jesus, where have you been?" I ask, facing her. "Why didn't you answer my calls and texts?"

She doesn't respond. Instead, she crosses her arms over her chest, her stance defensive. I tense up, my gut telling me I'm about to be yelled at—again.

"Do you have something to tell me?"

I sigh. "Listen, Dakota, I really need a friend right now. Can we put whatever I did to make you mad on hold? I think Rowan just broke up with me and—"

"What did you say to Isla?"

So much for putting a pin in whatever I did. Nope, she's addressing it right now.

"Uh, I've said a lot of things to Isla."

"She told me she really appreciated the walk you guys took yesterday because you told her all about Isabella, and now she knows why I'm acting the way I'm acting."

Oh, the walk.

"I didn't say anything bad; I just told her about Isabella and how she was manipulative and vindictive. How you weren't sure if you knew how to be in a same-sex relationship. How you've been confused."

"Why would you tell her that?" Dakota asks, distress in her voice.

"She asked what Isabella did to you. What was I supposed to say?"

"Nothing. You were supposed to say nothing and then tell her that's a conversation she should have with me."

"What does it matter?" I ask, my brow furrowed. "It's the same information, and clearly you weren't telling her. It's something she needed to know. She was worried about you. She said you weren't clueing her in on anything."

"Because I wasn't ready to talk about it!" Dakota yells. "This isn't easy for me, Bonnie. I'm still self-conscious from my relationship with Isabella, and finding my authentic self has taken a long time, but I've made strides. I was just starting to feel like this soul I've buried for years is starting to flourish, and then you had to go and do that."

"Tell her to be patient with you?" I ask. "How is that hurting the situation?"

"You took my story away from me!" she shouts. "That is my story to tell, not yours. Now, instead of her coming to an understanding with me, listening to how I might talk about my past, she heard it from you, and it changes the narrative in her head. Instead of understanding . . . she pities me."

"What? No." I shake my head. "She doesn't pity you."

"And you don't fucking know everything," Dakota says, with such venom that I actually take a step back. I've never seen her this angry. "You weren't there. You didn't see the way Isla looked at me. You had no right to say anything to her."

"I was just being a friend."

"You have no idea how to be a friend." Her words slap me across the face.

"Excuse me?" Anger sears through me. "I don't know how to be a friend? You're the one who's never around when I need you."

"Exactly, Bonnie. When *you* need *me*. What about when I need you? Have you even asked me how things are with Isla? Asked about the weekend? Have you even remotely thought about how this is my second female relationship ever and wondered if I'm doing okay? Have you listened when I say that some of the things you say to Isla embarrass me? No, because you're too busy playing coffee shop and throwing yourself at Rowan."

"I don't throw myself at him."

"Okay," she scoffs, letting out a sarcastic laugh I don't like at all. "He wanted nothing to do with you, but you kept pressing and pressing—"

"Did he say that to you?" I ask, feeling my stomach drop. "Did he say he wanted nothing to do with me?"

"He told the Murdach twins he wanted to stay as far away from us as possible."

I bite my bottom lip, tears gathering in my eyes as the emotions of today pile on top of me, as the feeling of not being wanted consumes me. A tear slips down my cheek.

"I didn't know that," I say softly, clasping my hands together.

"It's because you never listen, Bonnie. You're self-absorbed, which is ironic, since you can't seem to figure out who you are or what you want to do."

I glance up, the truth in her words stinging. "You encouraged me to fix things up around here, told me that maybe I could find myself—"

"This is not your life!" Dakota shouts, flinging her arms out. "And you're making it your life. You came here to reflect, to figure out what you're good at, but instead you've just become so immersed in a project that you lost sight of everything around you and buried yourself in a relationship at the same time. You haven't found out who you really are."

"But what if I have? What if this is what I'm good at? Ever think about that? What if this is what I want to do?" I shout back.

"Is it?" she asks.

I open my mouth to answer, but I have nothing.

"Exactly," she says, as if to prove her point. "You came to Scotland to reconnect with yourself, but you've just pushed me away, gotten lost in a man, and focused on someone else's project without establishing who you actually are."

Is she right?

Have I gotten lost in something that isn't me?

I glance around the coffee shop, taking in all the small touches I've added, the baked goods I made, the pictures I took, and I can honestly admit . . . pride surges in my chest.

I might have gotten lost in someone else's project, but this project helped me see exactly who I am.

A hard worker.

Someone who finishes what she starts.

A baker.

A designer.

An idea creator.

A heart for a small community.

A businesswoman.

I might have gotten lost, but on the way, I found myself.

I know I did.

Looking her square in the eyes, I say, "You're wrong, Dakota. I have found myself. Maybe you're the one who's too blind to see it." I straighten up, feeling a little stronger. "You've always treated me like the lesser one in our relationship. The fuckup. And I'm sick of it. If you opened your eyes, you'd see that I've grown since we've been here. I've put in the work, I've reflected, and I've grown. And along the way, yes, maybe I forgot to ask about your relationship, and I'm sorry about that, but I'll be damned if I let you step on my growth."

"I'm not stepping on your growth, Bonnie. I'm trying to help you realize—"

"That I'm not the one with problems anymore?" I ask. "Maybe it's you who needs to reflect before you start seeing someone else. Maybe you need to figure out exactly who you are before you try jumping into another relationship. If you're so angry about me talking to Isla about all the trials and tribulations you've gone through, then maybe you weren't ready to start dating in the first place. Don't blame your insecurities on me."

"Unreal." She shakes her head, stepping away. "You know what, maybe you did find yourself, and that's great, good for you, Bonnie. But I don't like the new you."

My teeth grind together. "Why? Because I'm not rolling over, like every other time we have a conversation? Because I'm actually sticking up for myself?"

"Because you're completely missing the point. Life isn't always about you. Take off the blinders and realize your actions have consequences." She crosses her arms over her chest. "Tell me this—why do you think Rowan broke up with you?"

My teeth roll over my bottom lip as a wave of embarrassment washes over me, the realization hitting me square in the chest.

"Did you do something he didn't like?" she presses as tears start to well up again.

"I snooped in his shed," I answer, so quietly I can barely hear my own voice.

"Sounds about right. You crossed a line and did something he didn't want you doing. Not everyone is like you—they don't put their lives out on display. They like to take their time, introduce every part of themselves in due course. But you're too self-absorbed to think about that. It's always what you want, when you want it. Well, guess what? That mentality just bit you in the ass."

She's turned to walk away when I call out, "Wait, Dakota, please— let's talk about this."

She shakes her head. "I'm done talking. I need space."

And then she takes off, leaving me to crumble to the floor and sob into my hands.

◆ ◆ ◆

Bonnie: Dakota, please, come back to the cottage so we can talk about this. I don't like fighting with you.

Bonnie: We don't do this; we don't stay mad at each other.

Bonnie: We always work through things. Please tell me we can work through this.

Bonnie: Rowan, I stopped by your place, and you weren't there (which I'm sure you are aware of). I want to apologize, talk through this. Please.

Bonnie: I miss you, Rowan. I don't want to be fighting. This is something we can work through, right?

Bonnie: I'm sorry I invaded your space. Please just talk to me.

Someone . . . please, someone just talk to me.

I'm looking down when the door to the coffee shop creaks open. I freeze behind the counter, holding my breath, hoping and praying it's Rowan or Dakota. But when I glance up, I find Leith walking in, and all hope fails, crashing down once again.

It's been two days, and I haven't heard anything from either one of them. Two days of baking and getting ready for tomorrow's grand opening while trying not to get lost in my thoughts. I'm failing miserably, of course. My mind is constantly going over every interaction I've had with Rowan and Dakota. Replaying my last conversations with them.

Self-absorbed.

Don't listen.

Too pushy.

Not a good friend.

Immersed in a man, not finding myself.

Have I really been doing that? Is that really who I am?

It's terrifying to realize that maybe I do carry those attributes. That I'm so deeply invested in myself that I don't care about the feelings and reactions of others.

To say the least, it's been a painful and torturous two days. Especially at night, when I'm alone in the cottage with no more baking to do, nothing to do but ruminate while I clutch my phone to my chest, hoping one of them calls or texts me back.

But there has only been silence on both ends.

"Hold back the excitement of seeing me," Leith teases, pulling me back to the present, where I can't even force a smile at his joke. I'm hanging on by a thread, and one little thing will break the dam that I've haphazardly built. "Hey." Leith walks up to the counter where I'm standing. "What's wrong?"

Damn him.

Damn those two words.

That's all it takes.

One blink, and the tears I've been holding back crest over my lids and cascade down my cheeks.

I bury my face in my hands. "I'm sorry."

"Shh, don't apologize," he says, coming around the counter and putting his arm around me. I turn in to his chest and welcome his warm but slightly unfamiliar embrace. I'm desperate for anything at this point, though. I haven't had anyone to turn to. My parents and I aren't exactly on great terms, and I don't know if we ever will be. It's sad to say, but besides Dakota, I really don't have anyone else to appeal to, and that's terrifying.

"What's going on?" Leith asks.

I wipe at my tears and pull away. "Just a few stressful days."

"Does this have to do with you and Dakota?"

I look up at him in surprise. "You know about that?"

"Isla spoke with me yesterday. She said she was concerned that you two were fighting." He tilts my chin up, just like Rowan would. "Are you okay?"

Lip trembling, I shake my head. "No, I'm not. Everything is falling apart, and I don't know how to fix it."

Taking my hand, Leith leads me to one of the tables and sits me down. Then he moves around the counter, gets us both some tea and a buttery to share, and then brings them to the table, where he sits across from me. With a knife, he splits the buttery and sets his half on a napkin, offering me the plate to use.

"What's going on?"

"You really want to know?"

He nods. "Of course, lass. You're part of the Corsekelly family now. We help each other out. Tell me what's going on."

Even though I'm at an all-time low, I'm still a sucker for a pastry, so I take a bite of the buttery, savoring the rich flavor for a moment. "It started with Rowan. He took a call when I was at his house, and it seemed serious, so I gave him some space. I was walking around, and when I saw his shed I thought—"

"Ohhhh." Leith winces. "You went in his shed?"

"I wanted to see if that's where he stores his power washer. Boy, was I surprised."

"Yeah, he doesn't let anyone in there."

"Why not? His pottery is breathtaking. He should be sharing that with the world."

"Agreed, but that's not something he shares with a lot of people. It's his story to tell, not mine." Leith takes a bite of his buttery, and I realize . . . that's what I should have told Isla when she asked about Dakota. And how easy was that? Simple, and I wasn't offended.

Man oh man did I screw up.

"I understand."

"What did he say to you?"

"Roared at me. Rightfully so. He was so angry I could practically taste his fury in the air. Told me to leave, and we haven't spoken since. Thinking back on it, I don't blame him. I was so . . . lost in my own head, I didn't take his feelings into consideration. I've tried texting him and calling and even going to his place, but nothing."

Leith scratches the side of his face. "I shouldn't say this, but I'm going to anyway, just so you don't lose your mind. He really likes you."

I shake my head. "Leith, I know he wanted nothing to do with me. You don't have to say things to make me feel better."

He smiles. "Trust me when I say that I've never seen him act the way he does when he's with you. There's something special between you two, and I wouldn't give up just yet. Hang in there—he'll come round."

"He did say he would show up tomorrow, no matter what. Maybe I could apologize then. Put my heart out on the line."

"What's tomorrow?"

"I'm opening up new drinks and the baked goods to the public." My stomach flips at just saying it out loud. "I emailed the tour bus companies that come through here, letting them know there's a new take on some fresh Scottish food in Corsekelly, which their tourists might enjoy after seeing the Boaby Stone."

"It's a grand opening?" he asks, looking impressed.

"I guess so, yeah."

"Congrats, lass." He glances around. "You did a number on this place. It will do well."

"Thank you, Leith."

"Now." He reaches across the table and takes my hand. "About this Dakota and Rowan business—the bonds you have with them, they're unmatchable. They're not something that will just fall apart from one row. Give them time, and they'll come around. Rowan and I have been in our fair share of fights, and we've always come through them. Honestly, they've made us stronger because we've been able to understand each other better." He squeezes my hand. "Hang in there, lass."

And in the meantime, tell me more about this heart-on-the-line thing. Do you love me lad?"

I feel my cheeks flush. There's no use hiding it. "I think I do, Leith. I've never really loved someone before, not romantically, but with Rowan, it's different. He challenges me, makes me happy, protects me—and, most importantly, he makes me feel special, like I actually have something to offer this world."

"That's because you do." He holds his hands out. "Look what you created. You are full of . . . potential—you just had to find where to funnel it."

I thank him but can't help but wonder, *What's the point of creating something if I don't have anyone to enjoy it with?*

Nerves eat away at me as I think about tomorrow, all the hard work I've put into the shop, and the possibility of it all failing. Of me failing once again.

Dakota's anger-flushed face flashes through my mind, followed by Rowan's.

Will they show up tomorrow?

Despite our disagreements, will they still show up?

CHAPTER NINETEEN
ROWAN

Not doing it, not this fucking time.
    Don't even ask.
    Not after everything that's—
    Fucking fine . . .
    Anger level from 1 to 10, 10 being the highest: 123.
    There, happy?

"Rowan, can I be honest with you?" Maw asks, setting a cup of tea next to me as I stare off at the red curtains decorated with gold damask. My parents' rented London flat is certainly posh in comparison to their Corsekelly home.

I've been here for the past two days, and Da has yet to speak to me. They went to an appointment yesterday, which I wasn't allowed to attend, and came back looking more sullen than before. My easy guess: it wasn't good news.

"Oh, you want to be honest? That's refreshing," I deadpan.

Maw sighs. "I suppose I deserve that."

I plow my hand through my hair, sticking it up on all ends. "What the hell were you thinking, not telling me?" I whisper-shout so Da can't hear me. "I might not have the best relationship with Da, but that doesn't give you two the right to keep me in the dark about his health."

"I understand." Maw shifts uncomfortably. "You know I love you, Rowan, but I've spent the last few years of my life trying to mend the relationship between you and your father, attempting to be the peacemaker. I'm tired. I'm tired of the bickering, of seeing the two men left in my life go at each other every time they're in the same room. It's exhausting." She wipes under her eye, and my heart lurches. I hate seeing my maw this distraught. "I know you want to be here, but I don't think I can handle any more rows. It might be best if you leave."

"Leave? You really think I'm going to leave? When I just found out my da's dying? I'm not going anywhere."

"Rowan, he doesn't want you here. It might put more stress on him."

"Well, that's too fucking bad."

My phone buzzes on the table, and before I can hide the name on the screen, Maw catches it.

"Is that Bonnie?"

"Seems so." I stuff the phone in my pocket.

"You know, Shona was telling me you two are an item."

"Shona needs to learn to mind her own business."

"Did something happen?"

"Doesn't matter." I stand from my chair and pace the living room. "What did the doctor say yesterday?"

"Rowan, the last thing I want to focus on right now is your father's health; I want to forget—"

"You can't forget it, Maw. Just like you can't forget about the fact that Callum died. Or that the coffee shop is dying, or that you're spending your savings living here. You can't just brush your problems under the rug, hoping they'll disappear. This is life, and you have to face it. You have to deal with it, whether you want to or not. That's why I'm here. Even though you neglected to tell me anything until a few days ago, I'm here because you are my family, what's left of it, and I'll be damned if I'm left out. I don't want to be the goddamn black sheep anymore."

"Then you shouldn't have wanted to leave this family years ago." Da's weak voice cuts through the living room. He shuffles in, using a cane, his body deteriorating faster than I ever expected. Maw quickly goes to him and helps him into a chair.

She strokes his cheek lovingly, pain evident in her eyes. "Can I get you anything?"

"Water, darling."

Maw goes to get it, but I stop her and nod toward the chair next to Da and get the water myself. The air needs to be cleared. We can't go on like this anymore. It's not only hurting my relationship with Da, but it's hurting Maw too. And I'm seeing it. The exhaustion in her eyes, the weariness in her voice. Her husband is sick, and that's enough to worry about.

Fuck, am I really going to do this?

I glance over my shoulder to where my parents sit, holding hands.

A loving couple I grew up watching, admiring. There's a light smile on my da's lips as he looks at Maw. I remember when he used to smile at me. Those days spent in the kitchen, when he was proud of what I could do once he'd taught me the MacGregor way.

Where did that all go?

And why the hell has it been gone for so long?

Time to find out.

I bring two glasses of water over for my parents and set them down on the side table between them.

Once they've both taken a sip, I clear my throat. "I never wanted to leave the family. I wanted a chance to explore, the chance to create something of my own, like you created with the coffee shop." I look my da in the eyes. "It was never about the family, Da. It was about me trying to prove my worth."

"Your worth was with this family, with Corsekelly. But we weren't good enough for you."

"I wasn't good enough for *you*," I admit, slapping my hand to my chest. "I wasn't good enough for the town. Everyone had something. Callum was the baker—he took after you, Da. Leith and Lachlan were bound and determined to make something of themselves with personal training, and they have. Isla has built the bakeshop to a huge success, winning awards all over the country. My friends and family were all doing something, and I wanted to do the same. I wanted something of my own, something to make you proud." I grip my forehead, trying not to get emotional over all this. "All I ever wanted was for you to look at me and my gift the way you looked at Callum, with unconditional pride and love."

He tosses his arm up in the air. "Of course I love you." He looks away, dismissing the proclamation as quickly as he made it.

"Do you?" I ask, walking up to him and squatting in front of him. "Do you really love me? Or do you still blame me for Callum dying?"

He looks down at his lap, and his shoulders sag, as if the question has completely defeated him.

"I'm *angry* about Callum dying." He looks up and meets my gaze. "I could have lost both of you that day."

I lean back, blinking as I catch the tears brimming in his eyes.

"Every time I think about it, I get furious." His fist tightens, and he tenses before falling into a coughing fit. Maw places her hand on his back and offers him his water. He takes a few sips and then meets my eyes again. "His death could have been avoided if you'd used your goddamn brains. If it were you who were dead and Callum who was alive, I would have treated him the same way. The choices you two made together just about wrecked your mother. You put a hole in my heart, and then filled it with worry. Worry that instead of losing one son, I could have lost two." He pinches his brow and slowly rests his head against the chair.

"Da, I . . . I had no idea. I thought—"

"I know what you thought. And it might have been my fault for never correcting your way of thinking, but goddamn it, I'm still furious about it. And I'll be furious until the day I die. Careless behavior with no thought for the people who love you."

"Da." I reach up and slip my hand in his. He squeezes it tightly and, to my surprise, brings it to his mouth, kissing the back of my knuckles and then holding them close to his cheek.

He lets out a strangled sob, and that's all it takes. I break down as well, moving as close to him as I can.

"I could have lost both of you."

"I'm sorry," I say, bringing my forehead to his. I grip the nape of his neck and hold him there, not wanting to let go, not ever wanting to let go. "I'm so sorry, Da."

"I love you, Rowan."

I let out a sob, and tears stream down my cheeks. "I love you too, Da."

◆ ◆ ◆

"Here, Da." I place a bowl of soup in front of him and adjust the cardigan across his back, noticing how I can feel every bone in his shoulders. "Do you have everything you need, Maw?"

She nods quietly and sips from her bowl of soup.

Once they're taken care of, I take a seat as well, and quietly we all tuck in. Together.

The last few hours have been mentally exhausting. We cried for a good hour.

Cried over the loss of time.

The loss of Callum.

The loss of a relationship with my da.

The loss of those little, boring moments that make up a life.

The end is near. It's thick in the air, chilling and heartbreaking.

Clearing my throat, I ask, "How much time is left?"

Da doesn't look up at me, and neither does Maw. Instead they keep their eyes on their bowls, but I watch as my da slowly reaches over and takes Maw's hand in his. Her lip quivers, and a tear falls into her soup bowl.

"It's not good," Da says.

"I want to know. Don't hide it from me. Please don't hide it from me anymore."

Da slowly nods and looks me in the eyes. "It's stage-four chondrosarcoma. There's nothing they can do at this point. They offered a treatment plan to prolong life expectancy."

"Then let's do that," I say quickly. "What does it entail?"

Da shakes his head. "It's no way to live, son. I would have to stay here in London, it would cost more than I'm willing to pay, and I would be miserable—for what? A few more months?"

"Yes," I say, my voice panicky. "Yes, Da, a few more months. Months I haven't had with you. Months I need with you."

His weathered eyes connect with mine. "Rowan, I don't want to be in London. I want to be in Corsekelly, in my home, with the ones I love. And you can't stay here either. The town needs you. Your maw needs the town for support."

"But . . . but what about the time we've lost? What about—?"

"Whatever time I have left is yours, Rowan."

"How much time?" I ask, voice wavering, my throat tightening.

He closes his eyes. "A month . . . maybe."

"A month?" I nearly choke on my words. "How long if you do the treatment?"

"Three, maybe. But it's not a promise, and I wouldn't want to spend the rest of my days in and out of hospital, being pumped with chemo. I'd rather spend it in the place I love, with the people I love."

I lean my forehead into my hand and blink back the fresh tears that threaten to fall. How can I possibly lose him? How can I ever forgive myself for letting this feud go on for so long? For never talking to him and letting years of stubbornness and pride fester between us?

"Rowan." I look up at him. "It's going to be okay, lad. The life I've had has been beautiful. I'm a blessed man, and even though our time is short, I plan on making the most of it." He reaches for my hand. "Take me back to Corsekelly. Please."

For the second time today, tears streak down my cheeks as I nod. At this point, there is nothing else I can do besides soak in the moments I have left with him.

Chapter Twenty
BONNIE

Broken heart: One . . . still.

    Times I've thrown up from nerves: Three.

    Texts and calls that have been returned: None.

    Amount of cake eaten to mask my feelings: Let's just say I've had to make a lot of cherry cake this week.

    Today is the big day, and I'm not sure if I want to cry, smile, or go throw up again.

❖ ❖ ❖

Deep breaths.

    In through the nose, out through the mouth.

    Everything is going to be okay.

    In *one two three*, out *one two three*.

    Tamping down the threatening nausea, I glance around the coffee shop one last time. One minute to open, and I don't feel ready—despite burying my head in work the last few days.

    I've baked, practiced drinks, perfected every last detail when it comes to the shop, and made sure to collect pamphlets from everyone around town so I can promote all the special points of Corsekelly to tourists. Even with all that, I don't feel ready, and I think I know why: I don't have my two rocks next to me.

I haven't heard anything from Rowan or Dakota, and it's slowly eating away at me. My only hope is that they show up today and let me apologize profusely in person, which will lead to us hugging it out and everything going back to normal.

My phone buzzes in my pocket, and I quickly pull it out to see the alarm I set for myself. Opening day.

With one more deep breath, I go to the front door, reach out my shaky hand, and open it. Expecting to see a few smiling faces, I put on a smile myself and step outside, where I'm greeted by . . . no one.

My smile fades, and my heart sinks. I glance around and look down the street, off toward the Hairy Coo Footpath, but . . . nothing. Not one soul.

Not one friend.

Not one boyfriend.

Absolutely no one.

Trying not to get upset—I just opened, after all—I place the **OPEN** flag in its holster, prop the door open completely, and then step back into the coffee shop, where I try to busy myself.

I move around the counter, straightening mugs for the tenth time this morning. Then I check to make sure everything is stocked up, confirm that there are plenty of butteries, scones, and cake in the pastry case. I tuck in the napkins to be sure they're not crooked. All set, just like it was a half hour ago.

Tables are clean.

Vases have fresh flowers.

Drinks are ready to be made.

There's nothing else I can do.

I glance down at my phone. Ten thirty.

My heart sinks.

I can't believe that not one person has shown up. But, most importantly, I can't believe Rowan and Dakota aren't here. Did I hurt them so badly that they won't be here for me? Are they so angry they refuse to come support me?

Dakota and I have fought before, but never at this level. She knows how hard I've been working. She knows how important this is to me. Is she really not going to show up?

Feeling distraught, I sit down in the chair behind the counter and bounce my legs up and down.

Please don't fail.

Please don't fail.

I'm not sure what will happen to my self-esteem if this doesn't work out, if I once again fail to pull it together to make something of myself. To make something of my life.

Time passes.

Ten minutes.

Twenty.

An hour.

And no one.

Not one tour bus. Not one customer.

I sink deeper and deeper into my chair, tears streaking down my cheeks, depression starting to sink in.

When the clock hits one in the afternoon, I crumble to the floor and lean against the wall, my heart shattering into a million pieces.

Not a single soul has come to the shop.

No texts.

No phone calls.

I'm not sure what hurts more—that Rowan and Dakota never showed up, or that I've failed. I pick at a piece of lint on my leggings as I consider it. There is no doubt in my mind which one hurts more.

Dakota and Rowan.

"Hello?" a voice calls out.

Shit.

I wipe at my face and stand from the floor as Leith walks up to the counter. "Hell, I'm sorry it took me so long to come in." He thumbs toward the door. "A tour bus got stuck in a ditch just outside of town, and we all went out to help."

"We?" I ask, just as Lachlan comes through the door, huffing.

"Are there butteries left?" he asks in a panic.

"Och, Fergus, out of the way," Shona says as she steps into the coffee house, followed closely by Hamish, Alasdair, and . . . Isla.

"There's still butteries!" Leith shouts down the line.

The little line cheers, and—God help me—I start bawling like a baby.

The community has shown up for me. At least there are some people out there who appreciate the hard work I've put in.

"Lass, you okay?" Leith asks.

I nod and wipe at my eyes. "Yes, sorry." I take a deep breath. "Just . . . no one came in, and I just thought . . ."

"Aye, we've been legs deep in mud all morning. There was a landslide just outside of town, and a tour bus got stuck. All the other tour buses had to divert for the day, but we're all cleaned up now, and the road is good to go. Trust me, I would have been here sooner after yesterday's buttery." He pats his stomach. "We might be personal trainers, but we don't mind a little buttery on the bones."

He winks as Lachlan slings an arm around his neck. "And butteries aren't the only things we'll shred."

"Well, thank you," I say, smiling through tears. "Would you like a drink too?"

"Tea, please. Earl Grey." Leith nods to one of the tables. "Gotta grab a table before Shona can."

"Och, that's very gentlemanly of you," Shona calls out.

They all laugh, and so do I as I prepare their orders, which I spend the next few moments filling. Hamish cleaned me out of the tattie scones, said he was going to take them to the locals who helped with the cleanup.

By the time Isla comes to the counter, I have two butteries left and a few slices of cake. She smiles kindly and reaches out to take my hand. "You did a great job, Bonnie."

"Thank you," I say, returning a sad smile while the elephant in the room practically chokes all the air out of my lungs. "How's . . . Dakota?"

Isla's brow creases. "What do you mean, 'How's Dakota?' I thought she was with you."

Panic tightens my chest. "No, I thought she was with you. We had a fight, and I just assumed she went to stay with you these past few days."

Isla's eyes look wild now as she shakes her head. "No, she said she was taking some time to think about things. I thought . . . I thought she was with you."

"Oh my God." I quickly grab my phone and try giving her a call. As expected, she doesn't answer. "Have you called or texted her?"

"No, I was giving her some space." Isla pulls out her phone as well. "Should I call her?"

"Yes, see if she answers." Panic turns into fear as my mind reels back to the weeks after Isabella broke up with Dakota. She fell into a deep depression, and it took her a while to climb out of it. There were a few nights when I slept in her bed with her, just to let her know I loved her, I was there for her, that she was worth so much more than the way Isabella had treated her.

Isla gnaws on her bottom lip as the phone rings. I hold my breath, terrified. I can hear her voice mail pick up, and my stomach drops. Isla glances at me, wide eyed, and when the beep sounds off, she says, "Hiya, Dakota, it's me. I know you wanted some space, but I'm just checking on you to make sure you're all right. Please call me." She hangs up and shifts in place. "What do we do?"

I glance around the coffee shop. "Find her." Clearing my throat, I face my very first patrons. "Hey, you guys, something has come up, and I'm going to need to close."

Leith lifts his head, halfway through eating his buttery. "Is everything okay?"

"Hopefully," I say. "I hate to kick you out, especially since you showed up to support me, but . . . do you mind?"

"Not at all," Shona says, gathering everyone and shoving them out the door.

Leith stays behind, though, and when everyone is out of earshot, he asks, "Does this have to do with Rowan? We haven't heard from him in a few days, and since he's not here today and didn't even respond to help with the tour bus, I thought maybe you two didn't figure things out."

"I mean, no . . . but . . . you haven't heard from him?" I ask, more concern growing.

"No, but that's normal too. He can get into these moods where he doesn't want to see anyone. He'll sometimes go up north and stay in the family cottage up there. If you two had words, he's probably up there."

Oh.

So . . . he's just mad.

"Okay." I clear my throat. "Well, thanks for letting me know." Leith gives me a quick nod and heads out of the coffee shop.

Isla moves to the counter and takes my hand. "Where do we start?"

I clutch my phone. "Find My Phone. We'll track her down."

I open up the app and quickly click on Dakota's name. Isla leans over, and when the app pinpoints her, Isla nods next to me. "Badicaul. I know where she is. Come on. I'll drive."

"Do you want to talk about what happened with Rowan?" Isla says as we drive to what seems to be an outlook on a beach in Badicaul, northwest of Corsekelly. When we spotted her on Find My Phone, Isla explained that it was a place she'd told Dakota about on one of their dates. She said she didn't think there was anything dangerous there—no cliffs or anything like that—which now eases my beating heart, slightly. Not that I think Dakota would hurt herself, but then again, I'm not sure what kind of mental state she's in at this point.

Staring out the window, I watch the rolling green hills pass by as I shake my head. "Not really. I don't think there's much to talk about, honestly. I already went through all of it with Leith."

"Did he say Rowan would come round?"

"Pretty much."

"Trust him—he's right."

I chew on the inside of my cheek, trying to rein in my emotions. I'm over crying at this point. I've shed way too many tears.

"But honestly, if he does come around, hasn't the damage already been done?" I ask, my mind racing with disappointment. Did I push him away by being too caught up with my own life problems, just like I did with Dakota?

"Is the damage so bad you can't work through it?"

"I don't know," I whisper as we pull down a dirt road and go toward the water's edge.

Nerves tickle my throat, tightening my vocal cords. We curve around a bend, and then our MINI Cooper comes into view, followed by Dakota, sitting on the flat ground overlooking the shore. She's staring out at the water, her legs pulled to her chest.

"There she is," Isla says, relief in her voice.

At the sound of the car approaching, Dakota looks behind her, and I see her ravaged eyes, bloodshot and sunken. My heart twists in my chest, and before Isla can stop the car, I'm unbuckling my seat belt.

"Do you mind staying in the car so I can talk to her first?"

"Not at all," Isla answers, understanding in her eyes.

"Thank you."

Once the car is parked, I hop out and head to Dakota, who turns away again. I have no clue if I'm looking at a loch or the ocean at this point, but whatever it is, it's pretty.

Not saying a word, I take a seat next to her and mimic her position, bringing my legs into my chest.

"Find My Phone?" she asks, her voice brittle.

"Yeah. I'm glad you were psychotic about losing me when we decided to move here and forced me to download it, just in case."

"Glad it came in handy."

She falls silent, and I allow the moment of quiet to hang between us. Sometimes you just need a friend beside you to ease the anguish in your chest before you can talk about it.

After a few draining minutes, I hear her sniffle. I look to the side and catch her wiping her eyes. Her tears feel like a punch in the gut. Dakota's pretty emotionally tough, almost stoic sometimes, and I've only seen her cry a handful of times. Today being one of them.

I wrap my arm around her as the wind picks up, making it chillier than I care for, and I pull her closer. She automatically rests her head on my shoulder and quietly says, "I'm sorry, Bonnie."

"Why are *you* sorry?" I ask, confused. "I'm the one who screwed up."

She shakes her head. "No, I screwed up. I made you believe you were the lost one, that you needed to find yourself, when in reality it's me who's lost." Her voice grows tight. "I have no idea who I am. I lost myself with Isabella, and I don't think I've ever recovered, even though I've been pretending that I have."

"Hey." I squeeze her tight. "Relationships don't define us, Dakota; they only help mold us into the people we're supposed to become."

"And what have I become?" She wipes at her nose. "I'm not proud of what I said to you, how I've acted, how I neglected to show up for you today because I was too embarrassed, too ashamed. I'm not proud of who I am when I'm with Isla, and not because there's anything wrong with her. She's perfect, actually, but she just reminds me how fucked up in the head I am. I second-guess everything. I'm terrified that after every conversation with her, she's going to judge me, scold me, tell me that's not how to be a lesbian, how to carry myself. She's so damn amazing, and I honestly don't think I'm healthy enough to have that kind of relationship."

"A loving one?" I ask. "Because I think that's exactly what you need. Someone to nurture you, remind you of just how special you are and everything you have to offer this world."

"I have nothing to offer."

"That's not true, and I'll tell you why—because the girl who's sitting in the car right now was worried sick about you. There is so much love in her eyes, Dakota. The entire drive here, she was telling me how much she cares about you, how happy you make her, how she wishes she hadn't given you space because she doesn't want to lose you." I squeeze her tight. "You offer so much value, and you can't even see it."

She lifts her head and wipes her eyes. "She said that to you?"

I nod, wiping at Dakota's eyes as well. "You might feel broken, but she doesn't see you that way, and neither do I. I see you as a strong woman, a strong gay woman who knows herself but is just wary of trusting her intuition." I press my hand to her heart. "This is your path, your guide. Follow it, Dakota, and don't let your mind tell you otherwise. You have value—you are worth everything to me, to Isla, and yes, it will take time to shake the damage Isabella has done to you, but guess what—she didn't break you, girl . . . she just bent you. It's time to straighten you out . . . well, not like praying you back to straight, but you know, keep the gay, but just straighten—"

"I know what you mean." She laughs and sighs. "Jesus, Bonnie, I can't believe I said those things to you. I'm so fucking sorry."

"I'm sorry I told your story to Isla. I never should have done that. I understand how important it is, and I think I was just trying to cling to anything that would keep you close. I felt you drifting away, and it scared me. I didn't want to lose you."

"I felt you drifting away too," she admits. "First with the coffee shop, then with Rowan. I felt like they were all more important than me, but instead of talking to you about it, I bottled it up and chose some painful words to shout at you—words I didn't mean."

"There was some truth to them, even though they hurt. There's truth."

"I'm proud of you, though." She faces me, sitting cross-legged. "I'm so proud of you, Bonnie, and I can't believe I missed the opening. It was selfish and wrong and—"

"It's okay." And I mean that. It's really okay. During the drive, I wasn't thinking about the coffee shop. I was thinking that I might lose my friend, my rock, the one person who's been through all the ups and downs of my life. I can't lose her. "I really, truly mean it. It's okay, Dakota."

She wraps her arms around me and pulls me into a hug. "You're all kinds of special, Bonnie. You know that? You don't need to figure out what to do in life, because you're damn near perfect as you are."

I shakily smile against her shoulder. "If only that was enough."

She pulls away and lifts my chin. "It should be. What did you say to me? 'Relationships don't define you; they only mold you'? Same goes for you. A job, a relationship, where you live—they don't define you. It's how you live your life, treat others, and take advantage of every moment presented to you." She grips my cheek. "Like right now, after everything I said, you're still here, showing up, letting me know that no matter what we say, nothing can tear us apart."

"Never. You're my person," I say softly as tears build in my eyes.

"And you're mine." She pulls me into another hug, and this time, I hold on a little tighter, letting the familiar embrace soothe my troubled soul.

After a few good minutes of holding one another, I help her up from the ground and call Isla out of the car. She tentatively walks over, but when I push Dakota toward her, they quickly embrace. I give them some space, though I can't help but listen in as I face away from them, watching the waves lap against the dark earth.

"I was so worried," Isla says. "I didn't want to give you space but felt like you needed it."

Dakota sighs quietly. "I'm not . . . all the way mentally healthy. Isabella did a number on my confidence. I want to be strong for you, Isla, but I just don't know how to be, and I don't want you to resent me for it."

"You don't need to be strong for me—you just need to be honest." I sway a little, turning slightly, because *good God* do I need to see what's happening. From the corner of my eye, I catch Isla cupping Dakota's cheeks. "I'm falling for you, Dakota, so hard, and I know it's going to be a journey battling your demons, but I don't want you to do it alone. Let me battle them with you."

Jesus, if Dakota doesn't snag Isla, I very well might. Talk about total jackpot.

"I don't want to put you through that," Dakota answers stubbornly. I'm seconds away from slapping some sense into her when strong Isla swoops in again.

"That's what relationships are for, though—to lean on each other and guide one another through the good . . . and the bad. There's so much more to you than what happened with Isabella. That's a small bump in the road that I know we can conquer together, but you have to trust me to help get you over it."

"I do trust you. You've showed me what kindness is in a partner. You've provided me with encouragement and strength; even through my insecurities, I can see how valuable you are. How important, the kind of graceful and positive impact you've had on my life. I'm just . . . I'm nervous. I don't want to be a burden."

"You're never a burden to me." Isla pulls her closer. "You're a blessing."

Yup, here come the waterworks. There's no way I can play incognito at this point. I fully turn around and stare just as Isla closes the distance between them and brings her mouth to Dakota's. Just look at them. Happiness wraps around them and shines brightly through every shared glance and touch. It's everything I could ever ask for when it comes to my best friend: happiness.

But as I watch them kiss, hold each other tightly, press their foreheads together while talking softly about how much they care for each other, one thought invades my mind: *Can I ever get there with Rowan?*

After what Leith told me, Rowan's absence, his anger as he roared at me to leave, my guess is probably no.

And that makes me incredibly sad.

"You know, I just feel weird being here," I say to Dakota and Isla, who are holding hands across from me at Fergie's, kissing each other every two seconds. After the grand makeup, I drove the MINI Cooper back to Corsekelly so Isla and Dakota could drive together. I didn't mind—until my head started spinning with thoughts about Rowan.

Before we drove back, I took out my phone and sent him a few texts, hoping I would hear from him, since today was supposed to be a big day, but when we parked the cars and I checked my phone, there was nothing.

It's put me in a weird mood, and sitting across from two freshly reconciled lovebirds is making me even sadder than before.

"I think I'm going to go."

"What? No, stay," Dakota says. "I don't want you to feel weird around us."

"I don't feel weird around you two. I just . . . I'm feeling a little sad over the whole Rowan thing, and I don't want to be a Debbie Downer. Plus, you two need some time together."

"I want to spend time with you too," Dakota says, and I can see the indecision in her eyes, trying to balance a friendship and a relationship at the same time.

Smiling at her, I reach across the table and take her hand. "There will be plenty of time to spend with me. Just promise I get a night sometime this week, okay?"

"I promise." She smiles back.

I turn to Isla. "Thank you for taking care of my best friend. I appreciate you so much."

"That means a lot to me."

We exchange quick hugs before I leave the pub and head back to the cottage. I know there's cake stashed in the kitchen, and I have a heavy inkling that I'm about to eat it all. The town is quiet, most of the noise and activity coming from the pub, with a few stragglers here and there. I take a deep breath, savoring the fresh breeze off the loch. I never thought I'd fall in love with a town, but here I am, head over heels for Corsekelly, and yet . . . it doesn't feel right.

Nothing has felt right since my fight with Rowan. It's as if that fight dug an empty hole inside me and I'm trying to fill it with whatever I can, but it's not working. Nothing is working.

I'm truly . . . sad. And I don't think it's because he didn't show up today. I don't think it's because he's not calling.

I think it's because I accomplished something. I proved my worth, I created a vibe, I brought something to life, and the one person I wanted to share this with won't return my phone calls and my texts, and it's all my fault.

I think it's because for the first time in my life, I fell in love, and the man I've fallen in love with doesn't love me back.

And that's more painful than anything.

I bite my bottom lip as I trudge through town, the magic of the stone-paved road losing a bit of its luster. Everything seems to have dulled around me, and I know it's because I love Rowan. I love him so much, and if he doesn't love me back, then how on earth am I supposed to stay here, in the smallest town I've ever visited, and act like everything is normal?

Surprisingly, I didn't fail when it came to my job this time—I thrived.

But failure still rests heavy on my heart.

The snap of a twig pulls my attention from the ground to a dark figure passing by.

Wait.

Is that . . .

Is that Rowan?

He's home? And he didn't let me know?

I quickly hop around the corner of the Mill Market and poke my head around, eyes trained on him as my heart tumbles into a pit of despair. I can't believe he wouldn't tell me he's here. Then again, it's really all my fault. I pushed him and pushed him and drove him away.

As he steps inside the pub, I consider going back to the cottage but realize I'll just cry to myself in my bed, so I opt for the coffee shop. As I approach, I have to blink a few more times. Finella is standing at the open doorway. She looks stunned, with her hands to her heart and mouth agape. Another twig snaps, this time under my foot, and she jumps, her eyes connecting with mine.

Oh God.

She's home early.

I wasn't prepared for her return.

Does she hate what we've done?

I haven't had a chance to prepare her.

I clear my throat. "Finella, you're back from vacation. I thought you'd be gone for six months."

"That was the plan, but Stuart wanted to come back."

"Oh." I twist my hands together.

She turns toward the coffee shop and then looks back at me. I gulp, wondering if she likes the changes or if she wishes she'd never brought Dakota and me into the mix.

"Shona told me you've been working hard, Bonnie, but I never expected to come back to this." She shakes her head in disbelief. "This is more than working hard—this is a complete transformation."

"Do you . . . do you like it?" I ask, my heart hammering for so many reasons at this point.

"I love it."

Relief washes over me as she steps closer and pulls me into a hug.

"Thank you," she whispers.

It's my undoing. I wrap my arms around her and sob onto her shoulder.

Rowan.

Home.

His complete and total silence.

Feeling like I no longer belong.

Experiencing success, but having it overshadowed by my own faults.

It all crashes together. She holds me tightly, and her embrace feels like a long-lost hug from my mom, something I haven't received in too many years.

"Shh," she says, stroking my hair. "'Tis okay, lass."

"I'm sorry," I say, trying to gain control of my emotions but failing miserably. Pulling away, I wipe my face and take a deep breath. "Okay, sorry about that."

Head tilted, she studies me. "About Rowan—"

I hold up my hand. "Please, Finella, I really don't want to talk about it. How about I just show you around the coffee shop, get you familiar with everything? We've made quite a few changes."

"All right, dear," she says, resigned.

For the next half hour, I show Finella around the coffee shop, listening to her appreciation of the hairy coo pictures. She fawns over the new tables and enjoys every bite of the buttery I serve her. She's grateful for everything I show her, even the small things, like the power-washed floors. And even though her excitement should be contagious, it's not. All I feel is a sense of finality.

My job here is done.

Dakota is happy.

Finella is thrilled.

There's nothing really keeping me here, especially if Rowan has moved on as well. There's only one thing left for me to do, and that's . . . call my parents.

It's time to go home.

CHAPTER TWENTY-ONE
ROWAN

Hanging on by a thread: Three; there are three threads left.

Times cried since found out about Da: Five. And I can remember every single one of them so vividly, as if I'm experiencing them now.

Conversations with Da since I've found out about his cancer: More than I can count.

And that right there is worth every hardship I've suffered along the way.

"Want to sit there?" I ask Sorcha, my dad's new nurse, completely dreading this conversation.

"That looks great." We both take a seat in a booth in the back of the pub.

"There aren't many food options here, but I would recommend the fish and chips."

"That works perfect for me." She smiles kindly and tucks a lock of red hair behind her ear.

"Do you want a drink?" I ask.

"Water is fine."

I nod. "Do you mind if I order a beer? I'm going to need it to get through this conversation."

"By all means."

"I'll be right back." I quickly go to the bar and put in two small orders of fish and chips and a lager for myself, which Hamish fills up quickly, along with a glass of water for Sorcha. When I make it back to the booth, I hand Sorcha her water and take a seat, bringing the pint to my lips and taking a large gulp.

When I set the beer down, Sorcha looks me in the eyes. "How are you doing, Rowan?"

"My father is dying. I could be better."

"Have you come to terms with it?" she asks softly.

"No." I shake my head. "He has, though."

"He has." Sorcha nods.

I take another swig of my lager. "So, what should we expect?"

"You want to jump right into it?"

I nod. "Might as well."

"Okay." Sorcha reaches into her purse and pulls out an envelope from the hospice provider we chose to help us make Da's last days as easy and painless as possible.

Da's doctor was instrumental in pairing us with a caregiver who will stay with Maw and Da through his last days. I can already tell she's a kind and gentle soul, someone who will be there for us every step of the way.

I know we're going to need it.

◆ ◆ ◆

"Good morning," I say, walking through the door of my parents' house. Sorcha is already here, taking care of Da and making sure he's comfortable in the hospice bed we set up in the living room. The room's large windows look out onto the loch, letting in light and a cool breeze, which was what Da wanted.

"Aye, good morning," Da says, sitting up in the bed and moving to the edge. His mobility is okay. He can move around the main level of the house with a walker, but if we go farther afield, he uses a wheelchair.

Maw comes into the living room, fully dressed and ready for the day. "Rowan, are you here for the grocery list?"

I nod. "Aye. I was going to run to the Mill Market quickly and then come back to help out Sorcha, like you said."

"Thank you," Maw says. "I'm running to Kyle to fill these prescriptions and pick up a few other things. Do you need anything, Sorcha?"

She shakes her head. "I have everything I need right here."

Maw hands me a list and quietly says, "Don't be too long."

"I won't." List in hand, I go to Da's bed, give him a quick kiss on the top of the head, and then set out.

Normally, I would walk, but given the circumstances, I hop in my pickup and drive the short distance into town, parking in front of the Mill Market. When I make my way inside, I grab a trolley and head straight to the produce section while glancing at the list.

Apples.

I need apples and—

Crash.

The trolley handle bumps into my stomach, and I look up to see a wide-eyed Bonnie looking straight at me, our trolleys perpendicular to one another.

Hell.

When was the last time I saw her? Thought about her? Returned a call or text?

The answer to the last one: never.

I've thought about her constantly, when my da hasn't been on my mind.

Last time I saw her . . . I pushed her away.

I saw red that day, took it out on her, and ran her out of my life.

"I'm so sorry," she says, trying to get out of the way. "I wasn't paying attention."

"Nah, I wasn't. I'm . . . sorry."

"Guess we both were buried in something else," she says, her voice wavering. "All right, well, I guess I'll be going."

"Bonnie—"

"See ya." She waves quickly and hurries toward the checkout counter. With a quick word to Shona, she abandons her cart and strides out of the store.

Fuck.

I drag my hand over my face.

What the hell have I done?

And then it hits me.

I quickly pull my phone from my pocket and glance at the date.

"Fuck," I mutter, pulling at my hair until pain radiates down my skull. "Fuck." I squeeze my eyes shut.

I missed it.

I missed her fucking opening day.

Not only have I fucked up what we had by displacing my anger, but I also broke a promise, one that meant the world to her.

"Everything okay over here?" Shona asks, appearing by my side. "Swearing in the produce is cause for concern."

"Sorry." I stick my phone back in my pocket. "Just realized I missed something."

"Aye, the reopening of the Hairy Coo Coffee Company."

"How did you know?"

"Just an inkling." She rocks back on her heels. "I was there, but not until the afternoon. None of us were able to show up till then."

"Why?"

"Tour bus got stuck, so we all went to help them out. No one was at the opening. Heard from Isla that Bonnie was devastated." My gut churns. "Don't blame the girl for going back home—she's had a rough go at it, what with getting in a fight with Dakota, losing you, the coffee shop . . . and now that your maw is back—"

"Wait." I hold up my hand. "What do you mean, going home? To the cottage?"

"No," Shona says, brow furrowed. "Going back to the States." *To the fucking States?* "She leaves Tuesday. It's nice she was able to patch things up with Dakota before she leaves. I guess Dakota wanted to go with her, but Bonnie told her to stay with Isla and help your maw at the shop. Finella tried to convince her to stay this morning, but I think she's too heartbroken." Shona looks me up and down. "Thanks to you."

Fuck.

She's going back home?

I . . . I can't . . . fuck, she can't leave.

"Maw talked to her this morning?" I ask, my throat growing tight.

Shona nods. "Bonnie was up early baking, getting ready for the day, teaching Dakota everything she knows. Not sure how long she'll last. Dakota doesn't seem like the baking type, but she's giving it her best effort." She shakes her head. "Such a shame you two didn't work out. Bonnie was perfect for you. Perfect for the town."

I chew on the inside of my cheek, trying to comprehend everything Shona is telling me.

"Anyhoo . . . need help with anything?" Shona asks, her gaze steely as she stares me down.

I shake my head.

"Well, if you do, you know where to find me."

Whistling, she casually walks back to her register as my mind whirls. I glance over at her, and a smile stretches across her weathered face. How convenient, I realize, that Maw sent me to the Mill Market just now.

Maw has tried to talk to me about Bonnie, but I've brushed her off every time, unable to even think about the pain I caused her. Every text, every phone call—I ignored them all because I didn't know what to say to her.

I still don't.

I don't even know if there is anything to say at this point.

She's going home.

She clearly is done with me, and I don't blame her. I haven't given her anything to hold on to.

◆ ◆ ◆

"I think it's going to rain," I say as I help Da out of my pickup and into his wheelchair.

"Let it rain." He looks up at me. "Just means Callum is here with us, right?"

I smile softly. "I guess so." Moving behind him to push him to my cottage, I ask, "Why did you want to come here?"

He holds his hand up to stop me. "I don't want to go to your house. I want to go in there." He points at my pottery shed.

"Da—"

"Don't argue with me. Bring me to your shed."

With a heavy sigh, I wheel him to my shed, open the double doors wide, and push him inside. I watch, a bit nervous, as he slowly takes everything in, hands folded on his lap. His eyes travel to the shelves, first landing on my completed work, which is ready for a home but has nowhere to go. Then they travel to the back, where I dry out my projects. Those shelves are empty. And then he takes in my workstation. Messy, with clay splatter everywhere, it's a place where someone creates. The only question is, Does Da see it that way?

I watch him with bated breath. I try to gauge his reaction, try to understand what's passing through his head. When his eyes return to my completed shelf, the corners of his mouth twitch upward toward the sky.

"That mug." He points to one on the edge of a shelf, glazed and fired already. "Bring it to me."

Of course he would pick that mug.

Reaching over to the shelf, I grab the mug and hand it to him. With shaky hands, he examines it. His fingers glide over the handle, the emblem of the hairy coo, the perfectly shaped cup I made for Bonnie. He checks out the bottom. "You don't sign your work?"

I shrug. "It's not like I do anything with it."

"Because of me," he says softly.

"Because I was afraid of doing anything that would cause the family more pain." I lean against the wall. "I have so many regrets, Da, but setting aside pottery, in the grand scheme of things, is not one of them. For a while, I thought it was. I thought I was supposed to make something of myself through my hobby." I shake my head. "I now realize how obtuse that is. I should have focused on you. On Maw. On mending our relationship."

"We both should have. You are not to blame for the rift. I didn't make it easy on you. And I pushed you away when I should have been holding on tighter."

"Seems like I get that from you," I say softly, looking out toward the leafy trees that surround my cottage.

"What do you mean?"

"Bonnie," I say with a sigh. "We were seeing each other before I came to London. The day you and Maw rang and told me about . . . about your cancer, I found her right here, in my shed, checking everything out that I've always kept hidden. I honestly can't remember what I said to her. I think I've blocked it out. All I remember is telling her to leave and the horrified look on her face. I haven't talked to her since, and I've been ignoring her attempts to connect with me."

He slowly nods and looks back down at the mug. "Do you love her?"

I don't even have to think about it. The answer is clear as day in my head, even through the fog of my da's illness. "I do. She's the first lass I've ever loved."

"Do you want her to be the last?"

I reach up and grip the top of the doorframe. "Yeah, I would, but I don't think that's an option. She's going back to America on Tuesday."

"Tuesday?" I nod. "Then that means you still have today." He smiles.

"Da, I can't—"

"What is your biggest regret, besides me?"

I glance away. "My fight with Bonnie."

"So what's stopping you? Your stubborn pride? Don't let a personality trait you inherited from me keep you from getting what you want. You love her, yes?"

"Aye."

"Then be the man I know I raised. Apologize, and beg her to stay. If there was one thing I noticed when we'd speak to you on the phone, it was the passion you had for that girl. The same passion I have for your maw. It's one-of-a-kind love, Rowan. Don't be an eejit and lose it."

"But, Da, I should be focusing on you."

His eyes narrow. "You and I are right where we're supposed to be. Do you understand? The best thing you can do for me, in these last days of my life, is make sure I leave this earth knowing that you're taking care of your maw, that you're a man of this town, and that you're happy. And I mean deep-rooted, to your marrow, happy. Can Bonnie bring you that kind of happiness?"

"She's the only thing that's ever washed away the pain and brought me joy."

"Then what the fuck are you doing here, talking to me, you bawbag? Go get her."

"Just like that? Go up to her and ask for her forgiveness?"

"Aye. Helps if you have a peace offering as well."

I glance at the mug in his hands. "I actually made that for her."

He holds up the mug and smiles. "Then it's very fitting." He holds it out, and I take it from him. I move to the back of his wheelchair, but he stops me with a hand to my forearm. "Rowan, come here."

I squat in front of him, and he places his hand on my shoulder, giving it a feeble squeeze. I know it's all he can muster, but it's enough for me, and I put my hand on top of his.

"I need to tell you something I should have told you many years ago." His voice chokes up and he coughs a few times before he steadies himself and makes eye contact with me. "Your talent . . . it's beyond anything I've ever seen. This"—he points to the shed—"this is what you should be doing, and I never should have made you think differently. I'm sorry, Rowan."

"Da, please don't apologize."

"I need to. I need you to know I'm ashamed of my behavior, and I would be honored . . ." His voice cracks, and my throat tightens. "I would be honored if you would make my urn."

"Da . . ." Tears fill my eyes. "I can't—"

"Do this for me, Rowan. Please. Make my urn. It would mean so much to me." He squeezes my shoulder. "Please."

Wiping a tear from my eye, I nod. "It would be my honor, Da."

Chapter Twenty-Two
BONNIE

Cake slices consumed: One full Dundee cake, courtesy of Isla.

Tattie scones consumed: Two; one was burnt, courtesy of Dakota.

Cake batter consumed: At least one cup, courtesy of my fingers, which couldn't stop scooping up gobs. Don't worry, I used the batter for my own cake. Which brings me to . . .

Box cake consumed: A measly half of one, thanks to my dippy fingers.

All of the above is because I'm headed home without my best friend and with something new: a broken heart.

"Are you sure you want to do this?" Dakota asks as I wipe down the coffee shop counter, my flight back home tomorrow looming over me.

"No, but I think it's what I have to do. I can't stay here. Not now that Rowan's back. It's too painful."

"But, Bonnie, don't you see what you've done?" Dakota motions to the now-empty coffee shop that was bustling all day. "You made something of this place. You created an environment, not only for tourists but for the locals too. You saw Hamish and Alasdair—they were here for an hour, just talking and enjoying some tattie scones. You brought this place back to life." Dakota shakes my shoulders. "You, Bonnie. You did that. No one else."

"I had help," I say, flushing as I allow myself a moment to feel proud of what I've created. I glance around the shop, my heart completely invested in these four walls.

Find yourself in Scotland.

I found myself . . . and so much more.

"You had help, but we just executed your vision. The success of the coffee shop rests in your hands. You're just going to leave that?"

"Would you be able to stay here if Isla wasn't talking to you?"

"I would at least try to talk to her before I left. Why don't you talk to him?"

"And say what?" I toss my cleaning rag into the laundry basket we keep under the counter.

"That you're sorry?"

"I've tried to do that. You should have seen the look on his face at the Mill Market. There was nothing there other than the desire to retreat as quickly as possible." I work my way around the counter and start lifting the chairs off the floor and onto the tables. "I can't stay here."

"So you're going to go back home . . . to your parents?" Dakota follows closely behind me but doesn't help.

"Yup, can't wait to hear them tell me 'I told you so' multiple times, every day, until they die."

"Bonnie, there has to be something we can do. Maybe you can find another town out here."

"And what? Work? Pretty sure I need some kind of work visa for that, and I don't think they're going to provide one to someone who just came from working at a coffee shop. Face it, Dakota, I'm bound for California, and there is nothing you can do."

I've finished up with the chairs and have started to move toward the counter when Dakota stops me.

"I'll come with you, and we can figure something out."

"We've been over this. You are not coming with me, not when you have Isla here."

"You can't go back to your parents—you'll be miserable."

"Not as miserable as I would be staying here and seeing Rowan all the time, working for his mom."

Dakota looks off to the side. "But you love working here."

I walk back over to the counter, where I hoist myself up and scan the space one more time. Regret fills me. I don't want to leave this, not even a little, not when I feel like I've found my purpose, what I'm good at. "Yeah, I know. Today was so amazing with all the tour buses pouring in. I can't believe we sold out by noon. Just the kind of send-off I needed."

Dakota is silent for a second, and then she turns to me, a serious expression on her face. "What am I going to do without you, Bonnie? I can barely keep it together around Isla. I need you here."

"You don't need me. You're so much stronger than you think you are, and when you do feel weak, Isla is there to build you up. I don't think I could have picked someone better for you. She's perfect, and when you two get married one day—because I know it's going to happen—and you're standing hand in hand, both of you wearing beautiful white dresses that blow in the breeze, I'll remember the day you showed me the ad for two coffee shop employees and know it was the best decision we ever made."

"But you're leaving—how was it the best decision for you?"

I smile. "Because I'm leaving here with confidence, something I haven't had in a very long time. I'm leaving here knowing I made a change, knowing I helped you, I helped Finella and Stuart, and maybe even helped this town. I'm also leaving here knowing exactly what it feels like to love someone. I'm a changed woman, Dakota. You were right: I needed to find myself, and Scotland might have been the place to do that." I smile to myself, tears welling in my eyes. "I found myself, and that right there will help me get through the heartache of losing Rowan." At least, I'm hoping it does, because it's going to take a long time to get rid of this burning, aching hole in my chest.

"I'm not saying I like that you're leaving, but I am proud of you. You've created such a brilliantly cozy space for the town and for tourists. Very proud of you, Bonnie."

"Thank you."

"And frankly, I know you're hurting now, but I believe you're strong enough to get over Rowan. You know . . . if you want to stay and give it a try."

I quietly chuckle and shake my head. "I appreciate your encouragement, but I think it would be too much. And hey, Finella gave me her email address and said to use her as a reference. For all future jobs. Not sure what I'll do, but at least I'll have that to help me out."

"Yeah." Dakota wraps her arm around me. "I'm going to miss you."

"I'll miss you too, but it's for the best. Honestly, I couldn't stay here even if I wanted to. I now truly know what a broken heart feels like." I blow out a shaky breath. "I don't want to talk about it anymore. How about we just enjoy some cake one last time?"

"Is there any left?"

I playfully nudge her. "I snagged one of the cherry cakes. You'll be short one tomorrow."

"Great, it only took everything in me to make those."

We laugh as I hop off the counter and take the cake out of my hiding spot in the bakery chest.

I pop open the top of the to-go box. "In my head, we each take a half, but I'm thinking we work our way to the halfway mark?"

Dakota reaches for the plates. "Let's just call it like it is. Split it and plop a half on each plate."

"And that is why I love you."

After cutting the cake right down the middle, I give each of us a half, and we lean against the counter. We clang our forks together and dig in—just as the door to the shop opens.

Both of our heads whip to the entrance as Rowan steps inside, closing the door behind him. Hair styled, button-up shirt hugging his torso, jeans clinging to his thighs with the cuffs rolled, making room for his classic boots. My breath catches in my chest at the mere sight of him, and I realize something: not only do I love him, but I really don't know if I'm ever going to get over him.

"Rowan," I say, sounding like a breathless fool. "What are you doing here?"

"Can I come in?"

"Uh, Dakota and I are having a girls' night."

"This won't take long." He walks across the shop, that stubborn, grumpy attitude I fell in love with on full display as he leans against the customer side of the counter.

"Didn't you hear me? I said we're having a girls' night."

"And I told you this won't take long, but if you keep making me repeat myself, it might take longer."

"Did you come here to be a dick, because if that's the case . . ." I slow-clap. "You're doing a good job."

"Still sarcastic, I see."

"You don't lose sarcasm in a week. Takes time to drive that out of someone. You might have broken my heart, but you didn't break my spirit."

His eyes soften as Dakota whispers, "Ooh, good one."

"Thank you," I whisper behind my hand. "Felt like an excellent comeback."

"It was aces," Dakota says, hopping up on the counter, where she sits and enjoys the show.

Rowan scratches the side of his jaw, looking between us. "Will the audience be staying for this entire conversation?"

I turn to Dakota. "He wants to know if you're staying."

"I don't feel like leaving, that's for sure. I like that he's uncomfortable."

"Not uncomfortable," he says, shrugging. "Just preparing myself for more obnoxious commentary."

"Tell him he's a dick."

"She already called me that." He sounds cockier than ever. I have no idea what his angle is right now, but it's not making me sad . . . it's making me mad.

"I wasn't talking to you," Dakota hisses at him. She nods at Rowan while speaking to me. "Go ahead, tell him."

I fold my arms over my chest. "Dakota and I would like you to be aware of our ill feelings toward you. We spoke, and we agree—you're a microboaby."

"Aye, good to know." He's unfazed. "When you're done acting like a child, I would like to have an adult conversation."

"Acting like a child?" I just about scream. "You're the one who threw a temper tantrum when I opened your man shed. News flash: I was just trying to get one more look at your power washer, not invade your privacy. Sheesh, you would have thought I'd found your collection of twisted-off nipples or something."

"From what I heard, the reaction was uncalled for," Dakota says.

"It was," he agrees. "It wasn't fair. I took my built-up anger out on Bonnie when I should have leaned on her for support."

Support?

For what?

"Did something happen?" I ask.

He moves from the counter and goes to the door, opening it a crack and lifting up a paper bag, which he apparently left outside. Confused, I watch him close the distance and hold it up to me. "I made this for you before I selfishly lost my temper. Thought you could take it with you."

Oh . . . a parting gift.

Huh.

Why did I think, and maybe even hope, that he was going to beg me to stay?

I take the gift. "Well, thank you. I'll be sure to send a thank-you card." I motion to the door. "If you'll excuse us, we have some cake to tend to."

"Open the gift, Bonnie."

"I think I'd rather save it for a surprise later."

"Open. It."

"I think he wants you to open it," Dakota whispers.

"I know what he wants," I hiss. "Fine, I'll open it." I tear the tissue paper out of the way and let it float to the floor as I reach into the bag and grip a round object. I pull it out, and my breath seizes in my lungs as I take in the beautiful hand-thrown mug. Covered in white glaze with pink dripping upward at the bottom, it's speckled and beautiful, with . . . oh God, is that a hairy coo stamped into the side?

"I wanted to give you something that reminded you of all that you've accomplished. All that you've done for this town . . . for my family," he adds quietly, and the confident alpha who barged in here quickly morphs into a shy human being.

"It's . . . it's beautiful, Rowan."

"Thank you." Growing serious, he takes a step forward and lifts my chin so I'm forced to show him the tears welling in my eyes. "That morning, the phone call I took, it was my parents." He clears his throat. "Contrary to what they told me, they weren't on holibags. They were in London, meeting with a specialist. My da has bone cancer."

"Oh God," Dakota and I say at the same time.

Dakota hops off the counter, clearly sensing the shift in mood. "I'm just going to give you two some space." With that, she hurries into the shop's kitchen, leaving me alone with Rowan.

"Could we sit?" he asks, and I nod, leading the way to one of the tables. We lower the chairs and both take a seat.

"Is your dad going to be okay?" I ask, clutching the mug.

His Adam's apple bobs up and down as he swallows hard, eyes cast down, hands folded. "I wish I could say that he is, but he only has a few weeks left. We have a hospice nurse staying at my parents' house, helping us through the process. We went to the pub the other night, and she walked me through everything to expect in the coming weeks."

"Oh my God, Rowan, I'm so sorry. How are you dealing with all of it?"

"Well, it's forced me to have some tough conversations—conversations I never thought I'd have with my father. I'm grateful for them, though, for this last week I've spent by his side, talking to him about everything and nothing. It's meant a lot to me. But it also made me forget about something important." He reaches over and taps the mug in my hands. "I was supposed to give that to you on Friday, on reopening day, but I wasn't there. I also forgot about—"

"Rowan, you clearly had more important things to deal with than a silly reopening."

"It wasn't silly. It was important to you, which made it important to me. And it was important to my family. I'm sorry I missed it, that you had to spend most of the day alone. Just thinking about you all by yourself, waiting for someone to come in, makes me feel ill."

"I was fine," I say. It's not the truth, but I'm not about to pile on the guilt.

"I should have been there." He pushes his hand through his hair. "Hell, I should have been a lot of things to you, Bonnie, but I royally fucked up."

"Rowan—"

"No." He shakes his head. "Please let me get this off my chest." His eyes plead with me, so I sit there . . . and listen. "Ever since Callum passed away, I've felt this dark cloud looming over my life. I lost touch with my da, and even simple conversation with my maw was strained. I had this town and my friends, but nothing ever felt the same with them. Everything just felt dark, and no matter what I did or didn't do, I was stagnant. Every day was the same. Every thought was the same. Every interaction was mundane at best." His eyes connect with mine. "And then you came into my life. A ball of energy and blonde hair ready to take the piss out of me any chance you got. You drove me crazy, and yes . . . you made me act like Kilty McGrumpyshire." I snort, even as my heart threatens to pound out of my chest. "But hell, Bonnie, you made me feel fucking alive again."

He takes my hand, and from the look of desperation in his eyes, I know I'm done.

"I love you, Bonnie. I don't know how it happened, or when it happened, but I'm glad that it did. You've forced me to step outside of my stagnant little world and learn to breathe life back into my lungs." He clears his throat. "The other day, when I screamed at you to leave . . . fuck, I don't know what I was thinking. I was out of control, and I took it out on you. I was too embarrassed, too angry, too blind to fix it with you. I needed to get my head on straight, and honestly, I'm barely hanging on at this point. But my da said I can't lose you, and he's right. I can't let a once-in-a-lifetime kind of love walk out of my life without putting up a fight. So please don't leave, lass. Please don't fucking go back to America. I need you here. I want you in my life, in my bed, by my side . . . forever."

Misty eyed, I blink a few times, but it's useless. Tears cascade down my cheeks.

He loves me. I'm not dreaming it. He actually loves me.

This man, who I once thought was the most irritating creature on the planet. The man who became an advocate for my success. The man who helped show me how special I really am.

He loves me.

I smile with shaky lips as he gently wipes my tears away with his thumbs, concern etching his face.

With a wobbly voice, I say, "I love you too, Rowan. I don't know how or when it happened either, but just like you . . . I'm glad that it did."

"Then you'll stay, lass?"

"Of course she's going to stay!" Dakota yells as she barrels out of the kitchen and throws her arms around me. I snort out a laugh, bubbles of grossness coming out of my nose. "She was leaving *because* of you, you big lug. But now she has no excuse to leave." Dakota has me in a viselike grip, practically climbing into my lap.

"I love you, Dakota," I say, laughing, "but do you think I can finish things up here?"

"Oh yeah, sorry," she chuckles and then turns to Rowan. She punches him in the arm, but he doesn't even flinch. "That's for stressing me out and nearly driving my best friend away." She points a stern finger at him. "You owe me one of those mugs."

He laughs. "I'm sorry, Dakota. I'll make you and Isla a matching set. Hers and hers."

"Oh, I see how you work, really reaching for the brownie points. Uh-huh. I see you, Rowan MacGregor." Dakota slowly backs away. "I see *you*." This time she leaves the shop, and when the door clicks shut, Rowan moves in closer.

"So you'll stay?"

"Depends." I smile. "If I stay, will you come to bed wearing a kilt tonight?"

"I'll do anything you want, lass, as long as I come home to you."

I stand up and place the mug on the table—carefully—and walk around the table, where I settle onto his lap. His wide palms span my back as I cup his cheeks. "I can't imagine being anywhere else." I lower my forehead to his. "I love you, McGrumpyshire."

"I love you, lass."

I lower my mouth to his and kiss him.

Gripping him tightly, I kiss him with passion, with love, with everything in me, because I'm grateful for him.

I'm grateful for this town.

And even though I blamed Dakota for talking me into this adventure in the first place, I'm grateful we flew to Scotland on a whim. I never would have found Rowan otherwise. But, most importantly, I never would have found who I am and who I'm supposed to be.

EPILOGUE
ROWAN

Fiancées since we last spoke: One.
Pregnant fiancées since we last spoke: One.
Pregnant fiancées who are ravenous for cake: One.
Pregnant fiancées who are ravenous for cake and boaby: One.
I'm feeling like one lucky lad.

◆ ◆ ◆

"Does this look crooked?"

Bonnie walks into the bathroom of our hotel room, wearing a gold dress that stretches tight around her terrific tits but flows gracefully over her baby bump.

Our baby.

Fucking hell, I still can't believe it. Da passed away two weeks after Bonnie decided to stay in Corsekelly, but within those two weeks, we were able to bring him into the coffee shop every other day, right up until the last two days of his life. He was able to sit and enjoy the atmosphere, speak with Shona and Hamish and all the rest—and enjoy butteries when his stomach was up for it. He got to know Bonnie as well, and he shared all his baking tricks, ones I already knew, but I let him tell her anyway. And on his deathbed, a day before he passed, he held my hand tight and whispered that I needed to marry her. To never let her out of my sight. She was the one for me. I promised him I wouldn't let her go.

And I haven't.

I only wish Da and Callum were here to witness Bonnie's pregnancy and our nuptials next month. But even though they aren't here in person, I know they're here in spirit. At least, they were with me when I proposed to Bonnie in my cottage, with a piece of cake and a ring as the cherry topper—because when she said yes, the clouds broke open and rain pounded against the roof like applause.

"Oh dear God," Bonnie says, clutching at her heart as she stares at me. "Why did Dakota do this to me?"

"Do what?" I ask, snapping back to the present as I turn and look down at my wedding attire. I'm wearing a MacGregor red-and-green-tartan kilt with a matching green jacket, vest, white shirt, and red tie.

"Make you wear a kilt. She knows it's my weakness. Does she want me palming your balls during her ceremony?"

"You will keep your hands away from my baws while I perform my duties. Do you hear me, lass?"

"You know, I hear you talking, but I'm not quite understanding."

I'll be honest—Dakota knew exactly what she was doing when she picked out my outfit for the wedding. Dakota and Isla, for that matter. They asked me to officiate the ceremony, and there was no way in hell I was turning down the opportunity. The moment Isla told me she was going to propose to Dakota, I knew I wanted to be part of the celebration. I didn't care how—I just needed to be involved. And they gave me the highest honor.

The wedding will be small, intimate, with just a few locals and Dakota's parents, who are quite thrilled for the happy couple. They've been in town for a week and have done all the touristy things, which include visiting the Boaby Stone and stopping into the Hairy Coo for a coffee and buttery. Dakota's parents also fawned over the shop's merchandise and snapped up a few of my mugs, which seem to sell out every week. We can barely keep up with the demand, especially since I started making boaby-like handles for the mugs. Everyone wants to be the Serpent Queen and claim that boaby. Can you tell it was Bonnie's idea? When she first proposed it, the last thing I wanted to do was carve penises every day, but I've become pretty good at it now, and I have to admit: it's kind of funny.

What I don't think is funny is when Bonnie pretends to stroke the mugs while making a horrible snog face. Let's just say her maturity level is diminishing the further she gets into her pregnancy.

"What are you two doing?" Maw asks, coming into the room. "Dakota is looking for you, Bonnie."

"Tell her to keep it in her pants. I need to stare at my fiancé for a few more seconds." Maw laughs and takes off toward the ceremony space.

I spin Bonnie around and lead her out the door. "You keep it in your pants," I whisper in her ear. "Behave, lass, you hear me? No lifting up my kilt."

"Are you wearing underwear?"

"Aye."

"Then I can't be held responsible for what I do."

We step outside and turn the corner of the hotel, where we find Dakota and Isla. They're standing together on the patio that overlooks the ceremony space, which rests right in front of the vast blue loch that stretches for miles. They're holding hands and looking gorgeous in their white gowns. Dakota's has more of a gold tone to go with Bonnie's dress, while Isla's features a tartan sash that cinches her waist and cascades down the back.

"Are you two ready? We would really like to get married," Dakota says.

Meghan Quinn

"You're the one who put him in a kilt." Bonnie goes up to her best friend and places a soft kiss on her cheek. I hear her say, "I'm so happy for you. You deserve all of this and so much more."

"Don't make me cry." Dakota waves her hand in front of her face, making Bonnie laugh.

"And that's what you get for putting my fiancé in a kilt. You know how horny I am."

"Such a beautiful moment," I deadpan.

Isla takes my hand, which is my cue to start the ceremony. Together, we walk down the aisle, smiling at the friends and family grouped on either side, and stop at the edge of the water—a place where Dakota and Isla find peace, a place they frequent often, and where they will forever return, knowing this was the spot that jump-started their life together.

I gaze down the aisle as Bonnie and Dakota walk down it together, holding hands. Bonnie meets my eyes and smiles, and happiness floods my whole body.

It was kind of mad of my maw to put out an advert, looking for two friends to run the coffee shop, but to this day, it was the most life-changing thing she's ever done.

Not only did the idea give the coffee shop a future no one could've believed possible, but it also brought Isla love. And it brought me a whole new perspective on life.

I made peace with my da.

I'm in love.

I'm engaged.

I have a baby on the way.

Bonnie will say she came here on a whim, but I felt the weather shift the day she arrived in town. I think it was more than just a whim. If I have to admit it—I glance up at the sky as clouds overhead start rolling in—I think Callum had a small part to play as well.

338

ACKNOWLEDGMENTS

So . . . Scotland is now on my list of places to go. I became obsessed with research for this book. So obsessed that late at night, my wife would find me watching YouTube videos about Scottish tourism, sports, shops, recipes. The list goes on and on. I would even tune in to learn the Scottish brogue so I could get it right. I had a dream where I lined up a bunch of Scots in a row and dragged a broom under their kilts. My brain is a terrifying thing, but Scotland has a little piece of my heart now. Lucky for Scotland, huh? If you hear about a crazy blonde lady dragging brooms under kilts, just know that it's probably me.

To Aimee Ashcraft, my agent, thank you for sitting through my neurotic texts and answering every single one of them as I tried to sift through this story. I'm proud of what we were able to put on paper.

Big shout-out and thank-you to Lauren Plude for being a cheerleader for all things Meghan Quinn, for acquiring my stories, and for loving them as much as I do. You make the process so easy.

Lindsey Faber, your enthusiasm and love for my stories puts a smile on my face and makes me believe in myself a little bit more every time we go through edits.

To all the bloggers and readers out there, I don't even know how to express my deepest love for you. You take a chance on my books every time I release one, which is something I could never show enough gratitude for. Thank you for being the best fans a girl could ask for. You make this job so much fun!

Thank you to Jenny for keeping me sane, for handling everything behind the scenes, and for being my number one fan. I adore you.

And lastly, thank you to my wife, Steph. You are the reason I'm able to do what I do every day. You keep me grounded, you make time and space for me to be creative, and you've always been by my side every step of the way. I love you.

About the Author

Photo © 2019 Milana Schaffer

USA Today bestselling author, wife, adoptive mother, peanut butter lover, and author of romantic comedies and contemporary romance, Meghan Quinn brings readers the perfect combination of heart, humor, and heat in every book.

Text "READ" to 474747 to never miss another one of Meghan Quinn's releases.